ONE OF THE MOST GIFTED [WRITERS]
IN THE ROMANCE GENRE TODAY."*

Praise for the bestselling novels of
Laura Kinsale

"Readers should be enchanted." —*Publishers Weekly*

"An absolute gem, virtually flawless . . . I can't find the words to praise it highly enough." —*Rendezvous*

"Poignant and sensitive . . . hard to forget."
—*Heartland Critiques*

"Once in a great while an author creates a story and characters so compelling that the reader is literally placed on an emotional roller coaster . . . Ms. Kinsale once again takes the reader on that roller coaster . . . The story is rich with life, the writing beautiful and the characters unforgettable. This is a book readers will long remember and turn to again and again." —*Inside Romance*

"Noted for her well-developed, complex characters, richly descriptive historical detail, and emotionally involving stories, Kinsale has written a number of award-winning romances, many of which tested the limits of the genre in characters and plot as well as setting." —*Library Journal*

THE
Dream Hunter

LAURA KINSALE

BERKLEY SENSATION, NEW YORK

THE BERKLEY PUBLISHING GROUP
Published by the Penguin Group
Penguin Group (USA) Inc.
375 Hudson Street, New York, New York 10014, USA
Penguin Group (Canada), 90 Eglinton Avenue East, Suite 700, Toronto, Ontario M4P 2Y3, Canada
(a division of Pearson Penguin Canada Inc.)
Penguin Books Ltd., 80 Strand, London WC2R 0RL, England
Penguin Group Ireland, 25 St. Stephen's Green, Dublin 2, Ireland (a division of Penguin Books Ltd.)
Penguin Group (Australia), 250 Camberwell Road, Camberwell, Victoria 3124, Australia
(a division of Pearson Australia Group Pty. Ltd.)
Penguin Books India Pvt. Ltd., 11 Community Centre, Panchsheel Park, New Delhi—110 017, India
Penguin Group (NZ), Cnr. Airborne and Rosedale Roads, Albany, Auckland 1310, New Zealand
(a division of Pearson New Zealand Ltd.)
Penguin Books (South Africa) (Pty.) Ltd., 24 Sturdee Avenue, Rosebank, Johannesburg 2196,
South Africa

Penguin Books Ltd., Registered Offices: 80 Strand, London WC2R 0RL, England

PRINTING HISTORY
Berkley mass market edition / December 1994
Berkley Sensation trade paperback edition / January 2006

Library of Congress Cataloging-in-Publication Data

Kinsale, Laura.
    The dream hunter / Laura Kinsale.
       p. cm.
    ISBN 0-425-20762-5
    1. Stanhope, Hester Lucy, Lady, 1776–1839—Family—Fiction. 2. British—Middle East—Fiction. 3. Mothers and daughters—Fiction. 4. Middle East—Fiction. 5. Explorers—Fiction. 6. England—Fiction. I. Title.

PS3561.I573D74 2006
813'.54—dc22

                                                                                              2005054557

PRINTED IN THE UNITED STATES OF AMERICA

10 9 8 7 6 5 4 3 2 1

Prologue

───❦───

London, 1838

"What do you suppose they did to the poor devil?"

"Beheaded him, I expect," Viscount Winter said indifferently. "If the mob didn't stone him to death."

"Good God." Sir John Cottle gazed with distracted anguish at the viscount, who sat beneath a stately row of ceiling-high windows, his long legs stretched out at ease and a decanter of sherry at his side. In what reading light was available in the cheerless fog of a December afternoon, Lord Winter's face had an elegant severity, the unyielding, impenetrable look common among men to whom sun and distance are familiar companions. The austerity of his expression was accentuated by a pair of very dark and diabolic eyebrows, high cheekbones and an uncompromising set to the mouth and jaw. A number of books from the club's fine collection were piled about him on the table and the floor.

Sir John cast an unseeing glance over such titles as *Narrative of an Expedition in H.M.S.* Terror *on the Arctic Shores; Voyages Dans L'Amerique Sud;* and *Around Cape Horn: Scenes, Incidents and Adventures of the Passage from the Journal of Captain W. M. Alexander.* His mind was not in the club library, or on books, but full of barbaric and violent scenes of the East. He turned in distress toward his sporting companion, Lord Gresham. "I feel responsible. He was a Christian, even if he did come from Naples. Perhaps we oughtn't to pursue the thing, Gresham."

"Nonsense." Lord Gresham's thin cheeks were flushed with high color. "The Italian claimed he could pass himself off as a Mohammedan. We paid him a king's ransom—if he didn't know his business, there you are! We lost our money, he lost his life."

"Beheaded, for God's sake! I just don't know if—"

"You want the horse, don't you?" Lord Gresham fixed Sir John with a determined stare.

"Yes! God, yes." Sir John chewed his mustache, his pale blue eyes troubled. "But to send a second man to his death—" He looked to the viscount, who had already turned his attention back to his books, evidently more interested in taking notes than in following the conversation. "What do you think, Winter?"

The viscount did not raise his eyes from his writing. "If he didn't know what the stakes were, your Italian was a fool," he remarked.

"But can it be done at all?" Sir John demanded. "The fellow had been in the East for years."

"He spoke Arabic like a native," Lord Gresham added, "and God knows he looked like one."

Lord Winter glanced up from his book, a slight smile curling the corner of his mouth. "How do you know?"

Both men gazed at him. "Well," Sir John said, "he put on all his Bedouin gear to show us. A turban, and so on."

"A turban!" Viscount Winter lifted one eyebrow, shook his head and turned back to his notes.

Sir John sent a fulminating glare at Lord Gresham. "I told you we should have consulted Winter in the first place!" he exclaimed, his savagery at odds with his plump, pleasant face. "How should we be able to judge whether the man really knew what he was about?"

"Well, we're consulting him now," Lord Gresham said tightly. "That's the devil of the thing, Winter. We need better direction. Someone in Cairo, or Damascus, to hunt down the proper agent to go into the desert for us and get hold of the animal. But the consuls are determined to put any stupid obstacle in our way. We hoped you might recommend a name."

Lord Winter raised his eyes. Their deep cobalt blue made a startling effect against his black lashes and suntanned skin. "You're wasting your time and money, gentlemen. I very much doubt this horse exists."

"We have a paper—" Sir John began.

"From your ill-fated Italian?" the viscount interposed. "A pedigree, perhaps? Unbroken line back to the stables of Solomon, the truth attested by white-haired sheiks—that sort of thing?"

"Well, yes. Rather that sort of thing."

"May I sell you a flying carpet?" Lord Winter asked politely.

Sir John made an inarticulate protest. Lord Gresham said, "If you would read it—"

"Oh, I have no doubt it is a very pretty fairy tale. No Bedui in the desert will lie about a horse's bloodline, because they all know every horse as they know their own mothers—but for your consumption, gentlemen, they will enthusiastically perjure themselves in high poetry on paper: signed, sealed and thrice blessed by Allah. How much did you pay the Italian?"

"A thousand," Lord Gresham said frankly. "Yes, yes, I know you take us for nincompoops, Winter, but the thing is, the paper didn't come from the Italian." He lowered his voice. "I got it from my brother-in-law at the Foreign Office. It came in a packet intercepted at Jeddah, mixed up with some secret documents or other." He waved his hand vaguely. "Turks and Egyptians, troop movements, you know the sort of thing. Palmerston's interested in 'em, God bless the poor devil. But he don't care about horses, and after they got it translated, and decided it wasn't some sort of code, he told Harry he could throw the paper on the fire if he pleased."

The disinterested expression in Lord Winter's eyes vanished; he looked keenly at the two avid sportsmen who had sought him out. "Where is this paper?"

Lord Gresham immediately produced a well-worn document, bound in rough cord, from his inner pocket. Wordlessly he handed it to the viscount.

Lord Winter scanned the flowing Arabic script. The club library was silent while the other two men leaned forward, waiting. He finished the document, rolled it and handed it back, his face expressionless. "Once again, I strongly suggest that you save your money and your time."

"You think it's a farrago?" Lord Gresham asked.

"No, I think it's true." The viscount's mouth hardened. "That is a message to a man named Abbas Pasha. He's a nephew of the Viceroy of Egypt, and desert horses are his passion. He is a young prince who conducts himself very much in the tradition of Ghenghis Khan—anyone who deceived him on the subject of horses could expect to find hot irons promptly applied to the soles of his feet."

"Then this mare called the String of Pearls does exist! And she's lost somewhere in the Arabian peninsula. There must be a suitable agent who could undertake to search her out. If you could just advise us as to what sort of man we need and where to find him."

"That letter says a faster horse has never lived, Winter!" Sir John said, all in a glow. "You'll have heard that Gresh and I bought Nightwind last year. He's lightning! By Jove, he's trounced every horse he's raced—and he's hot-blooded too, just three generations from this same Eastern line. There's not a thoroughbred mare in the country can measure up to him, but if we can obtain this String of Pearls and breed back to the desert blood, I know we'll have a cross the like of which the world has never seen."

"We'll spare nothing to locate her," Lord Gresham declared.

"There is not the remotest hope that you can locate her," the viscount said with finality, leaning back in his chair and reopening his book. "Believe me."

"But if you say it must be true, that letter—"

Sir John looked up, his voice breaking off quickly as an elegant gentleman paused at Lord Winter's chair. "Naturally I would find you here," the man said coldly.

Viscount Winter's face did not visibly change, but he put aside his book and rose, not requiring to look behind him to identify his father. "It is merely the Travellers' Club," he said, offering his hand to the Earl Belmaine. "Hardly a brothel."

The earl ignored the greeting and gave Lord Winter's companions a curt nod. He looked remarkably like his son, but for the well-bred whiteness of his face and hands, and the thinner build of a man who made far fewer demands on his physical strength. His lip curled in disgust as he inspected the volumes scattered about the viscount's chair. "May I have the honor of a private word?"

"As you please," Lord Winter said.

"A nauseating place," the earl said, leading his son to a secluded corner of the library.

"Resign," Lord Winter suggested cordially.

"And lose my last means of holding converse with my cherished heir? I daresay I should forget what you looked like. I believe your mother already has."

"No such luck," his cherished heir remarked. "She managed to bag me neatly in Picadilly just last week, with one of her singularly tedious debutantes in tow."

"I collect that she is reduced to meeting you in the street," the earl snapped, "as you have not seen fit to call on her at home!"

"Alas, my courage fails me." Lord Winter gave his father a dry glance. "It's not as if we should have anything to talk about, after all. I am not interested in what she served at her last ball supper, or which girl she particularly desires me to marry, and she is not interested in anything about me but my defects. A topic which is too well-worn, you may be sure, to require further discussion."

"I should think that the natural affection of a son for his mother—"

"Yes, we are all agreed, long ago, that I am an entirely unnatural son!" the viscount interposed with an edge of impatience. "I'll have my profile taken in silhouette. She may hang it in her parlor, and point it out to her acquaintance in proof of my existence."

"Very attentive of you," the earl said ironically. "But I've not sought you out to compliment you on your celebrated courtesy to your mother. I've just come from the boardroom of the Royal Geographical Society." He reached inside his coat. "You will be pleased to be the first to see the names listed for Captain Ross's expedition to the Antarctic."

Viscount Winter's expression changed subtly. He stood looking at his father. The earl tossed two folded pages onto a table between them.

They lay half open. H.M.S. *Terror*, one was headed; H.M.S. *Erebus* the other, with a list of names beneath each. Lord Winter had no need to read them. His name would not be on either.

"I believe I recall that today is your birthday," the earl said. "My gift to you."

Still Lord Winter said nothing. A remote, blank aspect had come into his face, a look of bitter reserve.

His father was goaded into further speech. "I calculate that you must be thirty-one today. If I had a grandson, he would be ten years old."

Lord Winter's mouth tightened. His dark lashes lowered.

"If I had my grandson," the earl said softly, "you might have made your grave in the ice of Antarctica with my blessing. Or in the sands of your precious Arabian desert, or in some stinking jungle—any barbaric place you may care to kill yourself."

With deliberate leisure, Viscount Winter lifted the expedition lists from the table. He held them in his hand with an alarming gentleness. There were several other club members scattered in the far corners of the library. They glanced up, and then lowered their heads zealously over their books. Sir John and Lord Gresham diligently engaged themselves in a dispute over the quality of the club sherry.

"As the matter rests," the earl pursued with stubborn venom, "so long as you are my only heir, unwed and childless, I am forced to concern myself with you, and crush these interesting plans that you concoct to bring yourself to an untimely end."

"Your paternal devotion is heroic, as always," Viscount Winter murmured, handing the papers back to his father. "I hope you didn't have to sell too many votes in the Lords to obtain this. My removal from the expedition list bought a tidy sum of funding for the Society, I expect?"

"We will be at Swanmere for Christmas," the earl said, apropos of nothing.

"You need not trouble the maids to air my room. I will be abroad."

Earl Belmaine stood facing his son, his teeth clenched beneath a smile. "Have no fear," he said courteously. "I would not trouble a swineherd on your behalf."

Lord Winter bowed. "May I bid you good day?"

"Good day." The earl turned away. At the pillared entrance to the library, he paused and looked back. "I wish you joy of your birthday."

Viscount Winter made no answer, still as carved stone.

The Earl Belmaine had meant to leave on that acid note. But he looked at his tall son, at the cold handsome face that did not betray a flicker of outrage or emotion, did not betray anything at all in the steady gaze, and the earl could not quite burn every bridge behind him. Even as he asked, his own weakness angered him. "May I have the honor of knowing where you will go?"

"So that you may find a way to prevent me?" the viscount inquired coolly. "No, I think not."

The earl governed his temper, well aware that he had already given sufficient provocation to spark any unpredictable consequence. He would not put it beyond the viscount to bring home some painted female out of a harem and present her to his parents as his wife. He understood neither his son's sense of humor nor his reckless wanderlust, but he had learned, with some difficulty, never to be careless of either. "Happy Christmas, then," he said dryly.

"The same to you," Lord Winter said. "Sir."

His father departed, leaving the long room utterly silent, without even the turning of a page. The viscount stood watching him go, his face perfectly composed. Then he returned to the window table where Sir John and Lord Gresham still waited beside the stacks of books and notes.

Lord Winter resumed his seat. He poured himself a glass of sherry. He gazed pensively down into his drink, then took a sip and set the glass aside.

"Gentlemen," he said quietly, "I am inclined to render material assistance in the matter of your Arab horse after all." A faint, cynical smile lit his strange eyes as he looked up. "In fact, I'll see to it personally."

THE TRAVELLERS' CLUB library remained silent after Sir John and Lord Gresham took their leave with effusive and passionate thanks. All through the afternoon, the only sounds were the hiss of the fire, the turn of the viscount's page and the soft snores of a French diplomat stretched upon a sofa with a Viennese newspaper spread over his face. At length, as the rumble of dinner conversation began to float down from the dining room, this signal seemed to insinuate itself into Lord Winter's consciousness. He stood and stretched, choosing a book to carry with him and leaving the rest open on the table.

He went up the stairs two at a time, passing other members coming down. A trio of clubmen lounged at the door to the dining room, leaning against the wall and laughing while one of them finished off his pipe.

"Here he is!" one of them declared, looking aside at the viscount. "Our noble Lord of the Desert!"

Lord Winter halted and glanced from one to the other. "Here I am," he said. "Good evening." He started to go past.

"Such an antisocial fellow Winter is."

They grinned at him. They seemed to mean well, but he felt his old stilted unease come over him. He gave them a quirked smile. "A wandering mind, I'm afraid."

"Well, reel it in, old fellow, and dine with us."

Lord Winter hesitated. Then he inclined his head. "Much obliged, but I'm devilish bad company." He lifted his hand in a brief sketch of salute and walked by them into the dining room.

His usual table was at hand, a single, a few feet behind the door. As he sat down, some eccentricity of acoustics brought their lowered voices clearly to him above the hum of general conversation.

"Damned solitary sort."

"You know him? Never see him with anybody."

"He's hardly in the country long enough to be seen at all. Been wandering about the Syrian deserts forever, but now he's off to the south pole."

"The south pole, by God. Now there's a facer for ye old Travellers' clubmen. What's his school?"

"Governesses and tutors, I imagine. Couldn't risk him at school. He's Belmaine's heir, don't you know."

"Ah!" The single syllable held a wealth of discovery. "Belmaine."

"The only son. No other children. Immense bloody fortune—and there's the title, of course. Lucky brute."

"How agreeable, to occupy your pedestal all alone."

"Seems to suit the bastard. Asked him to dine with us, didn't I?" There was a pause; an all but audible shrug. "Devilish poor company, like he said."

Lord Winter riffled through the pages of his book and began to read.

One

———∞∞∞———

June 25, 1839
Syria

THE REVEREND MR. Thomson was understandably shaken. Indeed, it was a few moments before he could compose himself in the face of a pile of human bones heaped up outside the crypt, the skull on top, the whole ghastly scene lit only by two tapers stuck through either eye socket of the grinning thing. Weird shadows flickered over the planked coffin and gloomy faces of the wild-looking throng of Mohammedan servants gathered around.

He had not meant to lose his way amid the labyrinthine garden within Dar Joon's fortress walls. But it was two hours past midnight, and after the servants, with their turbans and drooping mustachios, had hefted the coffin to carry Lady Hester Stanhope to her final resting place, Mr. Thomson had lingered behind just a few moments to familiarize himself with the funeral rites of the Church of England, so that he might say them without any disrespectful hesitation or scrambling for pages.

This had proved to be most ill-advised. Immediately after the funeral cortege with their torches and lanterns had left the court-yard, vanishing into Lady Hester's black jungle of a garden, a misfortunate draft of hot wind had left the American missionary in utter darkness. He had been forced to feel his way through a maze of winding pathways, the soft voices and occasional dim glow of a torch always just beyond another oriental screen or a turning that seemed to go nowhere. For some time he had wandered, stumbling upon roots and brushing hanging jasmine vines aside, until at last he came upon the arbor.

The macabre sight that met his eyes caused him a strong degree of agitation. But the English consul Mr. Moore moved to his side, gesturing vaguely at the bones, and murmured, "Never mind him. It's only a Frenchman."

Mr. Thomson rolled his eyes toward the consul like a nervous horse. "I see," he said.

"Name of Captain Loustenau," Mr. Moore whispered. "Took him out to make room for her. Poor sod came here on a visit, got a pain in his belly and died all of a sudden. Years ago. She doted on his bones." He gave a slight shrug. "Lazy, encroaching rascal, to hear it told. But rather in her style, if you understand me."

Mr. Thomson cleared his throat in faint question.

"Young and good-looking," Mr. Moore amplified.

"Ah," Mr. Thomson said dubiously.

"Old Barker was the consul in her glory days," Mr. Moore added in a suggestive murmur, "and he used to say Michael Bruce was the handsomest devil that ever walked on two legs."

"Indeed," the missionary said.

Mr. Moore gave him an amused look. "Her lover, you know."

Mr. Thomson pursed his lips.

"Took him to her bed when he was twenty-three, she did," the consul remarked. "She was—oh, must have been thirty-four, thirty-five, if she was a day. Regular spinster by then. Traveled all about Turkey and Syria together, the two of them. Proud as a lord, she was; didn't care a button for what anybody thought. Dressed in trousers and rode astride like a Turkish pasha. Never would marry Bruce, though they say he begged her. Made him leave her here alone. Old Barker said she was boastful of it. Considered it a noble sacrifice, so that he could go home and become a Great Man." Mr. Moore shook his head. "Not that he ever managed that, more's the pity."

"I see," Mr. Thomson said. "How—singular."

The two men gazed at the coffin, each thinking of the withered white corpse they had found, after a fast day's ride from Beyrout, lying uncovered in the oppressive heat. Mr. Thomson felt that he should make some comment upon the wages of sin, but this pathetic end, dying abandoned among unchristian strangers and rubbish and the ruins of her desert fortress, seemed punishment enough for a transgression that must have taken place a quarter century ago. Mr. Moore merely thought it incredible that peculiar old Hester Stanhope, the mad Queen of the Desert, could ever have had the power to enslave such a lady-killer as Bruce was said to have been. Although Mr. Moore had never clapped eyes on her alive, he well knew Lady Hester by her reputation, not to mention her relentless feuding with any English consul, including himself, so unfortunate as to be posted within the orbit of her concern. But Mr. Moore's imagination failed him when he tried to envision Lady Hester as anything but an elderly recluse declaiming prophecies and interfering with consulate business, sending out scathing letters to everybody and complaining about her debts from the unbreachable sanctum of her mountain fastness.

"Devilish odd woman," he muttered. "Nasty sharp tongue in her head, too, let me tell you."

"May God have mercy on her soul," the missionary said softly.

"Amen," Mr. Moore said. "Best get on with it in this heat."

Mr. Thomson took firm possession of his wits, lifted the prayer book and began to read. As the stentorous words echoed about the arbor, another English gentleman moved quietly into the edge of the flickering light.

The consul glanced over at him, gave a courteous nod, and then piously lowered his eyes again. Reverend Thomson paused in his recitation, in case this should be a mourner with some real attachment to the deceased, who might wish to console himself with a nearer position to the coffin. But the latecomer did not join him in the front, instead remaining a little removed from either the servants or the officiators.

He was a tall man, well built, dressed in boots and an English shooting jacket, a powder flask clipped on the belt slung across his chest. His hair was as black as the mouth of the crypt. In the uneasy light, his eyes appeared quite dark as pitch, and his general aspect, to the Reverend Thomson's already frayed nerves, rather uncomfortably satanic.

"Lord Winter," Mr. Moore muttered under his breath.

As this name meant nothing to the American missionary—and since Lord Winter returned Mr. Thomson's nod of invitation with nothing but a silent stare—he resumed his service. The reverend was still feeling ruffled, but reflected that this bizarre funeral, along with some other incidents of his sojourn among the benighted of the East which he had recorded in his diary, should at least collect nicely into a volume of travel memoirs when the time was ripe.

For his part, Lord Winter manifested no hint of surprise or dismay at the novelty of the scene. The body was laid to rest in a dignified silence, only one of the black maids showing any sign of real sorrow in her quiet weeping. Beside her, a Bedouin boy stood straight and still, his wild elf-locks falling down on his shoulders, his dirty feet bare, a dagger at his waist and an ancient wheel-lock musket resting over his shoulder as if he had just come in like a young panther from the desert. Lord Winter's searching gaze paused on him a moment, took in the girlish kohl-lined lashes, full lips and delicate chin peculiar to nomad Arab youth, and passed on. Familiar with the Bedu, he did not doubt this superficial frailty was a complete illusion, and the boy capable of the most arduous exertion and cold-blooded banditry. But he was not the man Lord Winter was looking for.

It was apparent that this particular individual had not chosen to grace the company with his presence. Viscount Winter did not allow the man's absence to concern him, for it was unsurprising that the presence of Frankish strangers would make such a person wary of entering the walls of Dar Joon.

His expression grew distinctly sardonic as the consul unfolded a Union Jack and draped the flag of Britain over Lady Hester's coffin. Of all her enemies, she had hated the missionaries and English consuls most fiercely: to be laid in her grave beneath the Union Jack and sermoned over by a Christian minister would have made her sick with rage.

Although the viscount's attendance at Lady Hester's funeral was chance met, coincident with his private engagement at her hilltop fortress, he was conscious of a feeling of regret that he had not come to her once more before she died. But his mouth lifted in a saturnine smile at the sentiment. No; if he had known the end was near, he would have hired the wildest Bedouins he could find and mounted an attack on the place, so that she could have died fighting.

She had always wanted that. She had told him.

He should have done it.

The service over, the Frenchman's bones returned to lie beside Lady Hester's coffin and the crypt sealed, Mr. Moore turned promptly and offered his hand. "Good evening, my lord! Or good morning, I fear. Wretched business, this. Decent of you to come."

"I was in the district," Lord Winter said briefly.

Mr. Thomson asked in a hopeful tone, "You are a friend of the deceased?"

"Yes," Lord Winter said. He paused. "I had that honor."

"A very great lady, I am sure," Reverend Thomson said, on a funereal note.

"Indeed," the consul said hastily. "A most extraordinary life. Will you take a late supper with us down in the village, my lord? They tell me we have beds arranged there."

"As pleasing as that sounds," Winter said, "I prefer to stay here tonight, if you will permit me."

Mr. Moore looked astonished. "Here? But I'll have to seal the place. I can't allow the servants to remain."

"Perhaps," the missionary suggested gently, "as a mourner, Lord Winter wishes to be alone to reflect on this melancholy occasion."

"Oh. Yes. Quite." Mr. Moore gave the proposed mourner a doubtful glance, not being accustomed to considering the Right Honorable Arden Mansfield, Viscount Winter, in the light of a very feeling man. "Well, if that's the case, I suppose it must be permissible."

"Thank you." Lord Winter bowed his head. "I am much obliged to you."

Mr. Moore looked as if he might toss some quick remark, but then held his tongue. He merely smiled wisely and made his bow in return.

The consul would have been very much surprised to learn just how deeply Lord Winter did feel this death. After all the servants were herded out, their torches ablaze—professedly to light the steep, rutted path downhill for the missionary and Mr. Moore but in base truth for the worthier purpose of holding off night-demons and hyenas—Lord Winter barred the gate and walked back through the dark garden to the grave. He broke a rose from a sprawling bush, gazing moodily at the trampled earth and muddy stones before the crypt. The filthy condition of the place bespoke the neglect of decades. And yet beneath the debris it was still Dar Joon, the fabulous palace of the Queen of the Desert.

The desert—and Lady Hester. They had been tinder to a boy's dreams, the spark and the flame of his manhood. English mist, the clipped gardens of Swanmere, none of it had ever seemed so real to Arden as the fierce air of the wilderness. And no woman had ever possessed his mind as Lady Hester Stanhope had done.

He could not remember a time in his life when he had not known of her. When he was five years old, she had defied Bedouin brigands and crossed the desert to become the first Englishwoman ever to enter Palmyra; while Arden was still in short coats, pestering his father's trout with a string and a stick, she had searched for treasure in the ruins of Ascalon; as he was learning to jump his first pony, she had commanded a pasha's troops, laying waste the countryside in sanguinary retribution for a friend's murder; before he became a man she had defied an emir, dared the Eastern prince to send his son to make terms with her, so that she might kill him with her own hands. She had dressed as desert tribesmen and Turks dressed; she had given shelter to wounded Druses and rebellious Albanians, to orphans and defeated Mamelukes. When the all-conquering, all-powerful Ibrahim Pasha had demanded that she render up his enemies to him, she had said only, "Come and take them." And he had not cared to try.

She had never disappointed Arden, though age had withered her into impossible metaphysics and flights of astrology and magic. In her twilight she was more majestic than any female he had ever encountered. They said she had claimed to be the bride of the new Messiah, but Arden had never heard her claim it— only that she would ride beside Him into Jerusalem. She had possessed a towering conceit and a biting wit, a mind distracted by absurd prophecies, but it was the heart of a lioness that had defended this one mountaintop, alone amid the vicious tyrannies of the East, and kept it free of any law but her own.

Arden tossed the white rose down before the crypt. He had been born too late. Hester Stanhope was dead. He would never in his own lifetime find a woman to match her, and tonight, the indefinable restless loneliness that drove him—always drove him to the empty, brutal places of the earth, as if he could find there whatever piece of his soul he had been born missing—seemed sharper than it had seemed in a long while.

With a muttered curse, he doused his lamp and turned away from the crypt. By starlight, he walked desultorily among the silent courts, picking his way through the serpentine pathways toward the strangers' quarters where he intended to make his bed, losing himself twice in the maze of screens and passages. Finally, more suddenly than he expected, he stepped round a corner into a grassy yard.

He stopped. In the quiet, the sound of weeping came to him—no simple crying, but the terrible, rending sobs of a soul in the depths of despair.

With eyes adjusted to the dark, he saw the dim glow of light from an open door across the yard. Intrigued by this unexpected sign of occupation in a room supposed to have been sealed along with all the others, Lord Winter walked over the grass, allowing his boots to scuff an audible warning. He looked in at the chamber from which sprang this desperate lament and observed a figure in a dingy striped *abah*, hunched down in an attitude of profound misery among open chests and boxes full of papers.

Lord Winter made no attempt to conceal himself, but stood openly in the doorway. Even so, when he spoke the boy leapt back, knocking over a stool and sending papers flying in his start. The clattering sound was like a gunshot echoing off the stone walls.

"Peace be with you." Lord Winter gave a greeting in Arabic, recognizing the Bedouin lad of the flowing elf-locks and primeval musket. The youth said nothing, only stared at him with dread, breathing in heavy, uneven hiccoughs.

The young Bedui had reason enough to look dismayed. The consul had meant to lock all the servants out. No one with the least acquaintance with the Bedouin would trust that this son of desert robbers had remained behind for anything but larcenous intent, weeping or not. The boy held himself poised, as if he might be sprung upon at an instant.

Lord Winter returned the frightened stare with a shrug. "*Ma'aleyk*, there shall be no evil upon you, wolf cub. Come and drink my coffee."

If he expected this offer of hospitality to engender any gratifying degree of friendliness or appreciation in his audience, he was mistaken. The youth did not appear to be of a confiding nature. He remained standing silently amid the shadowy chaos of papers.

"*Yallah!*" Arden turned away. "Proceed with the sacking, then. God is great!"

"Lord Winter," the boy exclaimed in a husky, perfectly well-bred English accent. "I'm not a thief!"

The effect of hearing his own name and English tongue fluently on the lips of this disreputable desert urchin was more startling than Arden liked to disclose. He looked back, one brow cocked.

"My lord," the boy asked despairingly, "will you give me to the consul?"

"It's no matter to me if you steal all this rubbish you can carry," he answered, reverting to English himself. "But it appears that her loyal retainers have made off with everything down to the last spoon already."

"I'm not stealing!" the lad insisted.

Lord Winter leaned against the doorjamb and gave him a skeptical nod. "As you say."

"The consul—"

"My dear child," Winter said, "if you suppose I babble everything I know to the likes of Mr. Moore, you are vastly mistaken in my character. I daresay even he would be astonished at the thought. Did Lady Hester teach you English?"

The boy hesitated, and then said in Arabic, "Yes, *ma'alem*. May it please Allah."

"She seems to have achieved uncommonly good success. How long have you been in her service?"

But the lad retreated into shyness at such pressing questions. "For many summers, *ma'alem*," he mumbled, turning his face downward.

From his voice and beardless face Arden thought him not more than fifteen, perhaps younger. He stood taller than the usual child of the Bedu—but he had the pure, gaunt look of the desert upon him, everything about him Beduish from his small, graceful hands beneath ragged cuffs to the shoulderlength braids of the two lovelocks dangling down beside his cheeks, emblem of a young nomad gallant, and the huge curved dagger tied to his waist. Slender as a reed, with a pensive, tear-swollen face and smooth sun-hued skin.

Arden was disposed to like him, for no reason but that he was Bedouin, and a member of the freest race on earth. "Come, little wolf, take your drink of me, and the Lord give you life," he said.

The boy glanced up under his wet lashes. He seemed reluctant to accept the invitation, his large dark eyes full of tears and as wary as a gazelle's. Lord Winter was not especially conversant with the science of weeping, since he had little to do with children and sought out feminine company for one purpose only, having a detached disdain for womankind in general and a violent dislike in particular for the sort of wilting, flower-scented young English ladies so frequently served up to him in the hope that he might do his aristocratic duty and select one for his bride. But looking upon the trembling lip and filling eyes, he feared an imminent relapse in this case.

"Son of the wolf, weep not—you are Arab!" he commanded, to forestall the impending flood. This bracing admonishment seemed to have the reverse effect, however, for the lad burst out with a sob and covered his face with his hands.

With a wry twist to his mouth, Lord Winter watched the slight figure for a moment. He shouldered his rifle and pushed off the door. "Suit your own convenience, then." He strolled back into the courtyard, leaving the boy to his determined woe.

Two

THE WRETCHED INDIVIDUAL he abandoned to tears sank down amid the piles of useless papers. Zenobia was still shaking with the alarm of discovery, unable to stop the crying which so disgusted Lord Winter.

Lord Winter! If only it had been faithful Dr. Meryon, or kind Monsieur Guys from the French consulate, or even one of the German travelers; if only someone had come besides Lord Winter, with his cold-blooded indifference and his humor as cutting as her mother's.

She had been sure he would give her to the consul for thievery. And the consul would give her to Emir Bechir to cut off her hand if he thought she was a Bedu boy, or demand the thousands of pounds outstanding to Lady Hester's creditors if he discovered who Zenobia truly was. The English had taken away her mother's pension to pay her debts, and Lady Hester had written in fury to the English Queen herself, resigning her citizenship in a nation of slaves. But if the consul discovered that Lady Hester had a daughter, what might they not do to her to recover the money? He would tell the Jewish money-lenders and Turkish merchants and the English Queen; Zenia might be sold as a slave herself to pay the debts, because beneath her shabby robes she was white-skinned and valuable, the only thing of value that Lady Hester had left. Zenia would never have a chance to escape, to reach England and find her father there; she would never see a whole land like a garden; she would never be among her own people or have a proper dress as English ladies wore.

The thought of the dress made fresh tears roll down her cheeks. She was twenty-five years old, and barefoot. It came as no surprise to Zenia that Lord Winter mistook her for a Bedu youth. In her childhood, her mother had never allowed her to dress in anything but the male costumes of the Turks. Only Lady Hester's maid Miss Williams, marooned by her despotic mistress among the infidels, had secretly made up English clothes for Zenia, and when Lady Hester was sleeping let the little girl practice her English bows and manners. But Miss Williams had died, and Zenia had been sent to the Bedouins in the desert, and never since then had she owned a gown or shoes or stockings. The Bedu gave Zenia a musket and a camel and an Arab name, and consulted her on magic, because she was the daughter of the Queen of the Englezys.

She hugged herself, burying her hands and calloused feet in the folds of her robe. Oh, a true princess, she: princess of the lawless land of famine, a miserable queen of nothing.

If she had believed for a few hopeful days, when Lady Hester called her back to Dar Joon, that her mother wished for her presence out of loneliness or affection, or thought to send her to England, such optimistic conjecture was soon set to right. Zenia was not allowed to discard her Bedouin garments; she was not even suffered to replace them, for there was no money. Somehow Lady Hester's spies were paid, presents made to pashas and beggarly dervishes fed at her doors, but there was no money for new clothes for Zenia. For the last five years she had served her mother's frenzied whims and lived hidden behind the screens again, listening as Lady Hester told such infrequent English guests as Lord Winter that she would rather sleep with pack mules than with women, which made him laugh and answer that she was too severe, that sleeping was the only undertaking he found to be tolerable with women.

If only it was not Lord Winter who had come!

Zenia clasped the miniature that hung about her neck beneath the striped folds of her threadbare *abah*. It was the single item she possessed, a fragile thread: the only thing, sometimes, that convinced her in the face of all experience that she was not this ragged Bedouin boy in truth. Years ago, in one of her mother's hysterical fits of melancholy, Lady Hester had thrown the keepsake from her window down the cliff, but Miss Williams had sent Hanah Massad to retrieve it. Her mother's gentle companion had pressed the small portrait into Zenia's hands with a scared look, whispering, "This is your father. Don't forget! She must not know you know it!"

To a child, the fear in the eyes of her only friend had made a profound impression. They were all frightened of Lady Hester's temper and her Eastern punishments. She would not hesitate to bastinado an erring servant, having the soles of his feet beaten until he was crippled for life, and she had prided herself on the strength with which she could deliver a slap to the face of an impudent maid. Zenia had crept about her mother's chamber with apprehension, quick to obey any order, for which she was derided daily as a spiritless milk-and-water miss.

Forewarned, Zenia had always taken the most extreme care to

hide the miniature painting from her mother. She cherished it. She took the portrait from beneath her robes only in the greatest secrecy, and memorized the features of the handsome young man with beautiful eyes and the shadow of a tender smile in his expression, as if he looked into the distance at something he loved. In Zenia's dreams, he was looking at her. Inside lay a lock of hair and a roll of paper written upon in an untidy hand: *For my dearest love, the most wonderful creature in the world, affectionately yours Mic. Bruce.*

His dearest love was her mother, of course. The most wonderful creature in the world. But his smile—Zenia pressed the miniature against her breast and stole his loving smile for herself.

She rose, holding the keepsake gripped in her hand, swallowing tears. Wiping her face with her sleeve, she returned all the papers to their chests and doused the lamp, curling up with her broken musket in a corner. Her mother had never suffered Zenia to speak of going to England in her lifetime. But once, after Lady Hester had been reminiscing about her girlhood among the greatest British statesmen of the day, smoking her fragrant *narguile* and telling Dr. Meryon reverent stories of her uncle Mr. Pitt and her grandfather Lord Chatham, Prime Ministers both, mimicking Lord Byron's lisp and laughing at the way Lamartine had kissed his poodle, she had called Zenia to her in the small hours of the night and promised that there was money set aside so that Zenia might go home.

She felt a great fool now to have believed her mother. Lady Hester had ever been able to command the imagination of those who sat through the long nights listening to her speak. Zenia had been too credulous of this, the thing she desired over all else. She did not believe now that there had ever been any such special savings hidden away as Lady Hester had pledged to her, or if there had been once, the money was long spent on a pair of dueling pistols or a gold-braided camel's harness to gratify some smooth-voiced lying pasha, or just as probably stolen by Lady Hester's rapacious servants.

She would make her way by herself. If she had not a penny, if she was barefoot, if she did not know where he lived or even if he lived, even so Zenobia was fixed in her purpose. She hated the desert and Dar Joon. She was going home, the home where she had never been. She was going to find her father in England, and live like the Englishwoman that she was.

She sought for a more comfortable position, leaning her shoulders against the wall. She had not lain down to sleep for the past four days, sitting up beside her mother while Lady Hester lay wrapped in her drifting white robes, coughing and gasping for breath as the servants prowled through Dar Joon and stole what scraps were left. Her mother had wailed hoarsely at her to stop them, but as soon as Zenia rose Lady Hester cried for her to come back.

Huddled in her corner, Zenia feared to sleep now. There were secret entrances to Dar Joon, and wolves sometimes climbed the walls. She had never been so alone, and wished that she had gone down to the village with the others. She couldn't leave now, with the dark and the demons. Her mother's frenzied weeping haunted her as soon as she closed her eyes. It wove into lifelike dreams, and she trembled, afraid that she would wake and find Lady Hester's ghost calling for her. Voices seemed to echo in the empty rooms, and white hands in pale robes reached out to detain her.

The crack of a gunshot made her body jerk. The voices were suddenly real, shouts and running footsteps. She hunched in the corner, staring toward the door. Light bobbled, throwing fantastic shadows in the garden outside.

A figure in white Eastern robes stole inside the door. Zenia gasped. It was her mother—Zenia pressed her spine against the wall, staring at her mother's ghost. She sat immobilized in terror, watching it sink into the blind shadows just beside the portal. For an instant she could see the gleam of metal, and then it too was lost in shadow. She heard the cock of a gun.

"Wolf cub!" a man's voice hissed.

The English words startled her. She panted silently with fear. She did not want to answer, or reveal her position.

"Do you know a way out?" he whispered. "They have the main gate covered, and the tunnel from the stable."

Zenia was too frightened to answer. She heard rough voices, the crashing sound of a door kicked in.

"Damn you—are you here?" he muttered.

"Yes," she whispered.

"Then bloody well give me some help!"

"Beside the fountain," she said, in a voice that shivered with her breath. "Under the vines."

He made a soft English curse. "Nothing closer?"

"No, my lord."

"Lead the way."

She sat against the wall, shuddering.

"Coming?" he demanded softly. "These aren't respectable fellows, my cub. They're deserters."

Deserters! She grabbed her broken musket and stood up, quaking in all her limbs. She could hear the others coming. The light suddenly increased as they broke into the court outside.

She saw the gleam on metal again, as he aimed from behind the doorpost. The explosion made her body jump, a yellow flash that lit his face and the room, burning it on her eyelids, then suddenly all was blackness and angry shouts.

"Go!" Lord Winter snapped, and Zenia moved, stumbling over boxes toward the door. From the dark he groped and grabbed her arm, shoving her out into the court.

Someone ran into her. She bit back a cry and cringed against Lord Winter. She felt him move as hard hands closed on her— there was an ugly whack, a grunt, and the clutching fingers dropped away. The gunstock hit her as Lord Winter recovered his balance, a hard jolt on her collarbone and a tangling of their gun barrels together, but she threw herself pell-mell toward the courtyard wall.

Lord Winter came with her, close at her back. Her toes dug into the dirt as she flung around a corner, making her way by memory and feel, for she could see nothing. Lord Winter's hand gripped her shoulder.

A shot blasted from behind them, echoing around the walls. Zenia tripped, her foot thrust under a root. Her ankle twisted. She fell hard, with cold pain flashing up her leg and thorns ripping into her hands and face as she smashed facedown amid a rose bush.

Lord Winter dragged her up, but another body intervened, a chaos of shoving and struggle. She could not tell if it was a knife or thorns that tore across her. She rolled over and staggered to her knees, leaning on her musket, as another report exploded in her ear. She saw the moment like a traceried still life: Lord Winter rising on one knee with his rifle at elbow level, the bright fireball of light from its muzzle thrust point-blank against the chest of a bearded man. The dazzling afterimage hid any more, but she heard the heavy crash of his body into the roses.

She tried to run, pitching onto her knee again as her ankle failed her. Lord Winter hauled her up. She used her broken musket as a crutch, limping heavily, groping ahead with her free hand.

She collided suddenly with the fountain, encountering the marble edge with a gasp and a splash. Feeling her way to the side, she scrabbled through a mass of honeysuckle to find the concealed door.

Light cast a shadow on the wall. "Down!" Lord Winter ordered sharply, and she dropped. She ran her fingers over the wall, searching, afraid that he must be out of rounds. He could not have reloaded the rifle while they ran, and she hadn't seen that he carried pistols.

Even as she thought it, he fired—twice in rapid succession. The light vanished.

Her fingers found the wooden latch. She pushed the trapdoor open.

"Here!" she whispered.

He came after her, rustling the vines, climbing down into the slanting hole. Zenia slid down on her belly with her musket beside her. At the lower entrance, she pushed the concealing brush away with her good foot, skidding into the open air outside the walls. In the starlight, the valley and the limestone mountains lay white and silent, the cliff falling away from the base of the wall in a shadowed jumble of rock.

Her ankle throbbed, a sickening pain that seemed to take her breath. Lord Winter stole past her, the Arab head scarf flowing back over his shoulders, his face lost in shadow.

Zenia tried to stand up and made a faint whimper. But long ago she had learned that in the desert those who fell behind were easily forgotten. She limped desperately after, trying to stay in his footsteps on the rough ground. They circled away from the main gate and the village, taking a barely visible goat track. Zenia used her hands and toes and fingernails to drag herself between the boulders.

For as long as she could she pursued his swift pace, losing ground with every excruciating step, until finally she was so far behind that she lost the pale shade of his outline.

She was alone in the dark. She kept hobbling quickly, even after she came to the valley floor, afraid of what she might see if she paused and looked behind her. There were eerie things abroad at night—this night, when her mother lay in her crypt. Lady Hester was angry: Zenia could feel it. She knew Zenia meant to leave her.

Her mother had chosen Dar Joon deliberately for its dreadful isolation, to prevent her servants running away any farther than the tiny village where they could easily be seized and hauled back. Between Zenia and the way to England lay a waterless mountain country haunted by jackals and wolves and civil war. She had nothing but the robes she wore, a broken musket without powder, and a horror of walking through the demon-plagued passes alone.

A wild cry came from somewhere on the ridges above her. She tripped, pitching to her knees and scrambling to rise again, trying to listen over the sound of her own panting. She could hear nothing at first, but as she sank down against the musket, a jackal laughed. She looked back in the direction of Dar Joon. The moon was just coming up, casting cold shadows that seemed alive. As she stared at them, they crept across the ground toward her until she had to close her eyes to keep from bursting into tears.

Then she heard the hooves. The sound came out of the dark, echoing from the rocks around her, so that she could not tell from what direction. She staggered to her feet just as the animal was upon her, a huge dark shape—a djinni, a hot-breathed devil, materialized out of the night with her mother mounted upon it in flying pale robes. Its hooves nearly trampled her, spraying sand and rock as it halted. Zenia cried out and scrambled away, but her ankle crumpled; nauseating pain stole her breath and rushed blackness up into her brain.

The next she knew, there was rocky ground against her aching cheek, her musket tangled awkwardly beneath her, and Lord Winter's cool voice telling her not to be a cocklehead.

"A djinni," she whimpered, clutching at his robe. "There was a djinni!"

"Nonsense." There was a firm arm beneath her shoulder. "On your feet."

Zenia was shaking, unable to let go of him. She struggled to stand, but her ankle kept failing beneath her weight. The pain made her vision hazy and wayward. "A demon—"

"You're all right, little wolf," he said tersely. "I'm here."

Looking up at his harsh face in the moonlight, his solid height and the breadth of his shoulders, Zenia experienced a conversion of mind as precipitate as it was complete. She no longer saw Viscount Winter of the acerbic remarks and black disdain. She did not see another of her mother's mysterious friends; she did not see a man whose dark temperament had always made her feel apprehensive even behind the screens.

She saw her savior.

Lord Winter had come to Dar Joon. And whatever else he might be, he was not afraid of demons.

Three

"BUT WE ARE in the mountains!" the thin youth cried, working to sit upright and clear of Lord Winter in the saddle. The viscount merely pulled him back, holding the slender, shivering body against his chest with little effort. The boy's slight frame was shaking like a leaf, so delicate that it had surprised Arden when he'd first taken the youth up before him in the dark.

"You are a wretched specimen," he remarked. "I shall have to see that you dine more regularly, or else lose you in a high wind."

"We are in the *mountains*!" the boy gasped again.

"So you have informed me." Lord Winter surveyed the looming peaks and ridges in the cold dawn light, having always an eye on the surroundings for more reason than the spectacular scenery. His mule was toiling up a narrow terrace beside the ruin of a burned-out farm, dragging an unwilling baggage donkey past sprigs of vegetation that swelled through the cinders. "Do you have some further disclosure to make on the topic?"

"We must turn back!" the boy exclaimed. "You cannot go this way!"

"This is the way I wish to go," he said calmly.

"Then you are a madman!" His passenger made a sudden and determined snatch at the reins. "We'll be killed here!"

The mule jibbed and swerved as Lord Winter yanked the boy's interfering hands back, holding them in a hard grip. The viscount steadied the confused animal while pebbles skittered down the steep terrace edge beside them.

"Turn around!" the boy cried, struggling against his imprisonment. "You can't know; you don't understand—this country is death!"

"You are cross this morning, aren't you?" Arden released his captive, halted the mule and swung down in a tiny patch of charred barley stems. "Hungry, I expect. And I suppose your ankle pains you, though you haven't taken much real hurt, by the look of it."

The Bedouin boy grabbed the reins. Wind blew his long tangled hair across his face as he kicked wildly at the mule's ribs, attempting to haul the animal about on the terrace ledge.

"There is an unfortunate circumstance—" Lord Winter stood back from the struggle. "If you are considering flight—I feel I should perhaps point out that you have a loaded donkey affixed in your rear."

The boy looked over his shoulder, where the little ass stood with all four legs planted, browsing determinedly on the nearest bush.

"I fear you won't be galloping away at any great rate with that in tow," the viscount observed, giving the mule's rump an affectionate slap. "Provided this animal could be persuaded to gallop

at all, which is an unsettled question. I've not been so far privi-
leged to see her attain more than a competent trot."

Forced to the same conclusion, and worse, Zenia let the reins
fall from fingers that were clumsy with terror and cold. She felt
distraught, waking from an exhausted nightmare to discover herself high up on the steep paths into the Jabal Lebanon, the mountains proper, in rebellious Druze country where she would not
dare to slide from the animal's back and set out alone even if she
ventured to brave the consul and Dar Joon. Her sprained ankle
throbbed. The mountains were infested with renegades from the
Egyptian armies, the farms abandoned, pillaged and destroyed by
marauding Druzes and Metouleys bent on vengeance against
their own emir.

Lord Winter seemed entirely careless of their danger, though
she found it improbable that he was as unaware of the peril as he
affected to be. He was dressed as an Arab in a flowing white
burnous, a kuffiyah bound upon his head by a simple gold cord-
ing. His eyes, of a clear deep blue, held an aspect of hardened
competence that was no product of inexperience. On his shoulder
he carried a rifle, a weapon such as Zenia had never seen, its satin
wood beautifully chased with gold and silver, its firing mechanism
strange and foreign: a gun that would rivet the attention of any
Arab who beheld it. A pair of pistols, similarly fashioned, and a
flintlock musket were holstered on the saddle, all finely made; all
clean and wicked.

Plainly Lord Winter knew where he was going and what he
intended to do. As she looked at him, the significance of his cos-
tume and gear struck Zenia with profound effect.

"*Wellah!*" she exclaimed in Arabic. "Why do you wear this
clothing?"

"Ah—have I not made myself known?" he answered fluently,
sweeping a bow. "You behold Abu Haj Hasan, the *Moghreby* of

Seville, a Spanish Moor returned to the religion of his forefathers. I've made the pilgrimage to Mecca and now wander into the desert as Allah and my fancy take me." He smiled up at her with disarming mockery. "By God's grace my mother was a white princess of Andaluz. You may have noticed that I have her eyes."

"My lord!" Zenia wailed. "You will not!"

"I think I will, wolf cub."

"You're a Christian! They will slay you in an instant if you're discovered masquerading so!"

"That," he said imperturbably, "is of course a mishap I shall strive to avoid."

"My lord, I beg you, I plead with you to listen to me. It is madness. Any Moslemin will know you for a *Nasrany* the first time you must pray!"

"Come, do you take me for a fool?" he asked with sudden impatience. "I know the proper prayers as well as any Bedouin—better than you know them yourself, if the lack of pious observance I've seen from you so far is any sign. Have you even yet endured the *muzayyin*, boy?"

Zenia well knew of what he spoke. As the daughter of the Queen of the Englezys, Zenia had been considered lucky among the black tents, and often invited by an anxious mother to witness the circumcision rites. She felt herself flush hotly. "Of course!" she lied in haste. "Allah be praised."

He nodded, with a flicker of new respect in his eyes, and then grinned suddenly. "I'll admit I resorted to chloroform," he said in English.

She gave a faint moan, horrified at the idea of an adult man and a Christian willfully enduring such a thing. "You are a madman! None will believe it. You are Lord Winter."

"*Ay billah*, it saddens me to inform you that Lord Winter has been murdered," he answered. "Those villains we left behind last night are already arrested, if Moore has the enterprise to act speedily on the information I laid for him. One should not, however, put much faith in the promptness of consuls."

"But you are not murdered, my lord!" Distractedly, she held the windblown hair back from her face.

"Am I not?" Lord Winter glanced up, his mocking blue eyes full of amusement, but his expression altered as he regarded her. His brows rose. Zenia instantly lowered her hand, turning away in fear he might see that her skin also was pale beneath the sun's browning, like his; that her eyes were dark blue, not truly black; that she resembled her mother even though Lady Hester had always denied the likeness.

He caught her arm, pulling her back around toward him. She let him see her profile, her heart pounding, her mouth turned down sullenly.

"But you are Adonis himself, child!" he murmured. "You weren't such a beauty when your face was sopped in tears." He gave her a shake, his jaw tightening. "Take care that you don't find yourself sold to the Turks, my cub. You're rash to wander alone."

"Oh, *ma'alem*!" she said, with a compulsive closing of her fingers. "It is my greatest fear."

She immediately wished she had not said so much, but he did not seem inclined to sneer at her. "Stay within earshot, then," he said shortly. "Don't wander off without me."

This brusque instruction threw Zenia into a welter of conflicting emotions. He was the first person who had ever offered her any protection at all, but he had stranded her here, nowhere, made it impossible to get to Beyrout and from there to England. In her alarm and despair, an agitated idea took possession of her mind.

She watched him as he cuffed the mule's nose away and stepped back to the donkey. She did not know how to use the strange pistols, but as soon as his attention and his hands were occupied with the baggage thongs, she dragged the musket from its saddle scabbard.

He turned. Zenia raised the gun, aiming point-blank at his head. She pulled back the cock.

Lord Winter looked steadily into her sights, unmoving. He made no shift to use his rifle or even let go of the baggage cord. She sought for words in her dry throat, words to force him to her will, but his complete lack of fear made it painfully obvious that the musket she held was not loaded and primed. They stared at one another over the dull gleam of steel. Her hands were shaking. Slowly, she let the barrel decline, pointing it at the ground.

"Uncock it, if you would be so kind," he said gently. "That is, if you have determined not to shoot me."

Zenia realized she had been wrong; it was loaded indeed. But she admitted with bitterness, "I will not shoot you."

"I rather hoped not." He nudged the muzzle aside with a brush of his hand and held it there. "In that case, let us aim this well to the outside, if you please."

She released the musket to half-cock. "I have not an ounce of spirit."

He laughed. "It's no matter—I have enough for both of us."

"I want none of yours," she said darkly. "You are mad."

"Too severe, wolf cub. My father merely holds that I'm a changeling. Or a malicious prank played upon him by Fate." As he took the musket from her and rested the stock on the ground, his grin faded to a smile, an expression of surprising sweetness on his sunburned face. "Reckon me as you like, but I'm a fair shot, and not the worst companion to have by you in a tight corner." He hefted the musket, cradling it in one arm as he looked down at the firing pin.

"Companion!" she exclaimed. "Do you know what is said of you here? You are driven from your home by an evil demon, who goads you into the most terrible deserts, so that you must suffer agonies for whatever dreadful sin you have committed. That is what they say of you!"

His hands stilled for a moment, his face hidden from her. Then he flipped the safety catch into place, running his thumb lightly over the hammer. "Now there's a useful premise. My own personal demon. Makes people rather nervous of crossing me, I expect. I wonder no one's ever mentioned it."

"They would not like to say so to your face."

"Ah, Turkish manners! But you are Bedu, and have no such scruples, I perceive." He lifted his head, handing up the gun to her. "That's yours. I gave the antique an honorable retirement some way back, in a little contretemps with a djinni."

She held the excellent weapon, its metal bleeding the warmth of his body into her palm. "Why do you give it to me?" she asked suspiciously.

"It'll serve you better than a demon, where we're going."

"Where," she asked in a fading voice, "are you going?"

"Oh, the worst of deserts, naturally," he answered with outrageous cheerfulness. "Across the red sands to the Nejd."

Zenia instantly held the musket out. "You must take it back. I'm going to Beyrout."

"Are you?" He gave her a dark and charming smile. "I wonder how?"

She wet her lips. "Please, my lord," she said. "You cannot have meant to bring me with you."

"No. But neither do I mean to haul you to Beyrout, so put any hope of that from your mind. I'll leave you in the first place we come to, if you like. Mezarib, perhaps. Or Bozra, if we've come as far south as I intend that we have."

"Bozra!" She had heard of it, a caravan town some days out of Damascus, on the hajj road to Mecca. She would no longer be in the mountains there—she would be in worse case than here, farther than ever from Beyrout, abandoned on the edges of the desert itself where the Bedu raided most frequently; and a part of the desert where she knew neither friends nor allies.

The dismayed expression of his companion was not lost on Lord Winter. "If you start blubbering again, I'll abandon you right here," he said caustically. "Get down and make yourself useful. And what the devil is your name?"

Zenia, well broken to the voice of command, ducked her head and dismounted. She choked back a sound of pain as her cold and swollen feet touched the ground.

"Selim, your excellency," she said, the first Arab name that came to her tongue.

"There's food in the packs," he said, "and the animals need grain and water."

She limped hurriedly to do his bidding, the rocks icy and rough beneath her bare feet. She was shivering so badly in the cold mountain air that she could hardly untie the donkey's halter.

Lord Winter seemed uninterested in her labors. He stepped up onto an elevated ledge and knelt there, overlooking the mountainside, the beautiful rifle balanced across one knee. Zenia had no quarrel with that: she was glad to know he kept watch. She led the animals to the spring and filled a goatskin with fresh water.

She carried it to Lord Winter. He took it from her. Zenia stood shuddering in the chill while he drank.

"Bring the food and sit here," he said, pointing below him. "Out of the wind. We'll rest an hour."

Wordlessly, she searched among the baggage, found unleavened bread and olives, and brought them back to the place where he waited. They ate in silence, Lord Winter still mounted upon the rock and Zenia huddled below, while the last stars began to disappear and the wind swept across the mountaintops.

"What Arab are you?" Lord Winter asked.

"I am Anezy."

"Oh, that is instructive!" Arden said dryly. It was a huge tribe, the largest in the desert, with kinsmen spread from Syria to his destination in the center of the Arabian Peninsula. "What tents among the Anezy?"

This time the silence was longer. Finally, the boy said, "El-Nasr."

"*Wellah*," Lord Winter murmured, somewhat disappointed. The Nasr was a small *fendi* of the tribe, greatly weakened since the days when they had been Lady Hester's old Bedu allies. Their sheik was still respected over all the Anezy, Arden thought, but they were a family of the north. He should have guessed—the boy was bitterly thin, but too tall, and too timorous, to be home-bred in the pitiless crucible of the southern deserts.

But still, a member of el-Nasr would have a passport to his distant Anezy kinsmen in the south.

"Does el-Nasr have any blood feuds?" he asked.

"No," the boy said reluctantly. "But I am not sure—I haven't been in the desert for—" He paused, and shrugged. "For a very long time."

"How long?"

"Many summers," he said vaguely.

Lord Winter smiled. "Just how many summers have you seen in your life, O ancient one?"

Selim appeared to be much interested in discarding the seed from his olive. "I don't know, my lord."

The viscount looked down upon the boy's dark head. A puzzle in many ways, young Selim. The Bedu made little of time—in the desert the seasons passed without remark beyond some extraordinary event or another, but Selim spoke English so well, with only a trace of accent, a little lisping slur here and there, that Arden supposed Lady Hester must have gone to some lengths to educate him. Surely he knew how long he had been with her.

"Can you read and write?" he asked.

"Yes, my lord!" The answer came quickly and positively. "In English and Arabic."

"So," Arden said, "I suppose you want to go to Beyrout and be a clerk."

"I do not wish to be a clerk. I wish—" The boy stopped abruptly.

"What?"

"It is no matter, my lord."

"Come with me," Arden said abruptly, surprising himself. "El-Nasr has no blood feuds, and pays everyone for protection. Otherwise I'll have to hire a new *rafik* to see me through each tribe."

"I do not wish to be *rafik* to you, my lord."

"Why not? I'll pay you very well."

"Because then I could not quit your company. I would have to share your journey even unto death, and I don't want to die."

He gave a short laugh. "A foregone conclusion, in your opinion!"

"They say there is no water for fifteen camel marches across the red sands."

"Ah, but only think of how you'll electrify all your acquaintance with the story, and be known ever after as a singularly intrepid individual."

"You are mad," Salim said grimly. "I wish to go to Beyrout."

"Why the devil this longing for Beyrout, little wolf? Did her ladyship make you too soft for the desert?"

"Yes, excellency." The boy bit down with savage effect on an olive and spat out the seed. "I hate the desert."

"A pity. She did you no favor there."

The boy turned on Arden suddenly. "My lord!" he demanded in English. "Are you a spy?"

"I am not. Though no doubt I'll be thought one, and you too, cub, if the pair of us burst out in English at any inconvenient moment."

"Then why is it you come here? What can you want in such a place?"

He looked about him at the huge clear sky and the desolate country. "It's beautiful, don't you think?"

Selim hugged his arms around himself, shivering. "You are absurd! When you could be in England!"

He laughed. "You sound remarkably like my maiden aunt. What do you know of England?"

"I know everyone sleeps in a feather bed there," the boy said pungently, "and not on a mule's back on a mountainside."

"Ah! So it's a feather bed you want in Beyrout."

"I do not want a feather bed in Beyrout. I want—"

Lord Winter observed the boy's intense face. Whatever it was, he desired it very badly. Such longing was no common thing.

"Gold?" the viscount suggested. All Bedu had a burning desire for gold coins.

Selim cast him a proud, uncertain look, a quaint mixture of disdain and interest. So, Lord Winter thought, whatever it is you want, my fine cub, it can be bought for gold.

"What do you suppose," he mused, "it would be worth in sovereigns—the price of a *rafik* to Nejd and back again?"

The boy said nothing.

"Two thoroughbred camels?" Lord Winter suggested. "I saw them selling for thirty in Damascus."

Selim scowled at the ground. "I have no use for camels."

"You may buy what you like with sovereigns. Say, a purebred Keheilan mare, for a hundred."

The boy began to look hunted. "I do not want a mare," he muttered.

Lord Winter raised his eyebrows. "Tell me what it is you do want, and let us discuss the matter. Perhaps we'll find ourselves in charity."

Selim stared at him, almost through him, breathing quickly, as if his mind was grappling with some desperate calculation. "You would pay gold sovereigns? English money?"

Lord Winter nodded.

"How much—excellency—what would it cost for a passage to London?"

Arden, his curiosity aroused, had been running possibilities through his mind: the price of a doctor or a magician for some sick relative, the cost of an expensive bride, the value of a grove of date palms—but this made him look down at the boy with astonishment.

"London! Whoever do you wish to send to London?"

Selim's delicate jaw tensed. He turned his face downward, his tangled hair falling forward to conceal him. "It is I who wish to go, excellency."

In a long moment of silence, Zenia felt herself the object of unnerving scrutiny. In spite of his sharp manners, she perceived that Lord Winter did not altogether despise his wolf cub. But she dared not let him discover she was female. Lord Winter was of one mind with Lady Hester in his contempt for the weaker sex. Only as long as she was a Bedu boy in his eyes did she feel any hope that he would tolerate her, or extend the shield of his protection. He would cast off a girl instantly, most probably into the custody of the nearest village governor, who would send her to the pasha if he did not marry her to the first man, Christian or Mohammedan, who would pay him for her. She might escape to the north, if she could walk so far, limping and begging for food, without being killed or enslaved. In the desert a poor stranger would meet with hospitality, for a few days at least, but here where rebellion and Ibrahim Pasha's soldiers had tortured the land for so long, there was no such certainty. And if she did by God's mercy reach her old tribe the Nasr, she would only be where she dreaded to be, sunk again in the brutal misery of desert life, with no faintest hope of England.

But Lord Winter—Lord Winter could send her to London if he pleased. Consuls would bow to him, showering golden sovereigns as he willed. Ships would arrive at the bidding of an English lord—she had seen it happen; her own mother had often commanded such things in the days of her power, before all her money was gone and the debts heaped up.

"You are a strange child," he said thoughtfully. "I suppose it is no wonder. A Bedouin who hates the desert and speaks English superbly—I cannot imagine what your mistress contemplated for you."

"M'lady never spoke of that, or made provision," Zenia said, with complete truthfulness.

"Did she wish you to go to England?"

"It is I who wish to go," she said firmly. "M'lady is dead, may Allah give her peace."

"Very true," Lord Winter said, amused. "By which I take you to mean that she didn't intend you to set foot there." He stood up, shouldering the rifle. "Well, I have no such scruples, little wolf. If you long to see England, then, *ay billah*, you shall go. After you conduct me to Riyadh and Hayil and back again as my *rafik*."

Zenia stared up at him. She had never been to the Nejd, to the very heart of the Arabian peninsula—all of her years with the Bedu had been spent in the hot plains north and east of Damascus. El-Nasr's small *fendi* of the great Anezy tribe had never had reason or will to traverse the red *nefud* sands to the south. No one Zenia knew had even joined the hajj to go to Mecca. The southern desert was like a fabled land to them, the place of their ancestors; Riyadh the domain now of the puritanical Wahhabi princes, who would take back the world for el-Islam by arms, who hated any infidels but despised Christians most of all, who had even cut out the tongues of simple Moslemin for singing, because their exacting sheiks said innocent song might tempt the devil. Such were the stories she had heard of the land beyond the sands of the red *nefud.*

"Excellency," she said carefully, "if you will send me to England, I will do anything, but I must see the money first."

"Oh ho, must you? Go and look your fill then, but unless you can get to Damascus and back within the quarter hour, you will find the bargain off."

Zenia wet her lips and lowered her eyes. He gave a chuckle at her discomfiture.

"Quite the cunning desperado," he murmured. "I don't carry bags full of coins for young ruffians to plunder. Two sovereigns now, cub, on your oath that you will not desert me without leave, and your passage to London arranged on our return." A sudden thought struck him, and a wicked grin lit his face. "By God, I'll take you there myself. We'll have tea at Swanmere with my lady mother, and be appallingly respectable."

Zenia lifted her eyes in wonder. "Would your lady mother receive me?"

"I don't doubt she'd receive the devil himself, if that's what it took to get me back in her clutches." He came down off the boulder with an easy stride and offered his hand. "What say you, wolf cub? Is it the Nejd and England for us?"

She swallowed, barely able to breathe. Such a chance, and such a hazard. And yet she had no other hope.

Hesitantly, she held out her hand. He took it in his strong grip. "As you serve as my companion," he promised in Arabic, "I will see you to England on our return from the Nejd."

Zenia stood with her fingers held hard in his. "Our fate is one while we journey," she said, her voice unsteady in the formal vow of a *rafik,* "whether we live or die. I will conduct you to that place you name, and by very God I will not forsake you." She felt his hand begin to withdraw, and suddenly clutched at it. "*La Allah*, the Lord sees me, that I enter under your protection!"

It was another kind of oath—*dakhilak*—that laid upon him the charge of her life if he accepted it.

She raised her eyes. He looked down at her, this mad English lord, and smiled his fierce easy smile. He could defend her from anything, she thought. She was terrified of him, because he laughed at demons and loved the desert. "Please, my lord," she said in a small voice, "don't let me die before I can see England."

His grip tightened, her hand bound in the strength of it. "By God and my honor, Selim," he said soberly, "you are under my protection. I will guard you with my own life."

Four

―――∞∞∞―――

"I DO NOT wish for a wife," Zenia repeated firmly, by no means for the first time.

"So does the camel not wish for a saddle, but that is its fate, by Allah," Haj Hasan the Moor responded, sitting Arab-like on the ground with his coffee cup in his hand.

The little ring of Bedouin men laughed intemperately at that. Ranged about the fire at dusk, they called out variations on the theme. Zenia did not recognize any of these Beni Sakkr tribesmen that they traveled with, but she kept her kuffiyah up to her face for prudence, in the day and in the night, for any one of them might know her, though it had been seven years since she had left the desert.

"I am poor, excellency," she insisted, "I have nothing for a wife."

"And have I not said I will give you the camel and kill a sheep, by my eyes? And make you a present of your rifle? How do you say you have nothing?"

"Haj Hasan speaks well," a Bedui said. "It is much, by Allah."

Zenia kept her face down. "It is not well," she protested unhappily.

"*Yallah*, and is it well that I have no beard?" Haj Hasan demanded grandiloquently. "I, who am as a father to you! It was a splendid beard I cut off for your sake. Behold me now a bare-chinned girl!"

"Then you may grow it again, *el-Muhafeh*!" she exclaimed, naming him warden and protector in Arabic. "I am too young for a wife."

"Too shy!" one of the men proposed.

"*Ay billah*, too ungrateful," another said sourly.

"Too modest!"

"Too ugly, by Allah!" a fourth cried. "That's why he hides his face. No maid will have him!"

"Let us see!" They leaned toward Zenia, eager fingers threatening her kuffiyah, but it would have been outrageous rudeness to lay hands upon her. She pulled back from them unmolested, moving out to the edge of the light.

"Nay, don't chase him from the fire," Haj Hasan said complacently. "Allah sends that Selim is comely enough. You're mistaken there."

Zenia did not mind withdrawing from the fire. The mountains were twelve days behind them, and the memory of their icy coldness had now become a pleasant one in the hot desert twilight. She stood up and walked away, busying herself with pretended work among the baggage.

"*Yallah*, little wolf! Come back," the Bedouin voices urged, but Zenia sat where she was. This was an oft repeated scene, for blue-eyed Haj Hasan the Irrepressible missed no opportunity to tell anyone how he had cut off his beard and vowed that he would not grow it again until he had seen his little blood brother Selim wed. He had embarked upon this fabulous tale at the first Bedu tents, without warning Zenia, and already it had spread so far that it came back to meet them in their path. She supposed half the tribes of the desert must know of it, for interesting news traveled like a high wind among the Bedouin.

Every night, he made the shaving of his face a ceremony, but would not under the most persistant questioning reveal more of the matter, so that it had turned into a game with the Bedu, their curious and excited natures raised to a fever pitch. Obtaining no satisfaction in the mystery of what had driven Haj Hasan to make such a strange vow, they pounced now on the enigma of Selim.

"The boy is a Persian," guessed one of the men.

"He is Arab," Haj Hasan said.

"He is an emir. A prince!"

"*Wellah*, a prince in rags," the dour one scoffed. "He's a poor Bedu like us, he only tries to make an intrigue by hiding his face."

"Nay, he is of Andaluz, like Haj Hasan," another ventured. "By my beard!"

"No, he's not tall enough to be a *Mogreby*. Look at Haj Hasan—the Lord lead you, Selim will never grow to such a giant."

Lord Winter rose, impressive in his white burnous, with the rifle always on his shoulder, and swept a European-style bow that made Zenia quake inside. None doubted his mother, the beautiful white Andalusian dove, or disbelieved him when he swore by the glossy beard of his father, a turbulent Algerian sheik of vague but noble estate, who for some motive Zenia had never quite got straight seemed to have abandoned his son to be raised in at least three different places in the south of Spain—no doubt because young Hasan had shown fair to become a prodigious lying rogue, she thought tartly. Lord Winter's tales of Cordoba and Seville and Granada struck the Bedouin with a fascination, for they dreamed of Andalusia and the old empire, centuries lost, and wept to hear that the courts and graceful fountains of the Moslemin were now made into Christian churches and palaces for the infidels.

All gathered about him whenever he called to Selim to bring his kit. They sat watching raptly as he shaved the day's growth from his jaw, his motions far too skillful for Zenia's peace of mind. She dreaded some small revealing misstep, feared that someone would wonder at a man who carried a fine razor and a mirror in a folding case, but Abu Haj Hasan the *Mogreby*, with his black hair and blue eyes and intriguing rifle, was altogether so uncommon that such things seemed to pass as beneath comment, at least in his presence. She dared not contemplate what tales were spreading beyond this camp into the desert.

She rode a fine strong camel that he had bought from the Beni Sakkr, and thought that she should steal away with it in the night to Damascus, sell it there for the money to go to England. But she had sworn to be his *rafik*—and besides, she had no strength of character, or courage for such a thing, and so instead she slept close beside him under his tent cloth, for safety and for shelter.

They left the Beni Sakkr now. Haj Hasan had already hired another young *rafik* from the Rowalla tribe, to serve as passport and guide as far as Jof at the edge of the red sands. Zenia felt he had chosen poorly and paid too much, but she held her tongue, unwilling to draw attention to herself by disputing openly with her master. It was impossible among the black tents of the Bedu to hold a private conversation—if anyone went aside to whisper, everyone else would follow to see what was said.

In the early morning they set out with the Rowalla, a small party of three while in his own tribe's territory. The young Bedui beleaguered her with curious questions. "Why do you not wish for a wife?" he asked, riding his camel close to hers. "Do you prefer boys?"

"Nay, I prefer my own company, the Lord give thee peace!" she said irritably.

He did not appear to fathom the hint, tapping his camel to keep it well up with hers. "By Allah, you have a wonderful gun. It is the best I've ever seen."

This was a broad hint of another sort. "And if that is so?"

The Rowalla sighed. "I have nothing."

"Haj Hasan has paid you a riyal, and another when we come to Jof."

"But I have no gun. Will you give me your gun?"

"It is not my gun. It belongs to *el-Muhafeh*."

The Rowalla struck his skinny camel, urging it forward. For awhile, he pestered Lord Winter to give him the rifle, but Haj Hasan evaded his begging deftly, turning it aside with a question about how far the Rowalla had been to the south. The boy answered readily. As they rode in the hot sun, traversing a rocky plain, the Rowalla admitted that he had not crossed the red sands, but he had been as far east as Baghdad. He boasted on his travels for a few leagues, declaring that Andaluz could have nothing to match the mosque of Baghdad. Haj Hasan merely said that he had not been to Baghdad, and so could not say. Zenia, who had, and knew it to be a shabby enough place, finally grew impatient with the Rowalla's ever-increasing exaggerations and said that he knew nothing of the matter.

"You are only an ignorant Bedu," she said disdainfully. "You've never been anywhere important."

The Rowalla immediately dropped back beside her. "And where have you been, by Allah?"

"Baghdad and Damascus and Beyrout," she said. "You think those are the greatest places in the world, but they're like a little stone to that mountain, compared to the cities of the Franks and the Englezys!"

"The Lord lead you, that's not true. The sultan would never allow *kaffirs* to have greater cities than his!"

Zenia would have liked to appeal to Lord Winter on this point, but it was too dangerous. The Rowalla, however, had no such scruples.

"Abu Haj Hasan!" he cried. "Say the truth of this. Have you been to the Frankish tribes?"

"*Wellah*, so I have," Lord Winter said, riding before them without turning his head.

"Then, O wise *Muhafeh*, what is the name of their greatest city?"

"London," he said promptly. "Where lives the queen of the Englezys, who sends her ships of war to aid the sultan in his need."

"The queen, by Allah! She aids the sultan to crush Ibrahim Pasha and the Egyptians! *Wellah*, this is good, but wherefore is a great tribe ruled by a woman?"

"Such is Allah's will," Haj Hasan said.

"But what of her husband the king?"

"She is young, and yet unwed. But her name is Victory, and a lion and a greyhound guard her bed."

"Nay, the Lord give thee peace," the boy snorted. "It is not so."

"By my life, it is true. And her city is greater than Damascus and Baghdad and Stamboul together, with fifty times ten thousand men, all armed with guns, to fight at her command."

The Rowalla's eyes were like saucers. "God is great!" he uttered.

"*Yallah*, God is great," Haj Hasan murmured.

"Such is the queen of the Englezys."

"So she is, by Allah."

"And you have seen her, O *el-Muhafeh*."

"I have seen her, by Allah."

"Is she beautiful? Will she marry the sultan?"

"She is a queen. Is not every queen beautiful? She will not marry the sultan, for she is no foolish *bint* to be shut up with the harem, but she searches even now all the world for a husband worthy of her."

"*Ay billah*, she should come to the Rowalla and seek! I am the son of my father a sheik, and if you will give me a rifle, *I* will marry her, even if she is a Christian!"

Haj Hasan threw back his head and laughed. "*Subbak*, you are a forward child!"

"Nay, but Selim does not wish to marry, though you provide him everything in your kindness! Give me his rifle, so that I may grow rich and take a bride. *Yallah*, leave him here in his poor spirits! I'll ride with you in his stead, O Haj Hasan, into the red sands. Your enemies shall be my enemies. I will never desert you!"

Lord Winter turned, looking over his shoulder at Zenia. "What say you to that?"

She felt a bolt of fear, that he would abandon her in the midst of the desert for this boasting simpleton of a Rowalla. But she would not let her fear show in her face or voice, lest the Rowalla pounce upon it. "I say, *el-Muhafeh*," she answered bluntly, "that he only wants a rifle of you."

Lord Winter gave her a slantwise look, the white drape of his kuffiyah hiding his face from the Rowalla boy. "But every morning you tell me you don't wish to go south."

"I do not, *el-Muhafeh*. It is a foolish thing to do."

"This young Bedu says that he will go willingly, by Allah. Come, how do I know that you will not abandon me in the sands, Selim?"

"We are *rafik*. I have sworn I will not."

Lord Winter gazed at her, what thoughts he had in his head unreadable on his face. "So is this Rowalla my *rafik*."

"Then let us come to the red sands, O *Muhafeh*," she said, "and see which of us goes with you."

He smiled slightly. "*Inshallah*," he said. "As God wills."

"*Inshallah*," the Rowalla repeated piously. "We will hire a hundred camels, and cross the nefud, and go to see the emir at ar-Riyadh."

"What is this, a hundred camels, by Allah's beard?" Zenia said. "*El-Muhafeh* has no need of a hundred camels. He travels under the protection of an evil demon, and needs only myself to serve him."

"A demon!" The Rowalla stared. "Haj Hasan, is it so?"

"It is so, by Allah," Lord Winter said soberly.

"*Wellah!*" This news appeared to dampen the Rowalla's enthusiasm for their company considerably. He began to ride a little farther from them, drifting ahead on a pretext of scouting.

Lord Winter waited until the Rowalla was well out of hearing. "Paltry fellow!" he murmured in English. "Floored at the first blow."

"He would not dare cross the nefud sands," she said sullenly. "He only wants a rifle. If you give it to him, he will find a reason to be gone."

"I begin to see how fortunate I am in you, little wolf. That you come with me, under threat of the sands and a bride, too."

"I do not wish for a bride, my lord."

"You confound me. I thought you would be eager. A beautiful girl, with eyes like the gazelle and lips like a rose—such a one does not tempt you?"

"No, my lord."

"Not even for a camel?"

"Are *you* wed, my lord?" she asked pointedly.

He grinned, his dark eyes amused. "A direct hit. You force me to confess that I am not."

"I wish to be like you. I think girls are silly."

"Indeed!" He rode along, looking at her with a strange quirk to his mouth. "I believe you must be younger than I thought."

"I do not want to marry, my lord," she insisted.

"Yes, we have established that point to our satisfaction. Rifles are as nothing to you, and camels and brides but dust in your mouth." He smiled at her in a way that made her feel queerly agitated and uncertain. He had admirable strong hands, his fingers resting easily on the gun as he held the rifle upright in one hand, the stock against his knee. "But why the devil England?"

"It is green," she said.

His brows rose. "I see."

"Like a garden everywhere."

"Who told you this? Lady Hester?"

"Is it not true?" She turned anxious eyes to him.

"I suppose it's true enough the place is green. Extremely green. Suffocatingly green, some might say. But you could see trees in Damascus. You don't have to go as far as England."

"You have promised me!" she exclaimed. "I don't care about the trees in Damascus!"

"Peace, little wolf! You'll see all the British trees you can stand, you have my word on it. I'm only curious as to where you conceived this extraordinary desire to do so."

She gave him a hot glance. "You desire to go to the Nejd in disguise, which is stupid and dangerous, and you are quite mad."

"I'm in search of a horse."

"What horse?" Zenia asked warily.

"She is called Shajar al-Durr. The String of Pearls."

She looked suspiciously at the profile of the man who rode beside her. "Who does she belong to?"

"Ah, that is the question—who has her, and where is she? You were not born, little wolf, and I was just a boy when Ibrahim Pasha brought the army of Egypt to the Nejd, to take Mecca back from the fanatics and break the Wahhabi's power. He captured their prince, ibn-Saud, and with him the greatest collection of horses that has ever lived in the desert—all the best bloodlines harvested from the Bedouin were gathered in ar-Riyadh, and when ibn-Saud lost his war, he lost his horses. Ibrahim Pasha demanded them as tribute, and took them back to Egypt."

"Yes," Zenia said, "I have heard of this. And Allah sent that the horses died in Egypt, because Ibrahim Pasha sinned in his covetousness and greed to take them from the desert."

"True. It was a tragedy for the breed, little wolf, verily. But when are the Bedu without stratagems, or bitterness among themselves? Not all of the horses were taken—some were hidden away, and a precious few were allowed to remain in the hands of the Muteyr tribe, who had made common cause with Ibrahim Pasha against the Saudi prince. Which did not make the Saudis happy, you may trust."

Zenia made a gloomy murmur of assent. The old Wahhabi prince had been beheaded in Stamboul—and if some of the tribes had fought on the side of the Egyptians to bring him down, the blood duty for vengeance would endure for generations.

"Once Ibrahim Pasha and his Egyptians got Mecca back for the sultan, Ibrahim took himself off after bigger game," Lord Winter said, "and so for the past twenty springs, the Saudis have been free to amuse themselves by taking their revenge of the Muteyr. They have relieved them of their precious horses, until the only few that remained were sent away for safety. Among them was the finest mare of the finest strain, the Jelibiyat."

"Sent where?" Zenia braced herself for the worst.

"The sheik of the Muteyr committed his last mares to the

hands of two of his most trusted men, and charged them to be taken to ibn-Khalif, on the island of Bahreyn."

Bahreyn meant nothing to Zenia; she thought it was far across the desert in the eastern sea. "So we go to Bahreyn?" she asked dubiously.

"Nay. When the Jelibiyat mare left the Muteyr, she was heavy in foal to their best Kuhaylan stallion. When she arrived, she had no foal at her side, nor carried one, and her milk was dry. She had lost it, the sheik's men said, on the journey." He looked aside at her, the kuffiyah shading his face and making his eyes seem as bright as the blue sky within shadow. "But some say that is not so. Some say that she gave birth to a filly that lived to be *khadra barda*, snow-white, with a dapple marking like a string of pearls about her throat."

"Some will say any foolish thing."

"That is so, by Allah," he agreed.

"Or follow any foolish mirage!"

He smiled slightly. "She is no mirage, little wolf. Abdullah ibn Rashid has her hidden in the mountains of Jabal Shammar."

"*Rashid!* The emir of Hayil and the Shammar?" Zenia made a moan of dismay. "My lord—you do not hope to buy her?"

"No," he said, "I have no hope of buying her."

"What do you intend to do?"

He said nothing. Zenia felt the hot air grow thick and unbreathable in her lungs. "My lord—please—" She could barely whisper. "You would not go to such risk only to see her."

"Well, no, wolf cub," he said apologetically. "I'm afraid I mean to steal her."

"Cry mercy of Allah!" she gasped.

As if in echo of her words, a shout rose from the far hill, where the Rowalla came charging back on his camel, shrieking, "*Ghrazzu! Ghrazzu!* A raid, *yallah!* Fly!"

Hard behind him a band of riders crested the hill, shouting the shrill war cry of their tribe. Before Zenia could turn her mount, Lord Winter struck his camel full force, propelling it directly toward the oncoming *ghrazzu*. Zenia cried out in dismay, for an instant reaching to stay the unruly beast—and then realized that he had the rifle leveled, that he was riding into them on purpose, the camel breaking to a ground-eating gallop.

His first shot took the spear from one of the raiders' hands. They came on, while Zenia gaped at Lord Winter, and then drove her camel after, screaming at the Rowalla to stop Haj Hasan while she fumbled for the powderhorn he had given her. She did not know the gun; she could not open the bouncing powderhorn while her camel galloped. She heard another shot as she finally grasped the horn and pulled the stopper.

She looked up in panic at the sound of gunfire. Lord Winter could not possibly have reloaded. But the *ghrazzu* had split, one rider down, and still he rode into their teeth with the rifle trained. Another shot. The fleeing Rowalla passed Lord Winter, yelling in a shrill wail. A fourth shot, and the nearest of the raiders was struggling to turn his mount away from the oncoming attack.

With a shock, she realized that all the fire came from Lord Winter's rifle. The enemy wrestled their camels around, a moment of confusion about the fallen man, but Lord Winter fired again, twice and three times, and they abandoned any thought of rescue. As he topped the hill they were bolting at full gallop down the other side.

Zenia passed the loose camel and downed Bedui, her gun barrel trained on him, even though it was not primed. He had lost his spear, and seemed to have no firearm. His wide-eyed face stared up at her as she swept by, and he cried, "I am under your protection!"

She raised the rifle overhead, acknowledging it, and came loping up to where Lord Winter sat his camel at the crest of the hill. She was gasping through the cloth of her kuffiyah, not with effort, but with frenzy. As her mount jolted to a halt beside him, she looked at the foreign rifle in amazement.

He was mad, utterly and entirely mad. Their eyes met. She stared at him, panting, and at his incredible rifle that had fired ten shots without a pause before she had even been able to prime her weapon. He unslung it and released the cock.

He grinned at her. She had known that he would, the madman.

"My evil demon, wolf cub," he said mildly, smiling with affection at the remarkable gun. "Mr. Samuel Colt of Connecticut."

Five

THE WATER SKIN tied on Selim's camel was sweating. It was a sinister drip; perfectly steady. Arden marked his steps by the drops, one dark spot on the sand at a time, as the beast floundered up a dune in front of him.

Leading his own mount, Arden labored through the deep red sand. The Rowalla had deserted them four days ago, fleeing from the raid without glancing back. Selim had given Arden a pungent I-told-you-so look, which Arden had been so irreverent as to meet with a wink, but neither of them had greatly missed the Rowalla.

Arden had not meant to attempt the nefud sands before halting at the town of Jof to replenish their water and find a guide. But they had a guide already, fallen literally into their hands—the Shammar tribesman downed in the *ghrazzu*. Bin Dirra was utterly docile in surrender. Drinking Haj Hasan's coffee and cursing his companions for deserting him, he had readily imparted the forbidding news that the Egyptians had garrisoned Jof and would certainly seize any strangers without "letters."

Arden had letters—forgeries of several varieties, in fact—but no intention of risking arrest. At all costs, he must remain out of Egyptian hands. The last news had been of a great battle in the north; England had openly backed the Ottoman sultan to challenge the Egyptian general Ibrahim Pasha and his army, and Arden devoutly did not wish to be identified as an Englezy by any soldier belonging to Egypt.

Bin Dirra, lacking a camel and outraged at his own comrades for abandoning him afoot, had entreated Haj Hasan to let him lead them south by the direct route to Hayil, where he could lodge a complaint against his perfidious associates with the emir Abdullah ibn Rashid himself.

Bin Dirra claimed that he knew the way through the red sands perfectly. Arden, cautious, had looked this time to Selim, silently asking his opinion of the Shammari. The boy made Bin Dirra hold out his hands and swear by the life of his son that he was telling the truth.

Arden thought he was. He hoped he was. They filled the water bags in a range of rocky hills, where Bin Dirra shoved aside flat rocks to uncover secret basins, little pools of sweet rainwater.

So they had turned south into the nefud. And it was like walking knee-deep through the coals of a burning furnace, red walls rising on all sides to reflect back the fire.

For four days they had traversed the horseshoe-shaped dunes; with Bin Dirra feeling his way, making a cast up one hill and then trying another, as a hound would follow a very faint scent. To Arden, every dune and back-dune looked the same as the next.

Heavy sand was the hell of camels. In the hollows of almost all the huge curved dunes were skeletons. There were bones of camels and bones of men. Nobody ever got buried in the nefud sands; they only got scoured by the hot wind. Last night Bin Dirra had told a delightful little tale of how the Bedu had led a company of five hundred Egyptian soldiers into the nefud, pretending to guide them toward Damascus. The next well was just a little way, they had told the Egyptians. Just a little way further! Until the soldiers had fallen down to their knees, and the Bedu had drifted away, only lingering to snare a few horses and camels as they wandered from the dead men.

The story was not, Arden hoped, a hint. But he did not waste energy worrying over unrealized terrors. He had a compass concealed in his baggage, and the nefud was not endless. Their camels were in good condition. And they were committed now.

He watched the water drip, and walked, lost in savage desolation and utter solitude. The long inhuman reaches of the desert, where his body found the limits of what it could endure, and his soul came near to peace.

He had longed for it, with a longing that was terrible. And yet even here, he was looking for something that he could not find.

All of his life, he had been looking. He did not know what for: not a horse, though there was a fine edge of pleasure in that added risk; it was not to spite his father, for that interference had merely driven him to a desert of rock and sand instead of ice. Sometimes he thought he found it in the evening, when they stopped to rest and the red sands turned violet and indigo, flooded with light like a frozen tossing sea, and he turned from that glory to where Selim cooked homely balls of flour in the bottom of the fire, and burned his fingers retrieving them from the ashes.

Sometimes he thought he found it in the morning, when he rose and walked to the top of a sand hill, and grew drunk on the pure clear arch of the sky and the silence. Sometimes he thought he found it in a dry mouth and a thimbleful of water swallowed in the shadow of his patient camel, and sometimes in the grumbling roar of the beast herself as she complained of rising to start again, as his body complained that it was too much, too hard, he was too hot and dry and weary to go on. And yet the camel went, and so did he.

He thought he found what he was looking for, in moments that came and vanished, that he could not hold on to. Even the endless labor of plodding in line behind Selim and the Shammari, his feet burning through the woolen socks that were all he could wear in the sands—he prayed for it to end, and he wanted it to go on forever.

They made their devotions in the last of light, and settled to rest until moonrise. Arden lay in the blessed cooling air, staring up at the stars. Bin Dirra's voice seemed raucous, echoing back from nowhere, asking questions that Selim answered with short mutters.

A grim wraith, Selim. Almost uncomfortably beautiful, with the exasperating habit of sleeping very close to Arden. At first it had annoyed his rest—though he knew that any Bedui abhorred solitude and would expect to share his tent, he was not prepared to share the very blanket he slept upon. He had spent night after night retreating by inches, only to wake and find Selim pressed against his back again, until they reached the limits of the tent. Finally, on the verge of ordering the boy to sleep outside, which would have drawn questions and attention, the ridiculous nature of the skirmish struck him.

He had surrendered to the inevitable, reconciling himself to Selim's proximity by thinking of the boy as something like a dog, that must always have one paw in contact with its master. But with that light touch on him in his sleep, he dreamed of women with irksome and inconvenient frequency. He had looked forward to the extremity of the red sands, where he knew that physical hardship would taunt him with visions of water and food instead. Which it had, except that now he dreamed of water and food and women.

Six camel marches to Jubbeh, and four beyond that to Hayil, Bin Dirra said, Allah willing. The water was a problem. Bin Dirra thought they had just enough, if they were careful, even with evaporation and the drip. There were wells at Shakik, but that would mean a sidetrack of three days, and the water was two hundred feet down, requiring more rope than they had, unless they met some Bedu who could draw for them. In the winter, the tribes wandered on good grazing in the nefud, but there had been no rain for two years, and summer was upon them now, killing all it touched. To hope for Bedu at Shakik was to bet against long odds. Better to make straight for Hayil, and replenish the water at Jubbeh, where there was a village and wells worked by camels.

Six days. In the morning Arden rigged a bowl beneath the sweating water skin, to catch the drip, and Bin Dirra laughed in white-toothed delight. At the end of the day there was a mouthful of sand and dirty water in the bowl, smelling of camel. Arden offered it to Selim, who shook his head and went on unloading the other camel.

Bin Dirra refused it, too. "It is yours, O Father of Ten Shots! Drink!"

The Shammari stood grinning at him as Arden upended the bowl. The water tasted vile, but it was cool and wet. As he lowered the bowl, Bin Dirra grinned and took a step backward.

Selim cried out, and at the same moment Bin Dirra shrieked. The nomad looked down, and for an instant it seemed that Selim was attacking him viciously with a camel stick and dagger.

The Shammari stumbled back, screaming, and Arden saw the horned adder writhing at his feet, trying to slither away from the blows of the camel stick. He dropped the bowl and grabbed his pistol from the saddle.

"*Yallah!*" He flung Selim out of the way. At close range his shot took the head from the snake and left a twitching carcass.

Bin Dirra sat down in the sand, panting, holding his foot. Arden seized the length of cord he had used to tie the bowl and dropped to his knees beside the Shammari. He tightened it about the man's leg above the bite. It was not out of humanity that he scored the skin and bent to suck—it was because he knew now that if the Shammari died, their chances of survival shrank from a knife's edge to nothing.

He spat blood, and found the bowl shoved under his face, full of water. He rinsed his mouth and bent again, and again, praying that he had no open cut in his parched lips. He worked until the leg was swollen and Bin Dirra began to shudder and faint.

Arden raised his head. Selim held the Shammari up by the shoulders, staring at Arden with great frightened eyes. He lifted the bowl and rinsed his mouth again and again, not even sparing water, but still the revolting taste of blood and bitter venom seemed to stick on his tongue, nauseating him.

"Damn," he muttered. "Damn, damn, damn."

He had spoken in English, but Bin Dirra was in no case to notice. Selim said nothing. Arden stood up. He looked around at the desert, at endless, trackless waves of sand.

Five days now to Jubbeh. Five days, and if they missed it by one mile, there was nothing to save them.

BEFORE HE LOST his senses, Bin Dirra had muttered that they must find the rocks of Ghota. When they could see the rocks, they could locate Jubbeh.

By firelight, Arden had slit the bottom of his shaving kit and unfolded the maps hidden there, but in all of them, as he had already known, the nefud was a blank. There was no location for Jubbeh or the rocks of Ghota. He had taken surreptitious compass readings as they traveled. He knew that Bin Dirra had trended south-southeast, but the guide's line had been so erratic and their pace so uneven that Arden could only guess at their present location.

Selim sat beside Bin Dirra, holding him as he thrashed in anguish, his leg swollen and discolored horribly. Finally, late in the night, the Shammari had fallen into a deathly stupor. Arden did not think he would be alive in the morning.

He refrained from drinking, to save the water, and looked on their dinner of bread and dates with loathing, unable to eat for thirst and the sickening aftertaste in his mouth. He tried to lie down and sleep, but he kept listening to Bin Dirra's labored breathing, expecting it to cease. Whenever Arden looked over toward the Shammari, he could see Selim sitting motionless beside the dying man.

Finally Arden gave up on sleep. He rose, walking out into the clear starlight beyond the camels.

He stood looking southeast. *Continuous Desert of Pure Red Sand*, the maps said laconically, and no more.

Stars, and the desert. Where the stars stopped, the black desert began. That was all he could see. He felt Selim come up behind him and stand silently.

"I can find the way," Arden said.

He turned. The boy's face was barely visible in the starlight. Arden thought it was full of doubt.

"I promised I would take you to England," he said. "And I will."

He thought the boy would say *Inshallah*, God willing, the Arab's devout remark on any future.

"I know that you will," the boy said quietly. "I brought you water."

Arden was so thirsty that he could have drunk the whole bowl in one breath. "Save it," he said. "We have to make it last."

"This is mine," Selim said, holding out the bowl. "I will drink camel's milk."

"No."

"It will be better if you listen to me in the matter of water and food, my lord. I have seen what the Europeans do. They deny themselves until they cannot bear it, and then they squander more than they need, because they cannot judge."

Arden hesitated. Then he took the bowl, and found that it contained only a few swallows. He drank, the musty camel-taste like ambrosia on his tongue, and then Selim offered him the bread and dates he had been too thirsty and nauseated to eat for dinner. They seemed somewhat more edible now.

THEY COULD NOT linger, though Bin Dirra lay in a coma all night. Before dawn, they tied him to the largest of the camels, laid his kuffiyah over his head to shade him, and set off as soon as there was light enough to read the compass.

Arden plotted their compass course, but it was Selim who ranged ahead and back, scouting the dunes for the easiest way, up along the crests of some, creeping around the foot of others, and finally, when there was no other choice, leading them in a toiling climb straight over.

On the first day, Arden began to think they would do well enough, as long as they did not miss Jubbeh. But by the second, the shape and outline of the sand began to require that they climb more and more often, or else go dangerously far out of his compass reckoning. Arden had to lead both camels, while Selim scouted—as the beasts grew weary, moaning and roaring, he labored to drive them on through the blasting heat. He reached the place that Selim finally chose for their camp with a shaking exhaustion inside him that he was loathe to admit.

Bin Dirra was still alive. His leg was blackened and swollen, his face mottled. As the night fell, the Bedui began to hallucinate, calling out wildly. Selim sat beside him, trying to make him drink.

Arden rested, dutifully swallowing the food ration Selim gave him. It was like chewing wood. He was so tired that he fell asleep sitting up.

He dreamed that an angel came and hovered over him, singing. It was the loveliest sound he had ever heard in his life. Like a sweet, soaring hymn in a cathedral. He woke some time in the night, his cheek pressed to warm sand, and saw by the faint light of the coals that Selim was dribbling water into Bin Dirra's mouth.

The Shammari's half-conscious moans woke Arden at dawn. As he breakfasted on the musty dates and camel's milk that Selim gave him, he dug a vial of laudanum out of his kit and put three drops in the sick man's water.

Selim picked up a load to struggle with it to the camels, but Arden lifted the burden from the boy's arms. "Did you sleep at all?" he demanded harshly.

"Oh yes," the boy said. "I was accustomed to serve my mistress all night."

Selim seemed so at home in the desert, milking the camel and going barefoot in the scorching sand, that Arden had almost forgotten he was anything more than a thorough Bedouin. Lady Hester had been notorious for sitting up at all hours, making querulous demands on her servants. Arden thought of the nights he had sat up with her, drinking the tea and eating the food she ordered. He wondered suddenly if Selim had been one of those flitting, cringing servants who had bowed before him then.

The idea angered him. He determined that the boy should not have to shoulder so much of the work, and ordered him to sit down. Arden finished the loading himself. Selim sat obediently, drinking milk. Another realization struck Arden: he had not seen Selim eat bread or dates for two days.

The boy was living on camel's milk. It was perfectly healthy; in a bad year the Bedu survived all summer on their camels' yield, but in this heavy sand, without grazing, the lone female was only producing a pint or two a day, and Arden had drunk half that much himself for breakfast.

"God curse you," he shouted at Selim, "if you get any thinner, I'll leave your bones for the wind to pick!"

The boy looked at him with a stricken expression. "I'm sorry, *el-Muhafeh*," he said, as if he did not know what to be sorry for.

"Wretched little beast," Arden muttered with savage injustice. He was sharply aware that without Selim he would not have had a prayer of survival. He jerked a leather knot tight on the camel's load. His absurd irritation sustained him through the slogging torture of the morning, but by midday all emotion had been burned out of him, leaving nothing but the pounding of his heart in his ears as he battled the camels upward through knee-deep sand. He had worn a hole in the woolen sock, and each step brought a spike of pain at his heel. When the drug wore off, Bin Dirra began to moan endlessly, whispering garbled prayers.

The sand cascaded down, pooling around Arden's ankles, imprisoning him. He had to push the female, who was roaring and refusing to go on, while Selim dragged on her headrope. By the time they reached the crest, the camel stood trembling with exhaustion and Arden sank to his knees, fumbling with the compass.

Ahead, he could see nothing but more red sand, endless waves in an infinite horizon. Selim stood next to him. Arden tried to take a reading, but the compass face swam before his eyes. His ears rang. He leaned against Selim. Just for a moment, he thought, just rest for a moment. The boy stood patiently, bracing him. Arden could feel the quick panting rise and fall of Selim's breath.

He pushed himself upright and took the reading. "There—" he said hoarsely, pointing at the next great curved face of sand in an infinite array. "That heap of brush, do you see?"

Selim stared to the southeast. "My lord," he said, with a little rise in his voice. "There is another on the one beyond it."

Arden hardly understood him, but he caught the note of excitement and hauled himself to his feet, the dune crest crumbling under him.

"It is a marker! There is another!" Selim cried. "Do you see them? We have found the road!"

Arden stared ahead of them. The dunes marched away, innumerable. But he could see the little pile of roots, and the one beyond, with heat waves rising around them.

If it was a road, he thought blearily, it was only in the imagination of some fiend out of hell.

HE DREAMED THAT night of the angel again. He wanted to beg it for water, and tried so hard to speak that he woke himself.

At first he thought he was yet asleep, because the angel vanished into the sensations of reality, his blanket beneath him, his empty belly and parched throat, but still he heard the singing.

It was unearthly, so lovely and real that it almost frightened him. An English hymn—he even knew the words.

He sat up abruptly, reaching instinctively for his rifle.

The singing stopped. Selim's voice said sharply: "What is it, my lord?"

Arden let go a long breath. He leaned back on his hands. "My God—is that you singing?"

There was a little silence. He could see the boy's black outline, sitting as always beside Bin Dirra.

"Yes, my lord," Selim said faintly.

He wet his lips. The unreal aura of the song still seemed to cling to him, so that he hardly wanted to speak.

"Bin Dirra will not remember," the boy said. "It quiets him."

Arden lay back down, staring at the sky.

"Do you dislike it?" Selim asked.

He looked up at the huge well of stars that seemed to hang so close and shimmering he might fall upward into them, passing weightless into a dark mirror with light reflected back on every side.

"It's beautiful," he whispered, his voice cracked by thirst and sleep. "Go on."

The boy paused. And then he began to sing again, a small, clear voice in the staggering silence.

ARDEN THOUGHT THE camels were dying. They trembled and hesitated, and every time the female lay down, he was afraid she would not get up again. He had to unload her, while Selim coaxed the male ahead with Bin Dirra lying weakly in the saddle.

Arden bore the water, what was left, which was only a gallon. The five days had gone; the afternoon sun was searing, burning down on their eighth, and he was certain that they had missed Jubbeh and now made their way by tortuous inches into the inferno. He found that he hardly cared.

They had lost the brush-pile markers two nights past, by trying to travel in the moonlight. He hauled on the grieving camel's halter, urging her to rise. He fell down when she came immediately to her feet. He stared at the blazing sand beneath him, vaguely amazed that she would rise at all, and sure that he could not. The heat scorched his palms and baked his chest. Then he hefted the water skin and baggage onto his shoulders. He stood up, reeling and weak.

The distance between him and Selim seemed a long way, a great stretch of level ground. He did not look up, but put one foot in front of the other. Selim was always ahead of him, moving, the ruthless angel of exhaustion, and he had to follow.

"Come along, camel," he mumbled in English, having come to love and hate the soft-eyed beast. "Come along, come along, poor girl. Not far now. Not far, my poor pretty."

She groaned and stumbled, the voice of his soul. Together

they moved by fits and starts and increments, until he reached Selim, who had stopped.

Arden thought in befuddlement that it was too soon to stop. He blinked at the boy.

Selim was weeping, shaking his head. Arden looked up beyond him, at a dune face that rose above and ran like a mammoth wall as far as he could see to the east and west.

Oh God, he thought. *We are finished*.

The boy gave a faint sob. Arden said, "Don't blubber. You're wasting water." He dropped the skins and baggage where he stood and stopped, lifting Selim up onto the female. The boy felt lighter than the water bags, hardly even a load for the beast. "Lead the other," he said, handing up the male's rope.

Arden drank deeply, lightening the skin still further, and then dragged the baggage onto his shoulders.

A foot at a time, he forced a way up the slope. He had learned what shape promised a little footing, and what would shear down under him, eating up two steps for every three. But he was dying. Halfway up the slope, the air was rasping in his throat, and dizziness pulled him down into a spinning well. His blood was going to burst in his head. He thought he heard church bells, and someone calling him.

"Stop," Selim was saying. "Stop, stop!" The boy had somehow gotten in front of him, off the camel, floundering in the sand, "Bin Dirra—" he panted. "Jubbeh!"

Arden held himself upright with a painful effort. He looked up at the Shammari.

"Where are you going?" the Bedui whispered. Arden could hardly hear above the laboring of his heart. Bin Dirra lifted his hand, gesturing weakly back along the trough of the dune. "There. I can see the rocks of Ghota. Why do you climb this?"

Six

Selim sat sullenly in the light from the doorway, plaiting hair that hung down below his shoulders. Outside, the streets of Hayil were busy and quiet, with that eastern quiet of whitewash and mud walls where no wheels ever passed. Even the voices seemed distant, swallowed up by the desert air, unless some argument erupted nearby and assaulted the ear with a sudden tumult like a donkey's braying.

The boy was in a high state of persecution, because Arden had bid him paint kohl about his eyes, given him a new robe and a pure white kuffiyah with a gold fringe, and bright turquoise beads to braid into his two long side-locks. Such was manly adornment in the desert. Arden thought he made a very pretty bachelor, even if the rest of his head was a hopeless rat's tangle of dusty curls under the kuffiyah.

"*Ay billah*, you will be the talk of the harem," he said, kneeling to tie the last touch in place himself: a single large pearl to dangle down behind Selim's ear.

The boy scowled. "I do not wish to be the talk of the harem."

"Reluctance will only send them into raptures, I'm afraid. Perverse creatures, females."

Zenia gave him a piqued glance as he leaned over her. In the sands, the sun had burned him to a deep tawny gold. "And I suppose you have a very great knowledge of females, my lord?"

"A vast knowledge. Silly bores, the lot of them." Lord Winter tossed the drape of her kuffiyah back over her shoulder. His hand brushed her throat without ceremony as he parted a lock of her hair with his fingers. "But sweet as honey."

"What can be sweet about them, if they are so boring?" she demanded sulkily.

"Well, it isn't their tiresome prattle, I assure you. But they can't talk all the time, by God's mercy." The back of his fingers pressed against her skin while he tied the pendant. "Their bodies are their honey, wolf cub."

Zenia stared down at her lap, her cheeks growing hot. Since the nefud, she had new and painful feelings about Lord Winter. She was no longer afraid of him. She thought about him every moment, worry and misery and longing.

He grinned and gave her hair a light tug as he sat back on his heels. "You'll figure it out, little wolf. When the time is ripe."

She felt suffocated and resentful, because she liked the touch of his hands on her. Because if he knew the truth he would scorn her for her sex. Because she did not have a body sweet as honey. If she had, he would surely have noticed by now. But no man noticed. And of course she did not want Lord Winter to notice. Her whole welfare depended upon him not noticing. And yet she was perversely unhappy that he did not.

"Arab women are silly," she said. "Englishwomen are more interesting, I think."

"I beg your pardon," he murmured, lifting his black eyebrows. "I did not know you were a connoisseur."

"Englishwomen are more beautiful. Their skin is like silk."

"All women have skin like silk if you look in the right places, my cub."

"Englishwomen have shoes," Zenia said, curling her legs under her. "Their feet are soft."

"That is true," he said, amused.

"They wear prettier gowns."

"More revealing, anyway." His mouth curled in a derisive smile. "One can at least get a look at the merchandise."

"They are not silly, like the Bedouins' harem."

"I'm afraid I must take issue with you there," he said. "Englishwomen are excessively silly."

She should have kept silent, but his easy disdain goaded her into saying, "You did not think my mistress silly."

"Ah, the old lioness. One among millions. Once I thought I could find—" He paused. His face hardened into dispassion. With cool venom, he said, "Once I was very young. Women make fools of us all, I fear."

Zenia looked at him warily. "I do not believe any woman could make a fool of *el-Muhafeh*. How could a silly bore manage such a thing?"

"Oh, with the most perfect ease!" he said, a sudden savagery in his voice. "Deceit doesn't require great cleverness—just a suitably virtuous expression."

She moistened her lips. "Deceit is very bad," she said. "But— perhaps—if a woman lied—she had some reason why she must."

"Of course." He smiled, but his eyes held a glitter of malevolence. "The most persuasive of reasons. She was entirely too frightened of what might happen to her if she said the truth." He shrugged. "A misjudgment on her part, as it happened. She should have been frightened of me instead."

"Did you beat her?" Zenia asked faintly.

He gave a cold laugh. "I killed her, wolf cub."

Zenia turned her face, looking at him slantwise beneath her kuffiyah. He seemed to have no expression, no hint of human feeling in his blue eyes.

He smiled, his teeth set together. "Why do you suppose an evil demon drives me to the wilderness?"

She busied herself with the ends of the kuffiyah, folding them and refolding them, terrified and desperate not to show it. "Still," she said, with a disinterested air, "I think the women of the English are the more comely."

"*Wellah*, think what you please. It's hardly worth disputing about." Arden rose, reflecting moodily that in a land where a man had the right to murder his own sister only because there was dishonorable talk about her, he should hardly be surprised the boy displayed no sign of horror. Glancing down, he saw Selim began to tuck the head scarf up to veil his face.

"No," Arden ordered, catching his wrist, "I do not want you to cover yourself."

"My lord," the boy said, "I must!"

"Nonsense. Why? They will think something is amiss with your appearance."

"Excellency—please hear me! I do not wish to marry!"

Arden flicked the pearl behind the boy's ear. "Are you so handsome that only showing your face will instantly burden you with a wife?"

"But I'm certain I won't want any of their daughters here—"

"God take you, Selim—if you have some broken-headed idea of an English bride, believe me that it is impossible! They will hold you in utter contempt in England."

The boy flinched as if he had been struck. For a moment his lips trembled, his eyes made large and dark and feminine by the kohl. "Will they?" he whispered.

"Be at peace, little wolf," Arden said gruffly. "And know that you are worth a thousand silly Englishwomen."

Selim gave him a brief anguished look.

"It is true," Arden said. He found difficulty in speaking. "Ten thousand."

The boy bit his lip. He gazed up with such an expression that Arden felt embarrassed.

"Come. Let us go," he said.

"But why must we go to the coffee-hall and—?"

"Hsst! Because I will it."

Still Selim closed his hand entreatingly over Arden's fingers. "My lord, you do not understand—I cannot—"

"*Ya* Selim!" Arden gave the boy a hard cuff on the shoulder. "Be a man!"

Selim instantly cast down his eyes, hiding his face behind the fall of tangled hair.

"And don't cry, damn you," Arden commanded in English. "Or I'll toss you down the nearest well, and you'll never get your teeth on a plum pudding."

This being one of the cub's burning ambitions, the threat had its effect. With all the straight-backed arrogance of the condemned resolved to face his execution heroically, Selim rose, turning toward the door.

Once the boy gave in, he did not cower. Arden had grown to treasure his little wolf, so full of baleful predictions of disaster—so hell-born brave that Arden had not yet found the words worthy of telling him. He took a possessive pride in the youth who paced through the bustling marketplace of Hayil beside him, moving with that free, graceful stride, the gold-fringed kuffiyah sweeping back with each step, as if they walked in the open desert instead of in the shadow of castle walls eight feet thick.

Bin Dirra's Shammar tribesmen awaited them in the wide market street, an escort of honor to the coffee-hall. For bringing Bin Dirra alive out of the red sands, the hospitality of his family and the Shammar tents had been pressed upon Haj Hasan and his little blood brother for weeks. At first, they had desperately needed the rest and recovery, but in the sweet welcome of the Bedu and the unchangeable cycle of nomadic days and nights Arden began to lose track of how long he had been in the desert at all. When he realized how he was drifting into the slow dream of the wilderness, he insisted gently that he must journey on. As he had departed the Shammar tents, eleven of the men had risen silently and come with him.

It was courtesy, for Bin Dirra's leg was still too black and swollen for him to travel to Hayil himself, but there was rumor in the air. It was whisper only, but the Shammar had drifted along in the desert, pausing at every Bedu encampment, diligently inquiring the news. The emir Rashid had called no one to Hayil, and yet the sheiks were finding reasons to gather there, and their men with them.

The Queen of the Englezys, it was said, was come in concealment, seeking a husband and a prince, and urging an uprising against Egyptian domination in the desert.

Selim had cast Arden such an unholy glance when they heard the rumor that he was hard put to keep a grave face. In truth, he was glad of the stir that this absurd twisting of his casual words seemed to have caused, counting on it to eclipse any undue inquisitiveness in Hayil about Haj Hasan the Blue-Eyed Moor. If the desert was disturbed, so much the easier to steal away with a certain purebred mare.

Here in Hayil the prince Abdullah ibn Rashid ruled, nominally in tribute and subjection to the Saudis of ar-Riyadh, but power hung in a delicate balance. The houses of el-Rashid and el-

Saud eyed one another with mistrust across the ten camel marches to ar-Riyadh in the south, and both brooded under the Egyptian yoke with a malevolence barely concealed. Though there were Egyptian soldiers in the streets, a garrison living in uneasy company with their vanquished foes, the Bedouin here looked to Rashid as the governor of their hearts and lives.

To such extent as the Bedu ever looked to any man as their governor, at any rate.

Arden's troop of Shammar stalked before him into the emir's coffee-hall, without pausing in the sudden change from brilliant whitewashed light to the darkness of a hundred murmuring voices and the bell-like ring of coffee mortars. The brilliant glare from the door shone on one massive column in a row of pillars that marched into the shadows. Light shafts fell from tiny windows high above. The Shammar went directly to a corner where slaves tended a multitude of huge coffeepots upon the fire, joining the guests seated on rugs or leaning against the wall. "*Salaam aleyk!*" was met amiably with, "*Aleyk es-salaam!*" as they wished one another peace.

"Please God, you are well?" someone asked ritually.

"The Lord be praised, it is so, good man!" came the proper answer—always the same, whether all a man's camels had been raided and his women stripped and his sheep stolen.

"Behold my brother," said one of the Shammar, nodding toward Arden, "Haj Hasan, the Father of Ten Shots."

Arden slung his rifle off his shoulder as he sat down. He put his hand on the leather-wrapped cylinder of the gun. "God is great!" he murmured.

His reputation had preceded him. "The demon is bound there?" They leaned forward over the rifle with a wary fascination.

"To speak of it is dangerous," he said. "*Wellah*, let us talk of benign things. Here is Selim el-Nasr, the son of my father. I've sworn by my beard to seek a bride for him from among the best blood of the Nejd."

"*No!*" Selim exclaimed loudly. "Life of Allah, I will *not* take a bride!"

A shocked silence fell. Arden glanced aside at him. The boy stared back defiantly, such hot anxiety in his eyes and color in his cheeks that Arden was struck anew with the bleak elvish beauty of him, the pure, hungry, exquisite perfection of his face beneath the Bedouin kohl and bright adornment.

A feeling of strangeness came over Arden; a feeling of alienness deeper than any he had ever felt, even in the wildest places or the tamest ballroom, an estrangement from all that surrounded him but this boy, this little savage with the great kohl-lined eyes, who looked up at him with appeal, and more. With a desperate, wordless adoration.

And suddenly Arden thought, *Oh my God*.

The boy's feelings were shining in his eyes. Arden turned his face away with a sensation of shock. But this was no time to lose his wits. Without answering, without a reproof or any sign that Selim's outburst had disturbed him, Arden accepted a tiny cup of greenish brown coffee from the slave and sipped. "What is the news?" he asked mildly.

As if the boy's eruption had never occurred, the Arabs began to talk again. Selim cast down his eyes, his mouth set in a moody curve. The boy held his head so low that nothing was visible of him but the top of his hair. The pearl and the turquoise beads dangled gaily.

His moment of protest was utterly ignored. As Arden sat beside him drinking, they were besieged with brides and rumors. The ibn-Aruks had four marriageable daughters, each more beautiful than the next. The Prince Rashid meant to unite the tribes and rise against the Egyptians. No, Rashid meant to fall upon the Saudis while they were weakened by the failure of their own rebellion last year. Ibn Shalaan's youngest daughter was better looking and better bred than the Aruk girls, but he doted on her and wouldn't let her marry until she was thirteen, though no doubt the proper bride price might make him reconsider. Rashid would not dare to attack ar-Riyadh, not while the Egyptians had their big cannon there, the guns of the Franjy infidels.

"But now the queen of the Englezys comes," a scar-faced Bedouin said confidently. "God willing."

"Ay, *wellah!*" everyone said in chorus. "The queen!"

"If the Saudis do not arrive first, by Allah," someone said grimly. "The Harb say that they ride here even now with Egyptian soldiers, to check any plan Rashid brews."

"God send that the queen brings her army with her, then." An untidy beard gave the Bedui a piratical air. "The army of the Englezys!" he said reverently.

"What do we need with an army of infidels?" another man exclaimed. "*Billah*, are we not Bedu?"

"My wife's sister is married to an uncle of the emir," a handsome young nomad offered earnestly. "Her cousin is a lovely girl, they say, and ready to be wed."

"The tribes are not in harmony. The Muteyr will not stay to fight the Saudis," someone commented. "Already they fold their tents, even before the queen comes."

"Aye, there is bad blood between Rashid and the Muteyr. They will not fight for him."

"But they hate the Egyptians."

"If the queen comes, God be praised, they will fight for her!"

"Will Rashid marry the queen, do you think?"

"Nay, she is a Christian!"

"No!" The chorus of denial on this point was vehement. "She is not Christian, or she would not come to help the Moslemin!"

A wizened old man wandered over and sat smoking silently next to the fire. In a pause, he reached to finger Selim's pearl. "*Ay billah*," he murmured. "If the young prince does not care for the virgins of Hayil, I have a cousin in Mogug who has a daughter . . . it is said, by God, that she is worth a string of pearls!"

Arden lowered his coffee and met the old man's eyes. Hoots of derision arose about them. "Mogug!" the others shouted. "There is no such girl in that poor place!"

The ancient made a deprecating gesture and rose, withdrawing. "Allah send me peace! Perhaps it was at Aneyzah, then."

Arden smiled at him. "When you remember, O my Father, *yallah*, hasten to come and tell me."

The old man touched his forehead and ambled away. Arden accepted another thimbleful of coffee, playing the part of a courteous guest, but while he sat with the rest on the carpet-covered floor, his mind was distracted elsewhere.

He felt quite certain that he would receive a visit from the old man—it was with that purpose he had braided the pearl, the token designated in the intercepted letter to Abbas Pasha, behind Selim's ear, and ruthlessly compelled the reluctant bridegroom through his paces. But it was the other revelation that forced itself into his reckoning, that made him stare so severely at a slave offering him more coffee that the servant moved away for fear of the *Mogreby*'s Evil Eye.

Arden was angry at himself. He had never considered himself an intolerant man, certainly not a righteous one, but he found that he was intensely discomfited by this new intuition. At the same time he thought himself a simpleton not to have considered it—the boy's air of delicacy had been plain from the start, and many of the Ottomans viewed such things with complacency, even considered the love between a man and a boy to be on some finer plane than that between man and woman. Arden made a conscious effort to view it in the same spirit, but he felt as if he had smacked face-on into a stone wall—there were many things he could accept, and a number of things he could deeply admire in the Eastern culture, but he found that he could not bear that Selim had come to think of him in that way.

Now that he was attentive to it, he saw that at least one man, a sleek-looking camel broker from Damascus, stared at the boy with something beyond mere curiosity—with a hungry look of recognition. Selim's anxious fingers clung to Arden's arm with even more apprehension than usual. Arden scowled at the fellow fiercely to warn him off. The camel buyer smiled and made a brief bow as he turned away.

When the *mejlis* was called, all rose to attend the emir's daily gathering in the wide street outside. Arden walked with Selim instantly behind him. He did not, could not bear to look at the youth as they found a place in the shade of a wall, settling down cross-legged with the Shammar, but he felt the Bedu and the townspeople observing him and Selim, some with a hard curiosity that he distrusted. He was fully appreciative of the company of his Shammar, for such looks could turn ugly.

The prince arrived, taking his place on a raised platform, a mud bench built into the wall and covered luxuriantly by Baghdad rugs and pillows. Princely enough he was, Abdullah ibn Rashid, dressed in Indian silk of purple and a long shirt of perfect white linen, with a loose black sleeveless *abah* over all. He wore a pair of golden-hilted daggers thrust in his sash. Colorful kuffiyahs draped his narrow, frowning face, one head scarf laid over the other, bound about his forehead with ropes of gold thread. With his beard trimmed to a neat and elegant point, he was the epitome of the desert prince, dark-eyed and lean, his look flitting restlessly over the crowd, always moving and searching even while he listened to the complaints and petitions and kissed the cheeks of tribal sheiks.

First among equals, Prince Rashid. He had won his position by arms, as the lieutenant of a rebellious Saudi who even now languished in Cairo, prisoner of the Egyptian viceroy. The Saudis, those old Wahhabi fanatics, were broken. The Egyptians garrisoned their capital of ar-Riyadh, a small island of soldiers surrounded by the enemy Bedouin, pursuing the ancient policy of encouraging hate and division between the tribes. And Rashid held his *majlis* with an Egyptian officer beside him—but they bound this hawk by fragile jesses.

The sheiks were gathering. If Prince Rashid could unite them, if he could hold them together even for a season, they could turn upon their tyrants and break the Egyptian's grasp.

One by one, the day's cases were presented to the emir and summarily decided. Once the Egyptian officer made a protest, and Prince Rashid added a beating to the fine assessed against a man who had spit at an Egyptian soldier. More often he consulted the *kady*, the man of religious law, for some interpretation or scripture from the Koran.

It was long and rather boring. Arden saw the camel broker who had stared at Selim rise and pass through the crowd, going forward to speak to a man who sat beside the emir—one of the prince's brothers, Arden thought. The brother leaned over and murmured to Rashid. The emir nodded. His searching gaze swept over the crowd and for an instant seemed to light on Arden.

The prince lifted his hand, beckoning.

Damn and blast, Arden thought.

"Come, I would ask the news of my beloved Shammar," Rashid said in a carrying voice. "Come, come, God be praised that you have arrived well and brought your guest."

Selim was all but hidden behind Arden as he and the Shammar rose, going forward to greet the prince. The boy would have stayed behind, but Arden reached down and hauled him up, pushing him ahead with a bit more force than necessary.

"*Ya* sheik!" the Shammar addressed their emir; or even "*Ya* Abdullah!" without courtly ceremony, in the Bedouin way. The prince had dismissed any townspeople with the proud gestures of royalty, but he was gentle with the desert nomads. Well he might be, Arden thought, for they were assembling in force, three thousand spears and camels outside his walls, and he was, in the end, no more than one of them—elected by violence and personal honor, his authority accepted while he was powerful and just, but easily abandoned for sufficient reason. And to the Bedu, any reason was likely to prove sufficient.

Arden was more polite, as a stranger at the emir's pleasure. He had not requested a private audience; he did not wish to draw attention to himself, but Prince Rashid's fretful gaze fixed instantly on his face.

"By Allah," he muttered to one of the Shammar, "I am told he is *Mogreby*, but he has the eyes of Sheytan!"

Arden cast down his devil's blue eyes. "I am of Andaluz, O Long-of-Life," he said. "My mother was a princess of that country."

"Look up at me! I am not afraid."

Arden lifted his eyes. He allowed a faint smile to touch his lips, a smile that said, *I didn't think you were.* But he spoke nothing aloud.

Rashid grinned suddenly. "Sit down!" he said, waving toward his right.

It was a mark of honor and preference, one that Arden would just as well have done without. But to efface himself now was impossible. He settled cross-legged on the rugs beside the emir. The prince's *kady* gave Arden a narrow, excited look. Arden hoped the man was not whipping himself into a religious fervor.

With a flick of his hand, Prince Rashid bid the rest of the Shammar to sit. Selim was doing his best to be invisible, slipping into a position at Arden's feet.

"And what is the purpose of your journey?" Rashid demanded.

"I must find this son of my father a bride, for I have vowed that I will do it, if I must come to the ends of the earth."

"You find him a bride, *wellah!*" Rashid repeated, bemused. "This is an honorable task, but why have you come so far?"

"Because the young *sheytan* will have no brides!" Arden exclaimed. "Ask those who were in the coffee-hall if it is not so!"

This raised a laugh and a murmur among the crowd. Selim

pressed back against Arden's knee. He thought he could feel the boy shaking. But he had no choice but to brazen the thing out, whatever Selim might wish.

"Let me see this one," Prince Rashid said, beckoning. "Stand up, boy."

Selim was trembling visibly now. He came slowly to his feet, his head lowered.

"Come here," the emir said. "Closer."

Selim took a reluctant step.

"Here!" Rashid exclaimed, scowling. Arden took Selim's elbow and thrust him in front of the prince.

For a long moment, Rashid looked on the boy. His *kady* leaned over and whispered in his ear. Rashid did not take his eyes from Selim, but his hard mouth curved downward. Suddenly he rose, taking the boy's chin between his fingers and jerking his face up.

Selim made a faint sob, a sound of such terror that Arden came to his feet. The boy lifted a slender hand, as if reaching out to him—but Arden was not looking at that.

He was staring at Rashid and Selim—at their profiles, one so close to the other.

Like a landscape lit by a bolt of lightning, he saw it.

Rashid: dark, hard, black-bearded, Arab. Male. And Selim: none of those things.

None of those things.

The prince turned his head, looked at Arden with his mouth pulled down in a cruel curve and his black eyes ablaze.

"Is it she?" he hissed.

Not until Rashid said the word did Arden feel as if his mind could encompass it.

She.

She! He wanted to turn his face to the burning blue sky and shout it in frenzy. She!

He had known it. His body had known it, dreamed of women,

dreamed of *her*; the soft hand in his sleep, the angel that sang in his burning visions.

She.

His throat would not manage words. He only glared back at Rashid, mute.

"Come!" the prince said, halfway to a snarl. "May it please Allah—you are mine!"

He turned, his robes swirling. But the Egyptian officer stepped in front of him. Rashid stopped, then put out his arm and flung the man aside. He turned to the crowd and lifted his hands.

"The Queen!" he shouted in a huge voice that rolled across the stirring crowd. "The Queen of the Englezys! She has come to me!"

"*The Queen!*" It was a murmur, a rushing wind in the mass of desert warriors. "She is come!"

They rose, the Shammar, the Annezy, the ferocious Kahtan and the Sherarat, the sheiks and nomads of a hundred tribes, with their legions camped beyond the walls. They began to press forward. The *kady* leapt onto the prince's platform.

"*Allah akhbar!* The holy war begins!"

"*Jihad!*" roared the crowd in return. "*Allah akhbar! Thibahum bism er rassoul!*"

The slaves and soldiers near the prince broke into confused fighting. Arden grabbed Selim's arm, but the emir had him— *her*—in a vise grip, hauling her toward a low door into the castle. Arden held on, staying with her, slamming the Egyptian officer against the wall with an elbow in his throat.

"*Jihad!*" the crowd kept howling, a thunder now against the echoing walls. "*Kill*, in the name of the Prophet!" The last thing Arden saw before he ducked into the black passageway was the Egyptian officer go down beneath the curved knives of twenty screaming Bedouin.

Seven

※

"Who are you?" Lord Winter demanded through clenched teeth.

Zenia sat down with her back against the wall, her face hidden in her knees.

"Tell me, damn it!" he shouted. His voice echoed back from the walls of the empty room, an unused harem filled with rugs and pillows, lit only by barred windows high above. "Tell me!"

"Lady Hester is my mother," she whispered.

"Of course," he muttered. "Of course it would be Lady Hester. The queen of the bloody desert! Queen of a bloody lunatic asylum!"

She could feel him staring at her. She could not look up; she was without even tears. Her hands would not stop shaking.

Suddenly she felt his fingers on her cheeks, forcing her face up as the emir had done. Lord Winter's blue eyes searched over her features, intense.

"Do you know your father?" he demanded. "Do you know who your father is?"

She moistened her lips. With trembling fingers, she searched beneath her robes, and handed him the miniature.

He didn't even look at it. "It's Bruce," he said, still staring at her face. "It's Michael Bruce, isn't it? God forgive me. You're English."

Zenia nodded.

"What have you made me do?" he asked wildly, thrusting up away from her. He paced the room. "You're English! You're an Englishwoman!" He stopped suddenly, looking over his shoulder at her. "How old are you?"

"Twenty-five," she said weakly.

He laughed. "Oh God." He put his hands over his face and tilted his head back. "God!"

Zenia stared down at her knees. "I'm sorry." She swallowed. "I didn't want to come here."

"You didn't want—" He gave a fierce laugh. "You're an Englishwoman! By God, how the devil was I supposed to—" He stopped suddenly. "No!" He turned on her. "No—tell me that it wasn't to get you to England. Tell me that you aren't such a god-damned little *fool!*"

She felt as if she could not draw breath. "My father!" she cried, unable to put together more of an explanation in the face of his vehement denial of her dream. "I was going to go to my father!"

The expression on his face frightened her. There was a strange glitter in his eyes, a cold fury that made her press herself back against the wall.

"Then why didn't you go?" he asked, in a voice so soft that she trembled.

"How could I?" she asked on a sob. "I could not tell the consul; I had no money; I was alone!"

"Couldn't tell the consul?" He was shouting again. "Why the devil not? It's his bloody *job* to take care of you!"

"My mother's debts!" she cried. "They would have sold me to pay the debts!"

He stared at her. "Fool!" he whispered. "You ignorant little fool! What do you think we are, barbarians? You had only to say it. Only once to say, 'I'm a woman, I'm English, I need help,' and we would have moved heaven and earth to get you out of there!"

"Oh *yes!*" she said with a sudden aching bitterness. "My mother needed help, and they took away her income, and left her to starve to death alone."

"Your mother," he snapped, "should have been shot!"

She scrambled to her feet. "I'm sure that would have been more your taste, O Great Father of Ten Shots! I'm surprised you didn't do it yourself!"

"I would have, if I'd got there soon enough," he said viciously. "If I'd known about you!"

She felt a wild desire to defend her mother, and so attacked him instead. "You were her particular friend! You could have helped her!"

"She was impossible to help." He tore off his kuffiyah and flung it away, pacing. "I gave her a thousand pounds every time I came, to pay some of her debts, but she had it spent before I ever got out the gate, buying French champagne and silk suits for her bloody pashas!" He stopped before her, looking at her with narrowed eyes. "I never cared a damn what she did with the money—it was her life, she could live it as she pleased, but my God, *look* at you! If you've had a new shirt on your back in the last ten years, I'll be devilish amazed to hear it."

A deep sob welled up in her, choking her angry retort. She pressed her fist to her lips.

"For Christ's sake, don't start—" He broke off, his jaw taut.

She tried to stop them, but the warm tears tumbled down her cheeks. "I wanted English sh-shoes."

His gaze flicked to her bare feet, and up to her face. He squeezed his eyes closed, shaking his head with a twisted laugh. "I would have seen that you were sent to England." His voice, when he spoke, seemed oddly helpless. "I don't know why you didn't tell me."

"I was afraid of you," she said weakly.

"But why?" He shook his head again, as if in bewilderment. "Why?"

She moistened her lips and looked down. "I've heard you and my mother," she said in a small voice. "You don't like females."

"What?" he asked blankly.

"You agreed with her. You said you detest women." She hesitated. "I was afraid you would leave me if you knew. Or—or . . . you killed a woman for deceit. I thought—as long as I was Selim—you would abide me for a companion. You would not leave me here."

There was a long silence. She swallowed in a dry throat and looked up. His black hair was tousled by the kuffiyah, touched with sweat and dust.

"Abide you." He scowled fiercely as he lifted his hand and wiped the tears from her cheek with the back of his knuckle. "My God, I'm alive because of you." His touch moved over her skin, slightly rough, tears and a few grains of sand on his fingers. "Little wolf! What's your name?"

"Zenobia," she said.

His fingers stilled. "Naturally," he said in a dry tone. "Oh, naturally!" He stepped back and threw his hands wide. "Zenobia, queen of Palmyra!" he said with a savage flamboyance. "I can guess whose vanity that was meant to serve."

"You can call me Zenia, if you don't like it," she said. "My mother did. She thought I was too missish to be a namesake for Zenobia."

"Did she?" He gave a scornful laugh. "I'll wager she never saw you drag a camel up a sand dune."

Zenia looked at the floor. "No."

"But you've lived with the Bedu. A long time."

"For eight years. She sent me to them. To live like this." She added violently, "I hate the desert! I hate it! I don't want to die here!"

He stood watching her. Zenia covered her mouth with the back of her hand, trying to hold back the pressing sob.

"You won't," he said, his blue eyes sober and clear. "I made a promise to you. I'll keep it, little wolf—unless they kill me first."

THEY WERE PAWNS. She was. Arden was not certain what his role must be, but he would go to whatever length he had to to get her safely out of here.

He was afraid it would require a brazen walk through the fire of revolt. Prince Rashid called him into audience without her, demanding to know what forces the Englezys could bring, and Arden lied flagrantly. Ships and guns and men—he described them in detail, and put their arrival at a date as far distant as he dared.

"Two months, *billah*," Rashid said, displeased. He drew on his long pipe.

"We could have made arrangements with you privately," Arden said. "You've made your move too soon."

Rashid's dark eyes widened a little at this blunt speaking. "There was no choice. The Saudis are a half day away." His lip lifted in scorn. "Those Wahhabi dogs come on the leash of their Egyptian masters. I will receive Prince Khalid el-Saud this evening."

"With hospitality," Arden asked, "or with fire?"

Rashid looked from one to another of the men who sat about him in the room. "We shall see, Englezy. We shall see. It is with God."

"Does my queen have your protection?"

He bent his head in acknowledgment. "She is under my protection." With a slight smile, he said, "Perhaps I should marry her today."

Arden said nothing.

"What is she to you, O Father of Ten Shots?" Rashid inquired mildly.

"My queen," he said. "I am her sword and shield."

"It is well, by Allah. She is a virgin?"

"Yes."

Rashid nodded. "We have heard of her mother, the English queen Esther. Her courage, it is said, would shame a man's. This daughter, too—she has ridden in *ghrazzu* and crossed the sands. It is a wonder of Allah. She will breed fearless sons, God willing."

"*Inshallah,*" Arden murmured. "You must protect her."

"And the bride-price?" the prince inquired mildly.

Arden looked into his black, shrewd eyes. It struck him that the case had gone far beyond caution. "A single mare," he said. "The String of Pearls."

For a moment Rashid said nothing. Then he shrugged. He rose abruptly, with a haughty move, and all his men with him. "When the time is ripe, I shall take you to see my mares. You will find pearls enough among them, by Allah."

IT WAS A damned quiet rebellion. The silence made Arden uneasy as he pretended to sleep through the midday heat.

He and the girl did not speak. After his first fury had subsided, he felt disarmed and awkward, unable to think of any word of reassurance that was not a lie. It seemed better to say nothing, the way they had said nothing in the sands.

Instead Arden had prowled the chamber, looking for escape, but the windows were three times his height off the floor, the central row of columns too wide around to be useful for anything, even supposing he could contrive some sort of rope, and the door impenetrable short of fire or axe. Finally he sat down, dropping onto his back against a dusty cushion.

For the hours that they waited, their fate swinging in balance, he lay on the rugs, listening and thinking and watching.

There was nothing soft or voluptuous in her. She was female as a she-animal was female, her beauty hard-edged; almost painful, keen as the blade of sword.

Zenia. Zenobia. He could not seem to make either name fit her. She was Selim; his wolf cub, his free-striding child of the desert.

He closed his eyes. And started to his feet when the shouts and the slam of the lock finally came.

ZENIA KNEW BEFORE any word was spoken that they were in grievous danger. In the barren guardroom, spears and weapons were piled high, the Wahhabi warriors and Egyptian garrison standing cold-eyed as she and Lord Winter passed.

She walked first, still in her ragged desert shirt and bare feet. Lord Winter came behind her; when they had left their imprisonment he had stood back as if in homage to her, and flanked her now like an honor guard.

She recognized the role that she must take, though they had not spoken of it. It was as if from the moment the soldiers had come for them, she was locked with him in sense and spirit, knowing his mind as she knew her own.

At the door to the emir's hall, she paused. The feast had already been partaken by the guests of honor, and now groups of men huddled around the huge trays, scraping up what was left of the rice and lamb. Prince Rashid stood overlooking all, his arms crossed, a solemnly courteous host. The Saudi emir sat upon a pile of rugs, his robes all purest white, austere beside Rashid's brilliant purple and green and red. The *agha* that was bound about the Saudi's head scarf was of plain dark wool instead of gold. To his right in an honored position sat an Egyptian general, conspicuous by his Turkish pantaloons, red cloak and tall betasseled fez. He held Lord Winter's revolving rifle across his lap, so absorbed in examining it that he did not even look up when all conversation ceased.

Zenia stood in the door. She felt Lord Winter's presence at her back. In the silence she could hear him breathing, soft and steady, his calmness like a firm hand on her shoulder.

Her chin was high. She thought of her mother; she *made* herself her mother, Lady Hester who had defied all danger, challenged Ibrahim Pasha himself. Her mother, whose whole life was unflinching, reckless, scornful courage. She walked down the center of the hall and stopped.

"Who are you?" she demanded of the Saudi prince in a voice that rang high to the roof.

His lean jaw dropped a little under the hooked beak of his nose. His black eyes grew furious, and for a moment, just a moment, he made as if to rise.

He caught himself in time. It would have been an acknowledgment of her rank if he had stood for her. The men grouped about him muttered softly, and then quieted as Prince Rashid lifted his hand.

"Khalid ibn Saud, of long life and prosperity, may Allah bless my prince," Rashid said, smoothing over the moment. He turned his head slightly toward the Wahhabi emir. "The daughter of Esther, queen of the Englezys, who searches the desert for a blooded prince to marry."

"Allah cut her off!" cried one of the men with Khalid, all in puritanical white too, one of their religious sheiks who expounded the laws of the Koran. "May she be blackened, and her parents blackened, and her family, and all of the Englezys, by the Prophet!"

Zenia took a step forward, lifting her hand as if she would slap him. The men nearest her shrank back, a faint start, but she held her hand erect a moment, and then dropped it. "Cowards," she spat at them. "*Billah*, do you flinch from a woman?"

"A woman in the clothes of a man! An abomination!" the sheik cried. "Cover your shamefulness, and may Allah rip up your belly in you!"

Zenia's throat was tight with terror. Her face was frozen in calm. She ignored the sheik, staring steadily at Prince Rashid. Lord Winter had said that the prince had taken them under his protection.

"Shall I suffer this?" she asked.

"You are my guest," he said.

"No." The Saudi emir's bitter voice interposed. "She has no appeal to the laws of hospitality. This woman comes before me accused of immorality and vice. She must be punished. And the man with her, as a Frankish spy."

The Egyptian general looked up. With an expression of boredom, he leaned on the rifle stock and watched the emir with dark unblinking eyes.

"At the proper hour tomorrow, before the assembled people of God, the man's head shall be struck off with a sword," Prince Khalid declared, "and the woman stoned until death. That is my judgment, in the name of the Prophet and of Allah, the Merciful, the Compassionate!"

Eight

⸙

THEY SAT SILENTLY, returned to the room of their imprisonment. Arden stuffed a cushion behind his back and leaned his head against the whitewashed wall. For a long time, he sat with his eyes closed. It was a battle within himself. His mind refused reality, and he concentrated on physical sensation for an anchor: the slightly rough pressure of the wall against his shoulders, the carpet beneath him, the occasional sound of a water wheel from outside the barred windows. He breathed the dry air, scentless, that whispered in off the desert.

He opened his eyes. The figure opposite him seemed too small, propped up against one of the two great columns that supported the chamber.

He saw a Bedu boy; beardless young Selim, timid and courageous, a handsome child with wild elf-locks and huge kohl-darkened eyes, small calloused hands and feet. A boy whose death sentence lay on Arden's shoulders, grieving him beyond speech.

But the perception was like a picture he had seen once, a black and white silhouette that in one glance appeared to be an ornate vase, and in the next a pair of faces looking at one another. The same way he had frowned at the silhouette and seen only a vase, he stared and stared and could not distinguish anyone but Selim, until in one instant of transformation his mind made the leap and he saw the other image.

A woman, full-grown. Willow-slender, with skin sun-dyed to darkest gold—and the same huge eyes that gazed back at him in distress—a woman that he did not know, and yet he knew. An Englishwoman. Her mother's daughter, but beautiful, so savagely unkempt and beautiful that his soul seemed to sink down in anguish, unable to bear the intensity of it.

He felt that Selim was lost already. He was angry, surrendering a friend; mourning the boy who had never been, but when he looked in this new perception and knowledge, his feelings were beyond enduring. He could not suffer them. He was numb.

"I'm sorry," she said, and he heard a woman's voice, pitched in a fair, clear timbre like the desert air.

He shook his head. Her lips parted to speak again.

"Don't," he commanded. He was afraid that she would say that it was her fault, when it was his. When he had been blind, blind, blind. Repentance was not a familiar sentiment to him. If one could die of an emotion, he was dying of it. Crushed and annihilated by it, until he could barely pull air into his chest.

She said nothing more. Only knelt, her feet tucked up under her, her delicate shoulder resting against the great pillar. The tangled locks of hair framed her face.

After a long time, she said, "I should have told you."

And what was he to say to that? That she should have; that he would never have brought her; that he would have abandoned her at the first possible place if he had known? Because she was female, and he would never have believed it possible that such heroism could quietly exist in a female heart.

She glanced up at him diffidently. The late afternoon light glowed on her hair, picking out the tiny flying strands, and brought rose to the deep gold of her skin. It was as if he had been traveling with a shabby cocoon, a secret, and something magical and fragile and brief had suddenly appeared from within it.

He thought—She's going to die tomorrow. They're going to stone her to death. If Prince Rashid, God rot him in hell, had stood up for them . . .

But he had not. He had bowed to his emir and fanatical sheiks and the Egyptian officers and given up his little stab at revolt with a calm smile.

There was a depth of panic in Arden that he couldn't touch, did not dare feel. He could think of his own death. A just penalty for this, for bringing her here. She had wished to go to England, and he had led her to destruction instead. And she had come so bravely, warning him, imploring him to turn back, and still riding beside him into whatever hell he chose to take her.

Even now she looked to him, without tears or recriminations. The way she looked at him—in sober trust, a wild creature wandered into the hunter's camp.

"Tell me," he said. "Do you wish to be known as Miss Stanhope, or Miss Bruce?"

As soon as he said it, he thought it an idiotic thing. He never knew the precise thing to say, the way to be easy and charming and comforting. But she answered instantly, lifting her face.

"Miss Bruce," she said. "I should like to be known as Miss Bruce."

He said, "Miss Bruce, come here."

She rose with a grace that seemed new to him, as if he had not seen her rise a hundred times before. As she settled on the carpet before him, folding her legs beneath her, he felt a brilliant rush of physical desire, a longing that seemed the culmination of all the days he had watched her and not known himself or her.

He lifted the braid that fell from behind her ear, fingering it. Such braids were the pride of young Bedouin men, their ornament to beguile the ladies. With his fingers, he broke the twist that bound the braid, and began to comb out her hair.

In silence he worked, his hands gentle. He spread her braids, and then began to draw his fingers through the wild disorder, unknotting a lifetime of tangles. He had never combed a woman's long hair before, but he found the way, tiny threads, with each snarl caught up in his fingers so that he would not hurt her. He was aware of her eyes upon his face, but he could not look directly into them. He kept his gaze on his work.

"Lord Winter," she whispered, "would you tell me what England is like?"

He smoothed her hair against his palm. "What do you mean?"

"What is it like? Your home—is there a garden?"

"Yes. A garden. A rose garden."

"And water?"

"A lake. With black swans on it." He turned her chin with his finger, to reach another tangle. "My home is called Swanmere."

A faint smile touched the corner of her lips. "And great trees? Is there a forest?"

"Several forests. Lawns of grass between them. And paths through the trees, that lead great explorers to silly little Grecian temples where the ladies like to take tea."

"Oh yes," she said, with a pleased glance up at him.

"And meet their lovers," he said.

Her eyes dropped shyly. She played with a lock of her hair that hung over her shoulder. "Where is your Swanmere?"

"Buckinghamshire. The green heart of England."

"Oh," she breathed. "And is the house very old?"

He had not been there for eleven years. But he found himself describing it in perfect detail, from the iron gates and the sweeping drive to the stone lions that guarded the stairs, the places where he had chased dreams as a boy and played alone.

"And the town?" she asked, and he described it, too, the wheeled carriages with rims painted gold and the farm carts piled with hay, the church and the green and the cottage dogs that chased the geese.

"London," she said, and as the sunset threw red light in a square against the wall, he told her of London. He wove a dream of an elegant place, left out the smoke and the smells and spoke of the tall houses and fashionable bonnets, of colored ribbons in shops, flavored ices and fireworks in the parks.

He combed out her hair, and held it up, coiling it in a mass atop her head. He tilted up her chin, turning her face from side to side, examining her judiciously, and said Miss Bruce must wear a white gown to her debut.

She smiled at that, but he saw under the smile, saw the terror and melancholy beneath. He stood up in the very last light, and raised her. Her hair fell about her shoulders, a dark, dusty cloud, still curling untamed. It blended with the shadows, so that he only saw her face.

"Miss Bruce," he said, bowing over her hand. "May I have the honor of this dance?"

She bit her lip. And then, with a shaky grip upon his hand, she made an awkward curtsy.

"It is a waltz," he said soberly. "Because it is May, and London, and you're the loveliest girl in the city, and I want you in my arms."

And she smiled up at him brilliantly. He smiled back, because he had said something pleasing for once, a lucky shot. Barefoot, upon the silent carpets, he drew her into the dance. She had a little of the way of it, as if she had long ago learned the steps, though he could not imagine how. With her palm lying in his hand, and his arm about her slight waist, they turned and turned without a sound.

"You dance splendidly, Miss Bruce," he said, another attempt.

"Miss Williams taught me," she said.

He could no longer see her face but as a pale shape in the dark. She was gone, lost to him. If their jailers came before dawn, he would never see her face again.

"There are candles," he said. "Two thousand candles in crystal chandeliers. Everything is light and sparkling."

"But why did you leave? It must be so beautiful."

"Well, you know, little wolf, I killed a girl there," he said, in the dreaming flow of the night and the dance. "And so I could not bring myself to stay."

She looked up at him without aversion or alarm. With simple gravity, a child born among wolves, accustomed to such things.

He hardly believed that he had told her. It seemed as if he hadn't, and yet he heard himself say, "I drowned her." He stopped the dance and put his face against her dusty hair. "I didn't want to marry her. I was drunk. Hellish drunk. And the boat tipped. I didn't try to save her. I didn't want her, and I let her drown."

Her hand curled about his. She said nothing. He lifted his head and looked up at the windows, where the sky still held a last flush of light against a black horizon.

"She was afraid of her mother," he said. "She was afraid of my father. She was afraid of her shadow. I hated her, because she was going to lock me up in her fear. But there was never so much as a kiss between us. God, I'd think they might have guessed, I was such an awkward devil—too shy to hold a coherent conversation. What a gauche pair we must have been!" He made a faint, cheerless laugh. "I don't think she cared much for me either."

Her face was upturned to his. He lifted his hand and cupped her cheek, sliding his fingertips over the smooth skin. "Where were you, little wolf? Eleven years ago, when I needed you?"

"With the Bedu," she said.

"Fate," he murmured. "Bloody fate. I've looked all my life for you." He touched her, tracing her face that he could not see. "And I find you today."

"I'm not what you think I am. I'm always afraid," she said into his chest as he drew her close. "I'm afraid now."

"I know," he whispered. "I know it, wolf cub."

She shivered, holding to him. He bent his head and kissed her cheek, but there was no comfort to be given. She made a small moan and turned her face down, burying herself against him, and he was instantly aflame.

It happened in the deepest chasm of his body and mind, a force beyond decency and civilization. Her clinging to him, her fragile shape, the darkness: her fear and his, that suddenly, acutely demanded life and fusion in the face of death.

He pressed her back against the column behind her, opened his arms and put his thumbs beneath her jaw. He pushed her face up, turned it up to meet his lips. He kissed her hungrily, angrily, deeply. He could not bear to face eternity having been so close and never part of her.

Zenia held to him, allowing his body to press her hard against the stone. She wanted him to touch her; she wanted it this way, roughly—his gentleness was near to shattering her into tears and fragments, and she wanted to meet fear bravely; she wanted him to be proud of her. He had not said he was, but she knew he was, and she was so close to collapsing into clamoring, babbling fear that she wanted his mouth hard and fierce upon hers. She pulled him closer, to stop the fear, as close as he could come, his body heavy and the rise of his breath crushing her. Beneath her fingers about his neck she could feel heat and the hard beat of his pulse—his life under her hands.

He made a sound of anguish and pushed back. The room had grown entirely dark, so that she could not see him but as a dim blur.

"Don't," she said, clutching with both hands at the drift of his robe. "Don't leave me."

"I won't," he said.

They stood unmoving, his hands upon her shoulders, as if some spell held them.

"I want to be brave," she whispered. "I don't want to cry." She swallowed. "I'm going to cry if you don't hold onto me."

"It's no matter." He sounded angry. "Cry, then! What difference does it make if you cry?"

"Please hold me!" she said desperately.

His hands rested on her shoulders. He tightened them. His fingers pressed into her.

Zenia reached up suddenly and pulled his head down to her. She thrust her lips against his, seeking.

Arden felt the edge perishing beneath his feet, his last honor crumbling. "I'm a blackguard," he said against her mouth. "I want you. I want inside you."

She understood him. He felt it in the way she stilled.

"Stop me," he said, his lips on her skin. "Damn you."

In his arms, she was perfectly motionless. He could feel her, every inch of her, fragile as a glass statue of a girl; so slender that he wanted to weep.

"Go on," she said calmly. "What difference does it make?"

Tomorrow they would not be alive. So what difference would it make?

He thrust away from her. He prowled into the darkness, feeling caged like a beast, and threw himself facedown on the rugs. He had always thought condemned men must be numb to feeling; they always appeared so. But how many of them had been locked up with the woman who was to die with them? To torment them, body and soul?

She had asked him to hold her. It was a plea for comfort. He could give her that, at least—he could hold her. Only hold her. He rose on his elbow, and suddenly she was there, falling to the carpet beside him, snuggling to him as Selim had nestled to his back for so many nights.

He held her tightly. He lay on his side and pressed her face into his shoulder and strained her body into his. Comfort. Comfort. He stroked her hair. "Go to sleep," he muttered. "Go to sleep."

Her arms were thrown about him. When he relaxed a little from the taut embrace, she moved to come closer. She pushed her hips against him, a slow squeezing pressure against his arousal.

It felt exquisite. It felt like life. His breathing quickened, and he spread his fingers into the mass of her hair. She smelled of sand and camels and woodsmoke and woman. He recognized it now, the source of all those taunting dreams in the desert where his body had known what his mind had not.

Unbearable. He was afraid he was the one who was going to cry.

What difference does it make?

None, but that he wanted her to want him. He did not want to take only. He wanted to give. But in a few hours all scruples were going to be nothing. "Go to sleep," he whispered again.

"I don't think I can sleep," she said in a small, muffled voice against his chest.

He drew his fingers through her hair. "Do you want me to help you sleep?" He ran his hand down her back, and up to cup her small breast through the rough fabric. So small, so slender, so soft. Like living glass. "I can help you sleep."

"Yes," she whispered. "Please."

He leaned over her. He knew how to pleasure a woman. That he had taught himself. He was always uneasy with other people, always aloof, but women were not people. They were an alien race entirely, one he could speak to with his body. With pleasure and sweet simplicity. With ecstasy.

He grazed his mouth over the tender skin behind her ear,

touching it with his tongue. He could see nothing, but his hand slid up the curve of her hip. He crushed the crude cotton in his fist, drawing it up. The first touch of her skin was a shock, it was so smooth and cool. It ignited the fire in him, like a cool dry leaf thrown on hot coals, bursting to flame.

"Zenia," he said, as if her name were a foreign word, so strange it felt on his tongue.

"Yes?" she asked faintly. She was cradled in the hollow of his arm and shoulder. He seemed large and powerful enough to hide in. From the beginning she had wanted to sleep beside him, sheltered from the world. But the world was going to kill him, too.

"I want to make you sleep," he murmured. His fingers tugged at the strings that tied her shirt at her throat. They had taken her rope belt with her dagger. The loose cotton moved easily as he lifted it above her waist.

The touch of his hand on her bare skin was new, the texture and life of his palm, roughened by the desert, and yet gentle. She was glad of the darkness, shamed and aching. She knew that he lifted her clothing so that he could go into her as a man went into his wife. But she was not his wife. And still she longed to have him touch her and hold her and kiss her as if her body was honey.

"Zenia," he said softly. "Like that flower, the one with all the queer little sharp petals, that grows anywhere." He touched her bare breast as he said it, stroking his finger across the tip. "Little pointed petals. Like this."

She drew in her breath with the sensation.

"A stupid thing to say." He gave a slight, wry laugh, burying his face against her hair. He bent his head down and kissed her nipple, drawing it between his tongue and his teeth.

She said, "Oh!" in a breathless gasp.

His arm beneath her pressed her upward in an arch. His mouth tugged hungrily at her breast. She gave herself to the feeling, gave herself to him.

And he gave her back pleasure. He gave her back oblivion. He made her forget her fear. He made himself everything in her universe, driving out terror with the circle of his tongue on her skin, with the heat of his breath at her ear. With the hard smooth substance of himself, muscle and male life, for he knelt beside her and pulled the loose Arab shirt over his head, and she could see the starlight on his shoulders.

Tomorrow—oh, but she would not think of it, she could not, it was beyond believing or knowing.

She reached up to him as he braced on his arms over her. She put her hands about his neck and felt his blood beating beneath the skin. She felt his jaw and the prickling of new beard, different and strange and yet himself.

He was looking down at her. She could not see him, but she could feel it.

"Am I like honey?" she asked, shyly, half beneath her breath.

"No," he said. He leaned down and kissed her, his whole body pressed against her. He pushed his hands up into her hair and held her face between his palms. "You're like water. Like bright water." He bent his face to her throat. "Oh, God, so bright and cold and clear that it hurts to drink."

She felt him, his body ready to mount hers. He was heavy, lying atop her. She had never seen a man unclothed, though she had lived among them, for the Bedu were painfully modest even among their own. But she had seen animals, and boy children, and she knew. It frightened her a little, but the terror that lay beyond, outside this small circle of their bodies locked together, was so huge that her fright seemed like elation.

"Is that a stupid thing to say? I could live without honey," he said, muffled against her throat. "I can't live without water."

Strangely, happily, she began to weep. She put her arms around his shoulders. "No. It is not stupid."

He was silent, his breath on her skin. Then he said, "You're crying."

Zenia slid her hands down his bare back. All of his strength seemed poised beneath her palms in powerful curves and suppleness. She touched his loins, her hands flat, learning his shape.

He groaned, pressing downward. A sweet thrill of sensation spread through her blood. He raised himself. And as he came into her, as he hurt her, thrusting painfully against her barrier, still she arched up to receive him. He held still a moment, his mouth locked over hers, his hand sliding down beneath her hips. He moved aggressively, forcing into her as he pulled her body up to meet him, rupturing her maidenhead.

She whimpered a little, becoming a woman, truly, completely, for the first time in her life, and he held her face and kissed her and stroked her cheeks and said, "Don't cry. Don't cry."

He was deep inside her, heavy on her. A sob of joy and pain escaped her. She wanted him here, a part of her. Impaling and stretching and invading her. It was enough to keep away the terror. She thought, *I can sleep now. Like this.*

But sleep was not what happened. She stroked her hands languidly down his back, and as if they held some message, the same message they had held before, he made that sound low in his throat and pressed hard into her, slowly, driving the sweetness again to her heart. Slowly, and again, as she caressed him. Slowly. She could hear him breathing through his teeth, the end of each breath and deep thrust a groan of pleasure. Her own breath was half caught in her throat, her body flexing in answer, reaching for the peak of delight that rode at the top of each aching penetration.

She began to whimper again, in eagerness. The pain faded as he filled her wholly. Her body clenched, holding him, holding his shoulders and his legs, holding him hard within her.

"Oh God. My God!" His hoarse whisper filled her ears as his body filled her, raw cadence.

Yes, she thought wildly, it was that, it was the tight clasp of her own body on him, as if she would not, could not let him go; it made him come deep and pull back and come hard again, until she was sobbing for breath, her head thrown back as he kissed her throat and her breasts, arching up to heaven and to him, shaking and shaking and shaking like a mindless thing, until the trembling gripped her in one long ecstatic moment, blinding sweetness, his pulsing life upon her and inside her and all around her.

He relaxed with a shudder and soft groan, lying over her, breathing hard. "Thank you," he said into her throat. "Thank you."

"Thank you," she whispered.

He laughed silently. She felt it in his chest. Except that there was a little wetness on her bare shoulder where his cheek lay against her.

They said nothing more, beyond that strange courtesy to one another. After a long time, as Zenia lay unthinking, only feeling him heavy and slack upon her, he lifted himself away.

She didn't beg him to come back, though she wanted it. With careful movements, he rearranged her shirt, drawing it down over her nakedness. Another courtesy, silent and sweet. He sat up, and she could hear the fabric rustle as he pulled his robe back over his head.

"Can you sleep now?" he asked, lying down beside her and drawing her close to him.

"Yes," she said. "Thank you."

He kissed her temple, and lay with his mouth against her skin, his arm around her.

Neither of them slept.

Nine

꧁꧂

ARDEN SAT BOLT upright at the first sound. It was pitch-dark, long before dawn. He did not think enough hours had passed—it could not be this soon.

His heart beat in his ears. He felt her hand curl about his at the quiet scrape of the bar being drawn back outside the door.

Too soon, too soon, not yet!

He gripped her hand hard. The numbness came over him now, the unreality he had expected. The moment had arrived. They were coming.

He stood up in the dark, supporting her as she rose beside him. He had expected light. Was it all to be in this blackness?

The door scaped softly. "Englezy!" a voice whispered. "Come, with the woman. There are camels waiting!"

Something like lightning seemed to flash through Arden's veins. The numbness shattered.

Rashid! he thought savagely. *By the Prophet and by the ninety-nine names of Allah and by the Hundredth Name, God blacken your face and give you long life and power, you old fox!*

"DHAI!" HISSED SOME voice in the starry dark, and Zenia's camel rose. It moaned, a blessedly familiar sound, its front heaving upward as she leaned over the frame for balance, then in two jerks the animal's rear swayed to full height while she inclined far back, as if descending a steep hill, then came the bumping thrust from its knees to its forefeet. Never had she so badly wanted to lean over and hug the long undulating neck of a camel as when this one moved out in the long smooth trotting stride of a thoroughbred racer.

They were already a long way outside the walls of Hayil, having walked and run swiftly through the dark streets, beyond the palm groves and out into the desert to where the camels waited. The guards at the gate had opened the way for them without a sound. *Prince Rashid*, Zenia had thought at first, but the two men with them were no Bedu. They were Egyptians, a black officer and a soldier of the garrison. And although this was clearly escape, there was something of arrest about it: their camels were led by others, urged on hastily by silent Bedu she could not recognize in the dark.

The night air throbbed past her cheeks. She rode like a man, as she always had, with her knee hooked about the crossed frame, but it felt for the first time a strange and sore position. She was vividly aware of her sex—she felt all wrong and yet right. The terror already seemed unreal, as if that could never have happened, that she might have died—but the feel of Lord Winter in her and around her was intensely real, as sharp as the scent of him on her skin.

She was embarrassed by it. The Egyptians might not notice, but she was sure that the Bedu could perceive it in the clear night air. With such a scent on her, she wished that she might hide in a proper camel litter, as the nomad women traveled. She wished that she could veil herself like the town women, but she did not even have a kuffiyah. She wanted to hide, and hold her femaleness to herself, and give the secret of it to no one but him.

"Where are we going?" Lord Winter finally asked in a low voice, barely audible above the shuffling thump of the camels' feet in the sand.

"You are going to Cairo, Englezy," the officer answered.

"Cairo!" Lord Winter exclaimed softly.

"To the *wali*. Mohammed Ali."

Zenia's heart clenched. The Egyptian viceroy, the father of Ibrahim Pasha, the most powerful enemy her mother had ever enraged. Lady Hester had set herself against Mohammed Ali years ago, and thwarted him and his armies at every turn she could.

But Lord Winter chuckled. "*Wellah*, God send that he recognizes your true worth!"

"*Inshallah*," came the officer's voice out of the dark, with good humor. "Khalid ibn Saud is a dog and a fool."

"Fool enough to kill a woman of the English," Lord Winter murmured. "There would have been bloody vengeance for that. Beyond what you can imagine."

The officer grunted. "You are more a fool to come to the desert, Englezy, and bring this woman in disguise. I cannot fathom this madness. But we save your broken-headed carcass, by Allah. My pasha sees to it."

"Your pasha might have spoken up yesterday, and saved us a wretched night."

"It is better this way. Even Wahhabi dogs can kill in packs."

Lord Winter chuckled. "Very true. And the Englezys will thank Mohammed Ali, eh?" he said. "To restore us with our heads on our shoulders. The Lord remember him for good!"

"And may the Englezys see the folly of fighting for the sultan," the officer added caustically.

"By my beard, you may be sure that I shall point it out to them."

The camels went jogging swiftly on under the stars. Zenia kept her worries to herself. She would have to find a way to communicate with Lord Winter, tell him that she did not dare trust herself to Mohammed Ali's whim. Not three summers ago, her mother had fired the Druze revolt with all the ingenuity and cunning she could command. Whenever a Druze sheik had come to Dar Joon, Lady Hester had greeted him with a sneering reminder of their submission to the army of Mohammed Ali's son without a shot fired. *What, hadn't you a single bullet for Ibrahim Pasha?* had been her constant gibe to the proud mountain tribes. The spark found dry and ready tinder. The revolt had exploded, spreading across the Lebanon, until Lady Hester had smiled to hear that Mohammed Ali had declared that the Englishwoman had caused him more trouble than all the rebellious people of Syria and Palestine.

Zenia could not submit herself to Mohammed Ali. But they were in the desert now, and it was a long journey to Cairo. She would find a way to speak secretly to Lord Winter, and they would escape, and come safely to some port and take ship for England. The two of them, as he had promised.

He spoke quietly once or twice to the Egyptians, but addressed no word to her. She wondered what he thought. She had felt that she'd known, back in the locked room in Hayil, that his mind and hers were as one, but now in the desert she was not sure. After the wild tension, the long hours, the frenzied silence of escape, the camel carried her along, carried her along, carried her along at an endless rocking trot. She clung wearily to the saddle frame.

Slowly the images of the pacing camels, the mountains and the sky, began to take firmer shape. She turned her head when she could see—they were nine, the two Egyptians, armed to the teeth with muskets and pistols and swords, a Bedu each leading Zenia and Lord Winter, a guide and a flanking guard trailing behind with two extra baggage camels. She saw Lord Winter's revolving rifle slung upon one of them, along with their own familiar packs.

Zenia had no idea of how far they had come. As the light grew, the Egyptian said something softly, and the guide touched his camel. They all moved more swiftly. The leader broke into a lope and the rest followed.

The translucent dawn showed them close under the sharp fantastical cliffs of mountains, a jagged line against the white sand dunes that swept up the sides of the ridges, cloaking the base of the tall rosy walls. Black shadows stood out sharp in the ravines and gorges.

The guide seemed to be making for one of these dark valleys. The camels loped along, skirting a huge dune, galloping in a great sweeping curve up into the rock-strewn gorge.

They halted in the chill shadow of the walls, with the last stars just fading in the slot of sky above. Zenia turned. When she met Lord Winter's eyes he frowned a little and turned away, swinging down from the standing camel with his foot on the creature's neck.

One of the Bedu clambered swiftly up the steep rock wall to keep a lookout. Zenia dismounted as Lord Winter and the Bedouins had, without making her camel kneel. She went and stood close to Lord Winter, but still he did not speak to her or look at her.

"We will wait here until dark," the officer said.

"So close to Hayil?" Lord Winter asked.

"My pasha has so ordered," the Egyptian said. "He will thwart the Saudis from pursuit. Khalid is a dog."

Zenia thought of the cold-eyed Egyptian general who had sat at the emir's right hand, silent and bored as a master with an ill-tempered puppy on his leash.

"You are not to be seen or spoken to by any of the tribes," the officer added. "If you give me your word to make no such attempt, I will leave you unconstrained."

"Upon Allah's life, I swear it," Lord Winter said immediately.

The black officer looked at Zenia. "And you?"

Standing a little behind and close to Lord Winter's side, she swore quietly and fervently.

"You are to dress and veil yourself properly as a woman," the Egyptian said, pulling down a pack. He dragged a black volume of cloth out and tossed it toward her.

Zenia felt herself grow hot and flustered. She bent down and took up the bundle, with all their eyes on her, and slipped behind a rock to put on the tent of dark clothing that covered her head to foot. She struggled to don the robes over her loose shirt, hardly knowing how to arrange the abundance of cloth. As she emerged, the officer said tersely, "Your face."

Zenia covered her face. And she saw how she altered before them—became almost transparent in her black covering; invisible. A woman. They looked past her and around her and never at her. Even Lord Winter did not lift his eyes to hers.

He seemed like a stranger. Zenia felt a surge of anger at him, an impulse to fling off the veil and force him to turn his face to hers. But she did not. Already knowledge was creeping on her—comprehension that the night before was not today, that they had acted without a future, and only now found there was to be one.

Blue shadows stained the high, pink walls at the entrance to the gorge. The men ate, sitting about, forming a circle that excluded her. Zenia stood beside her camel, watching from within her muffling. When they rose, there was food left for her to eat alone.

Lord Winter sat a moment after the others. She thought he was waiting for her. But as she took a step forward, he suddenly shoved to his feet. He began to run toward her.

Zenia took a step backwards at the expression on his face.

There was a pop—the camel beside her groaned and stumbled—and in a moment of paralyzed shock she realized that it had been shot.

Confusion broke around her. Everyone was running toward the milling camels. A shout came as the lookout flung himself down the sand dune that swept across the mouth of the gorge. He fired. Lord Winter's camel sprang forward and fell among the disorder of animals and men. But Lord Winter was in front of her; looming over her—he seized her about the waist and hurled her upward. The ground and the sky seemed to whirl as she pitched into the arms of one of the Egyptians atop a moving camel. As she fell in between the officer and the saddle frame, the camel bellowed and broke into a gallop for the entrance of the gorge, driven by a savage beating.

The other camels stampeded with them, the Bedouins dragging themselves onto their mounts as the animals charged. Zenia tried to turn; she caught a glimpse of Lord Winter yanking his rifle from the baggage camel as he swung atop it. As he fired at the traitorous lookout she lost sight of him. They burst from the gorge, mounting the dune with sand flying.

In the still dawn sky a pillar of dust revealed the pursuers on their tracks, yet unseen below the high crest of the dune. She heard the officer issue a curt command; the other Egyptian and a Bedu turned their camels away, heading back. The man she rode with did not break out into the open past the dune, but urged his camel along the base of the cliffs, keeping in the cold shadows.

Zenia heard the crack of gunfire, but the Egyptian officer whacked his mount, driving it on at a ground-eating run over the blue-tinged sand. She tried again to turn and look behind, but he shoved her brutally back.

"Keep still, or I'll strangle you!" he hissed at her ear. "Allah curse you! Curse the Englezys, and all treacherous Bedouin dogs!"

THE OTHER SOLDIER, hot and bedraggled, guided by a somber Bedui, caught up at midday. In a landscape of white sand and low black mountains, as stark as the moon, Zenia squinted and stared to see the oncoming party through the heat haze.

There were only two men. They had one of the baggage camels with them. As they came close, she could see a dark stain on the pack, and blood crusted on the animal's hair.

Zenia stared at it. She looked up at the weary Egyptian with dread.

"He was already fallen to them, my aga," the man said, with a brief bow and salute to his commander. "Shot from off this camel. They held the entrance—we could not come into the ravine to save him."

"El-Saud?"

"Pure white dress, my aga, and rags of cotton on their heads."

"Wahhabis for certain! God curse you! The Saudis will execute him, if he is not dead already."

The soldier bent his head in shame. "It was no simple *ghrazzu*, my aga. They tracked us from Hayil."

The Egyptian officer sat silent for a moment. Then he turned his camel toward the west. "As God wills," he murmured, and slapped the beast with his stick, pushing on hard.

Ten

⊸⊶⊷⊶⊸

ZENIA SAT IN the Alexandria office of the Peninsular Steam Navigation Company, her hands folded in her lap to keep them from visibly shaking. She wore black still, a black veil and dress, but now it was Frankish dress, with shoes that were agony on her feet and layers of hot petticoats.

She felt that the other passengers must be staring at her. She knew they were. In Suez, amid the silent bedlam of the bazaar, she had simply walked away from her Egyptian captors, mingling with a passing group of women, all dressed precisely as she was, all covered toe to head with black.

She had heard the shouts behind her when they realized she was gone. But in an alley she had thrown off the women's garments and become Selim again—then found a scoundrel of the sort her mother had often made her pet, an Algerian merchant, a rogue with friends in every crevice and no love for the local pasha. She'd paid for shelter and secrecy while the pasha's men and the soldiers scoured the town and cursed the women of the harems for hiding her. Once, they had come so close that she had taken up a broken copper pot and banged ruthlessly on it, pretending to mend the thing, while the pasha's agent shouted at the Algerian above the noise.

"Lord Winter?" the clerk of the Peninsular Company looked up inquiringly, his long Greek mustachios bobbing.

Zenia stood. She felt wildly conspicuous—the black dress had been the only Frankish lady's attire to be procured in all of Suez, pulled wrinkled and musty out of an unclaimed trunk off some long departed Bombay packet. It was made for someone so much larger about the waist that it hung in loose folds around hers. She was thankful for the net veil that drooped over her eyes, obscuring the upper half of her face, and the black gloves that covered her dirty fingernails.

As she walked forward to the desk, the clerk rose. He held Lord Winter's passport for a steamer ticket, cut from inside the seam of the viscount's shaving kit in one of the many nights Zenia had slept isolated behind a curtain in the Egyptian officer's tent. She had ten gold coins in her purse from the same place.

It was hers, she had thought as she stole it. He had promised to take her to England. He would have done it.

It was as much hers as Mohammed Ali's, anyway.

"Lord Winter, he is not with you, madam?" the clerk asked.

She stood there, looking through her veil at the Greek clerk. This was the only ship for a month; this was her single chance— if they would not let her exercise Lord Winter's open passport for a return passage, she had not enough money to pay.

"No," she said. Her voice was hoarse and grave, half-broken with fear. "Lord Winter is not coming."

The clerk hesitated a moment, and then his face took on a strange look, a sort of grimace of solemn agony. "Ah! I be so sympathy, Lady Winter!" He looked down at his manifest. "The ship is booked, but you wish return your family, yes? So you must! We will contrive!"

Zenia bit her lip. She could feel the eyes of the other English people who waited, the passengers who had disembarked at Suez and come overland with the mail to Alexandria. None of them were alone as she was; even the ladies who traveled without their husbands had maids and children with them.

The clerk was consulting the passport letter. "There is a horse to embark, Lady Winter?"

"No," she said. And for no reason, her eyes suddenly blurred and she felt hot tears slide down her cheeks. She swallowed. "There is no horse. None."

"Please sit," the clerk said. "I must speak captain."

Zenia sat down. She bent her head, willing the tears to cease, but they just kept falling, making dark marks on her dirty black gloves. She felt ill and dizzy.

For many weeks she had not wept; she did not know why now, in front of English people, that she could not stop. The humid heat of Alexandria seemed to press in upon her until she thought she could not find her breath. She had never felt so hot, even in the desert. Her feet felt as if they were locked in burning vises, and her head floated in stifling vapor.

She thought that she must go outside for a moment, and pushed herself up. But her vision seemed to fall in upon her. Blackness poured in from all sides. She heard voices, distant, and then everything seemed to come back, and her nose hurt, and she was on the floor with faces and excited voices all about her.

"Well, there is hardly anything to loosen," a man's voice was saying irritably. "This dress appears several sizes too large for the poor girl."

Zenia blinked. A young British officer in a blue naval jacket was leaning over her. He pulled out a pair of spectacles and set them on his nose, peering down owlishly.

"I'm all right," she said, trying hastily to rise.

"Indeed, you must lie still a moment, madam," he said firmly. "Just rest, and be calm. Here, the captain says that you have a cabin." He dabbed at her nose with a handkerchief and looked up at someone Zenia could not see. "It might be best to take her aboard directly, sir. It's cooler. I believe she may be—well—" His neck turned red. "You know what I mean, sir?"

"I'll help her, poor babe!" A woman knelt beside Zenia, all pink skirts and fresh powdery scent. "Come to Iris, my poor dear! Come along."

Zenia rose, with the woman's arm about her waist. "I'm all right—truly—"

"Nonsense. I've had four, all in Bombay! I know what this heat will do. It will kill you and the child both, if you don't take care. Come, just a gentle step—these gentlemen are going to show us the way. Baggage? I don't—" The lady's dark head turned. "Where is your maid, my love, and your boxes?"

"Oh!" Zenia lifted her hand, pointing at the battered trunk she had made sure to buy, to seem as if she were not entirely without possessions. It was empty but for enough sand to make it seem as if it had clothing inside.

"But your maid? She has not gone off and left you alone in your condition?"

Zenia felt her lip quivering. She shook her head hard, and began to cry again. The lady named Iris held her about the shoulders and patted her arm. "Never mind! You shall tell us all about it later. Come, my love. Poor little thing—you're skin and bones. Why, I could carry you myself!"

* * *

ZENIA FOUND HERSELF aboard the steamer *Edward Rule*, sharing a cabin with Mrs. Iris Smith, whose maid had been unceremoniously displaced. The coolness of the sea air did not surmount the rocking of the first boat she had ever set foot on, and Zenia spent the four days to Malta in such a misery of confused illness that she could hardly speak. She was vaguely aware that Mrs. Smith nursed her heroically, but even thanks were beyond her.

It was not until the ship lay anchored at Malta for coaling that Zenia gathered enough of her reason to sit up and speak with weepy gratitude to Mrs. Smith. This imperturbable lady, who declared herself an Anglo-Indian *par excellence*, and by no means stymied by a little seasickness, merely urged Zenia to look to her soup.

"For it's very likely you're eating for two, aren't you, my love?" Mrs. Smith gazed at her keenly. "You know it, don't you?"

Zenia sat on the berth, her face turned down to her lap. She did not answer, but only kneaded her hands together.

Mrs. Smith put her cool hand on Zenia's forehead, stroking back her damp hair. Zenia began to weep again. "I'm sorry!" she said helplessly. "I'm sorry to be this way!"

"It is very difficult, I know. It is so difficult." Mrs. Smith began to weep a little, too. "I lost my first husband when I was eighteen, and all alone in India, and in just your condition. Who are your people, my dear?"

Zenia swallowed, wiping at her eyes. "Mr. Michael Bruce is my father."

She was in dread that Mrs. Smith would ask more, but the lady only said, "Here, take another spoonful of soup. And we have an excellent melon. There are some compensations in the tropics, aren't there? That's a good girl." She waited until Zenia had forced herself to finish, and then rose. "The mails are leaving tonight, and I want to put a note in. It should arrive ahead of us," she said. "Do you feel up to going ashore? I've bespoken a room and a shampooer, and we can both have a nice bath. Much needed, on my part. There is nothing like a cool bath and an Eastern shampoo; one feels utterly refreshed."

Mrs. Smith's brother met her in Gibraltar. He looked a little oddly at Zenia. Piecemeal, she had told Iris Smith how she had come to be traveling home alone to England, leaving Lord Winter in the desert. She never said that she was Lady Winter—they had all begun calling her that from the start. She never said that she was his widow—they just looked at the black dress and veil and expressed their sympathies. And she thought wearily, *What difference does it make?*

He was taking her home. He had promised that he would.

"Iris," she overheard Mr. Harrow say softly to his sister one night, "do you know who she is?"

Zenia paused, gripping the stair rail while the ship rolled gently on the heaving swell of the Atlantic.

"That Stanhope woman, yes, I know," Mrs. Smith said. "Even in India we heard of that affair, Robert! But I'm not going to be a gorgon about it."

"Yes, but—"

"She needs help." Mrs. Smith's voice had a little edge. "You may believe me, I know what it's like to be alone and increasing in a foreign place!"

Mr. Harrow left a little pause. "I'm sorry," he said stiffly.

"Well, it is all water under the bridge now," his sister said. "But I will not abandon her for some scruple about her background! I mean to see her safely to her people."

Mr. Harrow's silence was longer. At length, he said ironically, "I only hope they'll thank you for it."

Zenia turned on the stairs and went away, lying down in the cabin and clutching the miniature of her father in both hands.

Don't cry, damn you, a voice chided her roughly. *It's a waste of good water.*

She closed her eyes and took a deep breath. She would not cry. She wanted him to be proud of her.

Zenia was paralyzed with excitement and fear and cold. She sat shivering in the berth, hearing all the sounds of London outside, smelling the smells, the air thick with smoke. It was so cold that she could see her breath even in the cabin, and outside everything seemed dark, the deck speckled with charcoal, the huge darkened buildings, the bleak, black-coated, shouting people. It was all ugly; horridly ugly and stinking.

"Don't cry, don't cry," she whispered to herself, a litany. "Don't cry, little wolf."

Mrs. Smith came bustling in the door with a cloak. "Now. It's all arranged."

Zenia went with her. She did not question Mrs. Smith's arrangements; they were the only reason she was still alive, she thought. Alive, and in England. Oh, it was so cold. It wasn't green—there was not a single tree to be seen, only the dead tall spikes of ships' masts.

She walked down the gangway with Mrs. Smith holding her arm and Mr. Harrow behind them. There was a little group of waiting people on the dock, standing still amid the bustle of the seamen. For an instant, Zenia stopped.

She saw a ghost; she saw Lord Winter in a tall man who looked up at her, his face half-hidden between his hat and his up-raised collar.

Then the illusion vanished, and she realized that it was someone much older, who looked at her without recognition. And

Mrs. Smith was leading her down, turning her to someone else, another gentleman who was clenching and unclenching his gloved hands.

Zenia lifted her eyes from the tight fists he made. She knew before she looked—she knew what Mrs. Smith had done; her heart flew up into her throat and she raised her eyes to see her father's face.

He was older than she had expected, with lines of worry about his eyes and carved into his cheeks, with the handsome features gone stark, the wind blowing his graying hair against his hat brim. For a moment he stared into her face, a searching look, at her and yet beyond her, as if he had expected to see someone else there.

She drew herself up and held out her hand. "Mr. Bruce?" she asked, with a proud lift of her chin, so that no one would see how she was dying inside.

Suddenly, weirdly, he began to laugh. "Oh my God," he said. "I remember." And he took her hand hard into his and pulled her up against him and squeezed her to his chest, muttering and laughing. He was much stronger than he looked; he almost smothered her in his arms, and then held her back and stared at her hungrily. "Please come home," he said, his voice shaking. "Please come. There is so much to make up for."

London transformed. From a bleak, noisy, gray place, it began to glow.

"This is Bentinck Street," her father said, as the carriage turned into a row of solemn brown-brick houses with white casements. "St. Marylebone. Home—such as it is." He smiled at her. When he smiled, she could see the young man in the painting, and she smiled back. "Are you quite cold?" he asked.

"Very cold!" she said. "I love it."

He laughed at her. All of Zenia's need to weep had left her, but her father kept sniffling and smiling, his handsome eyes reddened with emotion. "Well, we shall keep the fires up this winter." The carriage had stopped, and he caught her hand. "Now, I must tell you, Zenia, that my wife suffers from ill health. But she knows you are coming, and wants you as much as I do. She is a very special lady. You must not be afraid of her."

Zenia nodded.

"You know that I was never married to your mother," he said, tilting his head down. "But you are my daughter." His hand gripped hard on hers. "When I received Mrs. Smith's letter—I have not slept one night since, for wonder and remorse."

"Miss Williams said—" Zenia spoke faintly, hardly able to get the words out. "She believed that my mother never told you."

He lifted his eyes, locking his fingers in hers. "Zenia, I have done things in my life that shamed me. Your mother—I can't make excuses, I left her when she told me to go—but one thing I want you to know and believe. I would not have left you there. I would not have abandoned you. I swear it with every fiber of my being."

"I'm glad," Zenia whispered. "I was always glad that you were my father."

"I wish—did you never think to write to me?"

"Oh, no!" Zenia shook her head. "Nothing left Dar Joon that my mother did not see."

His eyes narrowed a little. "You were afraid of her."

Zenia gave a small shrug. "She did not like to be disobeyed."

He held her hands for a long moment. Then he said, "You do not have to be afraid anymore." He knocked on the roof with his cane, and the cabman came down and opened the door.

HIS WIFE INSISTED that Zenia call her Marianne. She was quiet and elegant, with a tender transparency. She had pretty, subdued manners that did not hide a generous welcome for her husband's illegitimate daughter.

Zenia could hardly keep from staring at her, fascinated. She could not imagine a woman more different from her own mother. Her father had a little tendency to hover about his wife, asking twice if she would like a shawl. Zenia met her half-brother, another Michael, an ardent youth of sixteen who shook her hand nervously, asked her about the government in Egypt, and talked for half an hour about European politics until his father chased him off with an awkward laugh, advising him to finish his Latin before tea.

Zenia felt unreal. She was welcome in the house on Bentinck Street; they offered her welcome so openly, as if there was a place that had been empty, and she had slipped in to fill it. No one asked more than simple commonplaces about her trip, and Marianne even expressed a discreet sympathy for her mother's death.

There was no sign of other children, and Zenia gradually came to understand, without being told, that they had died. When Marianne led her up to a bedchamber, it was clearly one that had belonged to a pair of young girls. There were two beds with embroidered pillows and lace coverlets, and two little beribboned silhouettes hung one above the other on the wall.

Marianne paused before she closed the door. "You must believe it when I say I am glad you came to us," she said softly. "Michael always loved my sons from my first marriage, and I am glad to love you, for his sake and your own."

"Thank you," Zenia said foolishly.

"Thank *you*," Marianne said, "for coming to us. I hope you will decide to stay. It would make your father very happy."

IN HIS WIFE's bedchamber, Michael Bruce stood with his hands behind his back, staring down into the barren fall garden behind the house. "I don't know what to make of it," he said. "I don't know, Mari."

"There can be no doubt that she is yours," his wife said, with a faint smile. "The Bruce looks are obvious, I should think."

"Are they?" He turned, frowning. "But—she is the most beautiful creature I've ever laid eyes on in my life." Then he made a wry face. "Excepting you, of course. So saith the belated knight!"

"I rest my case," Marianne said, leaning back in the bed.

He gave an ironic laugh. "Flattery, my dear? After all these years?"

"Why should I not pride myself on my conquest of the splendid Mr. Bruce?" she said gently. "You are a superior man, and your daughter is a diamond of the first water. When we have restored her complexion, and filled out her thinness, she will be beautiful beyond anything."

"If the world thinks so, then pray God that she has more sense than I ever did at her age," he said. "She must be twenty-five, Mari. Twenty-five! And she is thin, isn't she? I hope she isn't ill." He made a turn about the room, and then stopped, sitting down beside her on the bed. "You have a lunatic for a husband. For the last three days, I've been a lunatic. You must think—" He broke off.

She laid her hand on his. "Michael. It is all right."

"But to bring her here, Mari; to force her on you and our son."

"She is as much yours as Michael is. I have only to look at her to see it." She squeezed his fingers. "I was never jealous, was I? You told me everything long ago. It was one of the things that I admired in you, that you did not seek to hide it. I will confess, I was a little afraid—" She shrugged. "I thought she might be more like her mother. I'm not sure I could have loved her as well then, though I would have tried. But she is not, Michael. She is yours. And that is enough for me. Besides—" She curled her fingers around the coverlet. "I have missed having a girl's voice in the house."

He leaned over and kissed her. "I don't deserve your goodness."

"Perhaps you don't," she said tapping his cheek lightly, "but it's your innocent daughter we speak of."

He frowned a little. "Not so innocent. Grown up and married," he said. He looked up, fixing a distant gaze on the window. "It is all so damnably odd. I've been making inquiries—Mari, do you know who this Winter fellow was? The heir to Belmaine, for heaven's sake!"

"Belmaine! Oh, surely you must be mistaken."

"I'm not. There was word at the foreign office. Arden Mansfield, Viscount Winter. Only son of the Earl Belmaine. Killed in some uprising in Arabia—the report came in from Cairo, with the same mail as the Smith woman's letter to me."

His wife sat silently, picking at the counterpane. "But she's said nothing?"

"Not a word. I know nothing but what Mrs. Smith wrote. But Mari—he was there. Belmaine. On the dock. He didn't come forward. He let me take her."

"They don't approve, then."

He shook his head. "Good God, how could they approve? She's—"

"The offspring of two prime ministers and several aristocratic houses," Marianne said tartly. "They can hardly complain of her bloodlines, legitimate or not."

"But why has she come to me, then? Surely he told her to go to his parents if she was left alone."

"Perhaps she wished to come to you instead, Michael."

"But Belmaine! She didn't even speak to him. I don't think she knew who he was."

"Why should she? She can't have seen him before, any more

than she's seen you. The poor child is distraught. I shall have to invite Mrs. Smith and her brother to dinner. We must be grateful to her."

"Yes," he agreed abstractedly. "And who married them, Mari? Where? It would be no easy thing, to make a Christian marriage in a Mohammedan country—a marriage that would be legal here."

"I read in the paper that there was an American missionary at her mother's funeral," Marianne said quietly.

He glanced at her. The death of the lady in the desert had gone unmentioned in the house in Bentinck Street, though the papers had been full of letters and obituaries for Lady Hester Stanhope. "Yes," he said, holding her hand. "I read it, too." He pressed his lips together. "I suppose one never outlives one's past."

"Not when it is moving in upstairs," she said wryly.

"My love," he said, "it is worse than you think." He sighed, and then set his jaw. "I haven't told you everything that was in the letter. She is—expecting."

"That is a natural consequence of marriage."

"My dear, don't you understand?" He stood up with a sudden move. "I don't think she *is* married. And I don't think Belmaine thinks it either."

Eleven

⎯⎯⎯∞∞∞⎯⎯⎯

"Oʜ, I sᴀʏ!" young Michael exclaimed, as the blazing Christmas pudding, adorned with holly, was borne in by Marianne herself, the platter only lightly supported on the other hand by the maid. "Now you will taste something you'll like, Zenia!"

There was holly and greenery all about the house. The rooms smelled of steam and baking and evergreen, and Marianne and Zenia had copied from a magazine that showed how the Queen celebrated Christmas at Windsor, tying up bonbons in crackling silver paper and bows to hang from the branches of a little tree. They would have a very quiet holiday this year, Marianne had said, just Papa's colleague Mr. Jocelyn, an advocate in Doctors' Commons who always came to Christmas dinner—but to Zenia it seemed splendid.

"A plum pudding," she said reverently, looking at the perfect half-round mold, flickering with the last blue flames, set before her father.

"Steeping since October!" Marianne said. She turned the platter, adjusting it in a precise way, and handed her husband the knife. "Zenia's piece first," she said, with her hand over his to place his initial cut.

He gave her a pursed, laughing look aside. "I believe I understand you, my dear." He cut into the pudding, then moved the knife. "Here?"

"The other way," Marianne said imperturbably, and he obeyed her. As he scooped out the piece, a silver coin fell from among the crumbs.

"Good luck!" young Michael cried, sitting forward in his seat. "She got the shilling! Good luck for Zenia!"

"Good luck indeed," Mr. Jocelyn said pleasantly. He was younger than her father, with intelligent brown eyes that smiled easily. His clothes were exceptionally neat and his manners gentle. Zenia had felt at ease with him immediately.

Her father winked at him as he passed the plate. "Merry Christmas, and a fortunate and happy New Year! Be so kind as to do the honors with the sauce, Michael."

Zenia chewed her lower lip, gazing excitedly at the pudding as Michael dropped a huge dollop of fluffy sauce upon it. She knew that they had arranged for her to get the coin, but that did not matter. It made everything better.

Young Michael set the plate in front of her. Everyone watched, quieting. Zenia glanced up with a tremulous smile, and took up a forkful of pudding and sauce.

She nearly choked. "Phew!" She put her hand to her mouth, laughing and grimacing. "Oh, no! Oh, no! It's awful!"

Everyone groaned. "Awful!" Marianne cried, and popped a cracker at her, spewing bright paper bits and sweets over the table.

"I'll eat it!" Michael cried, pulling her plate toward him and taking a huge bite. He rolled his eyes in extravagant satisfaction. "Perfect! Delicious! Utterly salubrious!"

Zenia picked up the little cardboard cracker by her plate and popped it at him, and laughed immoderately when the bang made him flinch.

"I'll take my coin back," Zenia said, picking up the keepsake and dusting crumbs from it.

"Keep your silly old coin, then," Michael said merrily. "If you have no better sense than to think our Christmas pudding *awful*! What an addle-brain!"

Zenia glanced anxiously at Marianne, hoping that her step-mother was not hurt, but Marianne was smiling, her color high. She had suffered a rheumatic attack not long after Zenia arrived, and Zenia had been glad to fetch and carry and do everything she could. The weeks of illness had made Zenia feel more at home. Useful. She was accustomed to serve, and more than happy to nurse such an undemanding patient. She would rather think of Marianne than of what was happening to herself.

The horrible black dress from Suez had been replaced, but Zenia still wore black, and the seamstress who had come to the house had matter-of-factly advised a style that could be let out easily in the waistline. No other mention had been made of her condition. Sometimes she looked up from sewing or writing a let-ter for Marianne to find her father gazing at her, a somber expres-sion on his face, but he always smiled immediately, and with such warmth that she felt her fears recede.

She chose not to think about it. She chose to live in the mo-ment, with holly and Christmas presents, to listen raptly to the carolers who came to the door, and bask in the pleasure of pour-ing out hot punch for them. She sang a duet that Mr. Jocelyn taught her as he played upon the pianoforte and harmonized in a rich baritone. She lost at forfeits, and won at Yes and No, and How and When and Where, and pantomime. For the last round, just as the church bells rang quarter to midnight, young Michael pantomimed a camel. Zenia did not win; she made herself laugh very hard, and then said that she must go upstairs for her shawl.

In her room, she put the shawl about her shoulders and sat down, fiddling with the ends, tying them in a knot and untying them again.

"Don't cry," she whispered to herself, staring into the coals behind the grate. "Don't cry!"

She did not know how much time had passed, until she heard the sound of young Michael's steps go up the stairs past her door. A little while later, her father quietly knocked. Zenia looked up and gathered the shawl about herself as he entered.

"Don't get up," he said softly. "It is high time for bed."

He closed the door behind him. She sat still, tying and untying the shawl. Her father came to the grate and stood with his back to it. He seemed awkward, as if he had forgotten why he was there.

"It was a wonderful Christmas," Zenia said. "The most wonderful—"

"Please," he said. "I know you mean to thank me, but it only makes me feel worse. It is the first you've had, isn't it?"

She did not answer, but looked past him into the fire.

"Zenia—I just want you to know that you are welcome here. When the child comes—"

She looked up sharply.

"Yes, I know of it," he said. "Mrs. Smith informed me. I haven't wanted to pry, or make you feel uneasy. I just want you to know that you have a home. We don't go into society much anymore; I've not cared for it for a long time, and Marianne—well, you know her situation. This is a liberal neighborhood, artists and writers and so on. No one much questions other people's business. I don't know what you have thought about for your future, but—"

"I would stay with you forever!" she said quickly. "If I might."

He smiled a little. "Well, forever may be longer than you think, but you may stay until you choose of your own accord to go." He tilted his head. "You are young yet, and may marry again."

She turned her face down. "Thank you," she whispered.

"Do you think," he said gently, "that your husband's family should be informed of your condition?"

She shook her head.

"For the child's sake, Zenia?"

That did not seem very real to her. Mrs. Smith had said so, and the seamstress, and now her father—she could feel the changes in her body, hard and soft, but everything was so changed; they were just a part of all of it.

"For Lord Winter's sake?" he asked, when she did not answer. "Is it fair to his memory, to keep his child hidden from his own family?"

She bit her lip.

He knelt down beside her. "Zenia—is it Lord Winter's child?"

"Yes," she said. It came out more clearly and firmly than she had thought she could speak.

There was a frown between her father's brows. He looked at her for a long time, and then he said, "Did he take advantage of you? Force you?"

"No." She closed her eyes. "Oh, no. He wanted me to sleep. I was afraid, and he wanted me to sleep."

She thought he was going to ask more. But he knelt beside her unspeaking.

"He promised he would bring me to England," she said. She looked up at her father's worried face. "He gave me his word he would bring me. And he has done it."

He put both hands over hers. "Zenia—I must ask. I must. Did he marry you?"

She clutched the ends of the shawl. "It will be very terrible if he didn't, will it not? Will I be beaten? Will they take me away from you?"

"No!" He gripped her hands. "No, of course not!"

"I used his letter, to get a passage home. And everyone began to call me Lady Winter, and to help me, and be kind to me. And I—what was I to do? I had nowhere—I wanted to go home! I wanted to find you! That was all that I ever wanted, to find you!"

"It's all right." He held her against his shoulder, rocking her. "It's all right. My sweet girl."

"I can't cry!" She exclaimed, pulling away and standing up. She was breathing hard and nervously. "He wouldn't like it if I cried."

Her father rose. His figure was blurred against the fire and the white marble mantelpiece. She gritted her teeth together and dashed her hand at her eyes.

"If I can stay here," she said. "If I can stay here and help Marianne and have next Christmas and tell Michael I'm happy when he gets his commission in the Grenadier Guards, which I'm sure that he will, he wants it so. If I can only stay here!"

"You can stay," her father said. "And I'll get down on my knees and pray to God every night in thanks for Lord Winter, because he brought you to me."

IT WAS THE end of March when Zenia sat with Marianne in the back parlor, pouring water on a forced pot of bright yellow daffodils. She set the watering can on the floor, bending awkwardly over her increasing bulk.

The door opened. Her father came in. "Zenia," he said grimly, "You must come downstairs, my dear. You have a caller."

The expression on his face made Zenia's heart freeze. Marianne stood up. "Who is it, Michael?"

"It is the Earl Belmaine."

"Oh dear," Marianne said. "Would you like me to come?"

Zenia rose. She looked at them both anxiously. "Who is the Earl Belmaine?" she asked in a timid voice.

Her father smiled at her, a sudden sweet warmth. "Ah, if he had only heard you ask," he said. "It might shake his sense of himself a little. He is Lord Winter's father, my dear. You need not be afraid of him. I'll stay with you, and Marianne will come if you like."

Zenia glanced at Marianne, who had been having a difficult week. "No. You must not come downstairs. If Papa will go with me . . ."

"I'll be there," her father said, holding open the door.

In her father's study a tall man waited, an elegant form standing beside the open drapes, the winter sun lighting a curve of cheek and brow that gave Zenia a start of memory, a resemblance that knocked all her desperately gathered poise into confusion. She stood before the door, lost.

He gazed at her for a long, hard moment, long enough for her to see that he was prouder than his son, his eyes blue but colder, his skin pale and his carriage unyieldingly erect, the black hair dimmed with silver. He looked directly at her waistline without embarrassment, with a frigid gravity, and then up into her face.

"I wish to speak to her alone," he said.

"My daughter has asked that I remain with her," her father said. "Zenobia, this is Lord Belmaine. Belmaine—my daughter."

"Lady Winter," the earl said caustically. "Or so I am informed."

"Allow me to make one thing entirely clear." Her father spoke in a soft and dangerous voice, one Zenia had never yet heard him use before. "I will not tolerate any rudeness or insinuation regarding my daughter in my house. She lives with me. She has made no claims on you." He held a chair for Zenia, placing it near the fire. "It is you, sir, who chose to call on her."

Zenia sat down, supporting herself on the arms of the chair.

The earl's nostrils flared a little. He looked at her as if he would eat her—angrily, almost hungrily.

"Well," he said to Zenia. "Do you have marriage lines? A record? Witnesses?"

"No," she said.

He made a sharp turn and stood looking at a candle sconce on the wall, his hands locked behind his back. "No," he muttered. "Just 'no'!" He stared at the sconce. "You used my son's name."

Zenia said nothing, ashamed of her subterfuge. It had been lies, though she had not told them herself.

"Did you see him die?" Lord Belmaine asked the wall sconce.

"No. He put me up onto a camel with an Egyptian officer, and went for his rifle, and I did not see him again, because the Egyptian took me ahead."

The earl's eyes narrowed. "Tell me the name of this—this horse he was to obtain."

"The String of Pearls."

"And what name he used in disguise?"

"Abu Haj Hasan, the Moor."

"And what place they arrested him?"

"Hayil, in the Nejd."

Lord Belmaine turned. "You were with him, then. You are this absurd Queen of the English. I've made inquiries; I've had letters from the consuls in Beyrout and Cairo. Every court from here to Calcutta is buzzing with it; Hester Stanhope's bastard, living as a filthy Bedouin in some tent!" He glanced at her father. "Hester Stanhope's—and yours."

"My *daughter*, Belmaine. Under my protection."

"I have no interest in your daughter, Bruce, unless she's carrying my son's child! And if she is—then she's under *my* protection. I've waited. I've thought an adventuress would come wheedling to me. I've had this house watched. For months I've waited. My son! My son is dead, and I've waited. But you aren't going to come, are you? You're not going to ask for money. Is it not his?" He swung away and sat down, his voice shaking. "Is this just a game to drive me mad?"

Zenia looked at the top of his bent head. She said, "Perhaps you will not believe the truth."

He looked up.

"I was with Lord Winter," she said coldly. "One night, when we both knew we were to be put to death at dawn. I have never been with another. He is the father of my child."

My child. It was the first time she had thought of it so. Hers alone. She sensed that this man wanted it, and a wave of ferocious possessiveness welled up in her. She had to lock her hands on the chair to keep from hugging her arms about her and holding the baby inside her to herself.

"I have no proof," she said, before he could ask. "I have no proof of anything. But I do not deny you the truth, because Lord Winter was your son."

He stared into her eyes for a long moment, his own that same familiar hue, but different. Paler.

He stood up suddenly. "You have no marriage lines," he said in a sharp voice. "They have been lost." He looked up at her father. "Do you understand me, Bruce? They have been lost in the desert. I myself feel that they will be recovered. I will make every effort to recover them. I will use all the resources at my command to see that they are found. Do you understand?"

Her father put his hand on her shoulder. He squeezed. "Zenia?"

She opened her mouth to say that there were no marriage lines to be recovered—but Lord Belmaine was frowning at her with his jaw set, scowling at her deeply.

"Madam," he said. "Do not speak. I admire scruple. I admire honesty. But before you speak, I lay before you the question of the higher principle at stake. You of anyone must know what it is to be a bastard. You have it in your power to give your child his father's name, his rightful name and place—or withhold it from him." He stood stiffly, his hands behind his back. "Madam—Lady Winter—I do not want you to lie to me. I believe that you married my son, and you have lost your marriage lines, and they will be restored in good order. I believe this. I will act on this belief. I ask of you only that, for the sake of your child, for the sake of his future—please—do not speak unwisely."

My child. She thought of her mother, of her own life, of shame and defenselessness. She turned her head and looked up at her father. He watched her soberly, a mirror of the miniature painting she had dreamed upon all her days. He had said she could stay as long as she wished. But the future was coming, relentlessly.

My child. With no name, as she had had none. With no father.

"No," she whispered. "I would not speak unwisely."

THE BABY WAS born at Swanmere, in a gilt and green room that smelled of age, with a doctor and two midwives hovering about, and Lady Belmaine standing beside the bed like a stately statue as Zenia sweated and panted and felt her body torn asunder. All through it, she kept opening her eyes and seeing Lady Belmaine, upright and grave, her hair smooth as dove's wings, her high cheekbones white as linen, her fine mouth unsmiling.

Zenia did not scream, though they told her that she should. She did not moan. She was Bedu, el-Nasr, Selim. She had crossed the red sands. She would not let Lady Belmaine see her break.

There was a surge of agony and then a flutter of exclamations: commands and advice that she could not hear. All she could hear was, *Don't cry, damn you;* all she could see was Lady Belmaine; all she could feel was pain.

"It is a girl," someone said from somewhere.

And in the silence Zenia heard it begin to cough and wail.

"Congratulations," one of the doctors said heartily. "A fine healthy babe. Good color; excellent lungs."

Lady Belmaine's mouth pursed. She looked down at Zenia, a brief impatient look that skidded over her face and down to her clenched hands. "I will tell Belmaine," she said, turning away.

Twelve

THE CALLING CARD lay on the hall table, waiting for the master of the house when he came in. Michael Bruce glanced at it as he returned from his monthly dinner at Lincoln's Inn—and stopped dead in the hallway. He pulled off his glove and picked up the card.

In small copperplate print on exquisitely thin pasteboard, the name was *Arden Mansfield, Viscount Winter*. And jotted in the corner in firm black ink: *Travellers' Club or Clarendon Hotel*.

Michael Bruce shook his head. For a long moment he closed his eyes and shook his head back and forth, a half-laugh of horror choked in his throat. "Good God. Oh, great God. I am too old for this," he muttered, and turned toward the stair. "Marianne!" he shouted, and went up them two at a time.

* * *

MR. MICHAEL BRUCE had not lived an entire lifetime in quiet peace in Marylebone. In his youth he had traveled the Continent at the height of Napoleon's power, he had witnessed the bombardment of Copenhagen at twenty and prowled behind enemy lines in the Peninsular battlefields at twenty-one. At twenty-two, he had lived with and loved a baffling, sensual, haughty, extraordinary woman eleven years older than himself, had sheltered her in his arms on a wave-dashed rock while their ship went down off Cyprus, followed her into Eastern palaces and smoked with pashas and princes straight out of the Arabian Nights, waited shoulder to shoulder with her in the desert, their pistols cocked and ready for Bedouin assault. He had been belittled and adored by her in the same sentence, had given way to her ego, walked in her shadow, implored her to marry him long after he had known it would be the greatest disaster of his life if she did. He had left her on the shores of the Lebanon because she screamed at him that he must go. He had traveled with the memory of her tear-stained face, and in Constantinople he had found a sweet, quiet girl to idolize him—the first in a series of affairs that took him home across France; because when he was young, women fell in love with him as easily as breathing, and he could never say no to them.

Even to Hester, he had never said a final farewell. Somehow, in his heart, he had always had the illusion that he could go back. He had even made plans to bring her to France, but she had refused to come—somewhat to his relief, he remembered ruefully. He'd had a taste for high tragediennes, he supposed: he was by then deep in love with little Algaé, and embroiled in the hopeless effort to save her husband Marshal Ney from execution. After that had come the famous—infamous—escape of Lavallette from a Paris prison—and Michael's arrest for high treason in France, the trial for his part in aiding the fugitive to flee; then his own imprisonment, six months in the Prison de la Force.

All long ago. So long ago. His daughter must have been two years old then.

He had returned to England something of a hero. For years, he had been "Lavallette Bruce" to the papers. And then Marianne—Marianne the quiet, smiling widow, who had suddenly and abruptly made all of his confused strikes and runs at life seem vain foolery. She had simply refused an affair. She would only see him with the permission of his family and hers. Modest, straightforward Marianne, who merely expected the highest standard of conduct, without explanation or excuse. Michael had been a master of explanations and excuses. He did not know if he would truly have gone back to Lebanon for his daughter, not when he was young and reckless. He hoped he would have—and he thought that Hester must have been sure of it, or she would not have kept her secret so well.

He walked through the rainy night, fingering Winter's card in his pocket. It was perhaps not so strange to have his past come back so him in the form of a daughter, considering the sort of past it was, but he felt exceedingly peculiar to be calling on a man supposed dead for two years, the father of his granddaughter, who might or might not be willing to admit it, who might or might not acquiesce in the convenient fiction they had built, who might or might not be someone whom Michael, at fifty-four, could possibly knock down for taking advantage of his innocent daughter, whatever the bloody damned extenuating circumstances had been in the bloody damned desert.

When the door to the private parlor in the Clarendon opened, Michael saw that he was not likely to knock down Viscount Winter. Moral principle was not going to outweigh twenty years' age difference and a fighting weight that looked to be fourteen stone. The man who received him was powerfully built, hard-tanned, with the look of a coiled spring about him.

"Michael Bruce," Michael said, taking off his damp bat.

"Winter." The viscount thrust out his hand. He looked straight at Michael with brilliantly deep blue eyes. "Did you come alone, sir?"

Some evil genius made Michael say, "Who would I bring with me?"

The expression on Lord Winter's face made him repent instantly. "She did not reach you?" the viscount asked in a smothered voice.

In that moment, Michael forgave him. He made him suffer a few moments more, deliberately laying his hat and gloves on a table beside the door.

"Zenia is safe," he said. "You have a daughter."

Viscount Winter turned white and then red beneath his tan. Michael thought he was not quite as old as the harsh imprint of his adventures made him appear at first glance. He seemed to have difficulty knowing what to do with his sun-browned hands, staring down at them and then shoving them behind his back, turning away.

"Well," he said sullenly, "if she will have me, I'm willing to make it right."

Michael's lips twitched. He really felt rather sorry for the fellow. "But you already have, have you not?" he said mildly. "Lady Winter is in residence at Swanmere, with Miss Elizabeth Lucinda Mansfield in the nursery."

Lord Winter looked back in clear astonishment. He seemed for an instant as if he would reject the statement, but then a scowl erased any hint of emotion. He gave Michael a veiled, appraising look. "Of course," he said.

"I don't suppose you would part with some of that sherry?" Michael asked. "Forgive me, but you are presumed dead. An old man's nerves, you know!"

The viscount's mouth twisted in a smile. "You've nerve enough, Mr. Bruce." He poured the wine out into a sparkling glass. "I nearly was dead. Several times."

"Good. Not that I wish you ill, particularly, but I should like to think that you did not seduce my daughter and then abandon her without some sufficient reason."

Lord Winter poured himself a glass. He looked up over it. "No," he said, and then pointedly: "I wonder if you can say the same?"

"I suppose you have some right to ask. I never knew of her until she came to me. I was told—how ironic it seems now—that Lady Hester caught the plague after I left, and was a long time recovering. You may be sure that I felt a suitable son of a bitch, but by the time I had the word, all was supposedly well." He tossed down the sherry. "Do you know that I think, Winter? I think Hester was waiting to see if it was a boy. She'd sworn to my father she wouldn't ruin me by marriage. She was too old; she always said she was too old. She screamed at me until I left her. But I think if it had been a boy—" He set down the glass and damned her. The rise of his own violent emotion took him by surprise. He had not meant to say such things.

Lord Winter stood looking down into the fire. "She was capable of anything, I daresay," he said neutrally.

"Well, I doubt you wished to see me to speak of that," Michael said, standing up. "What else can I tell you? Your daughter is a fat, jolly, healthy little charmer. Lady Winter is grown beautiful beyond anything, now that she's had some proper nourishment. You will be astonished—and pleased, I hope. She was terribly wasted when she arrived. I go up to Swanmere twice a year. They live very retired. Your father does not like them to leave the place. He is a little inclined to be overprotective, perhaps, but then he has thought you lost to him. I'm glad—what an inadequate word!—I'm overjoyed to find that it is not so. Does your father know yet?"

Lord Winter shook his head, still watching the fire.

"I think that you should write to him. Perhaps I should do it for you, to ease the news. He is in health, and your mother also, bus it will be a stunning shock."

The viscount looked up at last. He had a closed expression, giving nothing away.

"Shall I write to your father for you?"

Lord Winter nodded slowly.

"Excellent. I shall say that you will be at Swanmere in—what—a sennight? That will give them time to prepare. Unless of course you wish to go directly. You must naturally wish to rush to your family. I'm sure there would be no harm done."

The viscount cast him a sudden vehement look. "There is no rush, Mr. Bruce. Oh, no. I wouldn't want to bring an apoplexy upon anyone, would I?"

GRIMLY, ARDEN PACKED up his small kit, having bribed the porter to get him a job horse at this late hour. He could not remain here, pacing the stuffy warmth of his hired rooms the way he had all day. He would have preferred violence, but he settled for movement.

A daughter! And *Lady Winter.* Somehow he had thought that she would come to him with her father. Why had he thought that? He could think of a hundred things that might have become of her; they all crowded in now, the possibilities—she might have died, never reached England, been rejected by Bruce, become one of hundreds of unprotected females on the streets; she might have entered a workhouse, gone into a factory, become a whore. Or an actress. Now there would be an outlet for her talents.

He might have looked all his life and never found her again.

The one thing he had never thought, in his wildest inventions, was that he would return to discover her installed at Swanmere as Lady Winter.

He wondered who she was, this Lady Winter. He couldn't see her in his mind. There was Selim, and then there was—a woman who had said to him, *What difference does it make?*

It was all he could remember clearly. He had misplaced the certainty that she was real, or ever had been. But he remembered what she had said before he made love to her. He could not recall her voice or her tone, but the words seemed infinitely cold and languid to him now.

Apparently it had made a difference after all, he thought fiercely.

He avoided Oxford Street, taking quiet back ways out of the city, for he led the Arab mare—Shajar al-Durr, the String of Pearls. She looked even more fairylike and fragile than usual in the bleak setting of narrow coal-blackened streets, all aglow in white next to the stolid liver chestnut hack the stable had provided, exhibiting her fright in twitching ears and soft snorts. And yet, though she trembled, she came with sweet docility, a princess dancing her delicate hooves upon the wet pavement, her whiteness reflected back by the stones.

She was his prize. What he had to show for three years of his life, for the cauterized scar and lingering shafts of pain in his left side, for futility and blood. It was Rashid, not the Saudis, who had shot him down and taken him like raided livestock from the Egyptians. Afterward, for some amount of time that Arden did not know, he had lain in the black Shammar tents, hung between living and dying of the wound in his side, his reason lost in the grip of weird and terrifying dreams.

He recovered, but Rashid had held him like a slave, friendship at knifepoint, until Arden had understood that he was still hostage to the fantastic image of the Queen of the Englezys. Myth and magic and legend was the lifeblood of the desert, and the prince a mixture of keen military pragmatism and romantic foolery. It needed only a figurehead, or some visible representation of it, and listening for hour after hour to Prince Rashid's bewitching certainties, even Arden had begun to half-believe that they fought for a queen hidden somewhere just beyond reach, a spirit over the desolate mountains and the long coppery sky, and that he was her earthly commander sent to Prince Rashid; a shield and spear and a demon-gun on the hot dirty ground.

Certainly the real woman had come to seem a dream. He could remember Selim; he desperately missed Selim, missed English words and quiet companionship. But that one day and night, when he had looked up and seen a woman—and such a beautiful, desirable, soul-wounding woman—it was too elusive. He lost the sense of it. He could not feel, or remember feeling what it had been like. He had to resist the dreamlike quality of it, to insist in his mind on hard facts, and as time passed he even lost the ability to remember those, or make them more real than the actuality of his life in the desert.

He was Abu Haj Hasan, riding under banners that unfurled like serpents' tongues with the words of Allah written upon them, shouting a war cry in one voice with the warriors of Shammar and Kheytan, galloping beside Prince Abdullah ibn Rashid as he rode on the mare they called the String of Pearls and took the desert in his hands. The rest of the world was gone, utterly vanished into dim, uneasy memory.

But one night, amid the poems and stories told over coffee and the fire, some Kheytani had spoken of an ancient Frankish stranger who had belonged to his tent when he was a boy. He had once asked his father who this man was, with his red beard and strange speech, and what he did there. And his father had answered that the man was *dakhile;* he had been a protected guest in his grandfather's tent, and when his grandfather had died, he became a guest in his father's tent, and if his father and his grandfather had not thought to ask him why he came or why he stayed, then it was surely a graceless discourtesy for his son, a mere boy by Allah's mercy, to inquire into something that did not concern him.

It was a tale for the children who sat about wide-eyed, a little parable of desert etiquette, not to pry into a guest's affairs. But sitting in the firelight, all Arden could see in his mind was that solitary old man who had come among strangers and lived a stranger until he died.

The next day, in scouting for a raid on Aden, he had seen British guns and British marines—and suddenly, strangely, his own self had come back to him with a jolt of painful realignment. By then it had been easy—Rashid had trusted him. Arden had caught the mare Shajar al-Durr in the night, released her from her hobbles, walked with her up to the sleeping sentry beneath the walls of Aden and nearly given the redcoat a seizure by addressing him in English.

He supposed that he should have expected these stunned reactions. He supposed that he should have known life would go on without him. It had done so before, and never made a material difference to him. He rode with cold rain dripping down his collar and seeping under his gloves, feeling lost.

On the journey home, he had longed for England. It was a new emotion, but this time the desert had nearly eaten him. He felt how close he had come to some fatal edge of his identity. He wanted home. He wanted the places that he knew by heart, the language that was his. And as he had traveled, gradually his sense of himself had been restored to him. His tongue remembered not to speak Arabic; his fingers remembered how to button his waistcoat and hold a fork; his body grew accustomed again to coat and confining boots. He recalled the things that were important to do and say with the European passengers.

Now and then, an abyss would open beneath him. He would face some trivial occasion and for an instant be unsure of the proper action: should he help himself to the dishes on the table or wait to be served? Should he shake hands? His hand would move—and he would have to consciously think the moment through. Small things, tiny things, but underneath them lay a black well of uncertainty.

Even now, he hardly knew where he was going. The streets were familiar; he knew the way home—but he was barred from the road north for a sennight.

He felt dispossessed. Bewildered. *Lady Winter* at Swanmere. Miss Elizabeth Lucinda Mansfield in the nursery. Clearly Lord Winter himself was not overly welcome in this cozy ménage. Bruce had all but said so to his face.

He had a spiteful thought of riding through the night—he could be at Swanmere by dawn, and let them discover just how strong their hearts were. He wondered by what means she had convinced his father that she was his wife. It must have taken some profoundly clever talking. His father was no fool.

But then, Selim had duped Arden without much difficulty, and Arden didn't think he was entirely a fool either.

At Hounslow, as the houses fell away from the road, Arden pressed the hack to a canter. The little mare followed like a ghost, her breath sparkling puffs of vapor against the backlit glow of the city. He was denied the gratifying outlet of shooting any footpads. Nothing more interesting appeared on the road but a little late traffic.

At Longford, he pulled up at the crossroads. It was rising midnight, and his last easy point to turn north and make Swanmere by morning.

He imagined walking into his "wife's" bedroom. And quite as suddenly his nerve failed him.

A crowd of reasons why he would be a fool to do it pushed into his thoughts. The servants would not know him; he had not been back for nearly thirteen years. He might find himself ignominiously denied entrance to his own home—worse, he would have to ask where his supposed wife was sleeping. He sat still, appalled at the thought of trying to explain who he was and what he wanted to some pinch-lipped hall porter of the sort his mother always hired to keep the inferior classes at bay.

Beyond that, there was the abyss. Who was she? What would she look like? He couldn't remember her.

He only remembered that she had said. *What difference does it make?*

He turned the horses west, away from Swanmere.

AT THE UNGODLY hour of five A.M., Sir John Cottle was roused out of his warm bed by a shout. He threw open the window, squinting down through a spitting mist, and saw two shadowy forms in the half-light of his yard.

"By George!" he uttered. "What the devil is it?"

"I've brought your mare," came a rough voice. "The String of Pearls."

Sir John sucked in his breath. For a long moment he stood very still. Then he shoved his feet into slippers, grabbed a coat and ran down to the hall. A sleepy butler came up from the back stairs just as his master threw back the bolt.

He hurried out onto the steps. "By God! Bejesus! Winter! Is it you?"

"Yes," Viscount Winter said, with a tinge of irony. "I realize it's a shock."

"And the mare—is that her, by Jove? Look at her! What a little darling!" His voice had a strange, anxious affability. "Winter, by all that's holy! We thought—well, never mind that, my good man! Would you mind—shall we just come away from the house a little?"

He trotted right past the horses, back down the drive in his slippers. Lord Winter looked after him, his brows rising, and then turned the hack and followed after.

When the house had vanished in the mist, Sir John turned. His round face was so full of distress that he seemed almost ready to burst into tears.

"I can't have her!" he cried. "I'm sorry!" He stood back, as if he did not even want to touch the delicate mare that watched him with ears pricked.

"What's amiss?" the viscount asked softly.

"I've married," Sir John said in despair. "I'm sorry." He lifted his hands helplessly. "I had to sell off all my stable. She won't have it. Hates racing horses with a passion. Oh, Winter, I could weep. Look at her! Look at those hocks!"

Lord Winter watched the ridiculous figure of Sir John in his nightgown and cap, standing in the drive.

"Gresham?" he asked, after a silent moment.

Sir John made a faint keening noise. "Duel. He's bolted to the Continent."

The viscount sat gazing at Sir John, such a forbidding expression on his face that the man in the nightgown and coat wet his lips.

"I'm sure I can find a buyer for you," he said quickly. "Nothing easier!"

With a faint laugh, the viscount shook his head. He turned the horses, wheeling past Sir John. "There is no need. Good day to you."

Thirteen

⚬⚬⚬⚬

"THE LORD LIFT up his countenance upon you, and give you peace, both now and evermore. Amen."

"*Amen,*" intoned the congregation. The minister turned up his palms, signaling a general shuffle and rising. As the mourners in the forward boxes began to file past the veiled and black-clad family, each bending briefly to express their sympathy, Zenia waited, her hands cradled in a sable muff. Her breath made faint clouds in the cold air. Beside her, the countess Belmaine was still and silent, her face composed, watching each row stand up in turn.

"We seem destined to meet at funerals," murmured a dry voice behind Zenia.

She knew him instantly. She had known he was coming; for a fortnight she had known, but not when. Her heart began pounding in her ears as she rose from the church pew.

His mother surely had heard him also, but the countess did

not betray so much as a flicker of emotion. She simply gathered her skirts and stood, walking out of the box as the usher opened it. Zenia could not be so stoic: she turned her head, looking back from beneath the ebony curl of an ostrich plume on her bonnet.

Lord Winter was dressed in black, with proper crape ribbon on his arm and hat, a perfect gentleman. But his skin was deeply tanned and his blue eyes striking—she had never forgotten his eyes. He was looking at her with cold intensity, with no more emotion than his mother revealed.

"My lady," he said softly, holding out his hat to direct her to go before him.

My lady. Zenia felt him fall in behind her. She felt his presence at her side as she took the hands of the family; she saw their reddened eyes and looks of shock at Lord Winter—few of them so lost in grief that they did not notice him. The deceased had been the scion of a county family; member of Parliament, supporter of Corn Laws and Tory causes. As a compliment, Lady Belmaine herself had arranged for the white sprays of flowers from Swanmere's succession houses.

The newly bereaved widow kept hold of Zenia's hand, and impulsively caught Lord Winter's in her other. "Oh, praise God!" she said brokenly, looking up at him through her veil. "I had heard the news, but—oh, how it does my heart good at this moment, to see you safe home with your dear, good, sweet wife, and your little girl!"

Lord Winter stood with his hand in the widow's. "I'm glad," he said brusquely, at the same time that Zenia said, "I'm so sorry." She glanced at him, flustered, and again at the widow. "For your loss," she added.

The widow was already looking beyond them to the next mourner. Lord Winter took Zenia's arm and drew her down the aisle after his mother's straight-backed figure.

"My dear sweet wife and little girl?" he asked tightly.

She felt unreal, walking through the vestibule and into the frigid air with his arm under her hand. The whole world was shades of gray; the somber stone of the church, the silver clouds, the bare trees.

"Yes," Zenia said. "I have a daughter." She did not dare look sideways at him under her bonnet. "You are her father."

He put his hand over hers and gripped. It was not a comforting hold, or a loving one. It was pure violent force, wordless. She could not tell what he felt, only that he hurt her.

His mother was waiting on the church steps. She gave Lord Winter a bleak glance. "How dare you choose such an occasion for your reappearance?" she asked in an undertone.

"I am so happy so see you also, Mother," he said mildly.

"For God's sake, Arden! Mr. Forbis's funeral! What will people think?"

He smiled slightly. "I suppose they'll think that I'm not nearly as dead as he is, poor devil."

"Save your impiety for your club. I will speak to you when we return home." She turned and walked toward her carriage.

"I wonder I don't run away again," Lord Winter murmured, watching his mother enter her coach, "with that treat before me."

Zenia said nothing. She looked down at her muff. A chill breeze swept her dark skirts. All the carriages waited in line behind the family's vehicles and the hired mutes with their draped staves and professionally solemn faces. At the head of the procession, four glossy black horses arrayed in black plumes and harness stood motionless before the ready hearse.

"I brought my own landau," he said. "Will you ride with me, Lady Winter?"

Panic consumed her. "I believe Lady Belmaine expects me to—"

His hard grip arrested her attempt to walk on. "No doubt Lady Belmaine expects all sorts of things, but you may find that the wishes of your *husband* and your mother-in-law are seldom quite in harmony."

Zenia looked quickly up at him. "I—"

"Not here," he said, drawing her with him as he bestowed a curt nod on a couple clearly bent on accosting them. He walked her down the long line of carriages, all the way out of the church-yard and across the village green to the last vehicle.

She was trembling by the time they reached it. He helped her up the step and sat down on the seat across from her. A footman in the Belmaine livery closed the door.

"Lord Belmaine insisted that I live—" she began, but he cut her off.

"God, how long will this take, do you suppose?" He looked out the window. "I detest funerals. Have you been unhappy here?"

"No." Zenia shook her head. She gripped her fingers together inside her muff. "No."

His jaw seemed to tighten. She gazed at his profile. The sun had burned lines about his eyes and mouth. His cheeks were as lean as a Bedouin's, the planes of his face more severe. The father of her child.

"It is so difficult to believe that you are here," she said.

"Is it?" He slanted her a look. "Am I very *de trop*?"

She had not thought Elizabeth resembled him at all, but her heart seemed to contract in the fleeting moment of likeness, the vivid image of her daughter somehow crystallized in an expression that was more than his blue eyes and black hair; his high cheekbones and hard mouth. He was entirely a man, sunburned and savage—and his plump, dark-eyed, rosy-cheeked daughter looked like him.

"I don't . . ." Zenia prevented herself from biting her lip. "What is *de trop*?"

"In the way," he said dryly. The carriage rocked forward, following the procession at a slow, stately pace.

"No," she said. "This is your home."

He made a sound of bitter amusement. He did not seem to want to look at her, watching instead the painfully slow progress of the funeral cortege past the church.

"God, how long will this take?" he asked again, dropping his head back against the seat.

"A quarter hour to the new cemetery," she said. "It's across the river. Then the service—and a luncheon at the Forbises' . . . your mother will not stay more than an hour. It should be over by three."

He lifted his eyebrows, an expression that brought a flood of memories. "You are an authority on funerals, I find."

"I've attended a number," she said shyly. "With your mother."

"Have you indeed. What a dutiful daughter-in-law."

"It is no trouble," she said. "I enjoy them."

He turned his head back to her. "The devil you say. You enjoy this?"

"It is the way English people do things." Zenia stroked the muff. "It's very sad for the families, of course. But—well, it hasn't been anyone that I know who died."

"Oh?" He made a wry face. "Did I not even rate a memorial service?"

She kept stroking the muff, over and over. "There was a memorial."

"Did you shed a tear, wolf cub?"

She lifted her eyes. His old name for her seemed to echo in the chill air between them. Abruptly he looked away, out the window again, the gray light harsh on his cheekbones and his profile.

"You've been eating well," he said.

Zenia was vividly aware that her figure had changed. Her

breasts and hips were full and round, still shaped by Elizabeth's effect on her body, and none of her bones showed anywhere. It was no more than a candid observation, no different than she might say that he had been long in the desert sun—and yet she flushed. He had made Elizabeth inside her, changed her body and her life.

They sat like strangers. They were strangers.

"Everything is different now," she said.

He gave a sarcastic laugh. "Certainly. You're wearing a dress. *Allah akhbar!*"

"I will not speak Arabic," she said stiffly. "I am done with that."

"I see," he said. "Pardon me, Lady Winter."

HE STOPPED THE landau at the gate and got down, sending it on up the drive without him. Ahead, the coach that carried his mother and her daughter-in-law had already disappeared around the curve of the landscaped grounds. He had let her escape—or perhaps he had let himself escape—at the funeral luncheon, making no protest when she went into the other rig with his mother.

He stood looking at the iron gates emblazoned with the crest of Belmaine, ignoring the keeper. The man touched his forelock, went inside the porter lodge, and then tried to stand out of sight behind the curtains to spy. Arden didn't know him. He had never paid much attention to the servants at Swanmere. There was little point; under his mother's exacting requirements, the turnover was so steady that all the employees were known in the house by their position rather than their name. Engaging and dismissing were two of her prime pastimes.

He turned, walking up the drive until he came to a familiar tree. The rhododendrons had grown higher under it, but beyond their arching branches, the path still wound down through the wood. He pushed aside dew-laden winter twigs with his cane. His breath steamed and vanished in the cold air.

He stopped before he came in sight of the lake. He was not quite ready for that yet. Or the house; he was not ready for that either. He was doing it in stages.

There was a little taste of smoke in the air, and wet leaves, and perhaps the first edge of a frost to come in the night. He closed his eyes, breathing the winter in an English wood. If he could have lived all his life in a forest, he thought, like some hermit, or a fox in a hole, he would not have had to leave England.

He remembered that he had dug a burrow once in this wood, tunneling back beneath the great roots of an elm, a den so deep that he could crawl all the way inside and turn around and curl up like a woodchuck. He had lined it with a horse blanket and laid there for hours, pretending he was a bear. Or sometimes a mole, squinting up his eyes and trying to smell worms in the dark.

He's rather a furtive boy, madam, said one of his governesses. *Perhaps a companion his own age would bring him out.*

And so the repellent cousin three times removed came and spent a summer, jumping up and down on Arden's burrow so that the roof caved, and peaching on him when he tried to put the horse blanket back. Arden had learned how to fight that summer, and run away on a dare. He only got as far as the local tavern, but that was merely the beginning. He liked running away. He got devilish good at it. By the time he was fourteen, he'd joined the army, and only the bad luck of being recognized by a footman who had just been dismissed from Swanmere and taken the king's shilling had prevented Arden from marching away with the Eighty-second Foot.

He came to the elm, still standing on the crest of its steep bank, its roots running out through the leaves and soft soil. The tunnel was long vanished, but he sat down on the thick root that had formed a lintel over the passage.

He took off his hat and put his face down on his crossed arms.

He dimly remembered a fragile, sun-kissed, dusty beauty—but she was utterly magnificent. The jet black silk, tight-waisted, with voluminously spreading skirts, the feathered bonnet, the net gloves and sable muff: all were formidably elegant. Her face was like ivory framed in this stylish black outline, cool and white, her dark eyes brushed with rich lashes, the curve of her cheek soft purity, her mouth calm perfection. She did not look like anyone he had ever seen before. She looked like a goddess of fashion and ice.

Between her and the dream in the desert, there was no remotest link. It dazed him to imagine he had made love to that stunning woman in black. He would not have had the presumption. In spite of her beauty, he thought that with the slightest effort, he could actively dislike her. He hated society ladies. He'd called her by his name for her, and she had only looked enquiringly at him, as if he had committed some faintly embarrassing faux pas.

If it had been her alone, he would have stood up now and turned and walked away from Swanmere. There was no more a legal marriage between them than pigs could fly. She was an actress indeed; she could transform from a Bedu boy to a vulnerable female to *Lady Winter,* but he could strip her of this new pretense in an instant.

And yet he did not walk away. They said he had a daughter. He was not, having seen what a remote stranger this woman was, instantly ready to accept her child as his own. But he did not deny that it was possible. He could remember the fact of having lain with her—he just could not in his mind transform the fact into the living existence of a child of that ephemeral union.

She had been a virgin. That was one of the more powerful imprints of the memory. He had never taken a virgin before. And he had not had a woman since.

A startling spike of desire ran through him. He lifted his head and contemplated the trunk of a tree. After such a long abstinence, he was living continually at a low-level smolder, but to meet it so suddenly and intensely, touched off by the thought of *her*—his own reaction unnerved and annoyed him.

He hurled a pebble and watched it strike the trunk and bounce back. Then he dusted the dirt from his hands and stood up. He could not put it off forever.

As he walked along the path, he could see the house appear through the trees. The lake reflected a gray sky, sheer silver with a long leisurely V spreading in the middle where one of the black swans paddled. Beyond, the handsome facade of Swanmere dominated the long rise of lawn, a white precision of form and adornment, tall pedimented windows and pilasters and urns in a calibrated sweep of majesty.

Arden stopped. His breath seemed to condense in his chest. His mouth and jaw hardened.

So long. So long it had been. And yet it looked the same. Always precisely the same. Huge and cold and flawless.

He closed his eyes and gave a silent, aching laugh. The elm tree and vanished burrow seemed more like home.

For a ridiculous moment, as he started down the path that circled the lake, he wished he had Selim at his side. The silent laugh escaped in an outraged chuckle. Selim! His mouth lifted in a sneer, and he thrust the tip of his cane deep in the damp ground as he pushed off.

ZENIA HAD GONE directly to change, not pausing with Lady Belmaine in the saloon. Let her tell Lord Belmaine that his son had finally come—Zenia wanted Elizabeth.

She interrupted her daughter in a game of nesting spoons together between her chubby fingers. Zenia dismissed the nurse and caught the child up in her arms, pressing her face into Elizabeth's tummy, making bubbling noises. Elizabeth laughed and grabbed for Zenia's hat plume. The leading strings on her blue-and-white pinafore dangled as Zenia carried her.

Elizabeth did not live in the nursery. Zenia could not bear to be separated so far from her. They slept together in Zenia's own bed, and the adjoining chamber held a crib and playthings and a cot for the nurse. Lady Belmaine did not approve of this arrangement, Zenia knew, but neither she nor Lord Belmaine seemed to take any deep interest in their granddaughter. Lady Belmaine had not favored Elizabeth since her birth, because she was not a boy, and Lord Belmaine's only comment had been that he was not much of one for babies, but he thought her a charming child—a remark that somehow implied that he would take a look at her again when she grew up, but probably not before.

Zenia did not mind. Elizabeth belonged to *her*. She was glad she had not had a boy—she well knew that Lord and Lady Belmaine would have exercised their authority to the utmost with a boy, and never allowed her to keep him with her to spoil and adore and cherish. But they let her do as she pleased with Elizabeth, as long as she did not take her daughter away from Swanmere. And on the baby's first birthday, the earl had called Zenia into his study and showed her the papers that made Elizabeth his sole heiress outside of generous jointures for Lady Belmaine and Zenia. "The title will go into abeyance, of course," he had said, sitting behind his great desk, never lifting his eyes from the papers before him, "but I have arranged that the entail shall be commuted. When she marries, her husband must take the Mansfield name, and with that proviso her male issue inherits. I need not subject you to the legal details, as they are rather tedious, but you may be assured that the girl will have everything."

He had been very cold and businesslike when Zenia had thanked him. "You need not thank me." He had looked up at her at last with his pale blue eyes. "Bluntly, madam, I have waited this long to be entirely certain that the child is my son's. But the resemblance is incontestable. That being the case, this is simply the proper and fitting way in which things must be left."

At the time, Zenia had not agreed that there was any resemblance at all, though she would never have dared say so. Now, she knew what the earl meant. And somehow it chilled and frightened her. He had come back, this man who was Elizabeth's father, and somehow in spite of utterly different features and coloring, she looked like him.

Zenia carried Elizabeth into her room and bounced her down on the bed. "You're mine," she said, wiggling her daughter's feet. "Mine, mine, mine. Isn't that right?"

"G' dow'!" The toddler immediately rolled over and maneuvered herself to crawl off the edge. She was a wayward and strong-willed child, inclined to tantrums if she was thwarted. Zenia caught her before she fell off the high bed, rolling her three times over to the bedstool, where Elizabeth very cleverly managed to climb down herself. She instantly headed back for her spoons, giggling wildly as she avoided Zenia's pass at catching her.

Zenia let her go, untying the black ribbon on her bonnet. Her fingers were not quite shaking, but they were still clumsy. He was back. He had come back alive. She threw the bonnet on her bed and rang for her maid.

The girl who attended her was silent but for a brief question of what ma'am would like to wear. Zenia stared into her wardrobe. All of the gowns were black or gray or lavender—at the end of a year Lady Belmaine had supposed, in her calm way, that Lord Winter's widow would not care to go entirely out of mourning. At first Zenia had not minded, but lately, she had begun to think wistfully of colors like the other ladies wore.

That was before they had learned that she was not, after all, a widow. Or even a counterfeit widow. Zenia had had two weeks to become accustomed to it, and still she had felt as if something was clutched about her heart, stifling its ability to beat. And the moment she had heard his voice in the church—she was surprised that she had not crumbled into a thousand quivering pieces.

He had taken a week longer to come than expected. A week longer in which to wonder how he would look, what he would say, whether he would denounce her openly as a fraud. Lord Belmaine said nothing of that to her; he had simply nodded to her and murmured, with a slight acidity, that they were all gratified by the news that Lord Winter had not after all met an untimely end. He seemed so unconcerned about his son's arrival that he thought nothing of suddenly plunging most of the great house into a state of repair and renovation, closing wings and giving over bedrooms to painters and carpenters. They were hammering now in the chamber beside hers.

Dressed in the least morbid of the dusky lavender gowns, with a small lace cap and her hair pulled back to fall in curling ringlets behind her ears, she hugged Elizabeth. She covered her daughter's face with desperate kisses in spite of wriggles and protests, and put her down. Zenia walked out of the room before her legs could fail her and descended the stairs.

Swanmere was the sort of house she thought her majestic mother must have grown up in. There was a great fresco, a tumble of activity among gods and goddesses and lesser creatures that cascaded all across the walls and ceiling of the grand staircase. At the foot, standing unsmiling beside a painted spaniel, a servant waited to escort her to the saloon they called the King of Prussia room, named for some visit of state a century before. He opened the tall door, bowed, and closed it behind her.

Lady Belmaine ceased speaking in her level, modulated voice, that tone that could sting with such discreet, unerring accuracy, and cast a glance at Zenia.

"Ah," Lord Belmaine said pleasantly. "Here is your wife."

The room seemed to be a hundred miles long. Zenia walked forward, her feet silent on the carpet, past gilt furniture and straw-gold drapes, to where Lord Winter stood leaning casually against one of the white columns that flanked the windows at the upper end of the room. She stopped, managing to look as high as his plain dark waistcoat for a moment, and sank into a curtsy.

"Never mind the formality," he murmured dryly. "We've met." She lifted her eyes.

"I want to see my daughter," he said.

Fourteen

⸺⸺

"She is sleeping," Zenia said quickly.

"Then I'll go to her." He had an implacable air, standing up straight from the pillar. "If you will pardon me."

Zenia felt a wave of anxiety. He seemed too ruthless; his expression too hard and unfeeling; she thought that he would frighten Elizabeth. As he walked past her without a look, she turned hastily to follow.

"She is not in the nursery, my lord," she said as he mounted the stairs. "She stays in my bedchamber."

He stopped with his hand on the carved banister, looking back at her. "Where is your bedchamber, Lady Winter?"

Zenia flushed at the question and the implication in his eyes. "On the second floor. The westernmost."

He seemed for a moment to consider that. "I see."

He turned, going up before her two steps at a time. In her voluminous skirts, she could not follow quickly enough to keep up. "My lord—please!" she called. "If you would wait—" But by the time she had reached the top of the grand staircase, he had disappeared up the back stairs to the uppermost floor.

She met the nurse in the hall. The woman was closing the door, but she paused as she saw Zenia and dropped a curtsy, smiling. "Her papa!" the nurse whispered, with a bouyant look. "Perhaps they will do better alone for a moment, ma'am."

Zenia ignored her, pushing open the door. She was in time to see Lord Winter lower himself onto the floor cross-legged next to Elizabeth. The little girl looked up at Zenia. She said, "Mama," with a smile, gave Lord Winter a brief distrustful glance, and turned back to her spoons.

"What is that?" Lord Winter asked, bending over Elizabeth's lap, his back to Zenia.

"Mah," Elizabeth said.

"She can't talk yet," Zenia said firmly. "She's only eighteen months."

"Spoons," Lord Winter said, tapping the silverware as if she hadn't spoken.

" 'Poo," Elizabeth said.

"Spoons!" he said.

Elizabeth handed them to him. He accepted the spoons and held his forefinger between the handles, making them chatter against one another. Elizabeth burst into a smile. She grabbed the spoons back, and then handed them to him again. He rattled them, and she seized the silverware, instantly offering it back again. " 'Poo!"

For ten rounds, the spoons went back and forth, Elizabeth punctuating every exchange with an emphatic, " 'Poo!" Then Lord Winter held up the pair and brought it chattering up to her face, catching her nose between the bowls.

Elizabeth yelped with pleasure. She seized a spoon in each hand and waved them at his face, crawling forward. She trundled herself into his lap and shrieked joyfully when he toppled backward, carrying her up in his hands so that she sailed above him.

Zenia bit hard on her lower lip. She had a passionate desire to rush up and snatch Elizabeth away. She was a difficult child. Everyone said so. No one had ever played on the floor with her daughter but her. No one else could make Elizabeth laugh so happily.

"She should take her nap now," she said.

"Go away." Lord Winter wriggled Elizabeth and swept her in wide circles and dives above him as she giggled and hiccuped. She was growing too heavy for Zenia to do that easily anymore.

Zenia leaned her back upon the door. She was not going to leave Elizabeth alone with this man. This stranger. "She will be sick if she continues to hiccup in that convulsive manner."

Elizabeth made a plunging descent, her squeals of laughter echoing from the walls. For an instant she lay facedown against his shoulder, nuzzling against him. He lifted his hand and cupped her head, his long desert-hardened fingers spread amid the honey-eyed curls as hiccups rocked her.

Zenia took a step forward. "She is inclined to emotional paroxysms if overexcited. I really think it would be better if—"

"Don't you have a ball to attend? Some calls to make?"

Elizabeth tired of her momentary stillness and pushed up to her feet. She looked down at her father with such a glow that Zenia's heart wrung. With pudgy arms outspread, Elizabeth pitched forward and let her dead weight fall onto his chest.

"Ummph!" he said, with a grimace that his daughter thought hilarious. She did it again. And again, and until he held her off, turning onto his side with a stiff, painful move. "*Allah yesellimk*, beloved. Let's try something else."

"Do not speak Arabic to her, if you please," Zenia said. "It will confuse her. She is not to learn Arabic."

He lay still a moment, while Elizabeth tried to reach him past the length of his hold. When her struggles began to grow frantic, he leaned forward and brought her up close, burying his mouth in the lace beside her ear and muttering something that Zenia could not hear.

Zenia frowned, and then walked to a chair and sat down. Her daughter and Lord Winter paid her no mind, playing on the carpet. They progressed to blocks, the viscount lying propped up on his elbow as he built a tower for Elizabeth to hurl down. After several steeples had gone to pieces, she abruptly turned and came to Zenia, crawling into her lap and reaching for her collar button.

Zenia felt a flood of mortification. Elizabeth lay down, snuggling in anticipation. Lord Winter sat up and turned toward them.

"Mama," Elizabeth said insistently, "Mama!" reaching again for her buttons and pressing her face into Zenia's breast.

Hastily, Zenia reached for a towel and spread it over her shoulder and Elizabeth. She looked down, unbuttoning her dress underneath. Her daughter, batting the towel aside, contentedly began to nurse.

For a long time, Zenia was too chagrined to raise her eyes. She felt all her face and neck burning with embarrassment. "You need not stare," she said angrily.

"You'll have to forgive me. It's an unprecedented moment in my life."

She pressed her lips together, keeping her face down.

"She's beautiful," he said quietly.

"I suppose you think she is much too old to be nursing still."

"I can't say that I've thought about it at all."

"Lady Belmaine disapproves."

"Well, then. I approve, out of mere perversity."

Zenia allowed herself to peek through her eyelashes up at him. He was sitting on the floor, his ankles crossed, his elbows about his knees. His fingers were interlocked in a strong, easy grip.

"Who named her?" he asked.

"She is named for Miss Williams," Zenia said, with a touch of defiance, "and my aunt Lucy."

"Miss—ah. Your mother's maid. My parents raised no objection?"

"No."

"And she was christened as a Mansfield?"

"Yes." Zenia drew a deep breath. Her milk was growing more scanty. Elizabeth gave up suckling and sighed sleepily. "Yes, she was."

Zenia rebuttoned herself and looked up. He was gazing at her, an unnerving stillness in his face.

"Everyone thought you were dead," she said. "Your father insisted on it. And I did not wish my daughter to be—without a name."

The question hung between them, unspoken. *Will you take it away from her?* She was afraid to ask it. She did not know him. And it was not his daughter only—it was her, Zenia, that he must accept. She could remember clearly all his biting opinion of women—most especially deceitful women. She could see that he detested his own mother. And yet he had played with Elizabeth, he seemed to like her.

A new and horrific thought burst into Zenia's mind. Could he somehow keep Elizabeth and not her? Could he send her away from her daughter?

"I came near to dying," he said in an even voice, watching her.

Zenia remembered a darkened saddle, and blood on the white hairs of a camel. She remembered him running toward her; the rough thrust as he shoved her into the Egyptian's arms. "I'm sorry."

One side of his mouth lifted in an ironic smile. He looked at her steadily. "Sorry for what? That I made it after all?"

"Of course not. I'm sorry that you were hurt. And I thank you for—what you did for me."

He frowned. "You should not have been there," he said in a rough tone.

She gathered Elizabeth tight against her. "I had no desire to be there, you may be sure! It was you—"

"Because you lied to me." He thrust himself to his feet, his mouth drawn taut. "The way you're lying now, damn you. Lady Winter! The perfect mother! My parents say you're devoted." His lip curled. "My God, you're so damned good at it," he said viciously. "I don't even know you."

Elizabeth wriggled restlessly. "Hush," Zenia said, "you're frightening her with such a voice!"

Elizabeth grabbed Zenia's skirts and crawled out of her arms, sliding to the floor. She toddled happily to her blocks and began to stack them.

"Perhaps it's you I'm frightening," he said softly. "Lady Winter."

She rose, ringing for the nurse. "You don't frighten me. I can take Elizabeth and go to my father if I wish. He promised me a home with him."

"No," he said instantly. "You can't take my daughter."

"You can't keep us prisoners here."

"Leave if you like. You don't take my daughter."

"Perhaps she is not even yours!" she exclaimed wildly. "How can you be sure?"

"She's mine," he said.

"She does not look at all like you."

"She's mine."

"Yours! She doesn't belong to you, like some possession!"

He turned on her. "Are you saying that you've been with other men?"

Zenia took a step back at the blazing violence in his eyes. "No," she said, "of course not."

"Then she's mine, isn't she? Because you've damned well been with me!"

They stared at one another. Zenia's lips parted. She saw his glance go to them—and vividly, intensely, she remembered him over her and inside her.

For an instant, she thought he would come to her. That it would all change, and this angry constraint between them would dissolve.

"I missed you," she whispered suddenly. "I grieved for you."

She astonished herself. She had not known until that moment what she had felt. All of her mind and heart had been occupied with Elizabeth. But before her daughter had come into her life, she had ached with loss.

"Did you!" he said, lifting his brows. "Which one of your many manifestations grieved for me? Not this one, I think." His eyes held a strange expression, wary and angry as a wounded animal. "Perhaps it was Selim." He gave a short laugh. "Selim might have missed me a little."

The nurse scratched at the door. Zenia dropped her eyes and turned to open it. "You will be wanting to dress for dinner, my lord," she said, careful to cover the hurt of his cutting answer by an expressionless tone. "I must do so now. The nurse will tend to her."

She held the door open to the hall, inviting him to leave. He did not. With a sideways smile, he said, "This is my apartment, I am informed."

Zenia felt her heart contract. "No," she said, mortifyingly aware of the nurse's presence as she bent over Elizabeth. "You have misheard—"

"Do you object to my sharing with you, Lady Winter?" he asked. "My father tells me that all the other chambers are closed for renovation. Quite thick with deadly paint fumes."

Zenia stared at him, sudden understanding washing over her.

"Heavy-handed, isn't he?" Lord Winter commented. "He is in full cry after a male heir, you know."

"Oh," she said stupidly, unable to think of anything more sensible in front of the nurse.

"It will be a trifle overcrowded, I daresay. Please do not suppose that I will disturb you until you're finished with your toilette, my dear. Elizabeth and I will entertain ourselves here, and then I can take my turn." He smiled, his eyes glittering. "Very civilized, you see."

CANDLES IN THE chandelier reflected back from huge gilt mirrors on the dining room walls. Arden had known he would require silk knee breeches for dinner at Swanmere. His parents always dined formally. Usually there were numerous guests, but tonight, with none, the table seemed even more huge than usual. Absurdly so, with his mother at the foot and his father at the head, and Arden face-to-face with Zenia across a snowfield of white damask.

The only concession to dining *en famille* was the absence of a towering silver centerpiece sprouting fruit and candles. He rather regretted that. There were only sets of candelabra at intervals down the table, so that nothing hindered his view of the woman who played at being his wife.

She wore black again. It seemed to place her at a cold distance, emphasizing her perfect beauty. Her dark hair curled smoothly about her throat, diamond earrings glittering against her skin. He could see her profile in one of the mirrors, pale and untouchable as she sipped delicately at the consommé with a silver spoon. The flatware that bore the Belmaine crest seemed too heavy for her hand.

He could think of nothing to say to her. All of his words stopped in his throat, sounding idiotic and churlish. *Did you miss me?* he wanted to ask, like an uncertain ass—to make her say it again, to listen instead of throwing it away. To hear how she said the words, if she meant them, if it was true. It changed everything, and nothing.

Did he want her? He had seen his daughter sitting alone in the middle of the floor, her head down—and he had instantly felt a powerful connection, a soul-deep amazement: he had not blamed her for her doubtful reception, only been shocked to the center of his heart by her smile. The woman in black across the table seemed a stranger, but Elizabeth was infinitely familiar, as if he had known her for all of her short life and his own. Already he was thinking of tonight and tomorrow and the day after, all the things he needed to do with her and know about her.

It did not take much sensibility to perceive that Elizabeth's mother disliked his regard. He felt it was a certain crack in her facade. He was not sure that she told the truth when she said she had grieved for him, but he was entirely sure that she had meant it when she said she could take Elizabeth and go to Bruce if she wished.

So. Let her mean it, he thought, setting his jaw. She would find that she had put herself in an untenable position. If his father did not explain it to her, Arden certainly would.

"I have been considering what would be suitable to make your return known to our acquaintances," his mother said over an oyster pâté. "Nothing with dancing. Would you prefer a light supper or an afternoon nuncheon, Arden?"

"Whatever is shortest," he said.

"Lady Winter has not yet been formally introduced," Lord Belmaine said. "Perhaps a dinner, to do so."

"If it is what you would like," his mother said indifferently. "For a dinner, anything under a fortnight is impossible. Three weeks, really, at this season."

"The night before Epiphany, perhaps. That will give Lady Winter time to have a gown made in color. I must admit, my dear," he said to Zenia, "that I would like see you out of blacks, under the circumstances."

"Very well," Lady Belmaine said. "Perhaps something in bottle green—a satin, with jet trim to match her eyes."

"Her eyes are blue," Arden said. They all looked at him. He turned downward to his plate, taking a bite of the pâté. "Dark blue."

"Indeed! You must pardon me. I'm afraid I have been unobservant," his mother said.

"Not nearly as unobservant as I was." He gave his "wife" a mocking smile.

She lifted her lashes. In the candlelight, her eyes seemed as dark as his mother thought they were.

"She should wear blue," he said. "Like the afternoon sky. And gold. Not diamonds."

They were still looking at him, as if he had lost his mind.

"I'm afraid azure is woefully out of season," his mother said.

"And silk slippers," Arden said, ignoring her. "Something pretty. She looks like a blasted ebony shrine. Make her something . . . pretty."

"I've never known you to take an interest in female adornment," his father said with a touch of amusement. "But perhaps Lady Winter has her own opinions on the subject."

Lady Winter was staring at her food as if she had never seen it before. "I should like blue," she said in a barely audible voice. "And gold."

"I do think you will be sorry with such a choice," his mother said.

"No doubt whatever you wish can be arranged, Lady Winter," his father countered.

"How people will talk," Lady Belmaine said. "Azure in January!"

"Will they?" Arden lifted his hand for another glass of wine.

"Then let her wear the green. You must forgive my interference in matters that don't concern me."

"You will admit that you know nothing of the mode, I believe, Arden."

"Yes," he said. "I will readily admit that."

"You would not wish your wife to be a laughingstock."

"No. I don't wish for it."

"I truly think you will be more satisfied with the bottle green."

He took a deep swallow of wine. "If my satisfaction with the bottle green will put an end to this topic, then I certainly shall."

Lady Winter picked at her turbot and said nothing. She seemed to eat very little. Not that he blamed her; dinner with his parents would damp the keenest appetite.

Do you dislike the fish? he found himself wanting to ask. It must not be a very familiar taste for her. But he was not going to start any more conversation. He sat through the second remove, mechanically eating roast pheasant and stewed hare.

"What do you think of Miss Elizabeth?" his father asked.

Arden put down his fork, gazing for a moment at the Belmaine crest painted on his dinnerware. Then he looked up at the earl. Over the long distance between them, he said, "Thank you, sir." He held his father's eyes steadily. "Thank you for bringing her here. Thank you for taking care of her."

Nothing changed in Lord Belmaine's expression. His long fingers tapped the tablecloth. Arden had never spoken so emotionally to him, except in anger. He felt strange, his throat tightening on his next breath as he waited for the answer.

Before his father spoke, Zenia said, "Lord Belmaine has been very generous, but I could have taken care of her perfectly well myself."

She was sitting very straight in her chair. Arden's expectation turned to annoyance and a queer disappointment. He picked up his knife and cut pheasant into small pieces.

"You are an estimable mother, Lady Winter," the earl said, surprising Arden with his approving tone. "I do not doubt you for a moment."

She gave his father a small smile and flashed a defiant look at Arden. "I would do anything for Elizabeth."

"Very proper feelings," his mother said. "I hope Arden will learn from your example. With a child, it is time and past that he gave up his heedlessness and remained at home attending to his responsibilities."

"Not at all," Arden said lightly. "I'm leaving for Siberia tomorrow, and taking Beth with me. We'll have a jolly time driving a *troika*."

"You will not!" Zenia gasped. "I forbid it!"

If she had not risen so seriously to such small bait, he wouldn't have lashed back. But her outrage, his parents, the surroundings, the prolonged torture of this meal at which he was the outsider, always the outsider—they all compounded and coalesced, sparking an old, old, unhappy anger. "And what have you to say to it, *Lady Winter*?" he asked, tossing back his wine and fixing his gaze on her. "You are merely my wife. The mother of my child, over whom I have complete authority and dominion. Has no one informed you of my lawful rights as your husband? You cannot take Beth away, as you have already threatened, not if I deny you permission. On the other hand, madam, I can take her wherever I wish, without consulting you at all in the matter. If you find this an undesirable situation, then you have only yourself to blame, don't you? We have a saying in English, Lady Winter—perhaps your mother taught it to you; she certainly knew the meaning of it. You cannot have your cake and eat it too."

She was utterly white, her lips working. Suddenly she pressed her napkin onto the table beside her. "Excuse me, I must see to Elizabeth." She rose and ran out so quickly that the footman just coming in the door had to make an abrupt step back, the silver vegetable dish rattling in his hands.

Arden did not look at his father or his mother. The vegetable dish appeared at his side—he could not have said at the moment if it was boiled carrots or cauliflower. He took a spoonful and then sat staring at it, revolted.

His father waited until the footman retired. When the servant had closed the door, he said, "I hope, Arden, that you will not regret those words."

It was the mildest comment he had ever made on one of his son's reckless follies.

THE EARL BELMAINE let himself softly into the carved library, where a distinguished and soberly dressed man stood up, barely visible amid the dark wainscoting and portraits and books.

"Good evening, Mr. King." The earl spoke with a small, wry twist to his fine mouth. "I fear that tonight will not be an auspicious moment for any meeting. My daughter-in-law is indisposed."

"I'm sorry to hear it, my lord," the attorney said, with an efficient nod of his head.

"Sit down. A little refreshment?" The earl poured wine from a decanter into one of the four glasses that stood ready.

"Thank you, my lord."

"Tell me," the earl said, measuring out a thick, greenish liquid from another bottle and sitting down with the cordial, "we are not so Gothic in these latter days that a wife and children are still considered the legal property of her husband?"

"Well, certainly not his property, my lord. We do not countenance slavery in the common law, I am happy to say. But the wife's legal existence is subsumed in the husband's. In return for his duty to support and comfort her, he has full rights to her property, and of course absolute paternal control over his minor children. Within the unbroken marriage, the husband represents the sole acting legal entity."

The earl nodded thoughtfully. He was staring at a portrait beyond the lawyer, a painting of his son, in which the artist had caught with full impact the arrogant, awkward solitude of a sixteen-year-old irritated beyond bearing by the hours of sitting motionless in formal dress at his father's command.

Lord Belmaine had never favored the portrait, though it was very like his son. It always distressed him in a vague way, but it was the only one he had. He had put off having a painting made of mother and young child in anticipation of his second and third and fourth children, envisioning a family grouping. But the others had never come, and by the time he had fully faced the realization that they would not, his son was an angry, sly, uncontrollable boy who eluded his governess for whole days. Arden had been utterly fearless, scornful of physical punishment; secretive and rash and defiant. By the time he was seven, Lord Belmaine had developed his sole permanent ailment: the very thought of his only son's disobedience and dangerous recklessness made him feel as if he had swallowed a burning rock that lodged just beneath his breastbone.

The doctors prescribed stomach elixers and special cordials. Lord Belmaine sipped at the latest, subduing a grimace. For some time, the pain had not bothered him, but the jolt of learning his son was still alive had smashed the strange sense of glasslike suspension that had held him since his granddaughter's birth. For the past two weeks he had endured strong pangs, and Arden's behavior at dinner had been of such a piece with his whole destructive childhood and youth that Lord Belmaine felt his ulcer fully inflamed anew.

"I had hoped that this would be no more than a formality, Mr. King," he said. "But I am afraid I was too sanguine."

"Indeed, my lord?" The attorney looked grave. "The couple

has an objection to renewing their marriage vows under English law?"

The earl smiled. "We have not got as far as discussing it, Mr. King. But my son has taken pains to point out to Lady Winter her legal disabilities as his wife. In particular he has emphasized his unconditional authority over her child. I fear this has not gone down well. In point of fact, Mr. King, at the moment I rather wish the Mohammedans had butchered him after all. It would spare me this singular desire to strangle my own son."

"It is a delicate situation, my lord." Mr. King lowered his eyes. "Do I understand, then, that Lord Winter seeks to convince the lady that she would be unwise to submit herself to a legal confirmation of matrimony?"

"I do not have the slightest notion of what Lord Winter seeks or wishes. He is the most perverse creature of my acquaintance. I have never understood him, nor pretend to."

"Perhaps, sir, the case is not so bleak as it appears. Whatever Lord Winter's personal feelings, if he attempts to convince Lady Winter to make the objection, it seems likely that he feels unable to do so himself. Else why go to the trouble to goad her? He could simply deny the union."

"The devil take him if he does," the earl said savagely. "What next will he put us through?"

Mr. King maintained an expression of calm. "Marriages celebrated beyond the seas are more or less exempt from our stricter laws regarding licensing and recording, as your lordship and I have very frequently discussed with reference to your son and his wife, but as I have also advised you, my lord, these undocumented unions are anathema if it ever comes to a question in the courts." The attorney shook his head gravely. "For a widow, we agreed that this was a tolerable situation, since there was no remedy—the child's legitimacy being countenanced by her baptismal certificate and the only important common law issues at stake being the wife's dower and the child's claim to her inheritance. Both of which we addressed in a routine and unexceptionable manner in your own will, my lord, entirely outside of any question of the validity of the marriage."

"Yes," the earl said, staring broodingly into his cordial before he turned back his head and swallowed the whole at once. He made a scowling face. "But he's here. And I do not understand him. I can't predict him."

Mr. King took a sip of wine and cleared his throat. "As we have also discussed, my lord, since the glad news of Lord Winter's life being preserved, the entire lack of evidence or witnesses makes the union and offspring vulnerable to attack—the greatest threat being a subsequent marriage conducted in a legal manner by either partner. In that situation, I could not be easy appearing before the bench in defense of this undocumented union. I was once privy to a case regarding an undocumented Gretna Green marriage, and it was a most unpleasant action. The law is full of anomalies and uncertainties in such instances—the outcome is no more sure than a throw of the dice. This is why I have strongly advised a prompt exchange of vows, extremely private but properly witnessed and recorded, and an acknowledgment and guardianship of the child by Lord Winter. The union will then be unassailable."

"And until then?"

"Until then, sir, we must fear that your son, or even Lady Winter herself, could act as unmarried persons, with the only recourse being a proof of the unprovable in the courts. Not a happy thought. If your son is unwilling to confirm the marriage, there is definite cause for concern."

Lord Belmaine leaned forward, resting his jaw on his spread hand, his other arm pressed against his waistcoat. "He wants the little girl. I think—I believe he has an ardent interest in Miss Elizabeth."

"That is better news, my lord. I can with perfect authority explain to him that he has no rights in her at all if he repudiates the marriage and a guardianship."

The earl lifted his lids. "See that you do so outside of Lady Winter's hearing, or it will be she who does the repudiating."

"Dear me, it is not to be supposed that she would actually contemplate such an unwise course."

"My son has done his best to precipitate it."

"I cannot believe he will be successful. There are not many ladies who would be so careless. It is true that she must submit to certain legal disabilities in marriage, but these are hardly such as to cause real affliction to the natural sensibilities of the female sex. Quite the reverse, in the opinion of most ladies. Certainly nothing so malignant as making a bastard of her own child and destroying herself by an open denial of her marriage."

"That, Mr. King, is to be your line with her if she balks." The earl sat up. "I had envisioned a meeting of all parties with you, but I believe that we must speak to them each separately. I hope you will find it convenient to remain a few days."

"Very good, sir. I shall be happy to oblige."

Fifteen

ARDEN HAD ALWAYS made it a point to charm the house-keeper. An endless succession of Mrs. Pattersons—they were all called Mrs. Patterson, no matter their real names—had hidden cold meat and bread tied up in kerchiefs or left plates of cakes and scones inside a huge dictionary that Arden had carefully hollowed out with a penknife at the age of eight. It had sat for years on a solemn podium beside the door in his room, its mild secret never discovered.

It sat there still. He had seen it when he went into his old bedchamber—the one she now occupied—to change for dinner.

He had coaxed a peace offering out of the present Mrs. Patterson, after a certain amount of fluttering fidgets at the invasion of her domain by the infamous son of the house. But he felt, as always, reduced to a scapegrace chub at Swanmere, so his old habits and stratagems came back easily to him. By the time he left, with a fork in his pocket and a hefty slice of plum pudding slathered with hard sauce balanced on his hand, Mrs. Patterson thought him a poor starveling who had never been fed properly in his life.

He went up the back stairs two at a time. He wouldn't have minded wolfing down the pudding himself—his appetite at dinner had not been precisely hearty. But he had not procured it for his own hunger.

He stopped before the door. It had occurred to him, as he paced the misty grounds until nearly ten o'clock, that the former Selim might be uncomfortable eating her fill in company. The courtesy and discipline of the desert demanded voluntary restraint, deliberate deprivation in the sight of others. She had eaten lightly even before he had said anything that could have upset her—and then he had driven her from the table with his biting words.

And he remembered that Selim had always daydreamed of plum pudding.

Standing before the closed door, he felt remarkably silly. She was not Selim. It was nearly eleven. There seemed to be no light inside. The door to his daughter's chamber stood open, the room dark.

Perhaps she had gone back down to keep his mother company in the saloon. Perhaps she had gone to bed. His body responded to the thought with a strong stir of carnal interest. It made him feel even more awkward, standing there with a fork and plum pudding like some lovestruck puppy.

Gently, he tapped the door with the fork. For a moment there was no answer. He felt relief—she was asleep, or not there. Then she said, in a wary voice, "Who is it?"

He put his hand on the knob and opened the door.

She was sitting up at the desk, muffled in a gown and woolen robe. "You cannot come in," she said in a sharp whisper. "I've had your things put in the next room. Elizabeth always sleeps with me."

She appeared to have been writing a letter, and made no move to lay down the pen. The fire hissed softly. A small snoring lump in the bedclothes was undoubtedly Beth.

A wave of emotions passed over him: warmth and exclusion, and a sudden strange homesickness—another of his burrows, this room, a safe den for the touchy, brooding boy he had been. But he was unmistakably turfed out by the new owner. She glared at him with a hostile, proprietary look.

"Eat," he said in Arabic, setting the plate and fork down on the nearest surface, the dictionary podium beside the door.

"I have told you that I will not speak Arabic—"

He closed the door.

It felt damnably like retreat. Or eviction.

As he stood in the hallway, a maid came swiftly up the back stairs. She was carrying a loaded tray. She hesitated when she saw him.

Arden stepped back. The maid ducked a little curtsy and knocked on the door.

"Who is it?" came the uncertain demand, from closer to the door this time.

"Your bedtime tray and tea, ma'am," the maid whispered, glancing again at Arden and turning down her eyes.

"Come," said the voice behind the door.

As it opened, he could see beyond the girl. Zenia stood beside the dictionary. Her eyes widened a little as she saw him still there.

She had not needed his offering—the tray was loaded with food. She did not require any service from him at all. She had made a cozy place for herself; she had respectability and comfort; she had his father's approval; she'd appropriated Arden's room and his name—and at the pull of a bell rope, he thought with savage mockery, she could get all the plum pudding she could possibly desire. Arden felt an unutterable fool.

He turned, striding down the hall to the stairs. It was easy enough to leave Swanmere after the doors were locked. He knew all the ways.

ZENIA SIGNED THE letter to her father. Her hand was still unsteady, and she broke the pen and had to mend it before she could finish. She had been expecting Lord Winter, though she had hoped that he would see the open door of the next room and draw his own conclusions.

Now he had come and upset all her decisions. She had torn up the first letter to her father, the one that said she must return to him directly, that she did not dare remain where this man, this stranger, menaced her and Elizabeth with his threats of taking her daughter away.

Then he had brought her food—he had looked at her with his intense blue eyes and said *eat*, the same way he had said it in the desert. She wanted to forget the desert. She wanted to forget how it felt to be hungry. But she had been hungry, even here, because she felt uncouth and greedy sitting at a table loaded with so much food. She always wanted to stuff as much of it into her as she could, as fast as she could. She wanted to eat like a famished beggar, and so she ate nothing. She was determined to be an English lady.

She had food brought to her in private. No one had ever said anything about it. She didn't think the earl or countess knew.

But Lord Winter had guessed that she was hungry. He had brought her plum pudding and commanded her to eat. Underneath the diamonds and the silk, he knew she was still a wretched, starving, dirty, barefoot creature.

She gave a small miserable laugh, wrinkling her nose at the

plate sitting on the dictionary. He might have asked what she liked, at least.

Oh, but he had remembered how she had longed to taste it. And he had pushed her atop a camel, and she had seen his blood all over the saddle. If he had not delayed his own mounting to lift her and shove her into the Egyptian's hold, perhaps he would not have been left behind.

Perhaps it was she who would still be there. Or stoned to death long ago. Elizabeth would never have been born. And he would be here. Safe in England, in his home, even married to one of the English girls that Lady Belmaine had selected for him.

Zenia knew she was at Swanmere for a single reason: because they had thought him dead, and Elizabeth was his daughter, to be protected and coveted as the only blood heir to Swanmere. Zenia had understood. And it had not troubled her—at first she had been lonely and intimidated, but after Elizabeth had come, Zenia had felt that it was right for his daughter to have what her father could give her. She had felt that he would have wanted it; that she owed it to him and to Elizabeth. On the nights she had sat in this room and remembered her first English Christmas and longed to be enveloped in laughter and affection with her own father and Marianne in Bentinck Street, she had made the best of it for Elizabeth. The only celebration of Christmas at Swanmere had been a large public dinner for the tenants, which Zenia had not attended. There had been no decorations or popping crackers. Lady Belmaine had said that Zenia would not wish to go out of mourning, and neither had the household done so.

Zenia's time with her father and family had been so short. As his visits to Swanmere were short. As the one night she had lain with a man's arms tight about her had been short.

Elizabeth made up for it. Elizabeth made up for everything. Zenia could hold her daughter close, make her laugh and comfort her when she cried. Choose her clothes, her toys. Take her for walks, though she very seldom left these rooms, for Zenia dreaded that she might become ill. Elizabeth was not a sickly child—she was rumbustiously healthy, because Zenia took the greatest caution to keep her safe from chills, infection and dirt. Zenia couldn't understand how Lord Winter could even jest about taking Elizabeth to Siberia. Besides that, she was just a baby still, not old enough to know what to be afraid of. Once she had escaped a nurse and crawled all the way down the stairs to the next floor. Zenia had found her tottering at the top of the grand staircase, ready to fall. Her heart still contracted at the bare memory of it.

That nurse had been dismissed. The new woman was more vigilant, but Zenia still disliked to abandon Elizabeth with her for long. The new nurse had even been ready to shut the door, leaving Elizabeth alone with Lord Winter when she knew nothing about him, merely taking his word for who he was.

Zenia gazed at her daughter. It was overly severe, she supposed, to blame the nurse for letting in Elizabeth's father when everyone in the house had known he was coming and it wasn't very likely that some dangerous escaped convict would be freely roaming the halls of Swanmere in elegant male dress. But the small body curled in the bed seemed so vulnerable, so painfully defenseless, and the world was so huge and full of hazard and pain and loneliness.

Lord Winter brought it with him, the world. All of the memories Zenia had tried to erase. The blue-charged light of his eyes as he turned from defying a *ghrazzu* all alone; his easy grin among the Bedu; he was a madman, and he loved the desert and the danger in the world.

Her tea was cooling in the pot. Under the silver covers, she knew there would be lamb and rice and buttered bread, with Queen cakes and macaroons for dessert, all of which she liked far better than plum pudding.

He had brought it for her, knowing she would be hungry. She rose, picked up the plate and carried it to the desk.

With a grimace for every bite, she ate the pudding. When she had done, she carried it to the door between their rooms.

Her heart was pumping madly as she knocked. There was no answer. After a second knock, she slowly opened the door and saw the room was dark.

Quietly she set the empty plate on the floor so he would find it and pulled the door closed.

GRACE WAS THE one who recognized him. Arden walked into the taproom of the Black Swan and sat down. The place was unchanged; smoked windows and beams and a pair of half-sotted carters who stared at him from their place by the fire. Harvey pulled the tap, his big bulk taking up most of the space behind the counter, while Grace sassed him good-naturedly as she shoved one of the carters aside to stoke the coals.

She turned from her task, wiping her hands on her apron, and saw him. An odd change came over her: she lifted her chin, tossing her chestnut head back with a gesture that he recalled very well.

"Is your mother here?" he asked.

"My—" She started to frown.

"You aren't Grace Herring's daughter?" He allowed the corner of his mouth to smile.

"Oh!" she said. And then, "*Oh!*" She untied the apron and started toward him, flinging it aside. "If you ain't the blackest liar in the county. My *mother*. Oh, lordy—just look at you, then!"

Arden stood up. Grace caught his hands, pressing them in her own. Harvey had turned; he was rumbling, "God bless us, my lord! We heard you was come home, and bedamned to them heathens supposed to murder you!"

Arden shook hands across the bar, his fingers enveloped in Harvey's great red paw. "I survived."

"Ay, but the good Lord give you as many lives as a cat, I reckon, my lord. What will you take, sir?"

"A pint of the homebrewed, if you will." Grace still had hold of his other hand. Her husband, as always, was oblivious. Arden had never been perfectly sure if this was intentional blindness. "Oh, Harvey don't mind," Grace had said to Arden once, "long as I don't make him bring up another man's brats."

Her eyes were pretty yet, with deeper smile lines about them, and her chestnut hair still tumbled a stray curl down beside a cheek that, in the dim light, was softly seductive. Arden's sexual initiation had been sudden and electrifying. He'd climbed the wall and been wandering through the woods outside Swanmere, prowling with an adolescent's ferocious aimlessness amid the greenery of high summer, when he had heard her laugh. He had seen her and Harvey through the undergrowth.

She was a few years older than he—perhaps seventeen then. And Harvey was huge; had always been huge, a widower newly remarried to his teasing kitchen maid. He had taken her dress down to her stays, and in the dappled sunlight Grace's breasts had seemed like dotted cream, her nipples large and brown.

Arden had been riveted. He had stood there, forgetting to breathe, while Harvey put his big palms over them and pulled Grace down on her knees. She was smiling, with a little look of concentration and expectation on her face, her hands braced in a green patch of grass. While Arden stared, Harvey pushed up her dress, holding one hand on her white buttock while he released his breeches.

In his fifteen-year-old innocence, Arden had been awed by Harvey's immense size. He had watched in hot, desperate fascination as the tapster mounted Grace from behind. She hung her head, her breasts swaying with the quick short thrusts as he entered, her palms digging into the grass. Arden had put his arm about a tree trunk and pressed his fingernails into the bark. The marks were probably there still.

Harvey was a quiet man, in speech and in sex. There had been nothing but the heavy sound of his breath and the slap of his brawny thighs against her. Arden had thought the man was going to burst, he turned so red, but instead he shoved himself forward and curled all about Grace as if he could devour her with his big body, the muscles in his arms standing out as he gripped her about the shoulders. He jerked and quivered, groaning softly, and Arden held onto the tree to keep his knees from buckling under him.

He had stepped quickly behind it as Harvey showed signs of life again. Arden stared at a moth on the bark, hardly even knowing what it was, while the bushes rustled and Grace said, "Let's stay a bit."

"Got work," Harvey said. There was the sound of a slap. "Lazy Gracie."

"Harvey," she'd said, in a coaxing voice.

"Work," he said. "New mouth be along to feed soon enough."

Grace had audibly sighed. Then rustling, and the sound of them going through the brush.

For a while Arden had not been able to move. He looked blankly at the moth, his nostrils flaring, since he had finally remembered to breathe. He was in a pitch of acute and untutored lust. He hurt with it. He had put his head down against the tree trunk and pressed it until his ears rang.

"I know you're there." Grace's voice had seemed like something imaginary through the bells in his head. He held still, swallowing.

"From the big house," she said. "You're the young lord."

Arden had been far beyond speaking. He closed his eyes, holding onto the tree.

"You want to do it with me?"

It was a whisper, a little shy. If it had not been shy, he would have turned and run.

He heard her moving, coming closer. When she spoke again, she was so close that he jumped.

"I've seen you. Goin' about quiet-like." She paused, and then said wistfully, "I think you're beautiful."

Arden had turned his head slightly, barely daring to look at her. Her face was flushed, her hair falling down. She held her dress up with her arms crossed and pressed against her, but it gaped in front, and he could see her breasts pushed together. His heart was beating so hard that he was afraid he was going to pass out.

"Beautiful eyes. Too beautiful for a girl like me," she had said, with a touch of regret.

She had turned away then. And to this day, he did not know if he had been deliberately lured by that strategic retreat or not, but as she started to go, he turned skittishly and said, "I've never—"

That was all that came out of his paralyzed throat. She looked back, and a knowing smile, age-old, had given her face a subtle glow. He had thought she was the most splendid female in the known universe.

" 'Tisn't hard. I'll show you. But I think you peeked already!"

She came back, and took his hand, and leaned forward, placing a little kiss at the corner of his mouth.

"You're married," he said desperately, through the feel of her and the scent of her and the soft, soft touch of her fingers as she carried his hand up to cup her breast.

"Mmm. And I'm going to have a baby." She touched his lips with her tongue. "My ma says that makes a girl get peculiar. I always want it, you know? And Harvey's working. I wouldn't do it with nobody else, but you're the young lord. Real quality. Are you afraid of Harvey?"

He was terrified of Harvey. All he could see was the size of Harvey's hand on her breast; all he could feel was her nipple swelling between his forefinger and his middle one. He pressed them together, and she made a sound deep in her throat, her breast rising beneath his hand.

She reached down for his trousers. He grabbed her hand, mortified beyond speech, hysterically sure he was going to go off if she touched him.

"You afraid of Harvey?" she had asked again.

"No," he croaked.

She had pulled him toward her, taking him with her to the grassy, sunny patch. He was trembling all over. And he had fumbled and gone to his knees behind her and slid his hands up beneath her skirt when she knelt, and done what Harvey had done, and in his adolescent excitement and degradation he had gone all odd and ill and strange, unable to move or breathe without being sick.

He could still remember the way she had wiggled against him and said, "Go on."

He hadn't; he'd said nothing, only pulled away and buttoned himself up and sat down with his face in his arms. And to his eternal shame he had shed tears of frustration.

"It's all right," she said, patting his foot. "It happens that way sometimes, Harvey says. That a man can't."

He could hear the disappointment in her voice. "I'm sorry," he said to his arms.

"Oh, well," she'd said.

He had thought she would get up and leave. He still didn't know why she hadn't. He'd waited, his head in his arms, desperate for her to go away and leave him to his mortification; still desperate to feel her again.

Finally, he had looked. She was lying in the grass, only having moved as far as rolling over onto her back. Her eyes were closed in the dappled summer sun. The dress was fallen down from her breasts and hiked up above her waist, showing everything. Her stays were loose—he vividly, vividly remembered the small bulge of her early pregnancy, emphasized by the way she lay flat on the ground.

He had stood up, looking down at her. His blood rose, a deeper, more powerful surge, as if it came from somewhere inside himself that he had never known existed.

He lowered himself onto the grass beside her, touching her, kissing her, his body leaning over hers. She'd opened her mouth to him, arching upward; he had no memory of how he had discovered her place, only that they had moved together, and he was on top of her, and she was panting and gasping, making sounds of surprise and delight and demand. She had clutched frantically at him. And it had gone on and on, until he had thought he was going to die if he could not reach the culmination of it; he was going to die of agonizing, blinding sensation—until at last, at last, her peak had released his, his muscles and his breath and his mind exploding, and then they had lain there winded, witless, both of them shocked by the power of it.

"Oh, my," Grace had whispered. "Harvey never done it that way!"

Long afterward, when Arden was considerably more enlightened about women, he deduced that it had been her first climax. Perhaps she had taught Harvey "that way." Or perhaps she had preferred after all not to be crushed under eighteen stone, and left things the way Harvey liked them in his own bed. At any rate, she had always shown a particular warmth for her shy and fervent young lord.

For several sensational years, until Arden's father took him up to London on his eighteenth birthday, he had lived in a haze of lust for Grace and a sweat of fear over Harvey. He could count on his hands the number of his sexual encounters in the affair. Precisely eight, though he had probably fantasized eight thousand, and he knew the place and context of every one of them. Grace had been an honest strumpet. She was always safely with child before Arden was allowed to touch her, much to his burning frustration. Harvey's children were authentic little Herrings.

Even so, Arden still was not entirely sure that he cared to have Grace cooing over him quite so openly in the Swan. But the big man leaned on the bar, smiling benignly at his silly and cheerful wife: an entirely innocuous cuckold.

An apple-cheeked girl bounced down the stairs, calling, "Ma—Jenny won't leave my ribbons—" She stopped and cast a wide glance at Arden.

"Make your curtsy," Grace said, standing up suddenly and wiping at her skirts with a quick embarrassment. "This is Martha, my lord—our oldest—you won't remember her but as no more than a scrap of a baby girl."

Arden rose, making a bow that brought deeper roses to Martha's cheeks. She was sixteen or so—and he smiled, remembering that charming belly dappled in the summer sun. He took her hand. "Miss Herring."

"La!" Martha said. "You're Lord Winter! Ma told me all about you!"

She was every bit the natural flirt that her mother had been, lifting her lashes at him speculatively. Arden leaned back against a heavy post and took a deep swallow of ale. As he lowered the mug, he caught Harvey's eye.

The tapster's genial expression had vanished. He looked at Arden with a cold, steady warning.

Arden bowed his head slightly, acknowledging the caution. Harvey watched him bleakly for another moment, and then turned to draw a glass. Miss Martha was babbling comments and questions about His Lordship getting himself killed in Ethiopia, a naive monologue that suggested her mother had not told her quite all about Lord Winter. Arden let her babble on. Grace gave him the trademark look under the lashes that had once consumed his reason and made him toss and dream and strangle his pillow at night.

She seemed older beside her breathless daughter, but not nearly so old that the village siren she had been was vanished. Remembering their first time had roused the heat in him to a sharp burn. But with a deep sense of dislocation and stress, he realized that it was not Grace that he wanted now. Or even pink-cheeked and rather willing-looking Miss Martha—eighteen-stone father or no.

Shortly after Arden had finished his mug, he bade the Herrings a good night, much to Miss Martha's disappointment, as he did not stay to see the retrimmed bonnet that she was about to model. Grace followed him onto the step. Their breaths mingled in the cold air.

"I was that glad, m'lord, to hear you was still among the livin'," she said, with the unexpected wistfulness that sometimes hushed her voice. "That glad."

He shrugged. "I'm quite all right."

She put her hand on his arm and said suddenly, softly, "You know that I can't anymore. Not with the girls all grown up. It wouldn't be—right. Do you think?" She glanced up at him anxiously.

He smiled. "No." He touched her cheek. "Besides, I think Harvey has my number."

"Harvey!" she snorted. Then she said, "He's been awful, awful good to me."

"And I prefer to avoid having all my bones broken." He smiled crookedly. "I've got a family now myself."

She looked a little brighter. "So you do, m'lord. So you do!" She patted his arm. "I feel better then." When he raised his eyebrows at that, she said, "You looked so dreadful lonesome when you come in. But you got a wife, and up at the big house they say that she's pretty enough to keep the cows in milk."

"Is that what they say?" he asked, bemused.

"A beauty," she said solemnly. "Not a candle to me, o'course."

"Of course not."

She giggled and poked him. " 'Ain't you Grace Herring's daughter?' " she mimicked him in a high voice. "Old cheek! You always was the cunning quiet one." Then she squeezed his arm and leaned up suddenly to kiss him on the mouth. "Real quality," she whispered. Before he had a moment to register the first female form pressed against him for more than two years, she had left him and run inside.

As he turned up the collar of his coat and walked down the street, the last leaded-glass window of the Swan squeaked open. "And you make sure she treats you proper, m'lord," Grace hissed, "or bless me if she won't answer to me and Harvey too! I can't have you in here makin' them fine sheep's eyes again. My Martha ain't got a particle more sense than me, m'lord, and I know just how much *that* is!"

IT WAS HOURS after midnight when Arden lit a candle in the room he had been relegated to. He undressed himself, having yet to engage a manservant, and tossed his clothes and damp greatcoat over the chair beside the crib. It was warm in the room, the fire kept up on Beth's behalf, he supposed.

Better if it had been cold. He opened the window and stood before it in his trousers, with the chill air flowing past his chest.

Oh, yes, I have my own family now. His lip curled derisively. *What a cozy little group we are.*

He rubbed his hands over his face, moving restlessly away from the window. He sat down on the cot. He'd slept on far worse. For a few moments he gazed at nothing, lost in an erotic reverie, mixing up Grace and the elegant dasher that the earl had arranged, three years too late, to put an end to his son's virginity—the Earl Belmaine desiring as always to take no unnecessary risks in any part of his heir's education or experience—and a few other females worth remembering, though not for their clever conversation. He found himself staring at the door to the next room.

She had looked less frosty in her gown and robe. Warmer. Her hair had been tucked up under a cap, but it would come down so easily.

He saw the plate lying beside the door. For an annoyed instant he thought of ringing for whatever careless maid had left it and delivering some pointed remarks on the folly of encouraging vermin in a house of this size. Then he knelt abruptly and picked the dish up.

He stood holding it. His mood rose—and then he thought it was an amazingly absurd thing, to read meaning into an empty plate. He pitched the crumbs out the window and set it down.

He sat on the cot again, slumped against the wall, his legs stretched out. He turned a red-and-yellow building block over with his toe and wondered why it wasn't so difficult to talk to someone like Grace.

Because there was nothing to talk about, of course.

Ah, simple lust.

He was much in favor of simple lust. He grew more in favor of it by the moment. So much so that he got up, blew out his candle, and very, very slowly tried the door handle.

It was unlocked. He had not expected that. The door opened silently, emanating warmth to the cool air behind him.

He could hear his daughter breathing, soft little baby snuffs. Nothing else. His eyes adjusted, picking out the black mass of the bed in the dark.

She might be awake. She might have heard him come in, seen the light of his candle beneath the door. He moved softly into the room. Everything was in its place, so familiar that he did not need to see it even after thirteen years.

He paused at the foot of the bed. She was awake, he thought. He couldn't hear her breathing.

"*Yallah!*" she said, so clearly that he startled—but the word held fear instead of anger. The bedclothes rustled as she twitched. She began to whisper, urgent babble that turned into low moans, like a puppy unable to howl. "Go!" she said plainly in Arabic. "*Yallah! Yallah!*"

Her body grew still then, but she kept moaning.

"It's all right," Arden said.

"Djinn," she whimpered. "A djinni!"

He knelt beside her, searching for her in the tumble of pillow and counterpane. He caught her hand. Her fingers twitched, closing convulsively. Faint yelps came from her throat.

"It's all right." He leaned over her, bending close. "You're safe, wolf cub," he said. "No demons. This is England."

The whimpering ceased, but she was breathing in deep short gasps, clutching his hand.

"I'm here," he murmured, kissing her cheek and her temple. "Don't you know I'm here?"

Her breath caught. She seemed to make an effort to wake, inhaling. Her hand relaxed. She lay still, so still that he thought she must be awake, but she said nothing.

He waited for her to realize he was there, to jump up and scream, or cast him rudely out at the least.

Tentatively, he touched her temple with the back of his fingers. She sighed, a sleeper's sigh, and turned over in the bed away from him, snuggling down with his hand caught in hers.

In the dark she was not Lady Winter. In the dark she was his game little wolf again, who dreamed of demons and had to touch him in her sleep.

He leaned against the bed frame. He didn't try to lie beside her, because then she would wake and break the spell. He put his head down, resting against her warm back. For a long time, while she sank far down in the depths of sleep again, he knelt on the carpet with his arm around her.

Sixteen

———✺———

ELIZABETH, AN ACTIVE child, found her mother entirely too dull to be borne in the very early dawn. She knew that if she put her small face up to Mama's, trying to wake her, she would only be snugged close and trapped, and then she wouldn't be able to fall out of the bed all by herself. But she did take a moment to investigate the unusual circumstance of an extra arm, large and brown, hugging her mother.

Elizabeth thought hug was a nice word. Hugging was a nice thing to do. "Guh," she said, touching the new arm.

A low rumbling sound came from somewhere the other side of Mama. The hand moved, and the arm, and a head of tousled black hair appeared. As Elizabeth stared in delight, a dragon lurked up from the floor, squinting and shaking its head. She pressed her hands together and smiled at it.

It blinked its blue eyes, and smiled back.

Elizabeth cooed. She crawled to the bed stool and turned about and let herself down very creditably. In her beribboned slippers, she ran around the bed and found the entire dragon, a great expanse of tanned brown skin right down at her level. She gave a squeal.

Mama murmured something sleepy. The dragon looked at Elizabeth with its laughing blue eyes and whispered, "Shhhhh," in a soft way, softer than the average hissing dragon that Nurse drew for her on paper. Very gently it disengaged itself from hugging Mama and rose.

It turned into a man as it did, and Elizabeth quailed back a little, less certain of men than dragons. But he didn't try to pick her up; he just walked, tall and impressive in padded stocking feet, into her playroom. He started to close the door.

Elizabeth instantly ran forward. She was not going to be shut out of her room. She smacked her chubby hands against the door before it latched.

ZENIA HAD AN excellent sleep. She drowsed later than usual, dreamily surprised that Elizabeth was content to sleep so long and quietly. Zenia vaguely remembered a door closing—she could not decide how long ago that had been, but the maid always came to make up the fire, which usually had Elizabeth up and bolting for her toys.

She moved to check her daughter's forehead for fever. Her hand swept across the bed. She sat up abruptly.

"Elizabeth!" She flung her feet to the floor. *"Elizabeth!"*

She ran for the playroom and collided with the nurse coming the other way.

"Oh, beg pardon, ma'am—"

"Elizabeth!" Zenia cried frantically, brushing her aside to see that the room was empty.

"Oh, ma'am, she's right as rain," the nurse said soothingly. "She's gone downstairs with her papa to breakfast."

"Gone down—" Zenia pressed her hand over her throat. "Oh!" She realized that the nurse held a man's shirt and trousers folded over her arm. "I didn't give permission for her to be taken down!"

The nurse's smile vanished. She curtsied deeply. "I'm very sorry, ma'am! But I—was I to say to his lordship that he could not take her?"

"Of course," Zenia exclaimed, turning. She rang for her maid, but she was already dressed by the time the girl arrived. She waited just long enough for her last button in back to be done up and her hair quickly pinned under a black cap, then ran downstairs.

There was no one in the morning parlor. Bright winter sun shone across the long table, sparkling on silver and crystal. It was still too early for the earl and countess, but two of the waiting place settings had been cleared away already. There was a napkin laid flat where one of them had been, with a large orange spot in the middle of it—obviously a spill. Several of the toast racks had been heavily raided. The room smelled of ham and coffee. A footman entered, carrying a fresh pot. He set it down and automatically pulled out a chair for her.

"Where is Miss Elizabeth?" she demanded, disregarding the chair.

The footman bowed his head. "I'm not rightly certain, m'lady, but his lordship mentioned going to the stable after breakfast."

"The stable!" Zenia whirled around and strode across the marble entry hall, the sound of her heels echoing from the red-veined columns and the floor. Another servant opened the door to the King of Prussia room, and Zenia broke into a trot as she traversed the great gilded length of it. At the end, she let herself out the French door onto the terrace, not stopping for a cloak.

The crisp air of morning struck her cheeks and lungs as she ran up a long path. The stables were a great distance away—they

crowned the hill behind the house, as formal and elaborate a facade as Swanmere itself. She was panting icy puffs of steam as she
reached the graveled court.

"Is Miss Elizabeth here?" She accosted the first groom she
saw, a little man leading a horse under the arched entrance.

He bobbed. "The grass school, mum."

"The grass school?" Zenia had never been into the stables; the
carriages were always brought round to the house, and she had
not ridden once at Swanmere. "Where?"

He seemed to sense her panic, for he threw the horse's lead to
a stableboy and bowed again. "This way, mum, if you please."

BETH MADE GIGGLING squeals as she bounced along, held in
Arden's arm on the front of the saddle. "Pa!" she cried. "Pa!" demanding that they resume speed when he halted.

Shajar instantly sprang forward in a canter, her ears pricking,
docile and pretty in spite of the strange surroundings. She rocked
across the grass, much too small for Arden's height, but perfect
for a young girl's mount. God willing, Beth would have twenty
years and more with her, for Arabs were long-lived horses, and
the mare was just now six years old. The Bedouins grew up with
their mounts. The greatest gift a sheik could give his baby son
was the mare that would carry him into battle.

Arden carried his own daughter on Prince Rashid's war horse,
turning and feinting and galloping in huge circles, ignoring the
shafting pain in his side. Beth would learn her first lessons on a
good solid pony, of course, but the String of Pearls would be there,
inspiration and reward—Shajar al-Durr, the splendid, perfect mare
that her father had brought out of the desert itself for her.

Beth was fearless. On the ground she had not drawn back
when the mare put down her muzzle and drew in great curious

gusts in Beth's face, but only reached out to touch the soft nose. She did not cry now, bouncing and flying, but laughed with joy. She might have been born in the black tents for the instant delight she took in mounting a war horse and jousting with the air. When Arden leaned his head down to squeeze her close and kiss her ear, she gave a squeal and then turned her face away.

"Oh, a cruel flirt!" he said. "You'll bedevil their dreams, won't you, *sheytana*?"

She made a chortle in her throat, as if she looked forward to it.

"*Elizabeth!*"

The shriek made the mare shy, leaping sideways. Arden clutched Beth tight while she laughed. As the horse steadied, he looked around.

Her mother stood frozen at the gate, her white hands up before her mouth. She seemed to have enough sense left in her to know that running forward screaming in a welter of flapping skirts was not the safest course. He made the mare stand still, and Lady Winter strode forward across the muddy grass.

"You are *mad!*" she hissed as she came close. She reached and tore Beth from his hold. The baby began to scream in protest, kicking to get away. Shajar threw her head, eyes rolling at the commotion. "You want to kill her!" Beth's mother cried at Arden. "You don't care if you kill her!"

Her face was mottled, her dark hair straggling free of an ugly black cap. She had not even worn a cloak. She spun away, carrying Beth with her.

He dismounted, watching her stride to the gate. All the air had left his chest, as if he had taken a hard blow.

Lady Winter turned, hefting the crying child. "Don't you *dare* touch her! Don't touch her again!"

* * *

THE EARL HIMSELF met Zenia halfway down the hill from the stables. "What has happened?" he demanded in a rougher voice than she had ever heard from him.

Panic and fury still drove her. "Lord Winter is not to be allowed to attend my daughter," she said. "She is not safe with him."

Lord Belmaine looked narrowly at her. "Tell me what has occurred."

"Ask him," Zenia said. "I must get her inside. She will catch her death. She doesn't even have a cap." She walked past, ready to throw off his hand if he tried to detain her, but he did not. Elizabeth had stopped crying and wriggling, and sat on Zenia's hip staring about her, pointing at items of interest. Her cheeks were chapped bright red. Zenia put up her hand to tenderly cover the baby's wind-pinkened ear as she walked.

Back in her playroom, Elizabeth began to cry again as soon as the door closed. She toddled to it when Zenia put her down, reaching for the knob. All the time that Zenia worked to get off her damp and dirty nightgown—he had not even dressed her, but just shoved her small shoes on over her knitted booties and buttoned her pell-mell into a coat—Elizabeth wailed, trying to reach the door.

Zenia bundled her in the warmest layers she had, ordering the nurse to build up the fire. When she put her in her crib, Elizabeth stood up, gripping the rail and screaming. She was going into a fit, Zenia could tell. She tried to cuddle her, but Elizabeth pushed her furiously away. Her screams began to mount.

THE EARL FOUND his son standing beside one of the paddocks, a saddle and bridle lying at his feet. Just inside the fence cavorted the loveliest little white mare that Lord Belmaine had ever seen, running with her tail held out like a streaming banner. She turned as she saw him and came to investigate at a floating trot.

The earl stood at the fence, a few yards from his son. "What the devil have you done now?" he asked, watching the horse sail along the fenceline. The mare halted, arching her fine neck toward him, her dark eyes liquid with inquisitiveness. Then she snorted playfully and thundered away.

"Oh, I've been trying to murder my daughter," Arden said. "What else?"

The earl felt the place beneath his breastbone begin to clench and burn. He would be forced to resort to a bland diet, he thought gloomily. "I ask myself," he said, still watching the paddock, "I ask myself why all your life you have made everything so goddamned bloody difficult."

"So disown me," his son said.

They stood in silence. The earl finally said, "May I ask in precisely what manner you are accused of attempting to do Miss Elizabeth an injury?"

"I thought she might like to ride with me." He shrugged. "She seemed to enjoy it."

"I must suppose that you did not consider the danger, should you fall?"

"This horse is the best blood in the desert," the viscount said coldly. "She's trained to perfection. She didn't bolt in the face of Ibrahim Pasha's guns—or when a screeching harpy in a widow's cap came screaming at her either. I wasn't going to fall off."

"Anything can happen on a horse. Even the best trained. You know that."

"Very true. And the house might burn down, and lightning might strike, and the sky might fall."

If the earl had not taken a secret pride in his son's superb horsemanship, he would have answered more pointedly. But he was aware that, in fact, Miss Elizabeth could not have been in more competent hands. Instead he said, "Lady Winter is an extremely conscientious and devoted mother. I can find no fault with her precautions regarding Miss Elizabeth. You will not discover that child roaming about unattended or neglected in any way."

"Does she ever get out of her room?" the viscount asked dryly.

"Lady Winter is very cautious of the peril of childhood illness."

His son turned his head. "Does Beth get out of her room?" he asked more sharply.

"Her mother takes no risks of infection. I believe that is wise of her, at this season in particular."

Arden stared at him with narrowed eyes, and then turned back to watch the horse. There was a dangerously forbidding set to his jaw and mouth.

"At least you might have put a cap on her," the earl said, attempting lightness. "There's a sharp wind."

"She didn't give a button for that." Arden smiled bitterly. "*She's* full of pluck. Maybe we'll run away together and join the gypsies."

Lord Belmaine leaned on the fence and gazed at his son's profile. The wind blew the viscount's dark hair across his forehead. He looked tired and angry, his mouth set hard, as if he endured a physical pain.

"I had hoped," the earl said slowly, "that you would not run away this time."

A muscle in the viscount's jaw twitched. He did not take his eyes from the mare. "I'm here," he said. And after a moment: "I will try. I am trying."

How hard? Lord Belmaine wanted to ask ironically, but he held his tongue. He was determined to remain on speaking terms. He never knew what would set his son off, and he was well aware of how often he wanted back the words that had done it.

"I would like you to speak to our attorney," the earl said. "Mr. King. Would that be amenable?"

"Perfectly amenable."

"He is awaiting your convenience in the map room."

"Fine." His son leaned down and hefted the saddle onto his hip, grimacing slightly at the move. He walked away.

THE ATTORNEY SAID nothing that Arden had not already surmised himself. He sat expressionlessly, listening, his gaze focused past Mr. King and his papers, out the windows draped in green damask and gold fringe.

"There need be no great inconvenience to it, sir," Mr. King said in a dry murmur. "With proper arrangements, the thing can be done with extreme privacy in the chapel here. His lordship and I, after considerable examination of the matter, feel that this would be the prudent and reasonable course. Do you agree?"

"Yes," Arden said.

The attorney, he saw, very nearly gave a sigh of relief. "Excellent. I shall put the matter in train, then."

"And if she doesn't agree?"

The man carefully pushed his papers into a perfect stack. "It would be extremely unusual, sir, for a female to be so misguided in her own and her child's interests."

"But if she were so misguided?"

"Lord Winter, these are merely formalities—I am informed that you have made a marriage to Lady Winter overseas, but have no proof of it that would be acceptable to the courts should the issue be brought before them for any reason. Which of course we must hope will never occur. We deal only with eventualities."

"What eventualities?"

"Ah. Should you or Lady Winter pass away, for instance."

"I already did pass away, Mr. King," he said mockingly, "and apparently that created no great difficulty."

"It created some." Mr. King cleared his throat. "But let me be blunt, Lord Winter. The main eventuality that must concern us would occur should either you or Lady Winter, some time in the future—regret your marriage. Seek a separation, judicial or private. Or perhaps—it has been known, I am sorry to say, that a married person will sometimes evince a desire to wed elsewhere. I am forced to say that the way might still be open even to that. And the guardianship of Miss Elizabeth is not as settled as I would like."

"What is my position as guardian now?"

"If it came before a court—and no marriage can be proved—" A small shrug. "Nonexistent, sir."

Arden's mouth tightened. "Have you spoken to Lady Winter about this?"

"No, sir."

"Do not," he said grimly.

"It would be foolish of her—foolish in the extreme, sir—to openly reject your legal relationship merely because it is possible to do so."

"She's a woman, isn't she? What's reason got to do with it?"

"She would bastardize the child. I cannot conceive that she would intentionally do so. I understand she is a most devoted mother."

Arden gritted his teeth. "Extremely devoted." Very faintly, in the dead silence, they could hear the hysterical screams of his daughter far away in the house. "Shockingly devoted."

"She can only hurt the child if she attempts to live in an unmarried state."

"You said she could marry someone else." Arden shoved himself out of his chair. "My God, she's so bloody beautiful—she could find someone to marry her, and bedamned to scandal!"

The lawyer was silent for a moment as Arden leaned his hands on the window frame, staring out unseeingly. Then Mr. King said, "May I ask you to be perfectly candid with me, Lord Winter? Do you see this as a credible possibility?"

He shook his head. "I don't know. I don't know her at all."

He could feel the lawyer looking at him. This painstakingly maintained fiction that there had already been a marriage "overseas" must be as transparent as water.

"I see. If the guardianship is your sole concern," the attorney said carefully, "it is possible that could be dealt with outside the issue of marriage."

Arden looked around at him, his hand gripping the window frame.

Mr. King rustled his papers. "It is conceivable that you can simply adopt the child—become her guardian—without confirming the marriage. If—ah—the mother opposed this, I'm not certain of the difficulty. A child born out of wedlock is legally a *filius nullius*, without relatives, but unquestionably in the mother's custody. I would have to inquire into it more deeply."

"I thought that's what I'm to do anyway—adopt her."

"Well, I use the word adopt, but of course since there *is* a marriage"—he gave Arden a penetrating glance—"and the child was born within it, we are merely making absolutely certain that the lack of record can never develop into a difficulty by instituting a formal guardianship. But if, for instance—and I speak entirely theoretically, my lord—if you had arrived and declared that there was never any marriage at all . . . then I'm afraid Miss Elizabeth would be a *filius nullius* in the eyes of the law."

"So I have choices," Arden said sardonically. "I can marry her, or I can toss her out and make a bid for my bastard daughter."

"That is to put it in a very ugly manner, Lord Winter."

"And her—she can marry me—or take Beth away, find another man to give her bed and board, and fight me through every court in the land to keep me away from my child."

The attorney lowered his eyes to the desk. "I think it more probable in that case that she would take the little girl abroad, rather than deal in the courts."

Arden felt as if something was pressing on his throat. *Abroad*, he thought, with a rising sense of panic.

"Give me some time." He shook his head, leaning it down on his arm. "For the love of God, don't tell her this. Give me some time."

"There is no particular limitation as to time, although the sooner a ceremony confirming and recording the marriage can be held, the better to feel easy about the matter. Your father has asked me to speak to Lady Winter of the legal advantages to such a course. I shall confine myself to that topic. I see no need to confuse a lady with the difficult forensic details."

Seventeen

❈

It was the most violent fit Elizabeth had ever had. She had rejected every overture; nothing Zenia could do seemed to appease her, not even the toys or the songs that she loved. It seemed to go on forever—just as Zenia would get her calmed, stroking the hot little forehead, Elizabeth would realize that she was falling asleep and burst into frenzied cries against it. The worst was when the door opened to let the nurse in or out: Elizabeth lunged for it, and once fell so hard against the rail of the crib that she shrieked with pain. Both Zenia and the nurse tried to pick her up and walk with her, but she would twist and shove so angrily that it was impossible.

The nurse said tentatively, "If you would leave her to herself, ma'am, perhaps—"

Zenia turned savagely on her. "I would not leave her!" she

snapped. "Go and fetch some cool water! And then don't open the door again!"

The woman turned as red as Elizabeth. She lowered her face and curtsied. "Yes, ma'am," she said, barely audible over Elizabeth's screams.

Zenia glanced out the window. She had lost track of time. It seemed as if the fit had gone on all day, but it was still bright, the sun high. As the door opened, Elizabeth's head turned toward it. She began to scream so frantically that she stopped breathing, her face going from red to blue, her mouth open wide and her body arched back, so that Zenia was terrified she was going to choke herself.

She tried again to pick her up, but Elizabeth's rigid limbs fought, her body rolling away. Elizabeth drew a strangled breath and screamed again, the sound ringing in Zenia's ears. Zenia tried again to sing to her, but her voice failed. Tears filled her eyes.

"Oh baby," she whispered, leaning over Elizabeth's frantic form, "oh baby, please baby. Don't cry. Don't cry."

She was vaguely aware that the door still stood open; she didn't look up, but wiped angrily at the tears that dripped off her nose as she turned to close it.

Lord Winter stood in the doorway. His daughter arched and cried, oblivious to everything now but her hysteria. And suddenly, before Zenia knew what he was about, he strode across the room and lifted Elizabeth from the bed.

She writhed, her eyes closed, her howl increasing to a pitch Zenia had not known it could reach. She fought for an instant, but he hoisted her easily in spite of it—and then suddenly she opened her eyes. She was swinging upward, her small mouth open. Before she could draw breath for another scream, she was perched atop his shoulders. He turned to the door, ducked through, and walked away down the hall.

Zenia hastened after. Elizabeth was crying, but softly now,

more hiccups than weeping. He went down the stairs with Zenia at his heels. By the time they reached the first floor, Elizabeth had ceased even her hiccups. She was silently clinging to her father's hair as he deliberately tilted her to one side and then the other, walking down the long hall.

At the great staircase, he descended in bouncing steps that had Elizabeth bumping up and down like an india rubber ball. She began to giggle.

He stopped at the foot of the stairs, turning to look up at Zenia. Elizabeth's tearstained face was wreathed in smiles. "Do you want her back now?" he asked coolly.

Zenia took a step down, reaching for her. Elizabeth's eyes widened. Pink flooded her face as she drew a breath to scream.

Zenia dropped her hands. She sat down on the staircase and put her forehead down on her knees. The absence of Elizabeth's screams was such a relief that she could not bear them to start again.

Arden looked at her huddled on the stairs. He set his foot on the lowest step and leaned over, catching her hand, exerting a pull. "Come. Let's take a walk."

She lifted her face, resisting. "I don't want her to go outside," she said quickly.

"We won't go outside."

She let him draw her to her feet. Elizabeth made a pleased sound. He walked across the echoing hall to an alabaster statue of a draped shepherdess. His daughter reached out and touched the marble fingers, making a surprised "Guh!"

"Yes," Lord Winter said. "That is a girl."

Zenia could have informed him that everything was "guh," if it was not "mama" or "pa" or "g'dow." But she did not. She felt as if she were resting in a calm after the storm. She actually felt— rather grateful.

Lord Winter walked through the great house, pausing at anything that drew Elizabeth's attention. He let her touch things that Zenia would not have dared to touch herself: silver urns and Chinese porcelains, gilt-and-enamel clocks. When Elizabeth tried to pick up a crystal vase, Zenia hurried forward to pluck it out of her hand.

Elizabeth drew a threatening breath. Her lips quivered for a moment, but Zenia said firmly, "No," and put the vase down as Lord Winter moved out of reach.

"If you let her touch, I fear she'll break something," she said, following him in anxious haste.

"It's just a lot of pretty rubbish," he said casually.

Zenia glanced around at the grandeur of tall pediments and draped windows, the polish of inlaid marble tabletops and silver candelabra. It came sharply home to her, for the first time, that he had been brought up to this. It was so familiar to him that he thought nothing of letting a baby play with a golden box from the carved mantelpiece—though he did move suddenly to catch it in his palm as Elizabeth let go.

He had appeared so stiff and distant here, so unlike the easy friend and protector he had been in the desert—he had not seemed to belong to the place.

And yet it was his. These were his possessions, his family's house that would belong to him after his father. Zenia caught a silver candlestick before Elizabeth could overturn it, amazed at his indifference. She would not have brought Elizabeth into these rooms if her life depended on it. She had let Lady Belmaine guide her in how to act and what to wear, learning to sit gracefully and straight, to pour tea and accept a cup. But he walked through the house with the negligent ease of ownership, introducing his daughter to Swanmere.

In the slow procession of high-ceilinged rooms and luxurious color, of footmen who opened doors and closed them silently,

Elizabeth's eyes began at last to droop. In the long gallery she fell asleep, her cheek resting on Lord Winter's black hair.

He walked on a little way, and then turned his head. Her plump fingers hung against his cheek, small and pink on the hard angle of his face. "It pains me to tell you, Lady Winter," he said, with a sideways smile that creased the tanned skin beneath her hand, "that your daughter snores."

Zenia reached for her, but he eased down in a window alcove. Elizabeth woke a little, only to make a faint complaint and cling to his neck as he lifted her down onto his shoulder.

"I'll take her upstairs," Zenia whispered, leaning to reach for her.

He caught her elbow. "Sit down," he said.

She hesitated. He looked at her steadily, such blue eyes— surprising color, like the blue beads that fell in the dusky caravan tracks, broken from a thousand years of camels' woven fringes. His lashes were black as kohl.

"Sit down," he said again.

Elizabeth snuffled at the soft, deep vibration of his voice. With a hiccup, she nestled into his neckcloth.

Zenia gazed at them a moment. There was still the jealous, upset part of her that wanted to snatch Elizabeth away. She swallowed, looking at her daughter resting against him so trustingly. Zenia had slept that way once—next to him. Knowing he was there. Knowing she was safe.

She perched on the edge of the window seat. "I had not realized you were clever with children," she said awkwardly.

He gave a short, dry laugh. "I don't know a bloody thing about children."

Zenia entwined her hands, looking down at them. "She has these—fits. Sometimes, I don't know how to stop them. But you—" Her voice trailed off.

"Don't care for female blubbering," he supplied. "Next time I'll just turn her upside down and shake her."

Zenia looked up quickly, but he had that crooked smile, and she could see that he didn't mean it.

"I'm sorry that I frightened you this morning," he said. "Zenia."

He pronounced her name carefully, as if it were difficult for him to use.

"I'm sorry that I—said what I said." Zenia pressed her lips together. "But you must not take her outside."

"I won't forget the cap next time, you may be sure."

"No! No, I truly mean it, you must not take her out of the heated rooms. It is much too cold and damp. Even here there is a draft. I hope she may not take ill from her exposure today."

He scowled. "Is she inclined to take ill?"

"Oh no, she enjoys perfect health," Zenia said, allowing herself a touch of pride. "I take every precaution."

"So I'm told." As he looked at her over Elizabeth's head, there was a faint gleam of mockery in his eyes. "My father thinks you the model parent."

"Does he?" She felt a gratified surprise.

Lord Winter toyed with the lace on Elizabeth's pinafore, smoothing it with his finger. Then he said, "The two of you have similar opinions on the care of children."

"He hasn't spoken of it to me. I'm glad if—if he doesn't disapprove of me."

"Never fear. You're the apple of your father-in-law's eye."

And what do you think of me? she wanted desperately to ask, but it was impossible. She was not certain of English ways in this. In the desert, a man could put away his wife by sending her back to her family—many did it frequently, taking a new bride when they tired of an old one. Especially if she had not borne a son. A wife could do the same, take refuge from her husband in any tent, and from pride he would not come to seek her as long as her family paid back the bride-price if she would not return to him. Her sons would never go with her, but her daughters might if she wanted them.

A Christian marriage allowed of no such easy divorce. The earl and countess were powerful evidence of that. There was not a Mohammedan husband alive who would have suffered to keep only Lady Belmaine when she gave him but one son, and he so urgently desired others. But Zenia and Lord Winter had made no Christian marriage. There was no sheik or emir to listen and judge among his own people. There were volumes of law books that lined the shelves of her father's study; there were courts and inns and temples—Chancery and Doctors' Commons; Arches and Common Pleas—their names had whisked through conversations between her father and Mr. Jocelyn; there were registers and church weddings and advocates and barristers. She had written to her father to advise her, for she did not trust what anyone else might say.

She wished to do things in the English way. But she was afraid Lord Winter did not want her for his wife. She was afraid he wanted Elizabeth alone. And she could not bear that. She would not. She would take Elizabeth away to her father first, or farther, as far away as she had to go to keep her daughter, even if it was to the desert itself.

But she looked at Lord Winter, with Elizabeth's hair curling softly against his jaw and her small nose pressed up against the folds of his neckcloth in her exhausted sleep, and Zenia did not want to go. She wanted to stay here, behind English walls of such sovereign height that nothing could penetrate them.

As if he read her thoughts, he said, "Zenia—I mean to remain here." He frowned slightly, looking away from her out the window. "You know that we must come to some . . . settlement between us."

Her breathing seemed to grow difficult. "I will not leave without Elizabeth!" she exclaimed.

The frown became a black scowl. "I have not said—I had no such thing in my mind." His eyes flicked to hers, a keen look. "I don't know why you mention it."

Zenia sat silently, clasping her hands hard together, her gaze fixed on Elizabeth's hair.

"Do you have some thought of leaving with her?" he asked tautly.

"Not at present," she said in a careful tone.

She was very still, her head bowed a little. To Arden, she appeared composed; entirely feminine and remote, that delicacy that awed and drew and baffled him. He had meant to place the thing before her in a simple, temperate manner. To say that a marriage between them would be the best—the only—course, for Beth's sake. It was so obvious; he did not see that she could form any reasonable objection, living already as Lady Winter in name.

And yet the words altogether escaped him. He was in dread that he would somehow say it wrong—almost everything he had said since he arrived at Swanmere had been wrong. And now from his first sentence she was already springing into a hostile answer. There had been, for a few moments, a fragile peace between them. A peace inside himself, walking through the house with Beth on his shoulders and Zenia at his side. It was the only time in his life he could remember that he had felt at home here.

He caressed his daughter's warm neck with his fingertip. Poor Beth, locked up in two heated rooms. For her own good, by her devoted mother. He knew nothing of children, but he had felt such a kinship and pain, hearing those frenzied screams, that he had simply acted. Let her out of there. He looked at her mother and thought, *You don't know your own daughter. You'll lose her that way.*

But he did not say that either. He had some sense.

In the end, he said nothing at all. He closed his eyes and

leaned his head back. The night was catching up with him: Beth's steady snores and the warm stream of afternoon light through the glass seemed like an invitation to serenity and sleep. He really did not want to fight with this person next to him; this beautiful black-and-ivory butterfly. He looked through his lashes at her and imagined her without the annoying cap and stiff bombazine. He tried for a moment to see Selim in her, but Selim was gone, cast forever into fantasy. Left somewhere far away, as Arabia was so far away that it seemed illusion now.

But Beth was solid and real in his arms. Her mother was sitting beside him. He imagined reaching out and drawing her close, into a circle of three.

He did not. He let himself drowse, while erotic images of her unbuttoning her dress to nurse drifted up unbidden in his mind. He felt her reach out and make some motherly adjustments to Beth's collar. Her hand smoothed Beth's hair. And he felt the brush of it, cool and soft as it whispered past his cheek.

He swallowed a silent moan of hunger. He wanted to turn his face into that white palm, kiss and caress it. He opened his eyes. She was leaning close, her fingers still on Beth's hair.

He moved, just a little. Just enough to bring his mouth in contact with her where her fingertips nestled in Beth's curls.

Their eyes met. For one instant, she did not draw back. And he felt a raw surge of lust, a passion to discover her, lay bare her body *now*; to take her on the floor as if it were the grass of a sun-dappled wood; as if by that he could learn the secret of her.

She turned her face, so that he could only see her profile. It was a modest move, but her hand drew away slowly, leaving him with honey-gold curls against his lips and a rage of desire in his blood.

He felt a huge distance between where he was and what he wanted, a rift that he did not know how to cross. Between his impulse to drown and bury himself in her and the pure, still contour of her cheek, the silence—an impossible reach. All the steps across that void were invisible to him, and so uncertain that any mistake would be the end. But he was burning all alone. He was going to do something wild if he stayed here.

He stood up abruptly, lifting Beth away from him, conveying her to her mother's arms. "You'd better take her upstairs now."

He didn't wait for an answer, but turned and strode away. A quarter hour later, he was shouldering his rifle and heading for his target range beyond the old dovecote, where he spent the remaining daylight putting bullets through glass balls hurled from a trap, concentrating all his awareness on the gun's report and kick, and the satisfying shatter of bursting glass.

ZENIA WAS CALLED down to speak to Mr. King in the hour before it was time to dress for dinner. He and Lord Belmaine rose as she entered. The earl set her chair in a position before the fire. He smiled and asked, with a surprising warmth, how Miss Elizabeth was faring now that she had quieted.

"She's sleeping," Zenia said. "There is yet no sign of an ague. I'm hopeful that she won't take any fever."

"Good," Lord Belmaine said. "Good. I'm sure you have her throat well wrapped up."

"Oh yes."

He nodded. "Lady Winter is a devoted mother, Mr. King," he said, sipping his green cordial.

"There is nothing so congenial to see as a mother's sincere tenderness for her child," the lawyer said.

Zenia felt again that small glow of gratification. She made a faint, bashful nod.

"With Miss Elizabeth's welfare in mind," Mr. King said, "we have a few tedious legal matters to dispose of." He smiled at her.

"Nothing complicated, but they will require your aid. For various reasons, it is a little worrisome that the written record of your marriage to Lord Winter has been lost."

Zenia's heart began to beat very quickly. She glanced at the earl, but he was also smiling, the tiny cordial glass clasped lightly between his hands.

"Of course, we could institute a search of all Arabia," Mr. King said, with a cough that was possibly meant to be a laugh, "but by far the simpler remedy will be for you and Lord Winter to confirm your marriage by a ceremony conducted under English law. Then there is a bit of paperwork for Lord Winter, attesting that Miss Elizabeth is his daughter and he her legal guardian, which you agree to—and then all will be done up neat as a pin."

They both looked at her with such blandly agreeable expressions that she was immediately suspicious. "I don't understand," she said, although she thought she did.

"Very simply, Lady Winter, you must marry your husband again," the attorney said, with another peculiar cough.

She sat very straight in the chair. "Is this what—" She almost found her voice failing her. "Is it what Lord Winter wishes?"

"Yes. I spoke to him this morning, and he is in full agreement."

But he was not here to tell her so himself. It was a lawyer and his father who called her in to tell her. She thought of what he had said to her today, that they must come to a settlement between them.

Was this what he had meant? Did he wish to marry her after all?

She would be safe then, she thought. His legal wife. A Christian wife, who could not be put away or divorced.

"Would that mean that I can never be separated from Elizabeth?" she blurted. "Or can he take her away from me as he said he could?"

"I'm sure no husband would ever wish to separate a devoted mother from her children," Mr. King said.

Zenia knew a platitude when she heard one. The attorney looked at her with that small, unblinking, steady smile—and she thought, *You're lying to me.*

"I wish to do what is best for Elizabeth," she said.

"Certainly you do." The earl rose, reaching for the bottle of cordial. "Would you like some wine, my dear?"

She shook her head. "No, thank you." Then abruptly she stood also, turning to the fire. She frowned into the gleaming reflection of red coals on the silver fender. "My father is a barrister of Lincoln's Inn, Mr. King. I do not think that I have any objection to doing what you ask, but if you please, I would like you to write it down for me, so that I may send it to him. I wish my father to advise me."

She turned about. Mr. King had risen. "I would be happy to do so, madam. I think you will find him readily in agreement."

"Yes," she repeated slowly. "I believe that I have no objection to what you ask, but I wish my father to advise me."

"Draft a letter immediately, Mr. King," the earl said. "I will have it sent down to London tonight, so that Mr. Bruce may have it in the morning."

"I must see it myself first," Zenia said.

The earl's brows lifted. He gave her another of the bland smiles, but this one had an edge to it. "Certainly, madam. I hope you don't think anyone means to deceive or cheat you, merely because we wish to do everything possible to confirm you as my son's wife. I hope it isn't a position which you have found unbearable in your time with us?"

"No," she whispered, daunted by the cool acid in his voice.

"I'm glad to hear it. I do not think Lord Winter is an entirely undesirable husband—but then I am his father, so perhaps I'm overly partial."

"I will do nothing that means I may be separated from Elizabeth," Zenia said.

"Will you make your daughter a bastard, Lady Winter?" the earl asked softly. "Because that is your alternate choice."

She took an involuntary step back. "I wish my father to advise me."

"That is perfectly acceptable. And if he advises any other course, I will be forced to think him a very great fool." The earl made a stiff bow. "I think it is time for us to prepare for dinner. May I offer you my arm to the stairs, madam?"

Eighteen

———⊗⊗⊗———

ZENIA WORE HER lavender gown, with pearls instead of diamonds. It was the closest she could come to blue and gold. They
said nothing to one another all through dinner. The earl spoke of
politics to his son, which did not appear to be a topic that much
interested Lord Winter, to judge by his terse replies.

His mother said that her dresser and the couturiere had
arranged to be available to Zenia in the morning, to make a start
on her new wardrobe in colors. Lord Winter made a little grimace at his plate—so brief that Zenia was not even sure that she
had seen it.

In a short silence, he said suddenly, "I saw that you've let the
carp pond fill."

"Ah," his father said, shaking his head. "Now there is a
tragedy. Frozen down to the bottom in '36. Broke my heart.
There were carp in that pond older than I am."

"I remember," Lord Winter said. "I used to feed them." He looked up at Zenia. "They would come when one rang the bell."

"Rye bread," his father said. "They loved rye bread."

Lord Winter sipped his wine. He set down the glass, turning it in his fingers. "I'll take in hand to have it cleared and restocked, if you like."

A fleeting expression of surprise crossed the earl's face, but he smiled, covering it. "That is an excellent notion. Do you know— I suppose I don't have the slightest conjecture as to where those fish came from. Never even thought to replace 'em."

"They're Chinese. I can obtain some."

"Indeed." The earl's pleasure suddenly turned guarded. "Not by going to damned Peking, I trust," he said sharply.

"No, sir. Liverpool."

"Eh?"

"The tea trade," Lord Winter said.

"Ah, I see. Direct from China, then, by George. I should like that. Fish from China. I like to have little odd bits of faraway places about. If you look in the Italian Grotto down beside the carp pond, Lady Winter, you will see some very pretty shells that a fellow brought me from the South Seas. I had them plastered into the wall."

"A veritable treasure trove of the world," Lord Winter said, with a very faint smile at her.

Her pulse felt warm and haphazard when he looked at her so, as it had when his lips had brushed her fingers in Elizabeth's hair. He looked at her as if they shared some silent understanding between them.

They shared Elizabeth between them. They had made Elizabeth. His body in hers, his mouth against her mouth.

She said the first thing that came into her mind. "Will you teach the carp to answer a bell?"

"You can do it," he said. "You and Beth."

Her heart lifted. He meant for her to stay.

"Would you like to do it?" he asked.

"Yes," she said, taking refuge in an intense study of her fruit fork. "Yes, I'm sure that I should like that."

AFTER DINNER, HIS father stood before the fire with a small glass of one of the revolting-looking cordials that he always drank. He had already tried the "Member of Parliament" overture, in which Arden was to be tempted into standing for some convenient borough by the dropping of appetizing political tidbits at dinner. There was a "Justice of the Peace" script which would follow shortly, probably before the arrival of tea, and then finally they would arrive at the one Arden intended to accept this time, much to his father's shock, he was sure: "Respected Landlord."

He was determined to find some use for himself at Swanmere. He had said he would try.

But the walls seemed very close as he stood with his parents and his not-quite-wife in the small drawing room, which was larger than the entirety of the apartments that he had used to keep in London. He had come to the fire, but it was too hot, so he drifted about the room, listening to the conversation between his parents only sufficiently to put in brief nods and "yes, sirs," at the appropriate pauses.

The dinner. The dismissed second-floor housemaid. The necessity of looking thoroughly into the characters of servants. The sad loss Mr. Forbis would be to the county; he had been an excellent magistrate. No, Arden did not suppose that he would care to consider the position himself.

He stood with his back to a window as the tea arrived.

"Will you pour, Lady Winter?" his mother asked.

He watched Zenia as she did it. She was a little shaky, carrying a cup to his mother. His father declined, only accepting a plate of biscuits.

She looked up at Arden. "Will you take tea?"

The irony of it seemed too keen. She brought the teacup and placed it silently in his hand. He thanked her—in Arabic. Though she ignored his words, she flushed bright pink.

"Pray tell us what he said, Lady Winter," his mother said. "I do think it is so uncivil for someone to speak a foreign language."

"He only thanked me, ma'am, for the tea."

"What a mouthful, merely to say thank you," his father said. "What are the words?"

His question met a long silence. She seemed rooted in place, blushing.

"It's hardly that risque," Arden said. "You can tell them."

"'May Allah reward thee, O my hostess,'" she murmured quickly, turning a deeper red, "'and multiply your children.'" She bit her lip. "It is a common blessing among the Mohammedans."

"A pleasant sentiment," his father said heartily.

His mother sipped her tea. "The heathens always seem inclined to multiply."

Standing beside Zenia, Arden saw her flush turn to white. She took it as a comment on herself—which it might well have been, knowing Lady Belmaine's stiletto methods. "I promised you would have tea with my mother," he said in Arabic. "Pleasant, is it not?"

She cast him a look, an unhappy appeal.

"It is quite rude, Arden, to speak in a foreign language," his mother said.

"I was merely complimenting Lady Winter on how becoming she appears in shoes," he said. "She was barefoot when we met."

Zenia's lips parted. She looked as if she would like to dash his tea in his face.

He didn't know why he said it. He had meant to be cordial. He could not afford to enrage her—his father had informed him that she was withholding her consent to their marriage—and yet he could not help himself. It was the only point of reference he could find with her, a shared language and memory. If they could speak of it, if he could tell her what he remembered and what had happened to him after she was gone, if they could talk of the red sands and the strange mountains of Jabal Shammar and the walls of Hayil; if he could discover his brave and graceful wolf cub in her . . .

He could love her. He would. He already did, but he couldn't find her.

He wanted her; her body inflamed him, even here in the somber dress and cap. But it was strange to him, formed differently, moving differently: he needed to find her inside this new shape.

"That is hardly a time Lady Winter can wish to be reminded of," his mother said. "You are shockingly impudent tonight, Arden."

Which of course he was. "I think I liked her better then," he said, recklessly digging his own grave deeper. "I liked her barefoot."

"What an ungracious thing to say." Lady Belmaine set down her cup.

"Does she always wear shoes?" he asked. "The way Beth always stays in heated rooms?"

"Of course Lady Winter wears shoes. Whatever has got into you, Arden?" His father was scowling at him in a familiar way. He took a long sip of cordial and set the glass down hard on the mantelpiece. "Or need I suppose it is anything more than perversity?"

"Is it perversity, Zenia?" Arden asked, looking at her lowered profile. "Am I to forget everything I knew of you, all the best things, so that you can be an English lady?"

She stood there staring down at her clasped hands. The small bunch of black silk flowers pinned at her throat rose and fell, the only motion about her.

"Tea and seedcakes!" He gave a short laugh, turning away to the window. "Such a very proper lady. You came to the right place for that. My mother is the highest authority in the matter."

"I really must see to Elizabeth," Zenia said—slipping away, escaping him once again. He heard her footsteps hurry across the carpet, and the solid sound of the closing door.

ELIZABETH WAS FUSSY and petulant. Zenia tried to calm her by nursing, but she found to her great distress that her milk was finally and completely gone. Elizabeth sat in her lap and cried. Zenia wanted desperately to weep too—it seemed such a cruel moment to lose the one thing she alone could share with her daughter.

But Elizabeth did not seem to want to share anything with her now. She refused to stay in Zenia's lap, she refused to be rocked or listen to lullabies, and she would not settle into bed, but kept sliding down and reaching to try to open the door to her playroom. If Zenia would not open it, she would begin to wail. So it was standing open when he came.

"It is only until she goes to sleep," Zenia said—but of course the moment that Elizabeth saw him, nothing would do but that she must be picked up and carried on his shoulders. He stripped to his shirtsleeves and hefted her up with a grimace and walked back and forth between the rooms, with Elizabeth cooing happily whenever he ducked under the doorframe.

There was a dangerous moment when she pointed at the outer door and began to whimper, but Lord Winter turned her over in a tumble onto the bed, and she was still tired enough that she lay laughing up at him, tousled and breathless and drowsy-eyed. To Zenia's dismay, he sat down beside her on the bed, then rested on his elbow amid the pillows while Elizabeth clutched his open shirt collar.

She fell asleep with it in her fist. He and Zenia had not once looked at one another.

There was a light knock on the bedroom door—Zenia's nightly tray. The maid came in and put it down and curtsied on her way out. Lord Winter stayed where he was on the bed, and Elizabeth barely fluttered her lashes before she was asleep again.

They must look a real family, Zenia thought. A father and mother and child.

"Eat," he said quietly. "I don't mind."

Her throat felt so tight that she did not think she could force herself to swallow. "I don't care for anything now."

He still had not looked at her. "I understand that you are not yet certain . . . whether you wish to be Lady Winter in fact."

"We will wake her, talking," Zenia said, keeping her voice low. "I think it would be best if you asked your father to arrange for another room for you."

He looked up at her then, a flash of blue. "No," he said.

"Your presence upsets her. I could not get her to bed with the door closed."

"Then leave it open."

"I cannot—" She stood, turning away so that she did not have to look at him.

"Do you think I'm going to ravish you, Lady Winter? Bring in a trundle for the nurse, if you feel the need of more chaperonage."

She heard the bed move, and looked to see him disengaging Elizabeth's fingers. As he rose, Elizabeth rolled over into the warmed depression where his body had been and sighed, relaxing.

Zenia was angry with him. Elizabeth had never let anyone but Zenia lie down with her. Never.

He lifted the silver cover from one of the dishes and ate a

thick slice of cheese. And then she was angry with him because he so easily made himself at home in her room.

"I wish you would leave," she said tightly. "A gentleman would leave, and arrange to sleep elsewhere."

"Oh, a gentleman." He glanced sideways at her. "I'm sure you know all about that."

"Please," she said.

"Beth likes me here."

"She only cares for you because you allow her to do what she should not."

He gave her a long look. "If you insist on keeping her imprisoned, you know, you may find that she doesn't care for you at all."

"I do not keep her *imprisoned*." Zenia expelled a sharp breath. "She goes out whenever the weather is fair. You know nothing of it."

"Zenia—" He moved to the shuttered window, his back to her. His voice was unexpectedly intense. "I know something of it."

"What can you know? You only saw her yesterday for the first time in her life. What do you know of how I've tried to keep her safe? What do you know of what it was like, after—"

He looked back at her. She turned her face away.

"They said the Saudis took you. There was blood on the saddle." Her voice began to shake. "You were dead. And I'm not going to let Elizabeth die! You aren't afraid of anything, you have no sense, you don't care if you kill yourself, and I'm not going to let—"

There was a whimper from the bed as Elizabeth lifted her head. Zenia realized how her voice had risen.

"Please go!" she whispered, sitting down at the desk and staring at the silver dishes. "Just go."

"Zenia—"

"Go. You'll wake her—and I can't bear it if she cries."

He walked past her to the other room. As the door began to close, Elizabeth pushed up on her arms and started to wail.

"Leave it open," Zenia hissed.

It stayed open. The light from the candle on the other side was suddenly snuffed, leaving the doorway dark. Elizabeth peered at it for a long moment, and then laid her small head down again with a satisfied sigh.

ARDEN STOOD IN the estate office, trying not to gaze out the window at the gray sky. His father was leaning over a map spread across the desk, his forefinger pointing at each field in turn. "This was a part of the Lyburn Abbey place, but your grandfather bought it when old gentleman Cole had a stroke. There used to be a tenant, a Mr.—I don't recall his name at the moment. We'll look it up. That red volume, there. No, the green calf. Here." The earl walked impatiently to the bookcase and pulled a ledger down. He opened it on the desk.

Arden flipped the pages. There were endless entries and transactions, all dated forty years before—he had no idea how he could find the name of a tenant from his grandfather's day, or why he was doing it. "Is this man still farming the piece?" he asked.

"Good God, no, he must have passed on a decade ago."

"Need we look him up, then?"

"You must start from the ground, Winter." His father sat down behind the desk again. "This is the sort of thing you must learn if you wish to be a responsible landlord. Help him out, Mr. Pinkney."

"The tenant was Samuel Brown, your lordship," the bailiff said. He was a silent man with a full white beard and a sizable paunch for his five-and-a-half feet of height. Arden was informed that he farmed a large portion of the estate himself, but Mr. Pinkney was not forthcoming on this or any other topic.

"No, no," the earl said. "I meant you must help him out in looking it up. He needs to learn—well, never mind that for the moment. What was in the Abbey field last year, Mr. Pinkney?"

"Wheat, your lordship."

"And what are we to put in this winter?"

"Wheat, your lordship."

"And I suppose that the rough plowing will begin soon?"

"The field is already plowed and harrowed, your lordship."

"Excellent." The earl nodded toward Arden. "You see that a good mild winter has us well ahead. No frozen ground to put us behind this year."

"Yes, sir," Arden said. He thought of taking Beth for walks through the winter woods, showing her the holes in the trees and the animal tracks, and caught his gaze stealing toward the window again.

"Are we plowing anywhere at the moment, Mr. Pinkney?" the earl asked.

"The clay bottoms, your lordship."

"Ah! We haven't talked about the bottoms. The drainage—very neccessary to keep the ditches in repair. Take him down this afternoon, Mr. Pinkney, and let him look at the ditches. He can watch the plowing. If you change into something suitable, Winter, you can put your own hand to a row. I daresay you won't find it as easy as it looks. Good lesson for you."

"Yes, sir," Arden said, feeling his jaw tighten. He exhaled and deliberately relaxed it.

"Mr. Pinkney, I trust you to take care that he doesn't get in a tangle with the oxen. They're not like horses, Winter. Quite the opposite—walk right over you if you don't watch yourself. Perhaps you'd best let the boys do the plowing after all. I wouldn't like to see you get hurt by a damn foolish pair of bullocks."

"No, sir," Arden said.

"Now, what's next? Here, put this volume back. The miller's

field. You'll want to have Mr. Pinkney show you the bounds and corners."

"Why?" Arden asked.

The earl paused. "Do you know them?"

"No."

"Then learn them. You must know the bounds and corners."

Arden's gaze wandered to the window again. He leaned against the sill. "Yes, sir."

"The miller's field is always in hay," his father said. "And the piece by the dairy. Where else?"

The question was sudden. Arden realized, belatedly, that he was being quizzed. "Where else?" he repeated.

"What else have I said is in hay?"

"Nowhere that you've mentioned."

"I believe I mentioned the second half of the Abbey place—did I not, Mr. Pinkney?"

"You did speak of the Abbey place, your lordship."

"I thought I had. You should be writing this down, Winter. Pull up that chair. Mr. Pinkney, get him a pen and paper."

Mr. Pinkney opened a plain deal cabinet and handed Arden a book and fountain pen. Arden sat down. He made a note. *Miller's, dairy, 2nd part Abbey—always in hay. Learn the bounds and corners.* He was perfectly sure that no one had said anything at all about hay on the second half of the Abbey place.

His father leaned over the map again. "Now, the old dairy—what have we done about replacing that poor fellow, Mr. Pinkney?"

"Mr. Fenton is grazing there until your lordship pleases to make a change."

"Yes, the bloody fence. I really don't see the need. What do you think, Winter?"

"I have no idea what you're speaking of."

"Should we enclose the west wood?" his father said, with a vague, impatient wave of his hand over the map. "I really don't see the need."

"Oh, neither do I," Arden agreed blandly.

"Mr. Fenton seems content," the bailiff said.

The earl nodded. "Good. We're all in agreement, then. I suggest you make a note about the tenant."

While his father watched him, Arden wrote *Old dairy—tenant content*.

"In fact, Winter, why don't you manage that yourself?"

"Manage what?" Arden asked.

"Putting in the new tenant," his father said in a tone of slightly strained patience. "Replace the old fellow who died."

"I suggest that Farmer Dingle would be the best choice, your lordship," Mr. Pinkney said. "He will take it for two and a half."

"Good. Good. That will do."

"But doesn't Fenton have it?" Arden asked.

"No, no, we don't want Fenton to continue grazing there," his father said. "Not at all. He complains of the fence."

"I thought he was content with the fence."

"Arden," his father said, "I'm afraid lack of attention has always been one of your besetting faults."

Arden turned his face down to the book. He set his teeth hard together. *Fence*, he wrote. *Pay attention*.

"Shall we have some coffee, gentlemen?" Lord Belmaine asked expansively as he tilted back his chair. "Ring the bell if you please, Winter. What a pleasant morning. A bit damp—I advise you to take your greatcoat this afternoon."

"Yes, sir," Arden said. He stood up and pulled the bell rope.

The earl looked at him, smiling warmly. "It's very fine to have you working here. It does me good to see it."

"Yes, sir," Arden said.

His father looked out the window. "What a pleasant morning!" he said in a glad voice.

ARDEN WASN'T ALLOWED to visit Beth at midday. She was conveniently sleeping, he was notified by the nurse posted at the bottom of the stairs. He could hear Beth shrieking, but he didn't press the poor woman, who looked so guilty and harassed that he took pity on her. He was feeling rather suffocated by authority himself.

"I'll come back later," he said, "Mrs.—?"

She curtsied. "I'm called Sutton, my lord."

"All my nurses were Sutton, and the governesses too," he said with a wry smile. "What is your real name?"

"Henrietta Lamb, sir."

"I'll come back later, Mrs. Lamb. When do you think would be best?"

She lifted her face. She had a worried look, her straight brown hair pulled back tight under her cap. "I'm not certain what would be best, my lord. My lady feels that—Miss Elizabeth's health requires complete peace and quiet, without visitors."

Arden felt a rush of anger. But he said, in a dead level voice, "That is very well, but since I am her father, and not a visitor, you may inform Lady Winter that I will come for Miss Elizabeth's daily walk at four. I expect both of them to be ready to accompany me."

"Yes, my lord."

"Thank you, Mrs. Lamb."

She dipped a curtsy and hurried up the stairs as he turned away.

HE SAID NOTHING at all when he came, promptly at four, as he had warned. Zenia was ready. She was exhausted, Beth was exhausted, they had spent the morning and afternoon in a series of tantrums about everything from putting on socks to eating carrots to changing napkins. Elizabeth had cried when Zenia had left her with the nurse and cried when she stayed.

Zenia had been determined that she would not give in to the fits. She tried soft words and teasing, she tried to be firm, she tried pulling Elizabeth in her wagon—she even spanked when Elizabeth bit her hand. But she had found that her daughter's will far outpaced her own. By four o'clock, for the first time in Elizabeth's life, Zenia was willing to relinquish her to someone else.

But she wanted to weep when her daughter's face lit at the sight of him. Zenia started to lift her from the crib, but Elizabeth pushed her away, reaching with a happy squeal for her father.

Zenia sat down by the window, looking out, chewing her lip hard.

"Please do not take her outside," she said, without turning.

"It isn't very chill—"

"Do *not*. She isn't dressed for it."

"Yes. All right."

There was a silence. She waited for the sound of his footsteps to carry Elizabeth away.

"Are you not coming with us?" he asked.

"She does not wish for me to go, I assure you."

There was another long and awkward pause. Zenia pulled the handkerchief from her sleeve and wrapped it around her fingers and hoped that he would leave before her composure broke.

"Well," he said, "I wish it."

He was scowling when she looked at him. She turned her face down at her lap, just for a moment, just to govern the threatening tremble of her lip.

"Then don't," he said shortly, angrily. And he walked out of the room, and she lost her chance.

Nineteen

———⟨∞⟩———

"IT's BEEN A week," Lord Winter said. His voice held a barely perceptible, unfamiliar slur. "Have you heard nothing yet from Mr. Bruce?"

He was handsomely dressed, having just come up from the Christmas dinner for the tenants. It had gone on all afternoon and deep into the evening, the long tables lining the marble hall, the rumble of conversation drifting up the stairs. Elizabeth had missed her daily walk about the house with him—she was moody but quiet, not even pleased with her father at the moment. She kicked her feet and turned away when he bent over the crib to kiss her.

He straightened, watching Zenia work the small woolen socks and tie the ribbons as she changed Elizabeth into her nightgown. There was a strong aura of tobacco smoke about him, and another scent, sweet and potent on his breath—neither of which

Zenia had ever perceived on him before. When he would normally move away and keep a space between them, he did not.

"No, I haven't had an answer," she said.

"It's been a week," he said again.

There was a faint undertone of accusation in his voice. Zenia was puzzled and worried herself as to why she hadn't had a letter from her father, but she only said shortly, "It is the Christmas season."

Still he did not move away. She could feel him looking at her. If she turned her face, his shoulder would be at level with her eyes, his black satin stock and velvet lapels so close she could touch them just by leaning toward him.

"Was your dinner congenial?" she asked impersonally.

Arden made a sound, not a pleasant one, deep in his throat. And because he was intoxicated for the first time in thirteen years, he muttered, "No. I'm wretched ill at ease in company."

Zenia looked at him in surprise. He rested his hand on the edge of the crib. His blue eyes held a glitter; his mouth was set in a mocking curl. But as he stood there watching her, something like wistfulness came into his face.

"I am perverse," he said. "Hopelessly perverse." He pronounced the words with a diligent clarity, as if they adhered to his tongue. "I should like to kiss you." He blinked at her, slow and lazy. "I would be a great fool to do it, would I not?"

Zenia felt the blood come up into her face. She looked down at Elizabeth. "Perhaps not," she said, so barely above a breath that she doubted he heard.

He pushed away from the crib, wandering off as if he had forgotten her. Zenia stood still a moment, and then finished tying Elizabeth's ribbons. She lifted her daughter from the crib. And this time, for the first time, Elizabeth turned away from Lord Winter and didn't want to go to him to ride on his shoulders.

"Mama." She snuggled her face down in Zenia's shoulder, curling her fists up and pushing them in her eyes.

Zenia left him standing in the middle of the playroom with an expression like a rejected suitor's and took Elizabeth into the bedchamber, laying her down among the pillows. She leaned over and put her face next to Elizabeth's sleepy one. "He doesn't smell so very wonderful tonight, does he?" she whispered into Elizabeth's pink ear.

"Gah-ha," Elizabeth said. "Na-na-na-na-gah!"

"I don't mind it," she whispered.

"Pah!"

"Perhaps I'm not so nice as you," Zenia murmured, with a daring rise of her heart, "to spurn a kiss."

Elizabeth reached up, pulling at her hair. A loose comb gave way, and dark curls fell down in a shower on her daughter's face. It made Elizabeth flinch and laugh. Zenia loved to watch her laugh.

Elizabeth turned over onto her front and Zenia pulled the bedclothes up, smoothing them over her. She was already dropping off to sleep, facing away from the door, when Zenia snuffed the candle beside the bed.

For a week, that door had stood open. He came at four to take Elizabeth for her walk about the house, then returned her. Elizabeth took her dinner in the proper nursery down the hall, leaving the playroom to him for an hour to change into his silks, and then he disappeared while Zenia changed and the nurse looked after Elizabeth. Zenia went up early after dinner and made all her bedtime preparations, and whatever Lord Winter made of his own was done in the dark after he had put out the light on his side. As the routine had crystallized, Elizabeth had become less fussy. But she still would not allow the door to be closed. Zenia looked around at it now, pushing back her hair.

She could close it. Elizabeth was already fast asleep and un-likely to wake, from the sound of her steady snuffling snores.

Zenia went to the door. He was sitting in the wooden nurse's chair, gazing away into a dim corner of the room. He had pulled his stock and neckcloth off. They dangled from his hand, black and white.

She held onto the doorknob. She could feel her own pulse in her throat. The candlelight made a seductive sculpture of his face, falling on his cheek and jaw and mouth; his blue eyes pensive, focused far away on nothing.

"I'm sorry that your dinner was not agreeable," she said.

His head turned toward her. He stood up. For a moment he looked at her with that lazy, strange lift to his black lashes. "Your hair is down," he said.

She had forgotten. But the way he looked at her—she suddenly became conscious. A woman's hair was her glory, to be shown only to her husband among the Moslemin. Even in England all women wore their hair pinned up under caps and bonnets.

She flushed, reduced to the barefoot Bedu boy with hair falling in a tangle to her shoulders. "I'm sorry. Elizabeth pulled it down. I'll put it up," she said, turning.

"No," he said. "Must you?"

She hesitated in the doorway.

"Sit down," he said, with a little stilted bow toward the chair. "Or—is she asleep? Should I put out the candles?"

Zenia pulled the door halfway closed behind her. "Light does not make much difference. She is either ready to sleep or not. I think she has already gone now."

"Ah," he said.

She hovered near the door. "But perhaps you are tired."

"No," he said. "Not at all. Quite rested." Then his mouth turned up in an ironic twist. "It's not as if I do anything all day."

Zenia sat down in the hard-backed nurse's chair. "Your father said that you are working in the management of the estate."

"Oh yes," he said. "What a prodigious great farmer I am." The ale confused his tongue on "prodigious," and he said it again, with an abashed smile. "I beg your pardon. I am—a little on the go."

"On the go?"

"Well," he admitted, "I am three parts drunk."

Zenia had once or twice seen servants of her mother's drunk, but it was a very unusual thing, only when they had managed to steal bottles from the gifts of wine Lady Hester had sometimes received from Christian visitors. In the desert, of course, there was no such thing as alcohol—it was forbidden to the faithful, and worth a man's life among the Wahhabis. She watched Lord Winter with a wary curiosity, never having seen him take more than a glass of wine at dinner.

Except for the scent and the slur, and the indolent drift of his eyelashes downward and up again, which gave him something of a piratical air, he did not seem affected. He was very steady on his feet. He didn't appear to be about to crash into any walls or hit anyone.

"I have been learning bounds and corners," he said, with a tilt of his head toward the window. "And looking at ditches. And keeping my distance from a pair of perilous bullocks, so they may not put a scratch upon me."

"Oh?" Zenia said, puzzled.

He sat down on the cot. "You are mightily impressed, I see. So you should be. It is hard." He leaned his forehead on the heels of his hands, pushing his fingers into his hair. "It is damnably hard." He shook his head. "I don't know if I can do it."

In the worst days in the desert, she had never heard that muffled note of despair in his voice.

Zenia pressed her hands together. "I have always thought," she said quietly, "that you could do anything."

He lifted his head. "Have you," he said, with a sideways look at her.

"Yes," she said.

He stared at her for a long moment. "I've thought the same of you. Zenia. The flower that can grow anywhere." He smiled slightly. "Even here."

She hugged her knees to her breast, curling in the chair. "It's not so difficult here. It's easy."

"Oh, it is that," he agreed. "Do you know—I think we're both changelings. You were born here, to be a lady, and I at Dar Joon to be a natural savage, but the fairies changed us." He shook his head. "It was a cruel trick."

She looked at him in wonder. "You would not wish to be born to this? You would prefer Dar Joon?"

"I am perverse," he said.

"You are a madman," she said in disgust.

He smiled suddenly. "Ah. Little wolf. Sometimes I discover you, still here. Still with me."

"I wish to forget all that," she said into the muffle of her gown and robe.

"Why?" he asked, in a low voice that suddenly made her throat ache. "Why do you want to forget?"

She lifted her head. "You will not understand."

"Because you want to be a lady?" His lashes made the slow downward sweep, his gaze traveling over her. "If you sit in that unladylike way, I must advise you, I cannot answer for my actions at present."

She sat up, putting her feet on the floor. "Perhaps I should go to bed."

He looked at her with a open gleam of hunger. "I've not

touched a woman since you. And now I have to sleep on this cot, knowing you're there, just beyond that door." He stood up, kicking a stray block aside. It landed with a violent thump against the chest of drawers. "If sleep is the word for it."

Zenia rose, moving toward the door, listening for a sound from Elizabeth. But none came, and she hesitated. He had already turned away, sweeping up his cravat and neckcloth from the cot and tossing them over the clotheshorse.

"I suppose it's different for you," he muttered, pulling off his coat. "I suppose fine ladies don't lie in bed and burn. A well-known truth, my boy!" He unbuttoned his waistcoat, as if he thought she was gone, and dropped it in the direction of the horse. The waistcoat missed, sliding to the floor. "An exceedingly well-known truth."

While Zenia watched, he pulled his shirt loose. With a faint groan, he dragged it over his shoulders.

His bare back was tanned a deep gold in the candle's glow, with deeper shadows across the play of muscle as he moved. But her eyes went instantly to the great scar that ran from his lower rib up beneath his right arm, a ruddy irregular wound that had not healed well, overlaid and extended to his chest by unmistakable burn marks, where red-hot brands had been pulled from the fire to sear against the lacerated skin, the Bedouins' answer to any injury.

He dropped the shirt, turning. When he saw her, he grew still. And the desert came back between them, sharp and real. She knew what had happened; she knew him, that he would not have made a sound as they cut and probed with a knife for the bullet and then poured boiling molasses in the open gash, or cried out when they laid on the brands. It was a wound that should have killed him, by degrees, a slow dying in heat and thirst.

He said nothing. He leaned over, pressing heavily on the cot, and dragged the blankets and sheets free of their neat tuck. Zenia watched him, the strong line of his back as he stretched, the little wayward step he took for balance as he rose. She could hardly remember how it had felt when he made Elizabeth inside her. It had hurt, but she had wanted him, wanted him as close as she could make him.

"If you keep at this pretty lingering," he said, taking a pillow from the wardrobe and tossing it down, "you may find yourself playing Lady Winter in the most intimate possible manner."

She was going to be his wife. He had agreed to it. There was really no reason for this waiting. She knew what her father must say; she knew what was best for Elizabeth.

He straightened, with that leisurely lift of his lashes, a sidelong look toward her. "I am dead in earnest, Zenia."

"You may kiss me, if you like," she said.

It clearly caught him short. He stood with his hand still on the wardrobe door. She lifted her chin a little. Her heart was flooding her face with heat.

"You realize, of course," he said mockingly, "that in England, if a gentleman kisses a lady, she must marry him out of hand."

"Well," she said, with a nonchalant shrug.

" 'Well.' " The ghost of an ironic smile curved his mouth. "A most ladylike answer." He leaned on the edge of the open door, crossing his arms. "Nothing so honest as yes or no."

"You said that you would like to kiss me. I said yes, you may."

His expression grew intense, his gaze traveling up over her, from her hem to her waist to her breasts and lips. "If I do it, Zenia," he said slowly, "I'll be damned if I stop there. And that will be the end of this farce. You will marry me tomorrow."

She stood still, feeling weightless, breathless—uncertain of what she wanted, unable to move. She ran her tongue over her lips and saw him instantly fix his gaze on her mouth.

He pushed away from the door and moved near her. She thought he was going to touch her, but he stood before her, looking down. She was as tall as any Englishwomen she had yet seen, as tall or taller than most Bedouin men, but gazing straight ahead she saw only the arc of muscle from the base of his throat, the line of his jaw and his mouth. She would have to look up to meet his eyes.

"Tomorrow, Zenia," he said softly, "we will marry. The license is ready; the parson will come on a moment's notice. Tomorrow this foolishness ends."

Somewhere in her mind, there was a reason why she should think, a consequence she would be reckless to forget—but she could only comprehend the magnetic heat of him so near to her. She could only remember his body lying over hers, the weight of him.

"You would not—" she whispered, and then no more, afraid to ask if he would ever send her away from Elizabeth—from him—afraid of the answer, helpless to turn aside from the touch of his fingers against her cheek, his mouth lowered to her lips.

"Zenia," he murmured. His hand spread in her hair, tangled in it, tilting her face up to his, drawing her to him. "Zenia. My God, please."

But there was no pleading in his kiss; there was only possession—the thrust and taste of him. The alcohol was a heavy perfume, filling all the air she breathed.

He slid his arm behind her waist. She felt the scar beneath her palm as she slipped her hands upward, over his bare back. She turned her face suddenly and leaned her cheek against his chest, holding him tight and close. She pressed her face to the deep rise and fall of his breathing.

They stood still. She could feel the slight, slight sway of his unbalance, the soft rocking of his hold in time to each indrawn breath. He played with the hair that draped down beside her cheek, stroking it back behind her ear, kissing the top of her head, her temple, her lashes as he made her lift her face again with his fingers beneath her chin.

He kissed her deeply. Her body seemed to tremble and ache with yearning as his hands slipped beneath the loose wrap of her dressing gown, outlining her waist, moving upward.

"So long," he murmured, "it's been so long." His mouth moved over her eyelids and her brows and her temple, soft heat as he spoke. "I can't believe you're real."

She felt him brush the hair back from her shoulder. As he bent and kissed her bared throat, he pushed open her robe and drew it down from her shoulders. It fell, leaving only her linen gown.

He touched her breasts. Zenia whimpered. Her own sensations, her own need for this frightened her. She had never in her life been held close, never by anyone but him. He somehow knew secrets about her, knew how to make her body suffer sweet agony, sweet electric pain. He caressed the tips of her breasts, compressed them between his fingers, and a jolt of pleasure sent light delicious throbbing all through her.

But will you stay? she thought desperately. *Will you always keep me with you?*

She could not voice those fears. Her mother, Miss Williams, Lord Winter—all of the pieces of her heart she had ever given had been scattered or lost or thrown away. All but Elizabeth. She did not think she had the courage to love beyond Elizabeth, and yet her body cried for his, to be held close, to be part of him again.

Do you want me? she beseeched him silently as he pulled her down beside him on the cot, as he kissed the back of her neck and slid his hand beneath her gown and drew it up to her hip. *Do you want* me, *and not just your daughter? Not just a woman to use this way?*

If she turned and lay back and opened to him, if he mounted into her as he had done before, as his hands and his body and his kisses demanded—if she took his seed inside her again, she would be consenting to his dominion forever. Tomorrow he would marry her. She would not have to fear hunger or want, never again. She would only have to wait until he left her.

Because he would leave. She knew it to the depth of her soul; had heard it in his voice. *I don't know if I can do it*, he said—and she knew that he could not. His demon drove him to wilderness and ruin; he only stayed now because of Elizabeth. And she feared—oh, she feared to desperation that he would take Elizabeth with him if he could.

She shuddered, alive with desire and grief as he ran his fingers between her legs. He laid her down, leaning over her, fumbling at the band of his trousers. She could feel the same tremor in him that seemed to weaken her—his hand was inept at the simple task of buttons.

"Too damn foxed," he muttered. Then he smiled at her—such a smile, charming and wicked, and drew her hand to the fastening. "Will you help me, beloved?"

He rested on his elbow, his eyes half-closed in anticipated bliss, beguiling and seductive and dark and warm, the cruel beauty of the desert softened and gentled to the shape of a man.

Zenia did as he asked. She had always done what he had asked of her, resisted and surrendered and fallen in love with him, followed him in misery and glad compliance. Her fingers touched his hard shaft, and he groaned as if he hurt. He bent and sucked her breast and pushed himself into her hand.

Her head seemed full of sound, the beat of her own heart in her ears. She arched upward, her fingers closing in a convulsive caress each time his tongue stroked over her nipple. He moved in her hand, a velvety thrust in rhythm with the low animal moan in his throat. She heard something else—but he was shifting eagerly to come on top of her, bluntly pushing to enter her—until the sound came clear to both of them.

He stilled. The quiet knock at the door of her room was perfectly audible.

"That will be my supper tray," Zenia said faintly.

He stared down at her with blank incomprehension. Then he snarled, "God damn it to bleeding hell," and pushed up abruptly.

She could see that he was going to shout something at the wall, and moved quickly to put her fingers over his mouth. "Elizabeth," she whispered, edging from underneath him. At first she did not think he would let her go—his hand closed on her waist—but then he released her and rolled back into the narrow space, lying against the wall with his elbow over his eyes.

The knock came again. Zenia grabbed up her robe and pulled it about her as she hurried into the other room, closing the door behind her.

ARDEN WAITED. THROUGH the wall, he heard the soft thud of the outer door as the maid left. At first he thought Zenia must come back immediately—he was in such a state of suspension and arousal that he could not imagine she would not instantly come back, that she had even summoned the command of herself to leave him.

In his drink-bemused brain, he thought she must feel as he did. But gradually, as she did not come at once, it occurred to him that she was female, and different. He opened his eyes and stared at the dark, unfocused blur of his arm lying across his face.

It was her supper, of course. She would be hungry. He could hardly conceive of any other hunger at the moment but the urge to bury himself in her, to hold her and taste her and die with her. But she was female, and different. He occupied himself with erotic thoughts, remembering the shape of her body—her breasts, full and womanly; remembering that moment he had seen her nursing Beth; seized at the thought of it by an intense and driving lust to put another child in her.

He turned over, burying his face in the pillow, waiting.

She didn't come. He had no idea of how much time had passed, but it seemed to him long enough to finish four dozen scones and drink ten pots of tea.

He sat up. Perhaps she had become shy. Perhaps she was waiting for him.

For a long time he looked at the door between their rooms. He kept thinking the knob would turn: his whole being seemed fixed on the expectation, while in his mind a slow, small doubt began to form.

He rose, walking to the door. And when he got there, a deep dread that it would be locked held him motionless, unable to touch it. He listened for any sound, any sign from the other side.

Only silence.

"Zenia," he said to the polished wood.

She did not answer. He knew it was locked. He touched the brass plate, traced the engraved curls with his finger. He stared dumbly at the fine golden grain of oak.

If not for Beth, he would have kicked it down.

Twenty

◦◦◦◦

ARDEN LAY WITH his eyes closed, unwilling to admit daylight and anger, but loathe to fall back into the dreams. In them, he kept trying to swim, trying to reach the gray shape among the murky waterweeds, but he couldn't make his limbs move. The girl's white dead face would change to Zenia's face, her voice silent, underwater, and still calling and calling him for help.

Sometime in the dawn, the maid had come in to make up the fire. He had sat up in the dim light, confused and so thirsty that he downed half a pitcher of water, but it made him dizzy and drunk again, dragging him back down into the dreams. He lay now with no clear idea of how late it was, only that it was very late, and his belly held a sick shudder and his head felt as if there was a ten-inch stake driven through it.

He felt wounded and demoralized in the aftereffects of drink.

It had been a long, long time—but the physical sensations brought acute recollection of a more horrible awakening. The dreams were dreams; he had no real memory of the girl calling for him to help her, or of seeing her beneath the water. It was a hole in time and space: he could remember starting to drink in his room, he could remember sharing the flask with a sympathetic stableboy, he could remember the way the neckcloth had seemed a confusion in his hands as he dressed to meet her, and filling the flask again and again from the decanters in the dining room— then a kaleidoscope of moments, the way she had looked at him, quiet and frightened, the still lake, the chipped paint on the oar, the way the black swan had paddled aggressively after the boat, hissing and lifting its wings. He had laughed. She had screamed when the swan hissed. And that was all. Except that he thought he remembered sitting on the bank, dripping and crying, but he was not sure.

They said that he had tried to save her. That she had foolishly stood up, trying to avoid the swan, and turned the boat over. His father and two gardeners had testified before the coroner that they had seen it happen, that Arden had tried to pull her to the bank, but she was so hysterical with fear that she fought anything that touched her. His father had had the swan shot.

Arden did not remember that. He remembered nothing more. And no one had thought it anything more than a tragic accident. What man would deliberately drown his fiancée, after all?

But the way his father had looked at him. It had been like this—waking up, sick and groggy, and his father waiting . . .

He turned his face into the pillow.

He had left Swanmere, and he had never come back. It had been years before he had touched any drink again, before he could smell alcohol without it turning his stomach. And then he had only sipped at it, a public observance, to be less conspicuous, less painfully alien among his peers.

He had killed her, and yet it had been his emancipation. He had loved his exile. He had felt alive and real, alone. It was with people that he floundered; it was living as himself that he made into a debacle. As Haj Hasan, he knew what to say and do. As the Honorable Arden Mansfield, Lord Winter, he was and had always been baffled and uneasy.

He should not have allowed himself to sit there drinking the ale they kept pouring last night. He had known he was becoming drunk. He was certain he had done nothing awkward there, if sitting in nearly complete silence with a diligent smile on his face was not awkward. All of the tenants had been excruciatingly polite to him, as stilted as he, while his father had shaken hands and slapped shoulders and asked about grain and bulls and probably corners as well—the perfect open-handed English lord.

No, it was after the dinner, in this room, that Arden had made a perfect fool of himself. And there was no merciful alcoholic void this time. It was all quite clear in his mind.

He heard a door open. The maid, he thought with an interior groan, but the soft thump of running feet and a bright inquisitive, "Gah!" followed closely. Two small warm hands hit his bare arm.

He turned his head, allowing one eye to show above his elbow. Beth's face was full of anticipation, her dark eyes round and her lips parted.

"Gah-on," she said, pushing at his arm.

As he rose onto his elbows, she laughed and squealed, and made his whole life worth living for that one moment. But he remembered that last night she had turned away from him, and he did not try to reach out and pull her into his arms as he wanted to do.

"Miss Elizabeth!" a voice whispered urgently from the crack of the door. "Come here this moment!"

It was the nurse. Arden stiffened, waiting to hear Zenia, but when the door opened a little wider, it was only Mrs. Lamb who peeked in.

"Oh, sir!" she said, still in a whisper. "Beg pardon! Come, Miss Elizabeth!"

"No need," Arden said, his voice hoarse with sleep and drink. "No—she can stay." He groped for his shirt, which lay on the floor beside the cot, and managed some degree of modesty.

Beth ran to her white-painted toy wardrobe and banged on the door. Arden rose, took a deep breath to conquer the dizzy lurch of his stomach, and opened it for her. Within a moment, she had blocks and balls and a rag doll out on the floor.

The nurse was still hovering just the other side of the door— he could see her fingers holding it cracked open. "Is Lady Winter there?" he asked tentatively.

"No, sir," the disembodied voice said. "She's gone to Oxford with her ladyship. If you please, I'm to keep Miss Elizabeth to-day, sir."

He had not really thought she was there. And yet to know that she was not—to know that she had gone away, deliberately, as she had shut the door between them last night . . . he felt his throat tighten in a painful mixture of rage and rejection.

He made a stack of clean clothing for himself, threw his razor and kit on top and pulled open the door, almost dragging a star-tled Mrs. Lamb off her feet. "I'll dress in the bedroom. Please put Beth in whatever it is she's to wear outside and bring her down-stairs in an hour," he said. "Then you may see to other things, or take the afternoon free, if you like. I'll look after her today."

"Oh, sir!"

He walked past her. "And we'll want a basket of food. Lots of sweet biscuits for Beth. Mrs. Patterson knows what I like."

The nurse was staring at him in dismay as he dumped his things on the bed. "Sir, I believe Lady Winter would be most displeased."

He smiled at her. "I am a truant by nature, Mrs. Lamb. And as the cat has elected to leave the mousehole unguarded—" He shrugged. "We shall have one day of freedom, anyway. When do their ladyships propose to return?"

"I'm sorry, sir—Lady Winter did not say."

"Perhaps you will keep a close eye on the drive, and send up a flare when their carriage appears."

"It is very bad, sir," Mrs. Lamb said with a severity that did not quite reach her eyes. "I do not like to deceive ma'am."

"Mrs. Lamb," he said, "you would not peach on us?"

She was a sweet-faced woman; the strict purse of her lips could hardly make her look rigid, besides the fact that she kept her eyes carefully averted from his half-dressed state. "I'll have you know, sir, that I raised three little brothers all quite on my own, besides two boys with the Hastings and four with the Thorpes. I know all about boys."

"Beth is a girl," he pointed out mildly.

"Yes, sir," she said with a curtsy, "but you and she together will be as bad."

There was a crash from the playroom. Mrs. Lamb nodded, exclaiming, "There, you see!" and darted after her charge.

BY THE AFTERNOON, Zenia was anxious to start home. She had never left Elizabeth so long before, and Lady Belmaine sat at length with her elderly cousins, holding the hand of the bedridden lady who could no longer speak above a whisper, talking to the lady's anxious sister, sending Zenia out for a particular physic from a particular apothecary so that the sister might sleep better, instructing the cook on precisely how to prepare the larder of special foods they had brought from Swanmere.

In spite of her apprehension about Elizabeth, Zenia was glad to help as she could; indeed she was surprised to see this new side of Lady Belmaine, the calm efficiency with which she put a house that had fallen to shambles back into order. She was not openly affectionate or sentimental—she cut short the sister's weeping with a brisk admonition—but by the time they took leave, the ladies were as comfortable as they could be made, and even smiling.

"We shall return next week," Lady Belmaine said to Zenia as the carriage rolled past the gray spires and towers of the university. "I shall arrange for game to be sent in the meantime, and some of our own eggs. It is not possible to obtain truly wholesome eggs in town."

The bells were tolling, and a few young men in flapping robes ran down the street in the clear winter sun, still at their studies even during the Christmas vacation. Lady Belmaine made a comment on the noise, and regretted that her cousins could not be removed to a quieter place, even to Swanmere.

"But they will not hear of it," she said, a little impatiently. "They have lived in that house since they were born, and their parents before them. I must say that I have never understood the appeal of such a limpetlike existence, but it is the widespread disposition."

"I can understand it, ma'am," Zenia said quietly. "To have a home, and not wish to leave it."

Lady Belmaine looked straight ahead at the elegant gray satin of the forward seat. "You are not very like your mother, then."

Zenia lowered her gaze to her lap. It was the first time Lady Belmaine had ever mentioned her mother. "No. Not very."

"At one time, I was a great admirer of Lady Hester."

Zenia looked toward her, surprised again. The countess kept her chin erect, her white skin glowing pure, only slightly wrinkled in the harsh winter light.

"She carried her independence far to excess, however," Lady Belmaine said. "Did you know that we are related?"

"No," Zenia said, shocked.

"At a considerable distance. We share a maternal grandfather at some four or five removes. Robert Pitt. The son of Diamond Pitt. My descent is through the Camelford line—yours through both the Chathams and the Stanhopes."

Zenia was well aware of her own lineage—her mother had spoken of her ancestry with endless arrogance and pleasure. Lady Hester had been the granddaughter of one prime minister and the niece of another; she had reveled in telling stories of the ruthlessness of the family patriarch, Diamond Pitt, that turbulent, reckless Indian trader who had defied law and the East India Company for his fortune, and of her proud, murderous cousin Lord Camelford: the most accomplished duelist of his day, champion of the poor against swindlers and extortioners with methods more suited to a bloodthirsty pasha than an English gentleman; a peer who had handed out a hundred guineas in the street to vagrants and whipped turnpike keepers for passing bad halfpennies, and died in a challenge at dawn before he was thirty. When Lady Hester had ordered a flock of goats shot because the shepherd was cheating her, or bastinadoed a servant for insubordination, or defied some emir's tyranny, she had cited Lord Camelford's example as her guide.

"I did not know that, ma'am," Zenia said.

"The blood of Diamond Pitt," Lady Belmaine mused. "The flame from the East. It is a difficult inheritance. Dangerous, some might say. There has been genius—I would not say your grandfather and great-grandfather were anything less—but there is a dark side. It is not to be trifled with. Your mother was inclined to go too far with her passions."

Zenia could not deny that. She stared away from Lady Belmaine, out the window.

"Would you say that your mother was imbalanced in her mind?" the countess asked calmly.

"No," Zenia said. "I know that to Frankish—that is, I know people here have thought so—but it is different in the East, ma'am. It is more fierce. She was made to fit that life."

"I see," the countess said. "But you are not."

"No, ma'am. Not at all. I hated it."

Lady Belmaine was silent for a moment. Then she said, with no change in her impersonal voice, "Are you very much attached to my son?"

Zenia felt a strange confusion flood her. She turned her face away, unable to think of what to say.

"I will be blunt," the countess said. "I would prefer that you were not his wife."

"Yes, ma'am," Zenia said. "I have known that."

"You will of course believe it is because of your objectionable birth and upbringing. If I had not come to know you, I should indeed be appalled by such a marriage in my family, but that is no longer so. I do not dislike you, Zenobia, in yourself."

"Thank you, ma'am," Zenia replied in a small, confounded voice.

"While we thought my son dead, I was quite willing to accept you as my daughter-in-law. You are quiet and tractable, and really, there was no alternative, was there? But now I am constrained to say that this tripling of dangerous blood, this uniting of the most wayward strains of the Pitt inheritance—I have listened to your daughter's fits in the past weeks, and it has made me fearful."

"Elizabeth is very good," Zenia said quickly. "It is only that Lord Winter allows her too much license."

Lady Belmaine's face was utterly expressionless. "I think that you have no understanding of your daughter, Zenobia. I think you have no understanding of my son. My husband has never understood, either." She took her hand from inside her muff and stuffed the handkerchief she had been holding into her reticle, but not before Zenia saw that the lacy edge had been shredded into oblivion.

"What am I to understand, ma'am?" Zenia asked uneasily.

"Why, if you cannot see it for yourself, I do not suppose I can describe it. But neither of them will be content with a home, Zenobia. Neither of them will be caged. I lost my son because my husband would not see that. I might have had him for a little while, in his boyhood. At least until his passions came upon him naturally, but that was not to be. I was deceived by my own up-bringing; I supposed that he could be disciplined and curbed as I was. But it was a very great mistake. I knew him as my husband never could. I knew him as myself."

"My daughter is perfectly happy," Zenia said sharply.

The countess turned, looked aside at Zenia with a lift of her eyebrows. "I do not say that every spoiled child is possessed of a demon—"

"She has no demon!" Zenia cried hotly.

"—but the fact that your volatile blood does not appear to manifest itself in your character does not cleanse you of it. And it runs entirely true in my son."

Zenia stared at her, breathing unevenly.

"Can you say that it does not?" the countess asked. "That he will not do any outrageous thing that he wills, with no care for the cost?"

Zenia dropped her eyes. She twisted the tassled ends of her reticule so tightly around her fingers that they began to throb.

"If you had been brought up under the most respectable roof in England, I should have opposed any marriage between you and my son," Lady Belmaine said. "There is no sense in courting disaster by compounding again the bloodline that produced your mother's unstable nature. You have a daughter already. We may pray that she escapes the danger. But if you were willing to set my son—and yourself—free of this blighted connection, I would be anxious to aid you, and see to your welfare and my granddaughter's."

Zenia watched the silken checkstrap sway in rhythm with the motion of the carriage. She thought of Elizabeth's wild tantrums, and Lord Winter's exultation in danger and liberty and solitude. Of her mother's screaming rages. Zenia had said to herself that he would never, could never stay, and yet to hear Lady Belmaine tell her so, in such certain, unflinching words, and assert that Elizabeth was the same—Zenia felt sick with fear.

"The earl said that if I did not do as he advised," she said tightly, "Elizabeth would be"—she could not say the word— "what I am."

"Your father and his wife spend a great deal of time in France, do they not? I think that you would find yourself quite comfortable in a neat house near Paris. Or perhaps at that Swiss spa where Mrs. Bruce plans to take the water cure. You may be certain that I would see that my granddaughter is brought up in proper circumstances, wanting for nothing. There will be money for a school, or a governess as you prefer, and whatever you may wish in the way of clothing and an establishment. You need not fear any social rebuffs; I shall see to that myself. These things are taken as a matter of course on the Continent."

Zenia was silent, staring out the window. She longed for her father and Marianne and the comfortable close days in Bentinck Street. She wanted to do what was best for Elizabeth. She wanted peace and security; she wanted her daughter to grow up in perfect safety—and yet she thought of him, the despair in his voice. *I don't think I can do it.*

He could not stay. With a wrench of her heart, Zenia knew that he could not, not without destroying himself—not without becoming what his mother was, all her feeling turned to ice. He would go, and when he did, he could take Elizabeth if she gave him the right.

When Zenia turned, Lady Belmaine was watching her with an

unblinking attention. "You need not mention this to the earl or my son," the countess said. "If you wish to speak of it further, we will be private together."

For the first hour, Mrs. Lamb had kept a wary eye out the window while she finished her mending, watching Lord Winter play on the lawn just beyond the terrace with his daughter. She kept her opinions strictly to herself, of course, but it was with some approval that she saw the little girl exercising happily outside. It was just the sort of thing Miss Elizabeth needed, a little rough and tumble in the bright country air. Mrs. Lamb had made very certain she was dressed warmly, and Lord Winter, it was obvious, was rather under the weather and not inclined to take her far.

Still, the nurse thought uneasily of Lady Winter. She had had one particularly bad moment, when she had seen the earl himself walk out onto the terrace and speak with his son. But they appeared to part amicably. Mrs. Lamb breathed a sigh of relief and turned back to laying out the pattern for a smock.

She had meant to call them in for a luncheon, in spite of the picnic basket. Miss Elizabeth would certainly need a clean napkin, and her father was unlikely to wish to have anything to do with that. But when Mrs. Lamb was finished with pinning the pattern, and looked outside, the viscount had picked up Miss Elizabeth and headed far out onto the lawn along with the wicker.

Mrs. Lamb watched them for a moment, her fingers pressed over her mouth. She had no right to an opinion—no right beyond many more years of experience with children than Lady Winter could boast—but she was persuaded that Miss Elizabeth's character required greater freedom if it was not to be distorted and crippled, like a vigorous seedling forced to grow in too small a space. She could understand a young widow's intense attachment to her only child—but now that Lord Winter was returned—well, Mrs. Lamb had no business holding an opinion on Lady Winter's marital affairs either, but it was difficult to be blind to the obvious tension between husband and wife. Mrs. Lamb disliked to see Miss Elizabeth become a pawn, but she very much feared that Lady Winter was inclined to assert her management over the child to a greater extent than was wise.

She would give the truant pair another hour, Mrs. Lamb decided, before demanding that they come inside to clean up and take a nap. She knelt again beside the fabric spread on the floor, taking up her scissors.

When the hour had passed, she checked again outside the window. Lord Winter and Miss Elizabeth had vanished from the lawn. Mrs. Lamb made a little cluck and went to fetch her greatcoat.

Twenty-one

ARDEN TOOK A worm from Beth as she was about to eat it and shoved a biscuit into her muddy hand instead. He could hear the distant shouts of their distraught jailers, but he ignored them. They had been calling since he and Beth had drained the carp pond—Beth having taken a great delight in pulling down the mud bank, wielding her own small shovel with enthusiastic futility as Arden dug deeply with his.

They were both exceedingly damp. Arden had misjudged when the bank would give way, and been standing in the middle of it as the brown water began to pour down through the weakened soil. Beth had thought his yelp of surprise a great show, and waded in herself, squealing and shrieking with excitement and cold. Shortly after that the urgent shouts from the direction of the house had begun. Arden, looking at the state of his trousers and Beth's smock, had judged that a little time to dry off would be wise.

Perhaps he did not know the bounds and corners, but Arden knew every secret path and passage at Swanmere. He had carried Beth, the basket and shovels down to the low end of the lake, staying carefully under the brow of the hill as he dragged the rowboat from the bank into the water. Beth followed the basket into it, and they crossed the narrow end in three quick pulls on the oars. Hearing the hounds closing, Arden had grabbed her up, disentangling her wet clothes from the rusty painter eyebolt—not without the loss of her bonnet and a bow or two—seized the wicker and jumped ashore. The boat drifted off from the bank, but he did not stay to secure it. With Beth giggling in his arms as the evergreen branches brushed her face, he had mounted the little cliff, well concealed in a cascade of undergrowth.

They made their escape. The shouts had dimmed as he carried her deeper into the woods, where they had a sword fight with dead sticks, threw dry leaves in the air and put flat rocks on their heads. At his elm, he'd set Beth down and handed her the toy shovel, and together they had made a respectable start on restoring the tunnel.

At least, Arden had made a start. Beth had found worms and grubs and flinging dirt more to her taste.

She sat in a mound of dead leaves munching the biscuit. Arden was forced to admit that her appearance was not improved for drying out—she was much the same texture and color as her surroundings. There were some soft, square white cloths in the picnic basket, but with no clean water the application of one to her face only made her more disreputable.

For some time, there had been a growing frenzy in the remote shouting, male voices added to the feminine. "It's going to be the devil to pay with us, I'm afraid," he said, squatting in front of

Beth and sharing his ham sandwich, which added a smear of mustard to the mix.

"Goo-at!" she said with her mouth full, reaching for more.

He gave her the rest of the sandwich and dug out his pocket watch. Half past four. The sun was getting low. Zenia and his mother would surely be back before another hour had passed, if they weren't already.

"Are we scared?" he asked Beth.

She smiled at him around a slice of mustard-slathered, leaf-coated ham, her dark eyes full of mirth.

"Quaking in our bloody boots," he said.

"Ma-ma." Beth dropped the ham and crawled toward him. She lifted her arms to be picked up.

"Yes, I know it's time to go." He stood up with her, her muddy feet adding more dirty stripes to a waistcoat that was already squalid. "You needn't rush me." Then he wrinkled his nose, sniffing. "Good God. Perhaps you should at that."

He stooped to lean the shovel against the tree and toss the remains of their meal into the basket. As he threw the muddy white cloth in, it occurred to him that it was a diaper.

"Ah, well," he said, turning down the path that would circle the lake. "What are nurses for? Let's go find Mrs. Lamb."

"Ma-ma," Beth said.

"If you prefer to have a living papa, I daresay we'd better hope we discover Mrs. Lamb first. But never fear, I know how to smuggle you in."

She laid her head on his shoulder with a baby sigh. He walked through the woods. The shouts seemed to have gone mostly to ominous silence, although as he neared the lake, he could hear an odd, somber call now and then.

He stopped at his first view of the water. There were boats on it. Men and boats, nets—and a knot of people at the head.

With a sudden drop of his heart, he saw his father among them at the edge.

They were dragging the lake.

For a moment he just stood there, staring. A nightmarish fear seized him—it was as if he had walked into his own past, seeing what he had only dreamed. His heart constricted in his chest.

Then with a start, a wrenching shift to a different reality, he recognized his mother and Zenia standing close together, the nurse and the maids huddled around them.

And the shock suddenly turned to realization. His breath came back; his jaw clenched hard.

"You precious jackasses," he exclaimed through his teeth. "You don't actually suppose I drowned her?"

He walked out into the open, standing where the woods stopped and the lawn fell down to the lake in a steep slope. No one looked up. No one noticed him. They were all intent on the men and the lake and somber ooze of mud stirring up from the bottom.

He could not believe it. At first, he just felt amazement, a sort of nauseated wonder, watching the slow drag of the net through the water. It did not seem real.

One of the men bent, pulling something shapeless and pale from the water. Arden heard a strange, terrible sound, a faint high keening.

It was Zenia. It was the worst sound he had ever heard in his life; it froze his blood.

He wanted to shout to stop it. But he stood paralyzed while they spread the wet thing out across a gunwale—it was nothing, some rubbish, a piece of canvas—and yet the awful sound did not cease.

"Stop it," he muttered. "Stop it, stop it. What are you doing?"

He could hear Zenia: her wordless keening—what they must have made her think he had done . . . he could hardly take in air for the ferocity of his reaction. Rage grew in him; blinded and deafened him to everything but that sound. They were making her think he had drowned Beth, letting her make that noise, letting her think he had drowned *Beth*.

He stood on the hill in full view of them, with Beth snoring on his shoulder and the picnic basket at his side.

It was the nurse who finally saw him. She gave a shriek and pointed.

The horrible shrill sound ceased, silenced as suddenly as everything else. For an instant they were all frozen, all but Zenia who came running, running in her full skirts, running so hard that she nearly fell when she came up the slope.

She began making the high, hysterical noises in her throat again, gasping as she reached for Beth. Arden let her go, watching Zenia crumple to her knees, holding her daughter so tightly that Beth squealed and began to cry.

He looked beyond, saw his father hurrying ahead of the rest up the slope—and the outrage inside him found a brilliant blood-tinged focus. "Get those goddamned nets out of the water!" he shouted savagely. "Get 'em out of my sight!"

His father stopped. Arden saw him look at Zenia and Beth and the wicker basket.

Arden's mouth curled in violent contempt. "Was it you who ordered this? Damn you to hell!"

For a long moment the earl looked up at him over ten yards of grassy slope. Then he turned his head, giving quiet orders. The men dispersed, heading for the lake, and Mrs. Lamb climbed up toward Zenia.

"Do you know how many hours you've been missing?" his father asked evenly, turning to look up at Arden again. "The boat was floating loose." He looked ten years older than when Arden had seen him that morning. "With her bonnet in the water."

"I don't care if the goddamned boat was sunk with her christening robe in it!" Arden's furious voice echoed back from the lake. Staring down at his father, he felt a darkness hover at the edge of his eyes, rage beyond his ability to utter in words. "How could you think this? How could you do this?"

"How could *you!*" Zenia's frenzied accusation rose above Beth's uncertain weeping. She scrambled to her feet. "How dare you say that! How dare you? Look at her! Look at you! She might have died!"

"Died of what?" he shouted. "Mud and a dirty diaper?"

Beth began to cry in earnest. Mrs. Lamb hurried up, prying her from Zenia's arms. "Let me get her into a hot bath, ma'am."

"You should never have let him take her!" Zenia cried angrily. "You were to keep her with you every moment! You may pack your things tonight!"

"Just so, ma'am. I am entirely to blame. Just let me get her into some clean clothes, and dry, and then I shall do as you say."

"Don't pack your things too hastily, Mrs. Lamb," Arden said in a cold voice.

Zenia whirled on him as the nurse carried Beth away. "What have you to say to it? It isn't her fault; it's yours! You have no sense; you don't know the meaning of it! You are mad! Can you imagine what I felt, when they told me—when I thought—you and Elizabeth—the lake—" She sat down hard, her face in her hands, her elegant, grass-stained gray skirts billowing around her.

"Zenia," he said in a cracked voice, looking down on the frail nape of her neck. "I would never let anything happen to her."

"I could not live without my baby," she said on that high shrilling note, rocking her body back and forth. "I could not!"

"I would never hurt her. I had her safe."

"I go away for one day—for one day!" she said into her hands. Her body shuddered. "I should never have left her with you. Never!"

She began to cry, shaking with huge tearing sobs. Arden stood beside her, damning his father, watching his parents turn and walk toward the house with Mrs. Lamb while Beth wailed in a small, lost voice. He stood as if he were unable to move while the boats and nets were hauled in and the lake slowly cleared. And all the time Zenia huddled at his feet, racked with anguished sobs.

"You will make yourself ill," he said. "Don't weep like this."

She lifted her ravaged face. "You frighten me so! Why do you always frighten me?"

"I'm sorry. I didn't intend to frighten you."

"They called and called for you, and you never answered."

He stared at the lake. He knew that he could have been back before this happened. He could have answered the urgent hails. He could have given himself and Beth up to the well-meaning, strangling grip of Swanmere.

"You heard them, didn't you?" Her voice was high and trembling.

"Yes."

"And you didn't answer?"

"No," he said.

"Why?" She swallowed a hiccuping sob. "*Why?*"

He sat down on the hill, staring at a black swan that emerged tentatively from the reeds at the low end of the lake.

"You should have answered!" she cried.

He tore up a clump of grass, shredding it in his fingers. "We drained the carp pond," he said. "She liked that. And then I took her to my tree. We were both wet, and I knew that you—we were trying to dry off before you caught us." He flicked a lump of dirt down the hill and added sardonically, "You frighten me a little too, you know, Mama."

"I could not possibly frighten you."

He made a slit in a stem of grass with his thumbnail. "Could you not?"

"No."

He tore the grass down its length, gazing at the two pieces.

"Not even demons frighten you," she said. "I've never seen anything frighten you."

He tried to tie the split stem together, but the pieces broke in his fingers. "Perhaps you have not seen every part of me there is to see."

"You even stayed behind when they came after us out of Hayil." She made it sound an accusation. "You stayed, when you knew they would take you."

"I would do it again. I would—" He shook his head. "There is no end to what I would do for you and Beth."

"I don't believe you. You will not stay here."

"I'm trying. Give me a chance."

"You cannot do it. You said so. And if you do, you'll become—" She made a small sound of despair. "Like my mother, or yours. Your spirit will not bear it."

"Then come with me—"

"There!" She turned on him, her eyes dark and passionate, the color rising in her cheeks. "That is what will happen! 'Come with me!' Come with me, you said, and took us into the red sands and into the guns of the Wahhabis and into the hellfire itself. I cannot come; I will not, and I won't let you have Elizabeth!"

He watched the black swan sail slowly along the shore, dipping its bill with graceful moves. "Perhaps it is impossible for us to understand one another," he said dully.

He felt her look at him. She looked so straight and long that he was afraid to turn and see what was in her face.

"I don't understand how I can love you and hate you at once," she said.

The grass stems fluttered from his hands. "Now," he said, "I am terrified."

"Of what?" she demanded with a haughty and disbelieving lift of her chin.

"Nothing, nothing," he said with false lightness. "Recall that I am impossible to frighten. I meant to make a joke. It's all so vastly humorous." He began to pull another stem of grass into rags. "You make it evident enough why you—dislike me. One is left to ponder—" He shrugged. "About the other thing. Why, that is. If you do. Why?"

She stared straight ahead. "Why do I love you, do you mean?"

"Yes." He rolled the grass tightly between his fingers, crushing it. "That's what I mean."

"Because you gave me Elizabeth."

"Ah," he said. He scowled at the swan as it drifted placidly toward the far bank. "How amazingly inventive of me. A feat hardly paralleled in the annals of the human race. I shouldn't suppose above two or three hundred millions of fellows alive have ever fathered a child." He flicked the ball of grass into oblivion. "Indeed, I seem to be at a singular loss for an equally obliging encore. Since you didn't come back last night."

She lowered her eyes. He did not look directly at her; only just enough to see her profile, pure and familiar, her skin golden in the late-angled sun. Her bonnet was gone and her hair had come loose in her frenzy: it fell down now in a rough cascade on her shoulders, a disheveled dark tangle.

Something about the clear winter light and the deep ruddiness of the setting sun tinted everything with crimson and vermilion, like a twilight in the red sands—it brought the desert back vividly—just so she had sat, just so, in silence, looking a little down, singing softly in the vast emptiness . . . and strangely, as if the light revealed some lost aspect of reality or memory or vision—he saw her fully, for the first time, as the same companion who had sat beside him there. The same face, the same person, the same heart.

All his memories conformed at last—the free-striding youth had not vanished, had not died, but been different all along. It was not a boy; it had never been: it was this woman beside him who had mounted a camel by a graceful athletic swing upon its neck, who had slept close at his back; who had let him braid turquoise and pearl into her hair; it was this sober, beautiful, pensive young woman who had rationed his water and food for him in the sands and labored up the endless dunes and wept as he lifted her up onto a camel's back, so thin and light she was nothing.

He had regretted, infinitely regretted what he had done to her by taking her with him—and yet it seemed to him now that in the pitiless struggle and silent, certain friendship, it had been the happiest time in his life.

"I wish we were back in the desert again," he whispered.

He said it before he thought: out of the crimson light, the clear air, the discovery of the moment—and instantly, the moment the words left his tongue, he knew he had committed a fatal error.

"I don't mean—" he began hastily.

"Of course you do," she said in a voice that seemed unnaturally calm. She gathered her skirts about her and rose. Without another word she turned away from him and walked down the hill.

HE WAS AT a comprehensive disadvantage when his father intercepted him shortly after sunrise in the passage outside Beth's playroom. Arden was unshaven and hungry and muddy and tired, having spent the night under his tree after a brief supper at the Swan—where it was abundantly clear that his presence was not pleasing to Mr. Harvey Herring, however Mrs. Herring and her daughter might feel. Arden had found the old elm as welcoming a home as any, and not as uncomfortable as a number of places he'd slept—but not a bed, for all that.

"Where have you been?" the earl asked.

"Out," Arden said.

"Are you drunk?"

"I am not," he said curtly, turning away toward his room. "Good morning to you, sir."

"Lady Winter has gone up to town," the earl said.

The door to the playroom was open. Arden could see the neat emptiness of it from where he stood just outside. He walked through and stood in the middle. The toy wardrobe stood ajar, cleared of its bright amusements.

"Of course," Arden said. "Having been persuaded that her daughter might at any moment be found at the bottom of the lake, she would think it well to remove her from the imminent peril."

His father followed him in, closing the door. "Yesterday was a rather trying day for all of us."

Arden pulled the jack out from under the cot with his toe and dragged off his boots.

"Perhaps I—" The earl hesitated. "My actions were overly precipitous. Perhaps I owe you an apology."

Not more than three times in his life that Arden could remember had his father offered him any regret or apology for anything. And every time, it cut all the ground from beneath Arden's feet. He generally wanted to hang himself when his father apologized to him, and this time was no different. He stood in his stocking feet, feeling disarmed and vaguely manipulated, and said, "No—it was my fault. I should have brought her back sooner. When I heard the calls."

"Still, I feel I should—"

"It was my fault," Arden said aggressively.

The earl locked his hands behind his back. "Well, I am sorry that it happened."

"What's one wife, more or less?" Arden stripped off his coat. "They seem to be the devil." He unbuttoned his mud-streaked waistcoat and the heavier flannel undercoat beneath.

"They do have their moments," his father said, with a touch of mordant humor.

In his shirtsleeves, Arden sat down on the cot. He looked at his hands.

"Arden," the earl said, "if the woman is entirely impossible for you to live with, we will buy her off and send her to the Continent. There's nothing she can hold you with. No witness, no certificate. Your mother has suggested to me a house for her in Switzerland."

"I want Beth," Arden said to his hands.

"That would be part of the arrangement. We will simply admit that we were falsely practiced upon by her claim to be Lady Winter, and now that you have returned, we find the truth to be otherwise. In return for a generous settlement and our pledge not to prosecute her for the deception, she must give you the right to see the child whenever you wish, and documents attesting that there was never a marriage, nor will she ever make any such claims upon you. Really, she has brought it upon herself by this obstinate and ludicrous delay." He shrugged. "But any repudiation must be done immediately. It will no doubt be a moderately unpleasant scandal, and I shall look a great doting fool for having taken her in—but as soon as she is out of sight it will blow over."

"For the love of God—the last I knew, you were inciting me to marry her out of hand."

"I had hoped—I thought perhaps you had some affection for her, given your—" His father looked uncomfortable. "The circumstances of your union. But however that may be—neither of you seems to care much for the other now. And the connection was always, I may say, beyond the pale. A gross *mésalliance*. Her sordid birth, her deplorable upbringing—I do not mention her destitution; I have never wished you to hang out for a rich wife. But I had supposed it a love match. I am not as proud as I once was. I should not have objected to a love match, provided there was some modicum of good breeding in the lady of your choice. And her blood is well enough, even if she was born on the wrong side of the blanket. But it is not a love match. And your mother is wretchedly unhappy about it. Women suffer these social calamities rather more acutely, you know."

"Ah," Arden said. "I am enlightened. Social calamities!"

"God knows you would not be the first young man to have a mistress, but to marry her—it is a crushing blow to the dignity of our name."

"Is it?" Arden tore his crumpled neckcloth free and held it taut between his fists.

"I think you must know that it is." The earl took a turn in the room, going to the window and back, and then back again before he spoke. "Now that you are home, and willing to remain—your mother mentioned that you might wish to be introduced to Lady Caroline Preston. Lord Lovat's second daughter, God rest him. I have met her; a very cultured and spirited young woman, well-traveled too, not one of your bread-and-butter misses. With a fine wit and a pleasant sense of the ridiculous. I think you might find her a congenial dinner companion."

Arden laughed. "Yes, wives are the very devil, aren't they?" He looked at the earl. "Yours must have given you a miserable night of it, to bring you to this drill."

Lord Belmaine pursed his lips. "You are disrespectful to your mother," he said, but there was a dry undertone beneath the annoyance in his voice.

Arden sat in silence, staring at the opposite wall, jerking the neckcloth between his hands.

"Arden," his father said gently, "if it seems cold-blooded—recall that you have honorably offered her the most that you can offer. Her motives are beyond my conception, but she seems to be rejecting it."

Arden stood up. He yanked the bell rope.

"Well," his father said, "I will leave you to consider." He opened the door.

Arden gave him a curt nod. "If you please, you may tell Mother that I will not be here for dinner. I'm going up to London."

The earl paused, his jaw tightened. "To what purpose?"

"To revel in my perversity." Arden shrugged. "To make an utter ass of myself."

Lord Belmaine stood with his hand on the doorknob. Then a faint smile curved his mouth. He inclined his head, went out and closed the door.

ZENIA LEANED FORWARD, looking out the carriage window as the footman knocked a third time at her father's door. The house looked ominously shuttered, though Bentinck Street was bustling at half past eight in the morning drizzle, and her father and Marianne should have been at breakfast.

At last the door opened a crack. The footman spoke to someone inside, but the gap did not widen. He turned and ran down the steps, holding his hat brim to shield his face against the rain.

"I beg your pardon, my lady," he said to Zenia. "But the maid says the family has gone to Zurich this week past."

"Zurich!" the nurse said faintly, holding Elizabeth and leaning forward to look helplessly at the footman. They had traveled all night, and her hair was straggling loose from her cap.

"Oh, they have taken Marianne to Dr. Lott!" Zenia exclaimed in dismay. "I thought it was not to be until spring!" Her lips trembled, the exhaustion and misery of the long night betraying her. She had thought, if only she could reach her father . . .

The footman made a little bow. "They say that all inquiries are to be made of Mr. Jocelyn, three doors down," he said. "Shall I ask there, my lady?"

Zenia made a gasp of relief. "Mr. Jocelyn!" She grasped the edge of the window eagerly. "Yes, indeed please do—but make haste, or he'll be leaving for his offices." She turned to the nurse and Elizabeth, who was staring with great eyes out the window at the busy street. "It is all right. It is perfectly all right. Mr. Jocelyn will advise us what to do."

"Then I hope he may advise us to go home," the nurse said under her breath, but just loud enough for Zenia to hear.

Twenty-two

—❧—

"In all honor, my dear, I can only advise you to return to him as his wife. It is plainly the best course," Mr. Jocelyn said, tapping the letter the earl had sent to her father. "Mr. Bruce gave this to me, with instructions to offer any additional counsel I might, but I supposed that he had answered it himself, or I should have written you directly. I wonder if his letter to you somehow went astray. They left in such a flurry that everything was at sixes and sevens, but there was word that the wind might turn and prevent a crossing for some time if they did not go at once."

"I do hope she was not too unwell," Zenia said unhappily.

The Bruce house seemed very empty and cold, with covers still on the furniture, the drapes taken down and the carpets rolled up. There was one shutter open, so that the dull light fell across the shoulder of Mr. Jocelyn's neat tan coat. They sat at the table in her father's study, with the letter unfolded and a pot of tea that Zenia had prepared herself and carried up from the kitchen, the cook having gone with the family.

"I fear there was considerable deterioration, but let us hope that the famous Dr. Lott will live up to his reputation."

"Oh, I pray for it," Zenia said, "I pray it may be so."

"But it is you that we must deal with at the moment, my dear," he said. "I think that this is a generous and honorable proposal to see to your welfare and Miss Elizabeth's. A private marriage, properly performed by license, and an excellently drafted settlement and guardianship with an acknowledgment of paternity—it is indeed all I could have asked if I had been handling the matter for you."

She stared down at the letter, biting her lip.

"I'm sorry that the house is closed up," he said. "I'm sure you would like a day or two of rest before traveling again, but what servants they did not take have been dismissed. I was just to come today and take the knocker down. But if you don't mind the inconvenience, I'm sure that the housemaid and Mr. Barret would stay another day."

"I have sent the carriage back to Swanmere," she said in a low voice.

She felt him examine her, well aware of his puzzlement. "You do not intend to return, then?" he asked.

Zenia clasped her hands in her lap, looking down at them. "Is it impossible for me to stay here?"

Mr. Jocelyn was silent for a moment. She watched the reflection of raindrops on the dark row of her father's legal volumes, watery patterns of light on the leather and the gilt titles.

The lawyer expelled a quiet breath. "I must suppose, then, my dear, that there is some very compelling reason why you have left Lord Winter. Has he mistreated you?"

"No," she said reluctantly. "Not me."

"Miss Elizabeth?" he asked in a shocked tone.

"He is entirely careless with her," Zenia said.

"Careless?"

"He is mad!" she said more strongly. "I was certain he had drowned her!"

"Good God," Mr. Jocelyn said.

"I do not want him to see her, or have any right to it. Above all I do not want him to have the right to take her away from me."

Mr. Jocelyn rubbed his fingers over his lower lip, frowning. "Certainly if there is any threat to the child, that changes the matter. Utterly changes the matter."

"I don't wish to go back to Swanmere," she said.

"No, I comprehend you." He nodded, still frowning. "In that case, we must reopen the house. You will need a cook, of course. Can you make do with the one housemaid? I—" He broke off. "Well, I will take care of all that, in any event. Your father left me with a certain authority to act in these domestic affairs. You have a nurse?"

Zenia nodded.

Mr. Jocelyn rose, folding the letter. "I must consider what will be best to do," he said, looking a little distracted. "I have to go up to Edinburgh—but no—certainly that may be put off until after Twelfth Night. If you write to your father, my dear, you might just like to put the best face on things for the moment, if you understand me. Until we are more certain of how things stand. When he left, he thought you well provided for."

"I understand," Zenia said, rising. She put out her hand. "Thank you, Mr. Jocelyn. Thank you so very much for your kindness!"

Mr. Jocelyn flushed, shaking her hand with a brief, negligible pressure. "Indeed, it is my pleasure. We will contrive, ma'am. We will contrive."

* * *

IN HIS PRIVATE parlor at the Clarendon, Arden glowered at the trim, gentlemanly lawyer that his note to Zenia had produced. He had expected her father at least, but they had come to this already—lawyers, ranks of lawyers put between them, to twist and warp everything.

"Mr. Bruce has misfortunately gone to Switzerland, where his wife is to be attended by an eminent physician," Mr. Jocelyn said, in a voice that seemed cordial enough. "I am charged with looking after his daughter's affairs in his absence. She came to me with your request for a meeting."

He opened the case on his knees and pulled out several papers. Among them Arden recognized his note; his formal, temperate and rational note, that had taken him an hour to compose.

"I hardly see that it is a legal matter," he said coldly, "for me to speak to my wife."

"I should clarify myself," Mr. Jocelyn said, with a nod toward his card that Arden had tossed on a side table. "It is true that I am a civilian in Doctors' Commons, but I am here at present only as a friend of Mr. Bruce and his daughter. I do not say that I would not take a professional position should it prove neccessary in the future. But I wish to be perfectly open with you, as Mr. Bruce's daughter has been entirely open with me regarding the history of your relationship with her." He gave Arden a significant glance. "I have also read this"—he flipped the corners of a sheaf of closely written papers—"and may I say that your proposal is entirely and perfectly in order. I do honor to you and Lord Belmaine for taking this position, given the circumstances."

Arden's spine relaxed a little. "Then why are you here, Mr. Jocelyn?" he asked tersely.

"To be blunt, Lord Winter, she has given me reason for concern regarding your treatment of Miss Elizabeth. It is a grave enough matter that I might—as severe as it may seem—feel constrained to advise her to reject your generous proposal."

"Bloody hell!" Arden exclaimed. "What does she claim I did to Elizabeth?" He flung himself out of his chair. "Tried to drown her, I'll warrant!"

Mr. Jocelyn raised his slender eyebrows. "Perhaps you will tell me your view of the matter."

For a long moment, Arden stood rigidly, fighting his temper at the effrontery of this stranger. But he had had a long and instructive session with Mr. King at Swanmere before he left. There were things she could do, if she were driven to it; ways she could put herself and Beth beyond his reach and leave him fighting through the jungle of the courts for the rest of his natural life.

He forced himself to relax his hands and sit down again. In the most passive tone he could muster, he explained Zenia's zealous confinement of Beth and their single day of freedom. "I should not have ignored the calls for us to come," he said, feeling embarrassed to admit it. "But for God's sake—she was never in the least danger. Never."

"I see," Mr. Jocelyn said. "I see."

"I want to talk to my wife," Arden said, forcing himself to stay calm. "I insist upon it."

The lawyer did not quite smile, but he looked down and shuffled the papers without any particular result. "Lord Winter, I must beg your pardon. I think perhaps I have unintentionally involved myself in a little disharmony between you and Lady Winter which is none of my affair. I must apologize for taking up your time, but my duty to Mr. Bruce—" He put the papers away and offered his hand as he stood up. "I hope you will forgive me as a benevolent meddler when I say that I only wish the best for your wife and daughter. I shall tell her that she cannot do better than to see you, as you urged in your handsome note, so that you may speak together sensibly about the situation."

Arden saw Mr. Jocelyn out. A few moments later, he followed himself, walking out of the hotel with his collar turned up against the damp cold. He was inured to London weather, but the wind seemed to cut through his coat, provoking a queer shiver. He put his head down, turning toward a bookshop in The Strand.

He was well known there. A pile of geographical and scientific volumes awaited him, but the bookseller was a little perplexed by his request for a book of conversation.

"Something in Greek philosophy, sir?" the man asked.

"No. English." Arden leafed through an atlas, keeping his face down. "Examples. How to speak to—various persons."

"Ah! A book of diction, I believe you mean, my lord. Elegant means of expressing oneself. Proposals of marriage, congratulations upon promotion, that sort of thing, sir?"

Arden frowned at Cape St. Marie on the island of Madagascar. "That sort of thing, yes."

Zenia had chosen one of her new gowns, a subdued silk striped in russet and fawn. She had no maid, so she had to ask Mrs. Sutton to help her with the corset and buttons.

"It's Mrs. Lamb, madam," the nurse said, yanking at the strings, "now that we are not at the great house. Which his lordship asked me long ago was I really called Sutton, and I said to him no, and he has called me by my proper name this age."

Away from Swanmere, Zenia had discovered that Mrs. Sutton, or Lamb, as she chose, was a considerably more militant character. She made no secret that she deeply disapproved of Zenia's removal to town, and had even ventured one or two remarks indicating her respect for Lord Winter as a father and a gentleman, which hardly endeared her to Zenia. But there was no choice at the moment—Zenia could not do everything for Elizabeth herself, not while she was alone in London, so she merely said, "I will be happy to call you Mrs. Lamb if you please. You should have mentioned it before."

"Will you wear the bonnet with the pretty orange scarf, ma'am?" Mrs. Lamb asked, lifting Elizabeth away from the open wardrobe, wiping her runny nose and catching up the bonnet in question with her free hand.

"It is only Lord Winter," Zenia said. "My everyday black one will do. I'm afraid Elizabeth is catching a cold."

"Ma'am looks a fright in the black one, if I may say so," the nurse remarked. "His lordship will be passing through Oxford Street on his way here, and certain he'll see ladies aplenty who know something of fashion."

Zenia was well aware of the insidious intent of this remark, but it was nevertheless effective. "You are to keep Miss Elizabeth strictly to the nursery in the attic," she said. She felt Elizabeth's forehead. "She seems a little warm. You are not to bring her down under any circumstances. Do you understand?"

"Ma'am." The nurse dropped a curtsey. She picked up Elizabeth and carried her out, muttering that any child who had been pulled from her bed and carried all about the country in the middle of the night would certainly have a fever. Zenia turned her head toward the door, and when she heard them reach the second landing above, she put down the black bonnet and reached for the one with the colored scarf for a tie—"capucine," the dressmaker had called it, but the color was the deep vivid orange of the nasturtiums that had grown in her mother's garden. There was a shawl that went with it, so sheer that Zenia could see through it, and a pair of fawn gloves with tiny matching flowers embroidered on the back.

She looked at herself in the glass and thought of all the fashionable ladies he would pass on his way. Her hair fell in ringlets against her cheeks, confined by the bonnet, perfectly clean and shining. The dress was tight at the waist and spread full over volumes of petticoats. It was fitted and trimmed and styled in the latest mode, entirely English, and yet she was afraid that he must still look at her and see the ragged Bedouin boy.

The knock came as she was descending the stairs. He was early—the housemaid hurried out of the dining room, stuffing a dust cloth into her apron, and answered the door. Zenia paused on the bottom step.

He stood in the doorway, a dark outline against the gray rain-soaked street behind him. He looked up as he took off his hat and stepped inside, lifting his blue eyes to hers.

If he could see beyond her English dress to her wretched barefoot past, he did not show it. His face was sober as he made a bow, handing his greatcoat and gloves to the maid. "Lady Winter," he said stiffly. "Good afternoon."

"Please come up," she said, turning on the stair. "Clare?"

The housemaid curtsied, instantly turning toward the back stairs to fetch the tea tray.

Zenia led him up to the drawing room. She and the maid had worked all day yesterday to hang the drapes again and pull the covers off the furniture and mirrors, but still the room appeared barren with no knickknacks or kickshaws set about. In the grim afternoon, the oil lamps cast a steady yellow glow.

"You look beautiful," he said in an abrupt way, and immediately turned as if he saw something that caught his eye in the street. Then he looked back at her with an air of detached survey.

Zenia's instantaneous glow of pleasure dimmed a little at his impersonal expression. "Thank you," she said. "You look very well." He looked as he always did to her: handsome, intensely masculine, darkness and cobalt blue. His physical presence carried with it a subtle impression of dominance; of solid strength. She had felt it in the desert; she had followed him there because of it. Slept near him because of it. She could have picked him out among a hundred men in the street outside because of it.

"Please sit down," she said, indicating an armchair near the fire screen.

"Where is Beth?"

"Upstairs. She has just fallen asleep. She is a little feverish, and I do not wish her to be disturbed."

He looked as if he might for a moment dispute her, but instead he made a bow, waiting for her to seat herself on the settle before he placed the armchair facing her and sat down. Clare came in with the tea and a plate of thin-sliced bread and butter. She set the tray down on the tea table before Zenia and closed the door behind her.

"I'm sorry that we have no cake," Zenia said, pouring for him. "Will you take sugar?"

"Is it possible," he asked, "for us to dispense with this sort of polite diversion for once, and simply talk together?"

She put down the teapot without pouring her own cup and laid her hands in her lap. "If you wish it."

"Zenia," he said, "I'm not good at it—tea and cakes. I have no patience with it."

She looked directly at him. "I suppose you would prefer to eat on the ground with your fingers?"

Her dry remark seemed to take him aback. He looked at her with a faint frown.

"Shall I sprinkle some sand on the butter," she asked, "to put you more at ease?"

He tilted up one corner of his mouth. "No." He lifted his cup, extending his little finger with an exaggerated delicacy. "I can play, if I must. How does your dear aunt do, Lady Winter? I hear she has the vapors once an hour. I have a receipt for a rhubarb plaster—most efficacious! Of course, if you prefer a more permanent cure, nothing can surpass a fatal dose of arsenic."

In spite of herself, Zenia felt a reluctant tug at her lips. She picked up the teapot, drawing her cup and saucer toward her.

"Do you remember when Chrallah woke me in the night?" he asked suddenly.

Zenia bit her lower lip. His camel Chrallah had grown spoiled with handouts of bread, and poked her long neck into the tent one night, her questing head hanging above them like a huge white serpent, her warm breath tickling his ear.

"Yes," she said. "It was a nice tent while it lasted."

"Unjust! What's one camel-sized hole?"

"One of her size, and one of yours," she exclaimed. "I did not think I would ever disentangle you."

"Rubbish. You were merely laughing too hard to be of any serious use."

Her lips pursed, and then spread irresistibly. "Poor Chrallah, standing there with a tent about her neck. She bore it with great dignity." Zenia glanced at him. "Quite unlike you."

As their eyes met, both of them smiling, she felt the blood rise in her cheeks. She looked away, flustered, and spooned sugar into her tea.

"When Beth laughs," he said, "I can see you laughing."

She kept her face down, sipping the tea. Her heart was beating hard, as if the next moment, the next thing he might say would change her life forever. Mr. Jocelyn had urged her strongly to marry him, in spite of all she had told the lawyer about her fears. He had made them seem overblown and foolish; he had not supposed that Lord Winter would separate Elizabeth from Zenia, even if the law gave him the means to do it as her husband. Every husband had the same ability under the law, when it came to that, Mr. Jocelyn said, and yet it was genuinely extraordinary to find any man cruel or mad enough to act upon it. The alternative, a life as a ruined woman with an illegitimate child, he stressed urgently, was far more to be feared, as much for Elizabeth's sake as Zenia's.

She was reassured, but not entirely certain. Lord Winter was no ordinary man. It would not be cruelty that drove him, but the diabolic force, the same djinni that had impelled her own mother to the East, to isolation and absolute liberty, the blood that Lady Belmaine said ran true in her son.

"Zenia," he said, with a seriousness that impelled her to lift her face again, "I want to say that I—"

She waited. Her look seemed to distract him from his sentence, though she was careful to keep any emotion from her face. He hesitated, watching her, as if he expected her to finish it for him somehow.

"I mean to say," he went on finally, with less authority in his voice, "that I have a very great . . . that I feel a particular . . ." He stood up, turning toward the fire. Looking at the screen appeared to restore his line of thought. He said abruptly, "I feel that you cannot truly have considered your position in a rational manner. That is why I wished for this meeting. All these damn—I beg your pardon—these lawyers have spoken to you, but perhaps no one has made you understand what it would mean for you and Beth to live outside my legal protection." He gripped his hands together behind his back. His voice hardened. "If a marriage to me is so abhorrent to you that it is your preference to be received nowhere, to live in poverty, to be out in the street, to have men— feel themselves free to approach you in an insulting manner— well, then, that is your choice. But you should understand that you will be condemning our daughter to the same indignities. You seem to think that I have no care for Beth's welfare—" His hands tightened; the veins stood out against his whitened knuckles. "But I believe you are far more to be condemned, by this foolish—this selfish, unthinking, damned stupid, mulish obstinacy in the matter." He took a few strides, stopped and looked back at her with an aggressive set to his mouth and his shoulders. "I would have to be a far greater monster than I am to justify it!"

"I am not selfish or obstinate or foolish! I mean to protect Elizabeth!"

Behind him, the rain began to beat in earnest against the windows. He scowled fiercely at her. "Do you truly think I am a monster, Zenia? What terrible crime do you suppose I intend to commit against her?"

She lowered her eyes. "I do not think you would deliberately cause Elizabeth harm."

"Thank you!" he said bitterly.

"But if I marry you, I should have no authority to protect her from whatever you might do. Mr. Jocelyn admitted it. Even if you weren't her guardian, even if you had no right to do anything, if I marry you, I cannot prevent you—because a wife cannot go to the law against her husband." She stood up. "You said so to me yourself—that you could do anything you pleased with her, and I could not stop you."

"I was angry when I said that!"

"Perhaps you will be angry when you take her away from me. Perhaps you were angry when you drowned the girl you were to marry."

He turned as white as if she had slapped him. "It was an accident."

"That is not what you told me."

He stared at her rigidly, his jaw taut.

"You said that you did not want her." Zenia had to force herself to stand still, to not step backwards. "That she was going to imprison you, and so you killed her."

His lips parted. Almost imperceptibly, he shook his head.

"Why should I trust you?" Zenia cried. "I cannot!" She turned away, her skirt sweeping against the settee. She hated now having spoken of it; she could not bear to see the brutal expression on his face: it frightened her, squeezing her heart with remorse and dread.

In a low voice, he asked, "Why does any woman ever trust a man?"

"I do not know," she said, swallowing. "I am sure I do not know."

"Perhaps because he loves her," he said, barely above the sound of the rain.

She turned. But he did not look at her; he was already walking toward the door, shoving a chair aside as if he hardly saw it. She heard his footsteps descending the stairs. A few moments later the front door slammed, a thud that echoed dully through the house. Zenia hurried to the window, but he did not pass below. She saw him ram his hat on his head and stride down the steps, careless of the rain, a tall shape that swung away at the iron baluster and vanished into the gray downpour.

ARDEN CURSED THE rain and cursed himself, falling back into the seat of the cab and shedding water over the cracked leather squab. He flung his dripping hat onto the opposite seat. He was breathing harder than he should have been, not so much from his effort to obtain a hackney as from the flush of emotion; the anger and the unnerving realization of what he had said.

He had meant to make a sane and logical statement of the situation, he had meant to see Beth, he had meant—anything but what had happened. He was the most maladroit blundering fool in nature; the more he cared for the outcome the more he butchered everything he did.

From a beginning worthy of a gawky schoolboy, he had found himself on the verge of his prepared declaration—and coward that he was, he'd shied off in the middle and made a cock of everything from there on. Every bloody thing. But he had the truth of what she thought of him now—what she feared—and in the black face of it he had heard himself say what laid him open and exposed, what he had known in his solitary heart, in his lonely heart, what he would not have betrayed for any prize on earth.

He was still breathing hard. He was nearly in a panic, because he had said that and she had not answered; he had not given her a chance to answer but run away.

He stared at his hat and the shabby hollows in the seat opposite him while cold water slid off his hair and down his neck. He had all his life been hunting, searching for some chimera that he did not know himself—he had thought it was anywhere but where he was. He had thought, usually, that it did not exist, and he was as much a fool as his father declared him. He had perceived, in a distant, disaffected way, that he was lonely, but there had been no other condition to know. He had always been that way, prowling the woods and the wastelands.

He rubbed both hands over his face, wet skin against wet skin, and opened his eyes, looking through his fingers like an animal looking out of a cage. He had discovered it, the thing he had never even known he was seeking—it was so close; for a breath of time he had possessed it: for a few months in the desert, for a week—a day—with his daughter. And the fear that it would vanish before he could reach it again made his muscles so tense that his head ached and his hands trembled in the seeping chill.

Twenty-three

ZENIA HAD NEVER supposed, after that single call, that he would not come again. Elizabeth's cold turned into a real fever, and Mr. Jocelyn's physician had pronounced it the measles. At first Zenia had been frantic, blaming Lord Winter's careless taking of her into the weather, but the doctor stated without question that the disease was certainly a contagion Elizabeth had caught from an infected young person. And indeed on the very afternoon that the physician left, a letter had arrived from Lady Belmaine with the information that the village children were full of measles, and it was now verified that the new second nurse-maid, the young one dismissed just a fortnight ago for sluggishness and stupidity, had come out in spots not three days after she had left the house. Lady Belmaine thought Zenobia would be wise to stay alert for symptoms in Miss Elizabeth.

Elizabeth came through it with ease, a mild case, with hardly any serious rash and only a week of drowsy fussiness before she was struggling to leave her bed. It was a blessing in disguise, the doctor said. If he had his way, all children would be deliberately infected before the age of two, so that they achieved immunity when the disease was so nearly innocuous. Zenia was not quite so sanguine—she had not slept for worry, and only the brief course of it reassured her that Elizabeth's first real illness would not at any moment turn deadly.

On the fourth night—the moderate crisis, as it turned out—she had even sent Lord Winter a note. She had not really thought Elizabeth in imminent danger, but she had thought that he would like to come. In her heart, she longed for him to come.

He had not. He had not even answered, although the boy had said he was still resident at the hotel.

What had come had been a packet from the legal offices of King and King, outlining a new proposal, since Miss Zenobia Stanhope appeared to reject the former one.

She sat again in her father's study while Mr. Jocelyn frowned over the papers, shaking his head. "I am afraid we have reason now for some concern," he said. "I do not like the threat inherent in this, my dear—I do not like it at all. Fraud is a very, very serious matter."

"I did not lie to anyone," Zenia said. "When Lord Belmaine asked me if I had proof of a marriage, I said no."

Her voice was weak. She felt almost ill, faced suddenly with the consequences of her indecision. *Unthinking, damned stupid, mulish obstinacy*, he had said, and she very nearly agreed with him. She was to be treated now as a criminal, or at best a case of charity, utterly dependent on the generosity of the Belmaines. She had her father's promise still—but she had learned, from the rather oblique hints of Mr. Jocelyn, that the Bruces were not so comfortably provided for that the lifetime support of a daughter and grandchild would be a light thing.

"I could wish that we had never got to this point," the lawyer said. "This is tragic, my dear. Tragic. I supposed, when I saw him—but if Lord Winter has lost patience, can he be blamed? From his point of view, if there is not to be a marriage, then that fact must be made evident immediately, so that he is free to wed elsewhere." He shook his head again. "No doubt his counsel has advised him to act with vigor for a resolution."

Zenia bowed her head. She had not described her interview with Lord Winter, only said that nothing had been settled. "Well," she said, "Elizabeth and I will go to Switzerland. At least my father is there. And there is to be a house, and money for her."

"Little enough of that," Mr. Jocelyn said. "This is hardly as handsome an offer as the other was, even in its pecuniary terms. And they have left themselves several ways out, in particular by making things dependent on your character and conduct. However, we may negotiate upon those points. Lord Belmaine is a little nervous of his part in this alleged fraud—and you see that there is a clause dealing with him alone. And of course Lord Winter's desire for access to Miss Elizabeth is a point of leverage."

"Oh," Zenia said, "this is horrible."

"This sort of thing is seldom pretty, I fear." He cleared his throat. "I am sorry to say that it will likely be even less pleasant before it is over."

She sat with her hands clasped tightly in her lap. As Mr. Jocelyn studied the contract, she felt her lips press and tremble. A tear slid down her cheek. "I only want to keep Elizabeth," she said in a painful voice. "Oh, God, will I be transported?"

"My dear!" He instantly produced a crisp handkerchief. "I am very, very sorry. I should not frighten you. Certainly you will not. If you must go to the Continent on these terms, you must, and well before any peril of such a thing. I am quite certain that the

Belmaines have no real desire to bring an action for fraud—that is simply to apply pressure to you to release Lord Winter entirely. But no matter what sort of paper you sign, they must be concerned that you might come back in the future and make some claim to be his wife." He gave her a perfunctory smile. "Indeed, if you could promptly move some fortunate young man to fall in love and marry you, we should have no concerns at all. I'm sure they would be perfectly delighted to drop these accusations, since your marriage to another man must remove any fears."

"I have come to hate the very word marriage," Zenia said. "And I am not fond of men, either."

He sat looking at her for a moment, his pleasant face cocked a little to one side, his brown eyes thoughtful.

"I beg your pardon," she said, realizing how she had spoken. "I didn't mean you, of course! But I do not think another marriage will answer," she said, rubbing her fingers on the smooth wood of the tabletop. "There is Elizabeth."

"Yes, of course," he said, as if she had started him out of a distant thought. "Miss Elizabeth. My dear, do you need to look in on her? I would like a little time to deliberate on a notion that has just come to me. I must leave for Edinburgh tomorrow, you know, so give me an hour now to ponder."

"I hope you still stay to dinner," Zenia said politely.

"That is very kind; I will be happy to do so."

She left him with his pen poised over a blank paper, glad enough to impart the burden to him. But even with Elizabeth, Zenia could not dispel the pall of worry. And pain. She could admit it, looking at Elizabeth's serious face as she worked to fit a beanbag through the tight neck of a tin cup. If Lord Winter could see Zenia in Elizabeth's laugh, she could see him with perfect clarity in his daughter's intensity and determination.

She had grieved for him once, but this was a different loss—she had demanded it herself, and yet the moment she had her will she had known with her entire being what a devastating blow it was. She had not expected him to relent; she had in some absurd way trusted that he would not—that somehow if she refused him and refused him and refused him, he would not go away, but change.

As if by taunting and taunting it, she could exorcise the djinni that compelled him to be what he was. As if she could erase the unhappiness in his eyes and make him want to stay. Glad to stay.

But he would not change. And by her folly she had ruined her own future—and worse, far worse—Elizabeth's.

Clare appeared at the door. "Mr. Jocelyn wishes to see you now, ma'am."

Zenia stood up from the floor and bent to give Elizabeth a hug. She ignored it except for a happy trill, never taking her eyes or stubborn fingers from her task.

In the study, Mr. Jocelyn was standing beside the fire, warming his hands. Still, his fingers were rather cold as he took hers and seated her in a chair before him.

"My dear, I have something to propose which will undoubtedly startle you. Let me say directly that you must not feel under any compulsion whatsoever—it is merely a suggestion, and if you do not like it, then there is no more to be said. You have said that you dislike the idea of a marriage—indeed, you expressed some distaste for men in general, although I know you only meant it lightly. But let me just put before you a plan to consider—merely to consider."

Zenia looked up at him in puzzlement. He seemed rather agitated, almost embarrassed. "I'm sure whatever it is, it is an excellent plan if you thought of it, Mr. Jocelyn."

He smiled suddenly, in a more natural way. "Well, it is not very professional, and I should not be in a position even to suggest it if I had taken any formal action in the case—but as yet I feel myself within the limits of honest truth to say that I am a family friend, and no more. My dear, would it distress you very much to contemplate a marriage to me?"

Zenia had been looking straight into his kind brown eyes. Hers widened; she looked away. "I—I had not thought—"

"Calmly, my dear. Calmly. Let me outline it a little more thoroughly. As it happens, I have been for some time pondering a marriage for myself. For professional reasons, and to add some comfort to my life—and for companionship, of course. But you see, I am not a very passionate man, nor at all in the way of making love to ladies, and so I have made small progress. Not to put too fine a point on it, out of pure indolence I fear I have made no headway at all. I had in mind that perhaps a widowed lady would be suitable—ah, I do not wish to offend you by my speech, but I do wish to be precise—I am not particularly desirous of physical intimacy with a wife." His cheeks reddened a little. "Children I greatly enjoy, but I am a second son, and have no need to be concerned with all the usual bustle about extending the line and so forth." He cleared his throat. "As I say, I am not of an ardent nature."

He was still smiling, but he looked ill at ease now, rocking gently from one foot to the other. He looked as if he wished that he could have the words back.

"I understand," Zenia said, earnestly desiring to make him comfortable again. "Oh, yes. I have lived in the East, Mr. Jocelyn, where it is perfectly comfortable to prefer a boy, you may be sure. But I understand that it is not openly done here."

His face flamed. He turned quickly away. "My dear! I said no such thing. I greatly desire that you will not put such a construction upon my words, nor mention such a thing again!"

Zenia looked at his stiff back, the high color in his cheeks and the rapid way that he blinked at the window. A strange tenderness for him stole over her. How lonely he must be! "Of course not," she said. "Please—I should never wish to distress my friend."

He took a deep breath, fumbling at his pocket kerchief and using it lightly. After a moment, he looked up at her with a diffident smile. "Yes, I think we could be friends, at any rate. It has been my pleasure to become acquainted with you and your daughter. If I could give you both a comfortable home and a little good company now and then, in return for the same, I should think myself honored. But this is not a fence that you should rush, my dear. While I am in Edinburgh, you must take the time to think it over. You will wish to write to your father, perhaps. I will send something to their Mr. King, a little hint, to reckon how they would take it, but no decision need be made until you have had ample time to consider. Ample time!"

MR. JOCELYN HAD not been gone two hours when Zenia was called down to receive Lord Belmaine.

She saw him in her father's study, desiring to have at her back all the solidity and dignified weight that his law books could provide. "I can tell you nothing yet," she said as she closed the door, not even risking him to say the first word.

He made a short bow. "Good morning, ma'am. I have not come to press you on anything. I simply wish to inquire into Miss Elizabeth's health, and ask if you know my son's whereabouts."

"Elizabeth has had the measles," Zenia said briskly, relieved and disappointed at once, anxious to show neither.

He frowned. "We feared that! How does she do?"

"It was but a mild attack, with little fever. The doctor says she is safely through it. Though I am going to keep her in a dimmed room for yet awhile."

"That is good news." His frown turned to a smile. He nodded. "The measles are no trifling matter, as some think. Lady Belmaine mentioned that there was an outbreak in our village, and we have been much concerned. How comforting to know that all went well! Would you like Dr. Wells to see her, just to be sure? He is our physician in town, and there is no one of a higher reputation."

"I don't think it necessary, thank you. She is doing excellently well."

He stood looking at her a moment, but she did not invite him to sit down. "I would be honored to pay my respects to your father, if he is at home."

"They have gone to Zurich."

The earl looked surprised. "So you are here alone?"

"Mr. Jocelyn, my father's particular friend, has been looking after us. He only lives a few doors down, and I may call on him for anything."

"I see," he said.

"He is an advocate in Doctors' Commons," she said.

Lord Belmaine's expression of fixed pleasantry vanished. "Indeed," he said.

"He has been very kind."

"Well," the earl said, turning his hat over in his hands. "You must call upon me if I can be of any service. You have only to send to Berkeley Square."

"Thank you," Zenia said, without warmth.

"I will not keep you, ma'am." Lord Belmaine made another small bow, matching her in coolness. "I presume you have not seen Lord Winter?"

"I have not seen him since before Elizabeth's illness," she said stiffly. "Perhaps you may discover him at his club, or the Clarendon Hotel."

"Thank you. I must not linger. Good day to you, ma'am."

* * *

SHE HARDLY KNEW what to make of Lord Belmaine's call. When she had heard who it was, she had been certain that he would begin a full assault on her to sign whatever papers they wished, but she was determined to do nothing while Mr. Jocelyn was gone. She was really angry that he had come on such flimsy pretenses—he had not even asked to see Elizabeth, and he must know perfectly well where his son was. He meant only to upset her, she thought, to put her off her balance, and when a boy arrived just after her noon meal with a note written on the letterhead of the Clarendon, she felt certain of it.

She stood in the hallway, breaking the seal with hands that were not quite steady.

It was not Lord Winter's handwriting, but his father's.

Please come instantly. Belmaine.

THE BOY HAD a cab waiting, and the porter at the Clarendon led her directly up to Lord Winter's suite. She knew by then that he was very ill, but still she was shocked by the look on his father's face when he met her at the door.

"Have you had the measles?" he demanded, before he said anything else.

"Yes," she said, "when I was ten."

He held open the door, and Zenia turned her head as she entered, hearing Lord Winter's voice raised. For an instant she thought he was shouting at a servant, but she realized that the words were a violent string of Arabic curses, falling away to muttering as she hurried into the bedroom.

"Dr. Wells, ma'am," said a gray-haired man with a cruelly hooked nose, his aspect of ferocity intensified by the heavy frown on his face as he tried to hold Lord Winter still with an arm across his chest. "Open that lamp and bring it here." He nodded toward the commode, where there was a strange small light with a tiny door. "My lord, if you will endeavor to hold him down on the other side. I shall have to tie him in a moment if we cannot do better than this."

Lord Winter's labored breathing seemed to fill the room; he tried to turn from side to side, straining against his father's hands. Beneath a growth of beard his face was gaunt and flushed, and low on his throat and his arms she could see the spots, much fewer and darker than Elizabeth had had, but some already turning to white dust.

"Hold the light up close to his face, please, ma'am," Dr. Wells said. "Very close—shine it directly into his eyes."

Zenia lifted the lamp. Lord Winter recoiled from the light, pulling back with a sound of anguish. When the doctor took his face between his hands and attempted to turn his head, Lord Winter tried to pull away from that too, nearly dragging Dr. Wells over top of him.

"A strong fellow," the doctor murmured, sitting back, his large hands still pushing down on Lord Winter's shoulder to curb his restless turning from side to side. "Let us hope very strong. The morbid principle has entered the brain. This is a more common sequel of the mumps than the measles, but his violent aversion to light, the stiffness in the neck, the maid's story of nausea and vomiting, the disorientation—together these suggest an inflammation of the tissues of the brain. Our task will be to prevent him lapsing into coma, and relieve the oppression of the lungs as best we may."

Lord Winter was still a moment, his eyes half-closed, his chest rising and falling rapidly. He spoke clearly, a long sentence, broken only by frequent deep gasps for air.

Dr. Wells frowned. "I am not pleased by this incomprehensible babbling. If it were accompanied by any limb weakness, I should not hope to see the day out."

"It is Arabic," Zenia said. "It is not—entirely incoherent."

"Is it?" The doctor's fierce face took on something near brightness. "That relieves my mind, ma'am, that greatly relieves my mind. As there is clearly no one-sided weakness in the limbs, I think we may put the fear of a rapidly fatal encephalitis from our minds, for the moment at least."

He bent his head, arranging his stethoscope, and then with practiced moves pulled Lord Winter's shirt up to uncover his chest. "Good God," he said, "here is an ugly wound! How old is this?"

"Almost two years," Zenia said. "It was a bullet he received in the desert."

"These are burn marks," the doctor protested.

"That is what is done for such things, among the Bedu," she said.

Dr. Wells shook his head. "Barbarians," he muttered, and leaned over, listening with his instrument to Lord Winter's lungs.

As the doctor tied him down and bled him, Lord Winter continued to speak hoarsely through his difficult breathing. Zenia sat beside him, stroking his forearm over and over below the tight knot of the binding, while his father sat on the other side, his fingers intertwined with his son's, gripping hard.

She did not tell them what Lord Winter was saying; how he spoke to her over and over, never by her name, but calling her wolf cub and little wolf and Selim, telling her that he would bring her home, that she must keep walking, that he would carry her if she could not, but they must go on.

"He is asking for water," she said to the doctor, when he had said fretfully for the fourth time that the bags were empty.

"He refuses to take it," the earl said unhappily. "I've tried to make him drink."

Zenia filled a teacup from the pitcher on the dressing table.

She leaned over him, stroking the damp hair back from his hot forehead. *"El-Muhafeh,"* she whispered, "this is your portion."

His restless motion lapsed a little. His lashes lifted. Without turning his head, he looked slowly toward her. "Now?" he asked, the question turning to a cough. His eyes that were such a deep blue seemed cloudy and dim.

"Drink it now," she said, still in Arabic. "I know how much you need."

"So hot," he said in English, closing his eyes again. He drank eagerly when she lifted the cup, and then said, "Where's Beth?"

"Asleep," she said.

"I'll bring her home," he said, jerking his arms against the bonds.

The doctor finished binding a pad over his patient's arm and said, "Come, if I may see both of you for a moment in the other room while he is constrained."

"El-Muhafeh, I will be very close," she whispered, touching his forehead. "Only call if you want me."

He heard her, she thought, for he opened his eyes, but then he closed them again and tossed his head, every breath a deep struggle.

In the parlor, Dr. Wells was writing instructions. "I will leave you with some tonic, and have the pills compounded and sent over within the hour. Lady Winter, do you have any sickroom experience?"

"Yes," she said. "I nursed my mother for many years."

"Excellent. A hot bran poultice would be highly beneficial, as often as you like to apply it to the chest. There is a little maid here who was most helpful in describing to me the course of his illness—I believe she had been watching out after him, according to her own lights, and will be eager to assist you in obtaining what you need. Any food of a nutritious and stimulating character that you can get down him, and as much water or wine. Keep some beef tea to hand at all times."

He went on with his instructions, writing them down. When he finished, the earl said in a hard flat voice, "Is it at all possible— that he may not survive?"

"My lord, I have hope that he can. I think he *will*, but I shan't pretend to you. He is gravely ill. An adult's course in these diseases that are more commonly contracted in childhood is fraught with peril. There is already a serious complication with the brain fever. If another develops in the next twenty-four hours, pneumonia or pleurisy or a worsening of the encephalitis, the outlook will be very poor. That is what we must avoid if we can." He began to pack his medical bag. "I don't scruple to say that it would have been far wiser of him to have got the measles when he was still in short coats."

The earl's face was pale and set. He nodded. When the doctor rose and took his leave, Lord Belmaine hardly seemed to see the hand that he held out, and shook it with a vague nod and murmur.

"Ma'am." Dr. Wells turned to her, as if he recognized that the earl's mind was not focused. "I will return this evening. Here is my card; you are to send directly if there is any change, in particular with regard to the lungs."

ZENIA DISPATCHED WORD to Bentinck Street that she would not be home that night, with instructions about Elizabeth's bath and what she was to wear in the morning, and a request for her own necessities. But it was a short note; she was fully occupied with sickroom tasks, and with answering Lord Winter's turbulent and rambling discourse. Sometimes he thought they were in the desert, and sometimes he seemed to be lost in some unknown place, looking for something, for her or for Elizabeth or a string of pearls. She spoke back to him in Arabic or English, and pulled the sheets into place as he constantly tore them loose with his ceaseless motion.

"I believe he is calmer since you came," the earl said, standing in the doorway of the bedroom.

She held the hot poultice to Lord Winter's chest, her hands rising and falling with each hard breath he took. He tried to pull it off, his fingers dragging at the muslin.

"Hot," he muttered. "It is so hot."

"I know," she said. "But we are almost there."

"Ghota?" he asked.

"Yes."

"I can see it," he said, lunging in the bed. "Christ! Get my rifle!"

The earl stepped quickly to the bedside, pulling his son back onto the pillows. "You don't need your rifle here, old fellow," he said firmly.

Lord Winter began to cough, his chest heaving under her hands. He turned his head toward the earl, his eyes focusing a little. "Father," he said hoarsely. Then a faint smile lifted his mouth. "I didn't think you would come."

The earl scowled ferociously. "Of course I came."

Lord Winter turned his head away, as he had when the light was too bright, his smile vanishing. "Here's my tunnel," he said sharply.

"Yes," his father said at random.

There was a long silence. Zenia watched Lord Winter's eyes drift and listened to his rasping breath.

"Do you want to come in?" he asked in a small whisper, hesitant as a child's.

The earl folded his son's hand within his own. "There is nothing I want more," he said, his voice cracking.

Lord Winter moved his lips, but an uneven series of deep pants overtook him. He began to toss his head again, breathing heavily. Zenia took up the cooling poultice and carried it into the parlor. It did not seem to have had much effect. As the night came on, she expected the oppression of his lungs would grow greater—it had always been that way with her mother. She tried not to think of that horrible time when both Lady Hester and Miss Williams had taken the fever, when Zenia was only twelve, and all the servants had stolen what they could and run away but for one girl of Zenia's age. From her bed, her mother had insisted that one of her black draughts be prepared for Miss Williams, but Zenia was sure now that the little servant girl had got the proportions wrong. It was after the draught that Miss Williams had felt such pain in her stomach that she had cried and writhed, and finally fallen into a deathly stupor that lasted three days before she died. When Lady Hester had heard Miss Williams was gone, her screams had echoed from the walls, as terrible as a wild animal or a devil shrieking in Hell.

It was after Miss Williams died that Zenia had been sent to the desert. She stood in the parlor, staring blindly at a small table beside the door, until she wrenched her mind away from old terrors and noticed the corner of a paper that had fallen beneath the table. She bent and picked it up—and found her own note, written to him days ago, with the seal still unbroken.

Zenia held the note. It might have been delivered under the door, and kicked aside unnoticed. Perhaps he had not simply refused to come or answer. He had been ill for some time, though the maid had told Dr. Wells he had not lost his reason until just today, after she had believed him on the mend.

Zenia thought of the legal papers that had been delivered to her. They must have been sent before he grew so sick—they would have taken some time to compose. But she could not concentrate her mind on them. It did not seem important; nothing seemed important but the arduous sound of his breathing, and trying to make him drink, and take the tonic and the pills, and keep the temperature in the room steady as the night came on and he seemed to lose even the strength to speak or toss, but lay still, his forehead dry and burning, each breath a heavy gasp. Dr. Wells had taken a room at the hotel, warning them to expect a crisis, and leaving instructions to call him when it came.

Lord Belmaine stayed in a chair beside the bed. He seemed to think Zenia knew much more than she did—he asked her more than once if she thought he was getting worse, and if they should call Dr. Wells.

"I believe he is asleep," she said.

"Oh, asleep," his father said in relief.

He sat looking at his son. In the dim light of a shielded lamp, his eyes had a glitter.

"I have never seen him ill," he muttered. "Never once!"

Zenia heard the panic underlying his voice. She said with forced calm, "He must have been very, very strong to survive the wound he had in the desert. He will be stronger now, having had a month of excellent food and rest in England."

"Yes, that's true." Lord Belmaine said, in his simple longing to be reassured. After a long silence, he said, "Miss Elizabeth suffered like this?"

"Oh, no," Zenia said. "No."

"I'm glad." The earl cleared his throat. "It is much easier in children, I take it."

"Yes, that is what Elizabeth's doctor said too."

Lord Belmaine stared at his son. He stood up suddenly and took a few steps, then stopped and turned. "It is my fault."

Zenia looked up at him. He was standing in the center of the room, with a fixed look of anguish. "It is my fault," he said. "I made sure that he would never get sick; I dreaded that he would get sick. Measles, God forgive me."

She shook her head in automatic denial, but he rushed ahead.

"I would not let him go away to school, or mix with the village children. He was never sick. I thought it a positive good—I didn't know—I thought these things were outgrown. I didn't know an adult could have measles at all, far less that—" He stopped. "God knows, I learned to know how I could lose him to all the damnably desperate things he does! To see that scar on him! But if I have done this; if he dies and I have been the cause—" He shook his head blindly. "I pray God to forgive me. I will never forgive myself."

IT WAS AFTER one o'clock that they sent for the doctor. At first it seemed that Lord Winter's breathing had eased, growing so quiet that Zenia set her hand on his throat to feel it. Beneath her fingers, his skin was fiery and dry, but she could not even feel a pulse, only the faint, faint lift of his chest in tiny soundless pants. She gripped his slack hand and shook him, but he lay unresponsive, his head rolling aside on the pillow.

She looked up at Lord Belmaine, but he was already out of his chair and striding for the door. The minutes Dr. Wells took to come seemed like hours—Zenia did not let go of Lord Winter's hand, squeezing so hard that her muscles ached.

The doctor came hastily in, calling for more light, displacing Zenia and leaning over to lift his patient's eyelids. This time, Lord Winter made no response at all to the bright lamp.

"He has slipped into a coma. Now, Lady Winter, I want you to talk to him. And you, my lord. On any subject; ask him questions, say whatever you think may evoke a response. The Arabic would be appropriate, since he used it in his dementia. I will see a hot bath prepared."

The earl looked terrified; he did not even seem able to follow the doctor's instructions, but stood back from the bed with his hands in rigid fists.

Zenia took a breath, sat down on the bed and began to speak.

* * *

HIS FEET WERE burning. He could not lift them out of the red sand; it swallowed him up to his neck in a blaze of heat. But he could hear a voice, a constant voice, familiar and beckoning, speaking words he could not understand.

He saw light everywhere, a cold white light. He was so hot that he wanted to rise up into that cold light; he tried to let go, to make himself so light that he would rise, ignoring the insistent voice that called him back. He was too hot; he could not bear it; he could not stay any longer; the red heat tortured him, filling up his head with agony.

But the voice kept talking. He couldn't understand it; it seemed he had once, but not anymore. He wanted to tell it to stop, to let him sleep, let him drift up into the cold. Sometimes he was vaguely aware that it had gone away, only because it came back again. And strangely, he heard his father talking to him. He heard death in his father's voice, and gave himself to it, floating easily toward it, cooler and cooler, until finally the voices faded away, along with all he knew.

SWEET AND SOFT, there was a song. There was an angel and a cathedral, and then the cathedral vanished like a waking dream, but the sweet song stayed. His mind sorted among fancies and visions, trying to put the song where it belonged. He saw a bright line and realized it was light; it hurt his eyes but he wanted to see the singer.

He lifted his lashes, blinking against the pain of it. There was a woman, holding his hand between hers, singing down at it as sincerely as if she were in a church and reading from a book of hymns. For a moment he could not remember her name, but he remembered her. He remembered her song.

He tried to ask her if she was an angel, and startled himself with how weak his own voice was. The words emerged in a faint whisper, barely audible even to himself.

But she heard him. Her head lifted. Her hands clutched at his.

He remembered her name. "Little wolf," he said, stronger, curling his fingers about hers.

And she smiled. It was like dawn breaking, like the light that suddenly struck over a mountain, spreading glory. "You came back," she said. And just as suddenly as she had smiled, she began to cry.

He closed his eyes. He could feel her wet face pressed on his hand. He would have liked to listen to her sing again, but he couldn't keep his mind connected with the world long enough to ask. Sleep drew him under, safe and deep while she held him tight, binding him to life.

Twenty-four

—∞∞—

"Ten days, the doctor ordered," Mrs. Lamb said, "and ten days in bed it will be."

In truth, Arden was not ready to leave the bed himself. He closed his eyes at this news and sighed, swallowing the tonic with a grimace. He felt weak and sleepy, and long periods of time seemed to pass that he could not remember. He was sitting up now, with pillows propped behind him, but he would have been glad to lie down.

"Zenia was here," he said.

"That she was," the nurse said, "and the doctor said she was a rare trouper, too, the good girl."

"Where is she?"

"In Bentinck Street, sir, and asleep if she is wise."

"When will she come back?"

"Now, shame, sir, you will not say she is a prettier nurse than Henrietta Lamb? She has her baby to see to, and I am to nurse you until you are upon your feet again. And a sensible system it is, too, for I've yet to see the man who would not make life a misery for the wife who tries to nurse him to recovery."

"She could bring Beth. They could take the next room."

"Fie, do you want her to see you still looking like something the cat dragged in? She has a very neat beau in that Mr. Jocelyn, and you, sir, are not fit to be seen by daylight."

"Mr. Jocelyn?" Arden asked sharply, and began to cough.

Mrs. Lamb cast him a keen look. "He has come by every day, and stayed to dinner often."

Arden pushed himself up in bed. Mrs. Lamb brought a tray with disgusting-looking mashed matter of various colors on the plates.

"What is this?" he asked hoarsely.

"Minced veal, pease pudding, and pureed turnips."

"I can't," Arden said, moving his head back.

She picked up the tray. "A fine-looking man, that Mr. Jocelyn," she remarked. "A bachelor; no doubt he enjoys a dinner in company with a lady for a change. He's gone to Edinburgh, but he will be back after Candlemas."

Arden cleared his throat, staring glumly at the tray as she paused. "You are a beast, Mrs. Lamb."

"There, you see how it is. But I'm accustomed to such nasty abuse from my patients, having brought up boys by the score."

But Arden was not a bad patient, in spite of Mrs. Lamb's predictions. Though they said he had been near to dying—for the second time in as many years—he had little memory of the past few days. He recalled getting a hellish cold, and vaguely remembered frowning at the sudden rash on his skin, but little more than that beyond strange dreams, and that Zenia had been there with his father. Compared to his nightmarish struggle to live through his wound in the desert, the weeks of agony and deprivation, this easy bed and accommodating service was perfectly delightful.

He felt no real pain, except his throat was raw, but his body and brain seemed sunk in lassitude. He did not even mind his father's daily presence; the earl came and sat reading and writing for hours at a time, but he said little and left the inquiries and beleaguering to Mrs. Lamb, who had an instinct for knowing to precision just how far she could go. Arden talked to his father now and then, on such innocuous topics as the weather and likely reward of partridge shooting in January, but the earl seemed strangely subdued, almost shy.

The doctor came and went, and pronounced Arden fit to sit in a chair, and then to walk about the parlor. He began to feel himself again, not so sleepy or inclined to want to lie down, not so nauseated by the sight of food. It was, in its way, almost a pleasant interlude. He waited patiently for his body to restore itself; waiting in a new and tranquil patience that he had never felt before, based on the certainty that Zenia loved him.

He was taunted daily with the threat of Mr. Jocelyn, but he did not take it seriously. His father, he knew, was sending daily reports to her of his progress, and if Arden rather wished that he could see her, he found that he was vain enough to hear the truth in Mrs. Lamb's description of him as something disgraceful to behold. With the shedding of the measle eruptions had come a general patchy peel of his desert-tanned skin, and he was not inclined to be seen looking like some sort of molting rooster. He thought of writing Zenia himself, to tell her what he felt, how he had woken to see her there singing—but he started it twenty times and every attempt seemed to falter into a stiff and hollow "thank you," that conveyed worse than nothing of what he meant.

So he waited. Once he asked his father if she had mentioned

anything about the future, but the earl shook his head. "No. When I first went to her—before I discovered you ill—she said that she could not give an answer yet. But she's mentioned nothing since. I've only called twice, though, and then only for a moment. She seems to be doing well, and Miss Elizabeth is quite recovered."

Arden frowned. "You never said anything about that damned plan to send her abroad, did you?"

"Nothing at all. Nothing, I assure you. In fact, Mr. King says he has all but lost the draft proposal he drew up about that—some new clerk came in after Christmas and seems to have mislaid it permanently. I told him not to bother drafting another."

"Good," Arden said. "You can tell him to tear it up if he finds it."

ZENIA HAD DECIDED that perhaps Mrs. Lamb was correct, and on such a quiet, clear day, Elizabeth would enjoy a visit to the park. It was still January, and quite cold, but Zenia's convictions about insulating her daughter from any possible ailment had received a severe blow. She had discussed children's health at length with Mrs. Lamb and the doctor, and was now deep in a number of recommended books of advice on the subject. Some of them were not quite convincing—but she found that she could agree with the idea that as long as violent changes in temperature were avoided when the child was broken out in a perspiration, exposure to fresh, dry, cold air was more beneficial than otherwise. Besides, the atmosphere of London had been ugly and damp for weeks, and this first radiant blue Sunday seemed impossible to ignore.

Certainly no one else was ignoring it. Zenia said nothing when Mrs. Lamb insisted that Hyde Park would surely be too crowded to be attempted, and Regent's Park was a far better choice. Ever since her return the week before from nursing Lord

Winter through his recovery, Mrs. Lamb had been subjecting Zenia to the most blatant matchmaking efforts. While she was not entirely deaf to them—not deaf at all—she could not forget the sheaf of papers from Mr. King's office. According to Mrs. Lamb, he was on pins to see her, but that, Zenia did not doubt, was mere hyperbole. If he wished to see her so badly, he could have called. He had been declared recovered and free to go about for a week. Every knock upon the door had sent Zenia hurrying to brush her hair or pull off her apron, but he had not come.

However, Mrs. Lamb's shameless gaiety about this Sunday outing seemed highly suspicious. So suspicious, in fact, that Zenia decided to wear the azure-colored dress, the blue wool that Lady Belmaine could not approve for a dinner gown, but had reluctantly admitted might make up into a walking dress. It had a tight, short-waisted spencer jacket with military trim of black braiding, and with her black cape and muff, and a black bonnet with a wide blue ribbon added to tie beneath her chin, she thought it was rather lively. Leaning close to the mirror, she wondered if it really did bring out the dark blue in her eyes, or if that was only her imagination. But there was no time to ponder that, as Mrs. Lamb came hurrying in with Elizabeth, announcing that the hackney was at the door to carry ma'am to church.

IT HAD BEEN arranged that Mrs. Lamb and Elizabeth would meet Zenia after the church service, since St. Marylebone was just outside the park. They were waiting, Elizabeth so shrouded in warm clothes that only her face and her feet showed, her bright eyes staring about her in fascination.

Zenia gave her a laughing hug, just because she was such a silly-looking bundle in her mounds of petticoats and pantaloons and little cape. Mrs. Lamb undertook the task of carrying her as they followed a crossing boy to negotiate the road and then entered the park gates.

Under a perfect blue sky, the long white facade of houses that lined the park's perimeter seemed to glow. Their spired domes were tinted a soft verdigris and tamed into the same perfect regularity of the houses themselves, face upon face all the same, stretching away along the boundary. Inside the iron fence, ladies strolled in cloaks as bright as Zenia's dress, scarlets and purples and golds, holding the arms of dark-coated gentlemen.

Elizabeth gazed silently at the packs of children running under the leafless trees, tossing crumbs to the ducks or drinking steaming chocolate from one of the refreshment tents. "I shall buy us a pie," Zenia announced.

"I'm sure she would like it, ma'am," Mrs. Lamb said amiably. "Though she ate all her porridge not an hour ago."

When Zenia returned, the nurse was sitting on a bench, watching Elizabeth and another small boy gaze at one another, both of them standing still and expressionless, not two feet apart. Just as Zenia reached them, a school of shrieking children ran past, sending both of the toddlers tumbling in heaps upon the grass. The little boy started to cry, but Elizabeth sat up laughing. She began to run in a bobbing circle, her arms out straight for balance, as the other children danced about her.

Zenia watched. Then she sat down next to Mrs. Lamb and shared out the pie, eating her own portion with relish.

Elizabeth fell down again, and by the time she stood up, the older children had passed on, yelling and shoving at one another. She stood looking after them. After a few tentative steps in that direction, she lost her nerve and looked back doubtfully toward Zenia and Mrs. Lamb.

Her face lit suddenly. "Gah-on!" she cried, and began to run back on an angle that would take her right past the bench.

Zenia turned. Lord Winter was bending down, the long skirts

of his dark blue greatcoat sweeping the ground; Elizabeth raced into her father's arms as fast as her bobbling legs would carry her. He lifted her up high in the air.

An army officer stood a few yards beyond him, gorgeous in plume and gold braid, but to Zenia there was no outfit more superb than Lord Winter's dark simplicity; no one handsomer or taller or with such a smile. Such a smile; it was still lingering when he settled Elizabeth against his shoulder and looked toward Zenia.

She felt her lips curl shyly. Mrs. Lamb put on a look of utterly blank innocence. He was paler than he had been, but he appeared fit. Looking at him now, Zenia could hardly recall the gaunt, suffering face of his illness—he had life in his smile and in his body; he moved with the same easy dominance, swinging Elizabeth down and sitting on his heels before Zenia.

"Hullo," he said softly, glancing at her and then back at Elizabeth.

"How are you?" she asked.

"Perfectly well." He took Elizabeth onto his knee, putting his head down to hers. "But I'll thank you not to give me any spots again, beloved."

Elizabeth crowed happily. "Gah-on!" she said, looking at him so closely that they touched noses.

"She seems stout," he said.

"Oh, yes. She came through it splendidly."

There was an awkward moment, in which the sound of children shouting and a distant band from somewhere in the park did not give Zenia any ideas for further conversation; at least none that she felt comfortable introducing in public. He seemed to find a duck waddling quickly after a fleeing child to be quite fascinating.

He stood up, letting Elizabeth slide off his knee. For a moment of panic, she thought he was going to take his leave.

"Perhaps you—" He cleared his throat. "I am a member of the Zoological Society. Would you like to walk in the gardens?"

Zenia lifted her face. Before she could answer, he added quickly, "The menagerie is open to members today. I thought Beth might like to see the animals."

She smiled. "That would be pleasant."

He took off his hat, reaching down and lifting Beth, perching her on his shoulders.

Zenia pursed her lips, frowning. "I don't think you should go without your hat in this cold."

He held it out to Mrs. Lamb to carry, batting Elizabeth's skirts away from his face as he cast an amused half-glance toward Zenia. "But please may I stay out another half-hour, Mama?"

She returned an arch look. "Someone must look after foolish children and madmen."

He smiled at her, clapped Elizabeth's hands over his ears, and walked ahead down the broad path.

MRS. LAMB AND Zenia made diligent small talk about the park and the weather as they strolled under the bare trees toward the Zoological Gardens. Arden felt happily at ease, listening silently, feeling Beth's warm weight on his shoulders.

He had reached a decision in the long, quiet days of his recovery. She had been badgered by lawyers; coldly informed of her best interests and Beth's; Arden had made love to her as if she were his by right—she was, but there were forms and conventions; there was a correct and proper way to go about these things, and he had grievously neglected it.

A lady, his book of *Polite Usage and Diction* informed him, had a right to be courted.

Without precisely planning it with Mrs. Lamb, the most flagrant of allies, he had resolved on this meeting in the park. The weather had done him a great favor, and Mrs. Lamb had done the rest—he had been walking here every day for the past three, in hopes they would come out, but it being Sunday gave him the excuse of the zoo, which would take hours to tour, if he had anything to do with it.

"Let me take her down to feed the ducks, sir," Mrs. Lamb said, as they passed out of the Inner Circle, where a scent of recently turned soil permeated the winter tranquillity of the beds. Without subtlety, she added, "You need not hurry. We will meet you the other side of the water."

Arden traded his hat for Beth, who toddled off willingly after a mallard that knew just how to stay a tantalizing few feet in front of her. Arden did not give himself time to grow ill at ease: he knew that the more time he allowed to pass the more difficult it would be to make his tongue form words; he would begin to hear how silly they would sound; how likely she would think him an ass—*God and St. George!* he thought sardonically, and plunged into his prepared speech.

"Miss Bruce," he said, dashing a look at her profile. "I would like to call you Miss Bruce, because I would like to begin again. At the beginning. I should like to—" He felt the foolishness of it begin to creep in, undermining his confidence. "You will think it ridiculous, perhaps. But if we could start as if we had just met—I have thought that the trouble between us might be a result of the unusual circumstance; the rather strange manner in which we—became entangled in this situation. That is—you do not know me in this setting, and I do not know you. And I hope—I should very much like—should be honored, that is to say—to make your acquaintance, Miss Bruce."

There, he thought. And it sounded just as absurd as he had feared. And she was not looking at him, or answering. And he stood holding his hat, frowning down at the brim, until he remembered the next part. He reached under his cloak and drew the white rosebud from his waistcoat.

"Because you are as rare as a rose in winter," he said—shameless plagiarism from his book of diction, "I thought of you when I picked this."

Of course he had not precisely picked the thing; he had obtained it on the advice of A Lady of Quality, the one who had written the book—and gone to the devil of a lot of trouble and expense to find the only florist in the city who did not laugh at the idea of a true white rose in this season—a small detail which apparently carried no weight with Ladies of Quality.

She accepted it, looking down at the flower. Arden could not see her expression.

He waited.

His breath frosted around him. He stared at a distant black dog that wove its way along the iron fence at the park edge.

"There are several petals damaged," he remarked, because the silence had become such an abhorrent vacuum.

She began to giggle. To his vast humiliation she began to laugh.

He stood rigidly before her, while passersby turned at the sound—he saw them grinning—it must be obvious she was laughing at him, at what he had done and said, for she was holding the rose where everyone could see it.

He felt as hot and ill as he had two weeks ago; flushed with stiff misery, his jaw set hard. He would rather have been facing a battery of Ibrahim Pasha's heavy guns than stand there, but he could not think what else to do.

"Oh!" she said, lifting her face. "Oh, did you truly think of me?"

He realized slowly that her cheeks were pink with cold and

pleasure, her eyes wide with a wonder as new and innocent as Beth's. She was still giggling, a strange hiccuping mirth from deep in her throat that he suddenly recognized was halfway to tears.

"Certainly I thought of you," he said gravely. "And if you are going to laugh at my rose, Miss Bruce, I shall take it back."

The rose vanished under her cloak and muff. "You may not have it, my lord."

It was hardly repartee of any great wit. He had not ever felt a particular need to banter with his lovers, nor to pursue any woman through flirtation. He had generally found that by looking at a desirable female in a certain way, he got his point across, and then they either sought him out or they did not. But they had been experienced women, always; they had not come for pretty badinage. Though he did not himself have any idea of it, Lord Winter, in his detached reserve, his satanic looks and intriguing travels, his well-known ruthlessness in ending any affair at his own convenience, had rather a reputation for being dangerous—even with the ladies who were considered dangerous themselves.

He felt, at the moment, more like a maladroit gawk. Women as objects of appetite were well within the range of his expertise; if she had been the usual amorous widow he would have simply let her talk as he walked her to his rooms or hers. But as much as he wanted to take her directly to bed and hold her and thrust himself inside her and use her until neither of them could move, Zenia was distinct and different; her rebuff could wound him; her disdain would exile him—he felt like a vagabond standing outside a lamp-lit room, liable at any moment to be invited in or driven away.

"May I offer you my arm?" he asked, on the advice of A Lady of Quality. As she accepted his escort, she said nothing. And the longer that she said nothing, the more he felt himself on the verge of blurting something rash or stupid.

"Do you like flowers?" he asked—uninspired but safe.

"Oh, yes," she said, smiling at him.

"What are your favorite kinds?"

"I think—" She bent her head so far down that he could not see her face under the bonnet. "White roses," she murmured.

Nearly, very nearly, he said in an ironical tone, *How gratifying!* But he stopped himself in time. "Then I'm glad I finally managed to locate one. It was no easy task, you may believe me."

She slanted a look up at him, a faint surprise. "Wherever did you find it growing at this time of year?"

"Ah," he said. "Ah."

She was still looking at him in inquiry after that splendid answer.

"I ordered it from a florist," he said, driven rapidly onto the rocks. "But if I had picked it, it would certainly have reminded me of you."

Still she looked up slantwise at him, her lips pursed gently. He could not tell if she was offended or amused.

"I bought a book," he said in desperation. "There is a recommendation for each month, you see—January is a white rose."

She turned her face away, looking straight ahead as they walked. "I think," she said slowly, "that you are right, my lord. Perhaps we should become acquainted. Perhaps I do not know you at all."

"Then allow me to advise you at once that I'm a saphead," he said jovially. "Supposing you have not divined it already."

She lifted her chin. "If you please, sir—I shall draw my own conclusions."

He bowed. "A lady's perogative."

As they neared the rustic gates at the entrance of the Zoological Gardens, Lord Winter's pace slowed abruptly. "Damnation," he said under his breath, and as Zenia looked up at him in inquiry, he turned to Mrs. Lamb. "I'll take her—"

"Winter!" cried a lady's voice, modulated in the most genteel accents, but carrying well for all that. "How do you do? Your dear mother wrote me the glad news of your return to us unharmed! All the angels rejoice, my dear, but what a horrible boy you are, to give us such a dreadful fright!"

It was a matron of some years and considerable stature who held out her black-gloved hand. As she stood with her companions, two younger women, Lord Winter turned from Zenia and Mrs. Lamb to make a brief bow over her fingertips. "Ma'am," he said. "How do you do?"

"Of course you have not the slightest notion of me, do you? It is Lady Broxwood, your godmother's first cousin," she said imperturbably, and cast a look toward her friends. "We have not met above five hundred times, but since I do not ride a camel, he will have nothing to do with me."

"Oh, indeed," said the younger of the two, a pretty, petite blonde girl several years younger than Zenia, "is it—" She stopped, looking self-conscious.

"May I entreat you, Mrs. George, to allow me to introduce Lord Winter to you," Lady Broxwood said.

The older woman stepped forward and gave Lord Winter's hand a firm shake, her heavily freckled face lighting with an open, contagious smile. "It is a great pleasure," she said. The wrinkles of sun and laughter about her eyes made a cheerful contrast to her plainly styled widow's weeds. "I should very much like to hear of your travels."

"Mrs. George and her niece are famous travelers themselves," Lady Broxwood said. "Lady Caroline, I present Lord Winter to you. Winter, Lady Caroline Preston."

The younger girl shook hands with the same confidence as her aunt. Her face was aglow with such enthusiasm that her prettiness became a positive beauty. "You have no notion how I have longed to meet you, sir! Arabian horses are my passion! Oh, Aunt—Lady Broxwood—you do not treat this gentleman with enough respect! He has brought the greatest mare ever foaled out of the desert, the Jelibiyat String of Pearls!"

Zenia saw the reserved expression on Lord Winter's face change. He held Lady Caroline's hand a moment. "You are familiar with desert horses?"

"Oh, a mere dilettante, I assure you," she said. "But I have an extremely knowledgeable correspondent in Cairo, and another in Bombay. The word, my lord, is that she is beyond price. Beyond imagination. How I yearn to see her! Will you bring her to London?"

"You must come to Swanmere to see her," he said immediately.

"How wonderfully kind! I should be—indeed, I can hardly express myself! I am euphoric! I had not dreamed of such a chance." She smiled at him, her hand still in his, and then at Zenia. This open look seemed to prompt the other ladies to her presence, and there was a moment of expectation.

Lord Winter paused, the corner of his mouth turned up a little; an ironic, half-smiling twist as he glanced at her. "May I present"—there was the barest instant of hesitation—"my good friend Miss Bruce."

"How happy I am to meet you, Miss Bruce. And who is this?" Lady Caroline asked gaily, turning to Elizabeth after everyone had politely taken Zenia's hand. She leaned over and pursed her lips, blowing out her cheeks with a great pouf that made Elizabeth squeak and laugh and reach out toward her face. "Is this your jolly little niece, Miss Bruce? What a beautiful child! And fortunate to have an auntie as good as mine, to take you everywhere."

"This is Miss Elizabeth," Lord Winter said, into the long lull after her innocent remark. That was all.

It felt a stinging blow. To be introduced as Miss Bruce, to have him fail to recognize Elizabeth as his daughter—a bitter anxiety settled in the pit of Zenia's stomach. Along with the papers, the contract that would send her to Switzerland, it put a new and chilling interpretation on his sudden gallantry and suggestion that they start afresh. She could not blame him; she had no one but herself to reproach, and yet, after his illness, after she had worried and feared and loved him so much—somehow it seemed that she would have another chance, that he had been giving it to her with his white rose and halting chivalry. For a few moments, for half an hour, she had thought—something. Something that she was not certain now that he meant.

She could see that Lady Broxwood was looking at her in that keen, expressionless way that the Countess Belmaine's friends had. While Zenia had not gone out into society during the Belmaines' mourning, she had always been introduced as his wife within the limited circle of Swanmere. If Lady Broxwood was an acquaintance of his mother's, she must suspect who and what Zenia was to him—and Elizabeth too. Zenia waited apprehensively for some cut or rudeness, but Lady Broxwood only turned her attention to Lord Winter.

"You are a godsend, Winter," she said summarily. "A fellow of the zoo society, are you not? We were just told to our faces that we must have a member with us to enter today."

"Yes," he said, rather coldly. "I am a member."

"Come, you hateful boy—has your lady mother neglected all your manners? You don't object to taking us through? We will pay our own shilling, I promise you, if your pockets are so much to let!"

"Oh, no—perhaps Lord Winter is engaged—" Mrs. George said calmly. "I have every intention of subscribing myself, now that we are back in London to stay. We shall go through another day."

"Nonsense," said Lady Broxwood. "And what has Lady Caroline been pining to do since you both got off the boat? Come, Miss Bruce, I'm quite sure Miss Elizabeth is *aux anges* to ride an elephant, is she not? Lady Caroline can show her the way."

Lady Caroline laughed. "Oh, indeed, but you must not look so horrified, Miss Bruce! I very well can, you know. I was riding an elephant when I was but four days old. You must not be frightened of them. They are the gentlest of creatures in the proper hands. They can pick up a feather off the floor."

"Or out of your hat," said Mrs. George. "Let us not blame Miss Bruce if she maintains a prudent respect for the creatures. You, my young lady, are entirely too sanguine, and will undoubtedly come to your just end one fine day."

"Why, when I have seen you ride Tulwar straight at a tigress, Aunt! Mrs. George is perfectly intrepid, I promise you—far braver than I, and cunning too! There is not a hunter in India who would not take her advice on tracking wild boar."

"Come, child, you are embarrassing me extremely," her aunt said, with a little sharpness under her amiable smile. "That is not at all true, and hardly the sort of thing that will draw admiration in polite circles."

"Then I think polite circles entirely foolish," Lady Caroline declared stubbornly. "If they do not appreciate you as they should, then I shall have nothing to do with them! What do you think of it, Lord Winter?"

"I believe polite circles are tolerably foolish," he said.

"There. Our oracle has spoken," Lady Caroline said. "Let us go in to the animals! Miss Elizabeth and I are on pins to ride the elephant!"

Twenty-five

The afternoon took on a nightmarish quality to Arden. He made abortive attempts to assert some sort of authority, some organization that might separate him and Zenia and Beth at least a few yards from the rest, but of all the things he had no notion how to command, a herd of women, he discovered, was the foremost in perversity and festive obstinance.

He found himself entering the Lion House carrying Beth, with Lady Caroline beside him and Zenia trailing behind in an ever-changing regrouping, sometimes with Mrs. George, sometimes with a stone-faced Mrs. Lamb, and now and then, to Arden's dread, with Lady Broxwood. He did not trust that woman to be kind, or even civil—he had no idea of what she knew or assumed, but Lady Caroline kept addressing questions to him, perfectly intelligent, provocative questions about the animals and the

Zoological Society's intentions in collecting them, forcing him to answer or to pretend he had not heard. She must think him remarkably deaf by now, but no matter how he tried to fall back and walk beside Zenia, he was cut out by one or the other feminine claim on his attention: Lady Broxwood's demand that he tell Mrs. George of the highest recorded temperature in the Arabian desert; Mrs. Lamb's curt mandate to give Miss Elizabeth to her for a change of napkin; Lady Caroline's questions about the different syllables used to command camels. Only Mrs. George seemed content to walk quietly, mostly beside Zenia—which finally seemed the least of evils to Arden, and so he ceased trying to rearrange it all and let them have their way.

The decided odor of exotic animals assailed them as he held open the door into the big cats' abode. The ladies filed past him. He held Beth close, walking well in the center of the long, wide corridor. It was dimly lit and stone cold, lined down both sides with barred cages.

On such a bright day in winter, there were not many patrons viewing the exhibit, only a few serious-looking gentlemen, one seated with a sketch pad before the black leopard, and a boy who was asking the attendant eagerly when feeding time would be. His high-pitched voice echoed in the hall, and somewhere down the row a lion's grumble escalated into an impressive roar. As the reverberations died away, Lady Caroline said softly, "That makes my heart go hot and cold."

Arden looked at her with some interest. She was an unusual girl; he would have liked her rather better than he did if she had not been such a damned inconvenience. For a female, she was easy to talk to; certainly charming to look at—in his present state of long privation he was extremely easy to please with regard to feminine anatomy, and Lady Caroline's pink soft skin and shapely bosom positively endeared her to him in that respect. He felt like a lecherous bastard, but he was so shy of Zenia, so afraid of a repulse, of saying the wrong thing again, and Zenia gave him no help; she did not chatter easily like Lady Caroline or ask him things to which he instantly knew the answer or come and stand beside him and breathe in that exuberant way that made her breasts lift and pull at the tight buttoning on her military-style jacket. No, Zenia hung back even when he tried to join her, slowing her steps until they were almost standing still, which made the whole group pause and gather about them, remarking on whatever bird or beast happened to be nearest, as if that were what had caused them to halt.

He had given up on it by the time they reached the end of the aviary. His afternoon with Zenia was hopelessly scuttled; he decided that he would at least enjoy the time with Beth, who was boisterously delighted by every animal, and perhaps then he could take them home, and go in, and talk to Zenia, and if he made himself particularly affable, perhaps if he was exceptionally fortunate and she was feeling particularly affectionate . . .

He stood holding Beth, contemplating the sexual act in powerful and vivid detail, hardly aware that he was staring at Lady Caroline as she stood before a tiger's cage; only conscious of the cat's rhythmic prowl and turn, back and forth and back and forth across the narrow limits of its cell, a vigorous beat to the cadence of his imagination.

Lady Caroline looked over her shoulder at him, frowning a little. "You will say I am a sentimental miss, but I cannot help but wish they could be free. Look at how he paces; how vehement his eyes are. He longs to be gone; to be back in his element."

Arden wrenched himself back from erotic invention to the present moment, profoundly embarrassed. "Yes," he said, his own voice sounding too loud in the echoing hall. He cast a guarded look to see if Zenia had been watching him. He thought she was, though he could not turn to be sure.

"You agree, Lord Winter?" Lady Caroline asked, smiling at

him. "But you would understand. People speak often of freedom, but I believe it requires a knowledge of the true cost of a free life to genuinely value it. If he were in the jungle, this fellow, every day of his existence would be struggle and savagery. Here it is easy. But still he longs to be free. He has tasted it, and anything less will always be torture to him."

"Certainly," Arden said, wishing that she had not worn quite such a tight bodice. "Torture."

Lady Caroline slipped her hand into the crook of his arm, turning to move further down the hall. "I'm glad you don't think my conjectures so odd as others sometimes do. I've not been into London society yet. My aunt warns me that I may not find it pleasant. People can be disagreeably severe, she says, and I fear I may not be quite the thing."

"I'm sure you will be the thing," he said, pausing to let Beth coo at an ocelot that was sticking its paw through the bars. "Whatever the deuce the thing may be."

She laughed as if he had made a great jest, the sound of it resonating against the roof. "That is reassuring."

He shrugged. "I'm hardly the one to know," he said. "I detest polite society."

Her hand curled tighter on his arm. "Do you?" She lowered her voice and bent her head toward him. "I should not say so, for Lady Broxwood has been so kind—but I'm entirely of the same mind. There is nothing so dull as a ball or rout—in Bombay we used to have them until I was ready to scream for the tedium of it. But then Aunt and Uncle George would always promise to take me on a hunt, or a trek into the mountains. Have you seen the Himalayas, Lord Winter?"

"I have not," he said.

She squeezed his arm. "I wish I might have the privilege of being there, my lord, to see your face when you do."

Arden began to feel a sensation of entrapment. He turned,

dismayed to find Zenia very close behind him. "You have her much too near," she said sharply, and for an instant he thought she was speaking of Lady Caroline's attachment to his arm, but he realized that she meant Beth and the ocelot, who were stretching toward one another.

"Of course," he said, using his move away from the spotted cat to slip free of Lady Caroline. "Am I the only one who finds this a melancholy exhibit? Let us proceed apace to feed the monkeys."

LORD WINTER WAS by no means the only one who felt melancholy. Zenia suffered every degree of jealous misery, from rage to hurt to despair, struck to the heart with the look of stark intensity on his face as he gazed at Lady Caroline and the caged tiger.

Zenia hated the zoological exhibits. She hated the yellow-eyed cats pacing relentlessly in their prisons: their beauty and their wildness; their frustration. She hated Lady Caroline for speaking of it, for standing beside him as he held Elizabeth, for detesting polite society, for being exactly and precisely and effortlessly the woman who should be his wife.

Lady Caroline loved the jungles and wild places, she spoke lightly of hardships and dangers. She was the first to feed the monkeys and bears, and pleaded with Zenia so prettily that Miss Elizabeth would be perfectly, perfectly safe upon the elephant that Zenia was constrained to let her ride. She had supposed it would be Lord Winter who took Elizabeth up, but it was Lord Winter and Lady Caroline, with Elizabeth tucked between them, squealing " 'Fant! 'Fant!" at the top of her lungs, while the animal's huge ears flapped languidly back and forth as it walked ponderously about the yard, each huge foot squeezing up a circle of mud. Lady Caroline waved at them, her skirts all akimbo so that her boots and stockinged ankles showed, though she pretended with a mischievous smile to try to push down her petticoats—

which only drew Lord Winter's attention to the whole business, Zenia thought angrily.

"I hope we have not spoiled your outing," Lady Broxwood said in a low voice, coming up beside Zenia as she watched.

"Of course not," she said coldly.

"Lady Belmaine particularly wished him to be introduced to her. They do suit, do they not?"

Zenia could not bear it; she looked aside at Lady Broxwood.

"I should not in general notice a person of your position, Miss Bruce," the older woman said, "but as I understand that you and the little girl are to go the Continent directly, and Lord Winter so rarely appears in society, I felt I could not scruple to pass over such a golden opportunity for them to become acquainted." She gave Zenia a piercing look. "You have been most discreet today; I am sure you will continue so."

"You need not be concerned, ma'am," Zenia said, her lips curling proudly. "We are going home as soon as Elizabeth is let down."

LORD WINTER ESCORTED Zenia to the front door in Bentinck Street, while Lady Broxwood's large, elegant carriage waited beside the curb.

"Zenia, I will come back as soon as I see them to—wherever the devil they live," he said, while Zenia stood holding Elizabeth, waiting for the maid to answer the door. Mrs. Lamb lingered at the foot of the steps, finding the coal hole of supreme interest.

"You need not," Zenia said. She had kept the tremble from her voice for all the time it had taken to disengage from the party, to suffer the discussion of whether they should all ride home in Lady Broxwood's chaise, to listen to Lady Caroline's enthusiasm and Mrs. George's invitation to dinner. Lord Winter had accepted the invitation, looking hard at Zenia—and she had refused it, of course, on account of her fictitious sister, Elizabeth's fanciful nameless mother. "You need not come back," she said to him now, hearing the tremble threaten.

"It was horrible, I know," he said low. "I am so sorry, beloved."

The door opened. The housemaid held it wide, curtsying.

"I am coming back," he said. "I want to talk to you."

Zenia stepped inside. She didn't turn to look at him. She heard Mrs. Lamb come in, and the door closed behind her. "Please change Elizabeth's clothes immediately." Zenia said, handing her to the nurse. "She smells like a menagerie." Without pausing, Zenia pounded up the stairs.

In her bedroom, she tore off her cloak and gloves, hurling the muff into the corner of the room. She pulled her bonnet off and began to pace like the caged animals had paced.

"I cannot bear it." She panted a little, biting her lip. "Impossible, impossible, impossible." Her eyes blurred. "It is impossible!" she cried.

She stopped, staring out the window down into the little garden. Angry tears spilled down her cheeks.

"I have done this! I would not listen to them. It is my fault. Oh, Elizabeth, it is my fault!" She pressed her fists and forehead against the cold windowpane. "If only—"

If only what? If only she was married to him now? If only it had been Lady Winter who had stood there and watched him with her? And if not Lady Caroline, then some other; some free and fearless woman of his own heart—he did not even know himself; he still believed in some connection that could bind them— Zenia did not know if he meant marriage still or the house in Switzerland, but it made no matter. She could not bear either. She would not.

She flung herself down at the writing desk. The letter to Mr. Jocelyn in Edinburgh did not take so long to write, it was only that she stared for so long at the blank paper, weeping, and finally laid her head down on her arms and sobbed until she was hoarse.

Mrs. Lamb came in quietly and laid a hand on her shoulder. Zenia sat up, turning her face away.

"His lordship promised he would return," the nurse said firmly. "You must have a little faith in him, ma'am."

"You don't understand," Zenia said, leaning her forehead on her hand.

"A mustard seed will move mountains. And this is only a little hill, ma'am, if you'll pardon me."

"You don't understand. She is right for him. Perfect for him. He doesn't even understand himself. Freedom is everything to him. It is his very life. Like those animals in the cages—he will fret himself to death if he cannot go. And if I—if I don't—if I don't have the courage to let him go now, I shall have to w-watch—" She swallowed. "It would kill me."

"What, do you suppose he will fret to death if he cannot ride an elephant in some nasty desert? When he has you and Miss Elizabeth at home?"

"He will take her!"

"Then perhaps you ought to go along too, ma'am!"

Zenia sobbed. "You don't understand! You don't know what the desert is—it is not elephants, or tiger hunts with servants, or whatever it is that Lady Caroline spoke about. It is life and death, and he must live between them or he is not alive at all."

"Nonsense. I never heard such talk."

"He has a djinni; he has a demon in his blood. My mother did. And I am afraid that Elizabeth has it too."

"Please, ma'am, a demon! Your own husband. I would spank a child for such folderol."

Zenia began to laugh and cry at once. "Oh, you have not seen him. You have never seen him when he is Abu Haj Hasan, and rides against the Saudi or the Rowalla. He is so beautiful and terrifying. I am the only one who knows." She shook her head. "The only one."

She stared into nothing, remembering what she had wanted to forget and could not. It was the demon-haunted man that she had first learned to love; the man she would trust with her life, and yet feared to the depth of her soul because he knew no fear himself.

"Now, ma'am," Mrs. Lamb said, "it's only that silly chit this afternoon has put you in a black melancholy with all her talk of elephants. Dry your eyes, for his lordship will be here soon."

Zenia jerked to attention. "No!" She turned to the paper. "I will not see him. I cannot." She scribbled, folded the letter, and handed it to Mrs. Lamb. "This is to go to the post office directly. Find a boy to take it immediately, do you understand?"

Mrs. Lamb opened her mouth, clearly intending to object. But then she closed it. She made a curtsy. "Yes, ma'am."

It was the nurse who met Arden at the door and slipped out onto the step, closing the door firmly behind her.

"Ma'am is not at home," she said.

"That bad?" he asked apprehensively.

"If you were one of mine, I would box your ears, sir. Box your ears! Why you allowed that horrid girl to hang all about you while you made such sheep's eyes at her, I can't conceive!"

"Did it seem that I looked at her so?" he asked in consternation. "I made sure that I did no such thing."

Mrs. Lamb snorted. "And after all the trouble I have been to, convincing ma'am that you cherish her!"

"She won't even see me?"

"Worse, my lord. I am to find a boy to carry this to the post office." She waved the note in her hand in such a way that Arden could see Mr. Jocelyn's name and direction on it clearly. "Of course, it being Sunday, the post office isn't open."

He held out his hand. "I'll take it."

Mrs. Lamb held the paper back. "Oh, God save me, sir—I have meddled far past my place already. What if she were to find out?"

"Mrs. Lamb," he said gently, "who would blame you for obeying the orders of your employer?"

She hesitated. "Indeed, sir. Indeed," she said, on a more thoughtful note.

"I have not generally found it necessary to interfere between you and your mistress, but now I do. I will take responsibility for this letter, if you will simply recall who pays your wage."

"Yes, sir," she said, smiling as she dipped a curtsy. She handed him the note. "She is most upset, my lord. Those ladies made the afternoon difficult for her, especially that wicked old biddy Lady Broxwood. My sister nursed her son's little girls, and she is a—well, sir, I should not speak ill of my betters, and I won't. But she is a tartar. Still, I think ma'am may regret whatever she has said in that letter by morning, and I do hate to send it off so thoughtless."

"All the more reason to protect her from some ill-conceived folly, Mrs. Lamb. What are husbands for?"

"I'm sure I sometimes wonder," Mrs. Lamb said. "You've near run the poor girl mad, I vow—all she can say of you is that you are a demon, pray, and she can't decide if you are beautiful or frightful! Now I ask you if that is a Christian fancy!"

"Beautiful?" Arden asked quickly.

"No doubt you are a well-looking gentleman when you have a care for your appearance," Mrs. Lamb said, looking him up and down, "though I don't like to encourage vanity in man nor child."

"Did she say she thought the djinni beautiful?" he asked.

"These heathen words," she grumbled.

"The djinni, the demon," he said urgently.

"She said," Mrs. Lamb snapped, "that she was the only one who knows." She turned to go back in. "And as a baptised Christian I will not stand on the stoop discussing such foolery. Good day to you."

Arden stuck the note in his pocket and bounded down the stairs. He strode rapidly along the street, and when he had turned the corner he abandoned all gentlemanly compunction and opened the letter.

Dearest Mr. Jocelyn, it said, *I am pleased to accept your proposal. As my situation here has become insupportable, I would be deeply obliged to you if we may be married as soon as arrangements can be made. Gratefully, Z.S.B.*

Arden stopped dead in the street.

Then he swore savagely. He took the muddy gutter in one violent stride, stopping traffic with no more than the mad force of his glare.

ZENIA STOOD IN her traveling dress, scowling at Mrs. Lamb. The nurse's stubborn refusal to accompany Elizabeth and Zenia north was the final straw. Since the day Mr. Jocelyn's answer had arrived, complete with railway tickets and detailed instructions for Zenia to meet him in Yorkshire for their wedding, as he could not come away from his business in Edinburgh long enough to travel back to London, the nurse had lost all her motherly kindness. Though she continued to treat Elizabeth with loving care, once Mrs. Lamb had finally understood that Zenia was not only not married to Lord Winter, but intending to wed another man, she was defiantly unequivocal about the proposed journey north.

"It would be plain murder to take that poor tyke on such a trip! All the way to Yorkshire! In January! When she has all but just risen from her deathbed!" Mrs. Lamb declared. "And on one of those horrid, dangerous railways that are exploding every day! I will have nothing to do with it. I will pack my things this moment if you wish, ma'am, but I will not go with you, nor will I put so much as a hairbrush into her little bag to help you to it!"

"I cannot leave her here!" Zenia cried, though Mr. Jocelyn's letter had strongly counseled her to do just that, for much the same reasons Mrs. Lamb quoted.

"Then I suggest that you reconsider the trip yourself, ma'am. It is monstrous impropriety. It is wicked. If it were not for poor Miss Elizabeth's sake. I should be long gone from this house, knowing what I know now."

"There is nothing wicked about my marrying Mr. Jocelyn!" Zenia felt herself on the verge of a hysterical fit. She had been wretched in the time between sending her letter and receiving his reply, alternating between repentance and determination, hardly able to eat for the sick ache of grief inside her. Now that the definite answer had arrived, she was edgy and miserable, afraid that if she hesitated one moment she would lose her nerve.

"It is wicked when you are already married!" Mrs. Lamb tossed her chin up with the haughtiness of the righteous.

"I have told you I am not!"

"You are married in the eyes of God. And you have your little girl to think of."

"Mrs. Lamb, please! It is only for a very short time. We must be at the station by ten, or miss the train we are to take!"

"I tell you, ma'am, I am not going. If you must do this unholy thing, then you may leave Miss Elizabeth with me. At least then she will not have her innocence blackened by her mother's sins."

"It is not a sin!" Zenia screamed. "It is *not*!"

The nurse's eyes widened. Zenia heard herself with shock; Lady Hester's vicious temper in her voice.

She drew a sharp breath, shaking. "I'm sorry," she said. "I'm sorry. But we must go."

Mrs. Lamb's lower lip tightened obstinately. At that sign of balking, Zenia felt violence surge through her, a mad desire to grab the nearest object and hurl it against the wall.

"All right," she gasped, afraid that she would lose control of herself. "All right, you may keep Elizabeth here. But you may not let Lord Winter call on her. And he must not take her anywhere!"

"He is her fa—"

"He has no right to touch her!" Zenia cried. "If I come back and she is gone, I'll make certain you hang for it! I will see you hung for the abduction of my child, do you understand me? I will see you hung!" Her voice was echoing back from the open door and the stairwell. She gripped her hands together and stood still, striving for command of her temper. "Do you understand me?" she asked, in a steadier tone.

"Yes, ma'am," Mrs. Lamb said, visibly cowed. "I believe his lordship has left London, in any case."

"How do you know that?"

The nurse curtsied, her eyes cast down. "I believe he said so when he last tried to call here, ma'am, and you would not see him."

"Good," Zenia said. She found that her breathing had become more regular. "That is good. I will feel easier then. I know that you will be responsible with her."

"Oh, yes, ma'am. I promise we will go along quite as we always do."

"I shall not be gone above four days."

"Yes, ma'am," Mrs. Lamb said meekly.

Twenty-six

⸻

"DOES YOUR GENTLEMAN have family at Whitby?" asked one of her carriage companions, a stocky man with a heavy northern accent and work-hardened hands that seemed at odds with his new silk hat, which he kept dusting with his handkerchief.

"I'm not certain," Zenia said. She spread Mr. Jocelyn's letter on her lap, verifying for the hundredth time that she was to take the train from York to a place called Grosmont where he would meet her. The corner of the paper shivered with the smooth rock of the railway carriage. Of course the letter said that she was on the proper train, in the neat handwriting of the secretary who had initialed the page at the bottom—no surprise, since the railway guard in York had taken her ticket, the last of the ones Mr. Jocelyn had sent, read it, smiled and showed her the correct carriage. "He does not mention it, but I am to get down at Grosmont."

All three of the gentlemen laughed. "That you will, ma'am," said the sea captain. "For the rail ends there. You must take a coach on to Whitby. There's little enough at Grosmont but a quarry. Whitby is at least a port town."

This brought about a friendly argument as to the merits of life on land or on sea, while Zenia looked out upon the wild moorland country with her lips pressed together in doubt. She had been traveling two days, hurled along by the new locomotives at thirty and even forty miles an hour. She was glad she had not brought Elizabeth, for it would have been impossible to rush between trains and eat and sleep sitting up in carriages with her daughter, but she was sorry that at the last minute, the housemaid could not be coaxed or threatened to come along on the extra set of tickets Mr. Jocelyn had sent for a female companion. At least there would have been someone at hand to hearten her as the comforting towns and fields and woods rocked past and fell away, transforming to this bleak, snow-dusted wasteland.

It reminded her strongly of the desert. Cold as it was, it was empty like the desert: the little train climbed out of snug valleys onto rock-strewn hills, the steam of its exertion flitting past her window. Compared to some of the big engines of the greater lines in the south, this one had seemed rather like a chuffing animal, a living elephantlike creature lifting its smokestack as if it were a thick trunk toward the sky. Zenia had felt rather inclined to give it a kind word and a pat, although she knew by now that everything about a train was covered with soot and cinders.

There was only one first-class carriage. At first she had been uneasy to see that her companions in it were all male, as she had found that by traveling alone, she was open to disagreeable advances from some gentlemen, but these three had turned out to be kind and friendly, without undue familiarity. Besides the captain, the others were a supervisor and an engineer at mines, not highly polished men, but very much inclined to treat her with anxious respect. One had already offered to take her to his mother at Egton Bridge, where Zenia could wait in case her "gentleman" was not at Grosmont to meet her.

She sincerely hoped that he would be. There was no set of return tickets—why this lack had not previously occurred to her she did not know—only that once she set out, the demands of the tickets and trains and their pell-mell schedule had compelled her forward with a kind of momentum of their own.

It was slowing now. Even this train was slower, as if it were in no hurry to reach anywhere before dark, though the clouds hung low and gray with impending snow.

"Look at that fellow," the captain said suddenly.

Zenia turned with everyone else, looking out past a brief hail of cinders as the train swung around the curve of a hill.

"By George," said the supervisor. "What is it, a gypsy?"

On the far side of a desolate hollow, a horseman brought his mount to a halt at the top of the rise. Against the leaden sky, he was a brilliant mark, scarlet and gold and turquoise blue, loose robes and a dark cape that drifted out in the wind. His horse was pale white, as brightly adorned, with long red tassles on its bridle and a tail that dusted the snowy ground.

"Must be a gypsy," the captain said. "What a magnificent animal."

The train rolled on, the figure lost to sight so suddenly that Zenia was hardly even sure that she had seen it. But her heart was pounding.

It was a gypsy, she said to herself. She bit her lip. "If you please, sir," she murmured, "what is a gypsy?"

"Why, have you never seen a Romany, ma'am?" the captain asked in great surprise. "Them that travel about the roads in caravans, and trade horses and tell fortunes and dance, and ain't above thieving?"

Zenia shook her head. For the next few miles, while the train ran along the bottom of the valley, the men regaled her with gypsy stories, descriptions of their clothing and odd ways, until she was reassured that they were right, and it had been a gypsy they had seen.

"Are we slowing down?" she asked.

"Oh, aye," said the mining engineer. "We're coming upon the incline. It will be tedious going awhile now."

"There he is again," the captain exclaimed. "Pacing us, the cheeky devil."

The horseman could be seen again, cantering leisurely along the ridge, closer now, the horse's white mane and tail floating out. Zenia could see the red head scarf bound about his face, covering all but his eyes. He looked toward the train as he rode. Suddenly he pulled up again, the horse dancing on its forefeet. There was a faint, fading cheer from the passengers in the open second-class carriage behind.

"We're slowing down," Zenia said anxiously.

No one answered her. They were all looking at the horseman on the ridge as he lifted a rife overhead, his arm raised against the sky. There was an answering roar from the second-class wagon.

"I am a little apprehensive about this fellow," the engineer said.

"Nonsense," said the captain. He scowled out the window. "Does anyone have a firearm with them?"

"The guards are armed, I believe."

The supervisor with the silk hat gave a scornful laugh. "With billy clubs!"

The rider turned, putting his horse down the slope at a long, lazy angle toward the moving train. The engine seemed to progress at a slower and slower rate. The horseman disappeared again, hidden by the lip of a valley.

"How many do you suppose there are?" the captain asked, with his jaw set in determination.

"A whole band, is it? They've chosen a good spot," the engineer said grimly. "The locomotive can't pull the incline before Beck Hole."

"What does that mean?" Zenia asked anxiously.

"The carriages must be hauled up, ma'am. The train will stop at Goathland, in just a moment."

Suddenly there was the report of gunfire, unmistakable above the ringing grind of the wheels.

"What was that?" the supervisor exclaimed.

"They're shooting at him!" Zenia cried.

"He's shooting at us!" yelled the engineer at the same instant, ducking below the window. "Get down, ma'am!"

Zenia shook off his hand, staring out, trying to find the horseman, terrified because she could not see him.

"It came from the second-class wagon," the captain said, kneeling on the seat to see out the high window behind him. "One of them has a pistol, thank God!"

The train began to roll faster. The shriek of the whistle assailed their ears as the carriage started to rattle with the speed.

"What's happening?" the captain demanded, looking around.

"By God, he's not going to stop at Goathland!" the engineer exclaimed. "He's going to try to make the incline!"

Their speed increased. A small huddle of houses flew past the window, scattered gray huts on the moor, two men running alongside the train and falling behind as it plunged down a sharp slope, flying ever faster. Over the sound of the rails, there was a sharp report and shouting from behind.

"Will they shoot him?" Zenia cried.

She craned to find the horseman; caught him in glimpses as the train hurtled down into a tree-studded ravine. He was a perfect target—color against gray and black, but the train was moving fast, swaying and jostling, and he was galloping, flashes of brilliance through the bare trees.

"My God, what a horse that must be!" someone cried.

There was another crack of gunfire that made Zenia flinch. "Madman!" she whispered under her breath. "Allah protect you!"

"Have no fear, ma'am!" The captain patted his heavy hand on her knee. "I believe he's alone, the crazy devil."

Zenia did not even turn to look at him. She was straining to see the horseman, listening for more shots. The train hit a short level space and charged upward, the slope suddenly becoming steep, robbing the engine of momentum. There was a third shot, and a fourth, as the trees thinned and the robed horseman broke into the open, pacing the train. A sound like a collective groan came from the second-class wagon. The horseman turned in the saddle. Zenia heard him yell a desert war cry, pointing his rifle in the air over the wagon and firing four shots one on another like a triumphant boast.

"I hate you, I hate you, I hate you!" Zenia sobbed under her breath. "What are you doing?"

"Damn, the fools are out of ball," the captain reported from his vantage. "They should have waited for a clear shot, the lubbers!"

As the train's speed was choked by the slope, the rider drew closer. The engine labored, slower and slower. She could see the horseman's eyes now, his eyes that seemed to laugh inhumanly within the mantle. The white horse moved in a powerful easy gallop, hooves flying over rock and snow, leaping a ravine, keeping a steady bearing with her window.

"The brakes, man!" the engineer cried. "For God's sake, if he does not prepare, we'll roll back!"

The brakes' squeal answered him. The violent rocking turned to a shudder as the train ground toward a painful halt. Zenia knew the horseman now with the certainty of blind fury, of terrible excitement. He reined the Arab sharply toward the cars, rang-ing close alongside, and leaned to open the carriage door beside her before the train's motion had ceased, holding his rifle trained for any threat from the men jumping out of the second-class wagon.

The train stopped with a jerk at the same instant the door flung wide. "Unhand her, you gypsy blackguard!" the captain shouted, lunging to prevent him as the horse jostled up to the door and the brilliantly robed and masked reincarnation of Haj Hasan reached for Zenia, his free hand closing on her arm and yanking her brutally forward.

She was so afraid that someone would shoot him, or he would shoot them, that she could find no voice but to scream, "No!" amid the struggle of bodies trying at once to interfere.

"Oh, yes," he snarled. "I *will* have you."

The gentlemen were all trying to pull her back, but he suddenly let go of her and leveled the rifle into the car, bringing all motion to an abrupt stop. The mare's nostrils flared, puffing jets of steam.

"Now," he said. "You will kindly free my wife to accompany me."

"Your wife!" the supervisor exclaimed.

Zenia could see some of the second-class passengers running up. A wave of the rifle barrel in their direction made them falter. The railway employees were shouting up near the engine, but amid the clash of metal and the anguished screaming whistle of the locomotive they seemed fully occupied with preventing the train from sliding backwards.

"*Move!*" Hasan bellowed at Zenia, tearing down the mask of the kuffiyah. "Will you give them the whole bloody day to reload?"

Seeing his face, the darkness and bright flame, his demon alive and burning in him, living on outlawry, on senseless peril—the hysteria that had been pressing and swarming at the back of her throat burst free. "Damn you!" she cried, her voice rising even above the wail of the steam.

The mare threw her head, eyes rolling amid the shouts and commotion. The dull pop of a misfire made him glance away toward it.

"Wolf cub!" he yelled. "*Yallah!*"

She plunged forward, tearing free of the sea captain, tripping, falling into Lord Winter's hold. "Damn you," she sobbed as he lifted her, denying her feet their last solid support. "Damn you, damn you!" she cried, clinging to his shoulders as he swung her onto the mare, burying her face in the free woolen folds of his cloak. "Why do you do this to me?"

She felt the horse whirl beneath her. She felt his grip holding her before him. A gust of wind sent the cloak flying back, showing her the train immobilized, suspended halfway up the overpowering slope, everyone gaping at them in the winter afternoon. And that was the last glimpse she saw of any of them, for he took her at a gallop up the slope past the paralyzed locomotive. At the top he halted, grinning like a savage back at the figures that bundled futilely after them on foot. The countryside echoed to the blasting cascade as he emptied the rifle at the moor and sky.

"VERY AMUSING," ZENIA said tightly, finally taking command of her voice as they rode through the falling snow. "And now if you will convey me to Grosmont, I will join Mr. Jocelyn as I intended."

The grip on her waist tightened. "Mr. Jocelyn is not there."

Zenia sat up straight, the cold wind stinging her cheeks. "What have you done to him?"

"Why, nothing. No doubt he is reposing happily in Edinburgh."

"But—" She paused. "Edinburgh?" she asked, with dawning suspicion.

"Why should he be anywhere else?"

She stared across the purple-gray moor. She thought of the letter from Mr. Jocelyn, written and signed by a secretary, the precisely assembled tickets that had brought her here to this exact time and isolated place.

"You stole my letter," she cried furiously. "My God, you will do anything! Anything to take Elizabeth. Were you so sure I would bring her in spite of any advice? How well you know me! I very nearly did, but Mrs. Lamb foiled you there! You might have had Elizabeth, assuming she was not killed in that mad attack—"

He brought the mare to a sudden halt. "I didn't intend her to come," he said sharply. "Nor did I intend there to be shooting. The guards don't carry guns; it was some pot-valiant lobcock with a pistol in second-class who started shooting, and that rattlepate of an engineer who did his best to smash the train!"

"Then why were you waving your rifle?" she shouted, dashing snow from her cheeks.

"Oh, for your amusement," he said caustically.

Zenia half-turned in the saddle. She could not see his face, only his jaw and mouth and the bright colored wool about his throat.

"Foolish of me," he said, his voice harsh. "I meant to ride down beside the train, meet you at Goathland, and carry you off. Very romantic, you see. Mr. Jocelyn would never think of it."

"Of course not," she cried. "He is perfectly sane!"

The flakes of snow flew against Lord Winter's jaw, white crystals that poised for a moment and then melted on his skin. "Yes," he said tightly, "and if it had been up to him, you'd still be cowering in a corner at Dar Joon, wouldn't you?"

"At least," she said, turning to face the front and pulling the edges of her bonnet close, "I would not be riding through snowstorms in the midst of nowhere!"

He brought his cloak up, drawing her back against his chest

and covering her with the dark, loose folds, lifting his arm to envelop her mouth and chin and shoulders. He pressed his open palm against her face, holding the cloak there against the wind. Through the layers of wool and silk, she could smell his scent. She could feel the pulse of his inner wrist against her cheekbone, the familiar life of him.

He bent his head, nuzzling his mouth to her jaw and throat. "There are other things you won't be doing with Jocelyn," he murmured, his voice low in his chest. "Because I'll kill him first, and then you."

Zenia drew in a breath, her body responding to his as it always did, against her will and judgment. "He told me that he prefers no physical intimacy in marriage," she said coldly.

"Then he's a liar," Lord Winter said, warming her cheek with his words. "Or something else."

"He is a good, kind man, who will give Elizabeth and me a safe home. He would not threaten to kill me."

"But does he know what he's bargained for? Does he know who you are going to be, once you have your fill of a safe little home in Bentinck Street?"

"I could never have my fill of it."

"You told Mrs. Lamb you were the only one who knew me." He held her, his arm taut. "But you've forgotten the other half of that balance, Zenia. You've forgotten that I know you too."

A strange shiver, something deeper than the cold, seemed to seep into her limbs and heart. "I don't know what you mean."

"I mean," he said softly near her ear, "that I am your demon. In you and beside you and over you. Run where you will, little wolf, but I am always with you."

Zenia began to tremble. "That is superstitious nonsense."

"Did you really think you could marry Jocelyn and live your paltry life in Bentinck Street? Did you think I would not haunt you and maul you to the death if you did it? I would not let you slip out of my claws. Look where you are at this moment."

"Enough talk of demons! It's Elizabeth you want, not me!"

"Elizabeth is made of you and me. And you've been mine since I dragged you up in the dark outside Dar Joon, crying that you saw a djinni."

She remembered the night and the demon coming for her; the sound of hooves and then his voice. Her whole body was shaking. *It is the cold*, she thought, but his heat radiated into her.

"All my life has been a hunt," he murmured into her shoulder and throat. "I have hunted for you over half the earth, and hell too. Bentinck Street is not nearly far enough to run."

She gasped, "I'm afraid of you."

He gripped her closer, his arm about her neck. "I tried to be a civilized creature. I tried to live your safe little life, and you ran to Mr. Jocelyn when I couldn't be what you want. Now I'm what I am, and I'll make you what you are."

Twenty-seven

⸺◈⸺

THE SNOW WAS flying so thick that she could only see the cottage as a glowing window in a black shape below them. It sat under the lee of a hill, a sudden lull in the wind, so that the flakes fluttered down gently instead of driving past as he guided the mare down the slope.

A few black-faced sheep huddled in the windshadow of the house, rising quickly to their feet and staring. He halted before the door, loosening his hold on her, his cloak crackling with icy stiffness. She gave a sharp whimper as her numbed toes struck the ground.

"There'll be a fire inside," he said briefly. "I'll put the mare in the lean-to."

Zenia could hardly make her fingers close as she pulled back the latch. But there was a startling transformation inside the thick

stone wall—outside was desolation: hurtling snow and near darkness; inside was an orange glow and the smell of warm bread, the
fire leaping in the huge brick hearth as if it had only recently been
fueled.

Its light showed the whitewashed walls of one room: clean but
haphazardly furnished with scarred chairs of ornate design,
mended and remended, their gilt worn away except in the deepest
cracks. A four-poster bed with three thick, heavily carved bed-
posts and one plain spar was hung with mismatched curtains,
some of watered sky-blue silk and some a faded brown check. A
thick Turkish carpet laid over the flagstone floor showed the
same hand-me-down history, apparently perfect except for one
large corner that the bed could not quite conceal, burned away to
an uneven, blackened edge.

Sweet-smelling loaves of bread lay on the table in a floury
pile. As Zenia stood with her cloak and bonnet drooping and
thawing, her hands and feet in agony with the return of warmth,
a white cat stared at her from the red damask seat of one of the
armchairs. It stood up, revealing a cat-shaped depression in the
upholstery. Zenia gazed back at it, dazed with exhaustion and
cold and hunger, hardly able to think what to do first.

Hinges squealed as Lord Winter pushed aside a long curtain
and came in through the door beyond the hearth, a strange figure, snow-crusted, alien to this English setting in his colored
desert robes and kuffiyah bound about his head by a gold-and-
black cord. He dumped a load of wood by the fire, loud clunks
that made the cat leap up onto a windowsill. Ice fell from his
cloak in small rushes onto the hearth.

Layers of wool and silk could be warm enough, even in the
sharp frozen nights of the northern deserts, but they did not keep
out the wetness. His black hair was damp, clinging in curls to the
back of his neck as he pulled off the headscarf.

"You may stand there dripping if you like," he said, facing the fire, "but I am going to strip down to a dry layer."

Zenia looked about, already aware that there was no privacy here, short of joining the horse in the lean-to. She watched, shivering, as he pulled the robes over his head, down to an English shirt and breeches under it all. As he emerged from the last long white desert gown, he looked over his shoulder at her.

"Shall I undress you before you catch your death, or will you do it yourself?"

Zenia pulled the bedraggled ribbon on her bonnet free. "I suppose it does not occur to abductors to provide dry clothes for their victims."

He waved at the bed. "You may have all the quilts you like."

With a surge of irritation, Zenia hung her bonnet and cloak on the hook beside the door and sat down, unlacing her boots to free her aching feet. He knew her, after all—quite every inch of her. What point was there in privacy? She worked to reach her buttons, but what was difficult in any case proved impossible with numb and clumsy fingers. She made a sound of frustration, turning away toward the bed.

"You must undo them," she snapped.

He came up behind her and released the buttons and hooks. Zenia stared at the bed, her chin lifted, ready at any moment to step away if he attempted to make love to her.

He did not. He only said, untying her corset, "I don't know how you can bear this rig."

It was far from her favorite item of Frankish clothing, but she said nothing. When it was all loose, she leaned over, dragging the dress over her head. She spread it carefully over a chair to dry and laid the corset across another.

She could feel him watching her. She still had more clothing on than she had ever worn with him in the desert, layers of petticoats and two shifts, one of thick linsey-woolsey, but there was something about the way that he stood still, an artificial stiff casualness in his stance, that made her well aware that she was offering a provocative picture.

So, she thought angrily, let him be provoked. As for his great worldwide search for Zenia—he had not even recognized her for a female the first three months she had known him. And she was too tired and shaken to spend energy on bashfulness. After such cold, the warmth seemed to wrap about her, seeping into her brain. She did not care if it was immodest; she only wanted to dry before the fire.

As he sat down, chasing the cat from its red damask chair, Zenia bent to pull off her petticoats and the damp woolen shift. For an instant the air felt cool on her bared skin, sending an uncontrollable shiver down her back. She could feel her breasts fill the linen undershift as she leaned over and lifted its skirt, releasing her garter.

He stood up again, with a faint curse under his breath. Zenia stretched out her leg and rolled her wet stocking down it.

"Are you hungry?" he asked.

"Extremely," she said, without looking up as she sat down and worked the stocking from her toe.

After a moment, a cracked plate adorned by the familiar Belmaine arms hit the table beside her with a chunk. It had a piece of bread and dollop of butter on it. A glass of cider from a small keg arrived with the same brusque thump.

Zenia ate, wriggling her cold bare toes, wincing at the pain. She glanced up to find him gazing at her with a look that burned like the painful new warmth in her limbs.

"What is this place?" she asked, avoiding his eyes.

"I used to come here to shoot," he said briefly. "Red grouse."

"What do you intend to do with me?"

"Marry you, little wolf. Unless you drive me to worse."

"And what is worse?" she inquired acidly. "Your contract in which I am to go to the Continent, or else be prosecuted for fraud?"

He looked at her sharply. "You saw that?"

"Of course I saw it. Mr. Jocelyn explained everything about it to me. Everything."

He swore softly. "You were not meant to see it. It was a mistake." His eyes slid away from hers. "I mean for us to marry."

"So that you may take Elizabeth if you please."

"Damn you, I mean for us to marry," he said angrily.

"Will you force me?"

"Yes." He made a hard chuckle through his teeth. "Oh, yes."

"You can't," she said. "It is not legal."

He smiled coldly. "You've been listening to too many lawyers." He sat back in the chair opposite, the soft high collar of his shirt falling open. With a slow look beneath his lashes at her, he said, "And you're living dangerously, for a reluctant woman."

Zenia turned away to the fire, watching the orange and yellow flames that cast shadows across his drying robes and her dress.

"But I think you like living dangerously," he murmured. "I think you're not quite the demure little lady Mr. Jocelyn believes."

"I am a lady. I can be one."

"A lady," he said, "would not sit there in her shift with a man who isn't her husband. A lady would have swooned aboard that train, not damned me while she threw herself in my arms. A lady," he said with particular emphasis, "does not intentionally show her garters."

"Did I ask you to stop a train?" she demanded vehemently. "Did I ask you to make a target of yourself for anyone who wants to shoot at you? Did I ask you to carry me for miles in a snowstorm, until I'm half-frozen and soaked to the skin? Did I ask you to steal my letter and send me on this preposterous journey?" She stood up, her voice rising sharply. "What choice do you ever give me in your madness?"

"Why, Miss Bruce, I had barely inaugurated the most decorous courtship, planned, scheduled and approved by A Lady of Quality and conducted entirely by the book"—he rose too, leaning across the table—"when to my dismay I discover you asking another man to wed you, by God!" He slammed his fist on the table. "So *that* for your damned gentlemanly behavior! Perhaps it works with real ladies, but it's a smashing disaster with you!"

"Because you are not meant to court me!" she cried. "Marry Lady Caroline! Marry someone who can go with you and be what you want!"

"I want you!"

"That's a lie!" she cried. "You want Elizabeth, and I can keep her from you!"

"Damn you!" he roared, moving around the table so aggressively that she backed up until she felt the fire behind her. "You're just like your mother!"

"I'm *not*!"

"Worse than your mother! At least she was honest about it! You want your stranglehold and a halo too!"

"I'm not worse than my mother!" she shouted, dragging her wet hair back as it fell across her face.

"Aren't you? Listen to you! Your father told me that she screamed at him until he left! She drove him off; I'll wager she rode him until he couldn't bear it, all that fine talk about how she would ruin his prospects, that drivel about her pride; Christ, and she knew she was carrying his child—I'll swear she drove him off the same way you're doing to me, hot and cold until I can't endure it! Because she had to be the master, she couldn't bear to let anyone else have a hold on her, she had to be the one in control of everyone and everything, and if she couldn't control it, she broke it or killed it or fought it till she died." His blue eyes glittered, his lashes still holding tiny beads of melted ice. "The way you fight me! The way you come when I'm too weak and out of my senses to talk, and then go off when I'm able—go off and marry Jocelyn! *Jocelyn!*" he yelled. "When were you going to tell me? When it was too late? For God's sake, Zenia! For God's sake." He shook his head, sitting down and leaning on his hands. "I would have put a bullet through my brain."

She stared at him. "It's Elizabeth you want," she said.

He gave a hoarse laugh, not lifting his head. "Of course I want her. Of course. I want to see her grow up, I want to know her. Why does that make me the greatest fiend in nature?"

"Because," she whispered, "you will take her away and leave me alone."

He shook his head. "I don't know how to make you trust me."

"I wanted to." Her lips quivered. "I wanted to. I was trying," she said. "But then I saw you with Lady Caroline. I saw the way you looked at her when she talked of being free. And I know I don't dare!"

He lifted his head. "How did I look?"

"As if—she were a goddess."

"A goddess." He rose, the firelight casting soft shadows over his tall figure. "Oh, a goddess," he said casually. "Of the philosophical variety, do you mean? The Greco-Roman sort, that dress in damped muslin and hold up torches for liberty, and make rather imposing statues? Is this how I looked at her? Rather pious as I worshipped freedom at her feet?"

"No," she said. "No."

"I don't appear suitably awed?"

"You look as if you are sitting through a remarkably tedious sermon. That is not how you looked at Lady Caroline and the tiger."

He dropped his gaze from a reverent contemplation of the mantelpiece. "Perhaps not," he said, "but I'll wager it's a fair representation of some fellow appreciating the drapery about winged Nike's bosom."

She turned her face aside. "You looked at Lady Caroline as if—she was everything in life to you."

He stood still. She felt him watching her. When she slanted a look at him, he had a new expression, one she had never seen before on his hard features—a faint, fond smile curving his lips as he contemplated her.

"I find you are remarkably naive, beloved," he said. "I wonder how A Lady of Quality would advise me to explain this."

She could not step back; the heat from the fire was already hot on her bared calves—but as he moved nearer she felt as if her feet were fixed to the carpet by some insensible force. He stood looking down at her, his smile fading into something else; a deeper attention.

It was as if she had been standing outside the prowling tiger's cage, teasing it because it was bigger and wilder and more savage than she—because she could—and suddenly found the bars that imprisoned it had vanished.

He did not lower his eyes below her face, and yet she felt as if he explored and uncovered all of her—her skin, her shape, her heartbeat as it quickened. The center of his look was on her and far away at once, his black lashes lowered in concentration. His eyes seemed a profound blue.

"Is this how I was looking at Lady Caroline?" he murmured.

Lady Caroline had already been fading from her consciousness. But at the question, recognition and jealousy rushed through her. "Yes," she said, drawing away slightly as she stared straight ahead at the open neck of his shirt.

He caught her hands, pulling them up against his chest, flattening her palms against him so that she could feel the taut curve of muscle beneath the linen. "As I recall, she was saying something about turning all the tigers loose."

Zenia curled her fingers, but he held her hands entrapped. "She said the tiger longed to be free. That it knew what freedom was, and that was its element. And even if its life was savage struggle, anything else would be torture to it."

"Ah, yes," he said pensively. "I suspected it was a lot of high-minded discourse suitable to a Greco-Roman goddess. Shall I tell you what I was thinking?"

Zenia lowered her eyes. "Will you tell the truth?"

"Oh, nothing but the whole vulgar truth." His hands tightened on hers. "I'm afraid you may be vastly disappointed to discover the true tenor of my character. Look at me."

She looked up. The dark energy was very strong and clear in his face.

"I was thinking of what I would do if you let me come into your house after the zoo. I was thinking that Mrs. Lamb would take Beth away for a nap, and you would probably be too modest and ladylike to ask me to go up to your bedroom to have one with you. So we would go into the parlor to talk a while. And naturally—" He shrugged. "I would be a mesmerizing conversationalist, remarkably gallant, strikingly clever, never at a loss for the right thing to say—I daresay you don't recognize me in this role, but nevertheless that's where I cast myself. And you were to smile at me rather a lot." His mouth curled sardonically. "This was all merely introductory, of course. A moment's contemplation. I think I had the tea tray expelled and the parlor door locked well before Lady Caroline got to the part about wishing all the darling lions and tigers could be free." He moved her hand, still clasped in his, and traced an upward curve on her cheek. "You were going to smile a lot. Perhaps you would smile at me now, for a realistic effect."

In spite of herself, she felt the corners of her lips tilt upward a little. "You were thinking of me," she said, "but you were looking at her."

He turned her hand over and kissed her palm and her wrist. "She was considerably more often in my line of sight. I shall make no essays into the feminine mind, but every time I looked about for you, all I seemed to see were throngs—swarms—I might say floods—of matronly ladies schooling between us. In the army, I believe they call what you were doing 'malingering,' and you would be shot at sunrise for such cowardly and treasonous behavior."

She bowed her head. "I suppose it was not very brave of me."

"It was not your boldest hour, wolf cub. Nor mine. Let us agree that we were both overrun and soundly thrashed by the enemy."

She looked up at him. "You were still staring at her. You were—you noticed her more frequently than her aunt or Lady Broxwood."

"Zenia, my beloved, I am going to try to engage your pity." He held her hands together between his, looking down at them. "I want you to imagine a fellow who has been two years and more leading an utterly celibate life. Who has the most beautiful, desirable, alluring woman sleeping in the room beside him, who sees her nurse his child, who lies awake thinking he'll die if he can't touch her again and dreams about her and imagines what he would do with her—who is in the midst of a most compelling daydream that takes place in her parlor—in a chair—did we arrive at the parlor chair yet?"

He drew her with him as he moved back a step, lowering himself onto one of the side chairs. With his hands at her waist, he spread his palms wide. His eyes were dark as he gazed up at her breasts, sliding his hands upward a little, pressing them together. Zenia drew in a breath. His lips parted.

"He's dreaming, you see—he is sitting in a chair in this daydream, and she is before him, with very little on, only a shift, with the light behind so that he can see her body through it. If I lean toward her, if I—"

He kissed her skin at the top of her chemise, as light as breathing, warmth that made her tilt her head back and close her eyes. She should not let him; she should not, but in the dim room, the soft temptation, it was hard to summon resistance.

"Somewhere," he murmured, "some person is talking about tigers."

"Lady Caroline," she whispered.

"I really have no notion who, and I think it's a stupendously silly subject." He skimmed his fingers beneath the shoulders of her shift, sliding the linen down onto her arms. "I am far more interested in how one goes about removing this fascinating garment. Do these bows open, for instance? Little pink bows. Girls are such amazing, wonderful, delicate creatures. I think they must sew themselves into their shifts, but it is the most charming picture." He ran his thumbs over her nipples, a sensation that made her arch toward him. He smiled in an abstracted way, watching her body as he did it again. "Beautiful plump breasts that make the cloth strain," he said. "I vaguely recollect—very vaguely, mind you—that perhaps Lady Caroline's buttons made a poor, a sadly poor, imitation of the same effect, and so it's possible that I did, for lack of a better model—" He pulled a bow open, watching the result intently. "For a moment perhaps I glanced at the lesser star, as it was so insistently thrust before me."

"More than once."

"Zenia!" He buried his face between her breasts. "I only looked. It's been two years!"

"It's been the same time for me," she said. "And I never thought of anyone else, or looked at anyone else, even for one moment."

He took a deep breath against her skin and bowed his head,

resting it against her. For a moment she felt the brush of his hair and the weight of him leaning on her. Then he sat back. "I've been led down the garden path, I see," he said with a new hardness in his voice. "I thought we were speaking of my religious awe of Lady Caroline, and how I must marry her because she wants to unshackle imprisoned tigers—but now I find the topic is common jealousy, and I am one count down, being so ignoble as to notice a female bosom forced on my attention." He flicked the second bow free, popping it entirely off with a sharp curl of his forefinger. "While you—pure as driven snow—merely arrange your wedding to another man, which I presume I am to accept with meek thanks for my deliverance." He spread the shift apart with his thumbs, baring her skin. "Perhaps you will now take your turn, and explain yourself, because I find your logic so far entirely unconvincing."

What he was doing hardly helped her tired mind to reason clearly. He had opened the bows to her waist, and though he did not kiss her, she could feel every breath warm her breasts. He touched her nipples again, and she arched shamelessly into his hands, asking for his mouth on her.

He pulled her closer, roughly. And it was like the sweet sensation of Elizabeth's nursing transformed, deeper and heavier, a man's demand to overtake her body. She leaned on him, her head thrown back, the breadth of his shoulders under her palms. He pushed her shift down her arms, baring her to her waist, and slid his hands beneath her skirt, dragging her down astride his lap.

"Very persuasive," he said with a dark smile. They were both panting. He held his hands at her hips, her shift rucked up so that she was all but naked.

Zenia shook her head miserably. "I don't want her to have you." She clasped her hands about his face. "I don't want to be there to see it."

"Lady Caroline?" His jaw was taut beneath her fingers. "Do you genuinely suppose I want to tour the world with some female preaching to me about independence and hardship?" His lip curled, showing a white flash of his teeth. "While sipping lemonade and issuing orders from her padded elephant cushion, no doubt."

"You say that now. But—"

"Christ, I know her sort, Zenia! I don't dare go to a lecture in London; they're lurking for me at the door." He gave a short laugh. "There must be a debutante's manual somewhere, with my name listed under 'Belmaine.' 'Be certain to mention his adventures in a worshipful manner, and wax positively exuberant over the geography of Asia. Vow you just dote on camels and don't forget to mention that you detest a waltz.'" He made a wry face, lowering his lashes as he gazed at her. "I think they've added a new line: 'Wear a tight dress and breathe deeply—he's pitifully vulnerable at the moment.'"

She put her arms about his head and held him close, laughing sadly, rocking him. "I do love you, you know. I do love you."

"I'm happy to hear it," he said, muffled in her embrace. "This is a damnable thing to do to a man you only hold in mild esteem."

She lifted his face between her hands, gazing down at him. He kissed the inside of her wrist, a faint scratchiness of his cheek against her skin. He slipped his hands down, pulling her closer, looking up steadily into her eyes.

"But you will go," she whispered, a litany to herself as she felt her willpower succumb to his. "You will go. If not with Lady Caroline, then alone."

"Zenia," he said, "Zenia. I only want to go as far as that bed." He moved his hand between them, breathing deeply. "Not even that far."

She felt the hard release of his sex between her spread legs. He kissed her throat and her earlobe, his arm behind her waist, curving her against him.

"Whatever you want," he muttered. "Whatever you like. I'll never leave you."

You will, she cried silently, lost in the sensations of delight he was creating, pressing away from him with her arms while her body arched toward the sweet urgent demand of his. She shuddered as he sucked her breasts, his hands spreading her, lifting her—she thought wildly that this would be another child, another part of him to keep—and suddenly she was eager to take him into her.

"I want another baby from you," she said, bending beside his ear.

"Oh God, yes," he said fiercely, "Zenia, yes."

She buried her face in his shoulder, brazenly touching his man's part. He drew air sharply between his teeth, his fingers closing hard on her buttocks.

He stilled, his body holding a deep internal quiver as she stroked him and guided him with her own hand. With each slide of her fingers that found the length and shape of him, all his muscles seemed to coil.

"You want to kill me," he whispered. "I know that's what you want."

She lifted her head. Her hair had fallen loose, drifting wantonly about them. She felt a strange giddy sense of domination as she caressed him; he was watching her face, but she could see the blue heat in his eyes lose focus, go distant and absorbed, as if when he looked at her he was looking at something far away and fascinating. He began to breathe roughly, his head tilted back over the chair, his hands gripping her.

Zenia's chin lifted. She rose and took him into her in a single deep impalement, pushing herself down as he stretched her. His throat worked with an inarticulate sound, and then he made a strong arch to drive himself further in, his hands at her hips.

But Zenia's position gave her control of him. It was when she moved, flexing her body and hips to find the source of her own pleasure, that he inhaled with swift ecstasy. She rocked against him, reveling in the deep ache of penetration. "You won't leave me," she said in a breathless hiss at the back of her throat. "You won't, you won't, you won't."

He opened his eyes. He frightened her with the fierce depth of his look. It was as if the djinni stared out at her, the wild djinni that she could never govern or resist, and her little chant was like a magic too small and weak to hold it.

But she could steal it. She could nurse his seed in her and take it with her and hold it to herself and keep it for her own, another child of his to love when he was gone.

She ceased moving. His whole body was hot and tense beneath her. He reached up and cradled her cheeks, slid his hands down her shoulders and her waist, under her buttocks, ardently urging her against him. "Please," he said, a grated appeal through his teeth.

She held still, held him in physical imprisonment. "You won't leave," she said—command and enchantment.

"Never," he said, wetting his lips.

"You'll stay at Swanmere."

"Anywhere. Anywhere." She could feel his hands up under her shift, his fingers pulling her desperately toward him.

She lifted her heels from the carpet, leaning forward. The motion drove him deep, so deep that it hurt, but with a piercing bliss that radiated from their joining. Her body pumped against him, eager to be filled, gasping, driven to shameless demand by the stark sound of ecstasy in his throat. His fingers closed with convulsive strength. He moved under her, arching back, meeting her with a powerful thrust at the height of her passion.

A radiant shudder seemed to seize her, a bright joy as his life surged into her, permeating her again. She held him to her, clutched his head to her breasts while their bodies throbbed together.

Zenia clung to him, whimpering. Her mind was blank and yet full of energy, sliding from wonder back to the present, slowly regaining awareness of herself; of him; the sharp stretch of her legs, the tickle of his hair against her skin, the hard press of his body bearing her weight.

He turned his face, rubbing it against her, drinking air with a harsh, hungry sound. "Thank you," he said. He rested his arms limply about her waist. "Oh my God, thank you." He took a deep breath, a rise and fall of his shoulders and chest against her.

Zenia bent to the top of his head. "Does one always say thank you?" she said into his hair.

"Hmm?"

"You always say thank you, after this."

"Do I?" he asked.

"Yes."

"What a polite fellow I am," he said with a faint chuckle. "The urbane Lord Winter."

"I thank you, too."

"Oh, any time! Your servant, madam." He sighed, relaxing against her. "Any time you please."

Zenia bit her lip. She curled her fingers through his black hair. She did not believe his promises made in extremity, promises that he would stay. He made them to get what he wanted; but she had thieved what she wanted. She felt a selfish, hidden triumph; an ugly little miserable joy that she could hoard a part of him to herself; that he could go but never really leave her. As long as she had Elizabeth, and now another—she was sure she had another by him now—and he could not take them, she was safe from the fear of being left alone, a force that lay so dark and threatening within her that it was like a djinni itself.

"This position is even more delightful than I had imagined it could be," he murmured, "but it seems that my toes are falling asleep."

Zenia pulled away, rediscovering shyness as she stood up and found herself with her shift all down about her waist. She turned her back to him, lifting the shoulders hastily.

He came behind her, enfolding her in his arms before she could restore her shift. "I'm not an entirely backward abductor," he said. "I forgot dry clothes for you, but I did remember to bring the license." He nuzzled her throat. "Would you like to wait until morning, or shall I go and fetch a curate now?"

Twenty-eight

———⚬⚬⚬———

Zenia stiffened. "Now?"

"If you wish," he said. "It can be done here—your friends the lawyers tell me that this license is good for any time or place."

"It's snowing," she said nervously.

"I don't mind," he murmured. "It won't take long to bring them." He rocked her back against him. "On the other hand, I'd be perfectly pleased to be snowed up here with you for days, if this weather turns to a serious storm."

"Snowed up? Trapped here, do you mean?" she asked, pulling away.

"It's not likely," he said. "But there's no danger. The place has stores and fuel enough."

"Elizabeth!" she exclaimed. "I can't be trapped here!"

"Beth is right as a trivet, and perfectly happy. You left her with Mrs. Lamb, did you not?"

"Yes, but—" She reached for her clothes. "Oh, these are still soaking wet!"

"You aren't going anywhere tonight," he said as she shook out the dress, flinging drops of water. "Zenia, don't be a fool."

"If there is to be a snowstorm! I cannot abandon her for so long!"

He pulled the dress from her hand and tossed it over the chair. "Perhaps you should have thought of that before you started north."

Zenia snatched the gown back. "It's your fault! You lured me here!"

"You came to marry Jocelyn," he growled. "Precious perfect as I'm sure he is, he's got no more control of snowstorms than I do."

"I want to go!" she cried. "I want to go to Elizabeth!"

"All right," he said. "I'll take you. By way of the vicarage. I want us married before we leave."

"There is no time for that," Zenia said, squeezing water from one of her stockings. "It may already be snowing too hard."

He pulled a lantern down from a hook on the wall and lit it. Striding to the door, he opened it to a swirl of wind and cold and stepped outside.

"It has stopped," he said, holding up the lantern.

Hugging herself against the frigid air, Zenia peered around the door. His shirtsleeves were plastered against his arms in the wind, his breath a bright frost in the circle of the lamplight. No snowflakes fell, and the lamp only sparkled on a dusting of less than an inch on the ground.

"It might begin again," she said, retreating toward the fire as he came back in. She sat down and began to work the damp, unpleasant stocking onto her foot. "We should leave now."

"And lose ourselves on the moor at night in a storm? A great lot of good that will do Beth. If you insist on making a start to-night, we'll go as far as the vicarage at Grosmont—I can find that. The priest can marry us on the spot, and we'll put up there for the night. Then we can take the train tomorrow."

"You dare not!" She looked up. "They will arrest you for attacking the train!"

"No they won't," he said.

"You can't be sure of that!" She stood up.

"I can be sure that I own half the bloody railway."

Zenia gasped. "You own it!"

He gave an impatient nod, reaching for his cloak. "I don't interfere in the thing—but no doubt they would think twice about prosecuting their leading stockholder. Particularly when I didn't do anything but ride alongside and get shot at."

"And pull me off!"

"My wife," he said. "I have a right to do that."

"I'm not your wife."

"Well," he said, with a dangerous gleam in his eyes, "we are about to remedy that, are we not?"

She avoided his hold. She gathered her shift up onto her shoulders and hugged herself. "I'm sorry. I should not have—I don't wish to do this."

His face changed, transforming from suspicion to a black rage. "I knew it!" He flung the cloak away. "I knew this wasn't about Beth! What have I done?"

Instantly, hysteria rose to her tongue. "I was wrong! I'm tired! I won't marry you! I want to leave!" She could hear her mother in herself, but it only made her more frantic. She burst into frenzied tears. "Let me go, let me go."

"No," he said, his voice a cold knife amid her weeping.

"I want to go," she cried.

"So you'll leave me," he said with a sneer. "So we all pay the price of your crazy fears! Beth, too. Just like your mother made you pay for her pride."

"I have to go. You have to let me go."

"No," he said.

"You're going to leave me!" Her voice reached a height of panic. "I'll be alone!"

"My God, you claim I'm the one who has to be free—but it's you!" His voice rose to match hers. "You have no faith in anyone but yourself! I've found what I was hunting out there! I found you. I don't need to search anymore."

"Don't, don't," she said, shaking her head. "That's not true. I can't believe that."

"What can I do to make you believe it? What can I say?"

"Nothing!"

"*Nothing!*" he shouted. "You've been living as my wife for two years; I want to marry you; you let me—" He pointed. "In that chair—that was hardly a rape, by God! What are you going to do after *that*—marry Jocelyn?"

"Yes!" she cried. "I'm going to marry him!"

"You're out of your mind! He won't have you now!" he said with a wild bewilderment.

"He will!" she shouted recklessly. "He will, he will! You could give me a hundred children, and he would still marry me! He wants children, but he doesn't want to do what you do!"

He stared at her. "You're as mad as your mother."

"I'm *not*!" she cried, covering her ears. "He wants children!"

"And what am I, then—the stud service?" he shouted. "Is that why you let me—" His raging voice broke off. He took a step toward her. "Is that why?"

"Yes," she sobbed, "yes, yes, yes!"

She was shaking all over, hunching with her hands to her head. Her eyes were squeezed shut. In the long silence, she fell to her knees, weeping.

There was no sound in the cottage, nothing but the wind hissing past the walls and muttering in the chimney.

"Very well," he said in a voice of ice. "Get dressed. I won't importune you any further, madam."

THOUGH SHE WAS chilled in her damp dress, he had wrapped the bed quilt about her, and she barely felt the wind as she rode before him out onto the cloud-lit moor. They had come so far from the railway that Zenia had expected it to be a long distance to anywhere. But it hardly seemed more than a quarter hour before she realized that the dark mass the mare was approaching was not a grove of trees clustered at the end of a shadowed valley, but a house.

The wind howled about it. It stood alone on the edge of the moor, outlined by the dull glow of snow and sky behind it. As they drew nearer, the tearing breaks in the cloud cover let moonlight through to glitter on a double row of dark tall windows.

It was not a huge house, like Swanmere, but still it was imposing, rising black and silent from a treeless prospect. He turned the horse in between stone columns and rode across the level expanse, the mare's hooves crunching in the snow crust. Instead of stopping at the balustraded double staircase, shimmering with streamers of snow that blew from each landing, he guided the horse around the corner to a smaller set of steps. He dismounted, leaving Zenia, and strode up to pound on the door.

After a long interval, someone opened it. The gleam of a light fell across the steps and the snow. She could not hear what Lord Winter said, but a man came quickly down with him, the collar of his coat turned up, carrying a lantern.

Zenia held the quilt about herself as the servant guided her up the steps and then left her with Lord Winter inside the door.

They stood in a dim, paneled passageway full of trunks and boots.

His face was remote. He held a brimstone match to several candle sconces. As the golden glow rose in the hallway, he lowered his arms.

"I suppose you saw that the clouds were breaking," he said, shaking snow off his cloak. He did not look at her. "It's not going to storm tonight. If you can possibly bear it, I suggest that you remain here until morning, and I'll have Mr. Bode drive you to the station then. Your case from the train is here, so you have dry clothes now."

"Where are we?" she asked in a small voice.

"My house," he said shortly.

"Oh. But I thought—"

"Welcome to my burrow," he said shortly. "My aunt left this to me years ago. There are mines and sheep, and the railway—an income independent of my father, bless her." His face was grim, but it lightened a little as an elderly housekeeper came into the passage, hastily adjusting her cap. "Mrs. Bode," he said. "Can anywhere be made fit for her to sleep?"

The housekeeper gave a little creaking bob of a bow, showing the hump in her back as she dipped her head. She managed to produce a strange combination of fluttery nervousness and authority as she said, "I'm sure my lady must go in the mistress's old room, though if the chimney will draw I can't say."

Zenia stood in her quilt during a conversation about the chimney and Mr. Bode's ability to start a fire—Lord Winter did not wait for the other man to return, but took up a load of firewood from the box by the door while Mrs. Bode fluttered and protested in a way that showed she had not much hope of preventing him. With the housekeeper carrying a candle ahead, Zenia followed them down the passage into the house.

It looked as her father's house in Bentinck Street had, every-thing covered in sheets and the doorways all closed, but this had an air of permanent disuse, an undusted and unused smell, the corridors lined with boxes and obscure items of furniture, the cold saturating the house as if no fires were ever lit there. Up-stairs, the bedchamber Mrs. Bode opened was dark and frigid, the wind rattling the windows, one sill dusted with snow where a pane had broken and been stuffed with cloth.

"She can't sleep here," Lord Winter said impatiently. He looked about the room with a frown. "I beg your pardon, ma'am," he said in Zenia's direction, "this is something of a bach-elor house. Mrs. Bode, I hope you will see to that window tomor-row. At least the shutters should be closed."

"Yes, sir," she said, with a glance at Zenia, one woman to an-other. As Lord Winter passed out into the hall, the housekeeper said under her breath, "Nor he hasn't paid me the least mind when I told him about that the shutter had fallen off, ma'am, and him and Mr. Bode all taken up with that gamekeeper's cottage like they been this past week, I don't know what he thinks I'm to do but take a ladder to it myself, and break my neck too." When Zenia nodded politely, the housekeeper seemed to take it as a ges-ture to unburden herself further. "A bachelor house it is, ma'am, and none but meself and Mr. Bode left, and at our age there's this great old place falling down about our ears while his lordship gads up and down the world, never here from one year's end to the next. I do me best, ma'am, but I've seventy and six years, and not even a girl to help, and I beg you'll forgive the state of the place."

"Please don't concern yourself, Mrs. Bode," Zenia said. "I'm sorry to put you out. I'm only staying the one night, and any place you can find for me will be quite all right."

"Oh, are you going off so soon?" the old lady asked, wringing her hands in disappointment. "I had hoped—with a new mistress—it was used to be a fine old place, it was, when Lady Margaret was alive, rest her soul."

"I'm sorry," Zenia said, "but I'm not—" She found that she could not bring herself to tell this fragile old woman that she was not the new mistress. "I'm sure it was very pretty."

Mrs. Bode went ahead toward the stairs, with Zenia following. "I assure you that it was, ma'am. But if a gentleman lives in two rooms of it like a hermit, why—" She lowered her voice as they began to descend. "The creeping damp will carry him off, I vow, as Mr. Bode and meself both tell him again and again, but he is— I'm sure you know what he is, ma'am. A good, generous master, but no sense of what is due to the house. He don't think a thing of it but a roof and four walls. He could live under a bridge, I daresay, and never know the difference. I tell you, ma'am, I took pity on him from the day he come here, with a lot of books and guns and nothing else—a reserved, shy gentleman like himself—I was mortal pleased to hear he was married and would have a lady to see after him, because he was right set to turn into one of them strange old queer gentlemen who never speak to a living soul, but only collect things and sit all alone in their rooms, only I'll never live so long as to have to worry about it much, but I thought it a shame."

Lord Winter came striding out of a doorway off the staircase hall, dusting wood chips from his sleeves. "This will have to do," he said. "Mrs. Bode, I'll find myself somewhere to sleep, if you'll bring her case here and clean bedclothes and all that sort of thing." As the housekeeper hurried away, he glanced at Zenia. "This is the best we can do, I'm afraid," he said abruptly, indicating the door.

Zenia walked through into a paneled room lined by books and strewn with a diversity of articles: rolled maps and boxes of shells and traveling tokens. A folded, tassled and embroidered umbrella of gold and red silk, the type used to shade a pasha on his camel, leaned against one window bay. Next to it, pinned to the somber green curtain, a huge cobra's shed skin dangled down to brush the floor.

Already a fire blazing up behind the elegant brass fender was taking off the chill in the library. Lord Winter picked up another log and threw it on, watching the flames.

The light pulsed on his face and a gilded clock set among pieces of broken statuary on the mantelpiece. Sheafs of hand-written notes waved gently in the fire's draft, stuck beneath a cracked marble head and a blue-and-white Chinese vase on the mantel. Zenia recognized a *hijab*, an amulet that would hold a charm to ward off evil, hung on a leather thong about the sculp-ture's stone ear.

Beyond him, in a corner near the fire, there was a Turkish sofa piled with cushions and wrinkled sheets. Mrs. Bode came in with fresh linens folded atop Zenia's traveling case.

As she bent to begin remaking the sofa bed, Lord Winter turned his rapt attention from the fire and said, "It should be warm enough in here. I will bid you good night."

He walked past Zenia and left before she could answer him.

"I beg your pardon, ma'am," Mrs. Bode said. "But his lord-ship's right enough; this is a good cozy room if you can bear with foreign snakes and that. Would you like me to have Mr. Bode take the snake out, ma'am?"

Zenia looked at her dubiously. "Do you mean the skin?"

Mrs. Bode burst into a quavering laugh. "Oh, yes, ma'am. That awful old thing. I don't mean to say a real snake, I declare! We aren't that bad!" She tucked in the blanket. "But bad enough, for all that. I wish I'd had word that the new mistress was to come, and I would have hired some girls and turned the place over right, and paid for it out of me own jar if I must!"

"The snakeskin is fine," Zenia said. "And I have slept in far worse places than this, Mrs. Bode."

The housekeeper gave the sofa a last pat. "That's kind of you to say, ma'am. More than kind. Would you like some buttered toast?"

"No, thank you. I'm very tired."

Mrs. Bode made her creaky bow. "The bell's there, then, ma'am. Perhaps we'll have a blue sky in the morning, and you'll see the place in a better light."

THERE WAS NO blue sky in the morning. There was only a leaden gray through the cracks in the curtains. Zenia sat on the sofa in her traveling dress, uninterested in the tray of toast and tea Mrs. Bode had brought, reading Lord Winter's note.

He told her the time she must leave to meet the train, that the carriage would be ready, and asked her to allow a moment to speak to him about a business matter before she departed.

She waited as late as possible. She sat looking about at the jumbled library, the desks and notes and maps; it was not home-like; it had more the appearance of a large closet used for random storage, and yet she breathed his familiar scent in the room and on herself. Inside her.

She knew that he would not ask her again to be his wife. She had gone too far; she had made her final choice. The creature of last night, that had screamed at him and cried, seemed distant now, and yet she felt the source of it still within her, driving her away from him.

It was an intimate anguish, a grief she had known forever—she longed to be with Elizabeth to assuage and forget it, and yet she knew that it would be there, unalterable, underneath all the happiness she could contrive. It was a pain that seemed more safe and familiar than happiness itself: happiness that she could lose, that would slip away, and leave a mortal wound for having once existed.

She understood her mother now in a way that she never had before. Lord Winter was right. Knowing that her father would not—could not—stay, her mother had forced him away. There was a terrible rage inside Zenia too, and fear. She picked at the dark fur on her muff, afraid even to see Lord Winter, with no certainty whether she would shriek at him or plead forgiveness for what she had said to make him let her go.

Finally it was Mrs. Bode who came to tell her that he wished to see her. She led Zenia into the next room, another elegant chamber that had been filled with books and odd objects. Here there was a long dining table, half devoted to maps and atlases spread open, and the other half cleared but for a coffeepot and the remains of breakfast upon it. In the dull places where paintings had once hung on the walls and over the mantel, an array of polished guns rested in well-kept racks: Frankish rifles and pistols, along with weaponry of the East, beautifully chased muskets and golden scimitars.

He stood beside the single chair at the table, dressed as she had first seen him at Dar Joon, in a sporting coat and high boots. "You must leave in a quarter hour," he said, without greeting her. "I want to come to an understanding about Beth."

There was a dangerous edge to his voice, a determination that seemed intensified by the gleaming armory that surrounded them.

"I thought about this all night," he said. "I don't know what you expect of me—what sort of agreement you have made with Jocelyn—but if it is in any expectation that you and I would"—his jaw was rock-hard—"continue as lovers, while you are married to him, that is impossible. If our—if last night results in another child, then anything we agree upon now about Beth applies to that also. Do you understand?"

Zenia nodded. She could hardly lift her eyes from the plates on the table, where it appeared that he'd had even less interest in eating than she.

"I want Beth to know who I am," he said.

"If you insist," she said. "If you think that will be best for her."

"Don't presume to tell me anything about what's best for her! Damn you." Then he shut his mouth hard, as if he would have said more and refused to allow himself.

"What else?" Zenia asked.

"I want to see her. Daily, if I like."

Zenia shook her head. "No," she said emphatically.

He turned to the window. "Are you so afraid I'll steal her?"

She was afraid of that; she was afraid of seeing him herself. "I think visitations would be too difficult. For her. She might learn to care for you—depend on you to come—and then be hurt when you don't."

"When I'm not allowed to," he said, low and savagely.

"Will you be staying in England?" she asked.

He did not answer that. Evidence of his traveling, drifting life lay all about them.

"So I am never to see her again?" he asked coldly. "Even once?"

"I will speak to Mr. Jocelyn about it, and see what he suggests. I'll have to consider it."

She half expected him to fly into a fury, but he only stood still, staring out the window, his face remote. "There is the carriage," he said, at the sound of wheels and hooves in the icy snow.

Zenia's heart began to beat very hard. She gazed into a cup of coffee, still full, that had gone cold on the table.

"I suppose," he said, "that you are right, and I will be leaving the country." As he spoke, his expression did not change, and yet he seemed to withdraw entirely from humanity. He looked out the window with an unblinking detachment. "I suppose that you are also right, that it is best for your daughter and all of us if I do not see her again."

"It would be less painful."

"Would it?" He smiled, a small inhuman smile. "Excellent."

"I must go," she said desperately.

He turned, almost as if he had forgotten she was there. The mantel clock began to chime as he stood looking at her. "Yes, of course."

He opened the door for her, and followed her across the front hall. Mrs. Bode was there, peeping out onto the steps. "Mr. Bode has put in a hot brick, ma'am," she said, keeping her eyes down as she held open the door.

Stepping out into the wind, Zenia saw that the Arab mare was blanketed and tied to the carriage. She glanced at Lord Winter.

"Shajar al-Durr belongs to Beth," he said, the cold wind blowing his hair. "She is Elizabeth's to keep. Not yours or Jocelyn's. Mr. Bode will see that she has a box on the train."

Zenia nodded.

"Good-bye," he said, with a small bow. He turned and went back into the house.

Twenty-nine

—◦◦◦—

ZENIA ENTERED THE carriage with the image of his face as he had turned away from her: dark and austere, showing nothing, not emotion or anger or regret. In the daylight, the house was a solitary gray rectangle with tall handsome windows, standing entirely alone on the moorside, the stables and outbuildings tucked in the valley below.

She heard Mr. Bode speak to the horses. The chaise pulled away, grinding over the snow. Beyond the gates, it turned to lumber slowly downhill, following a narrow drive cut into the side of the hollow.

She tried to think of Elizabeth, of the journey ahead, but she could not banish the image of him as he had closed the door. It would be the last thing now; the last memory, to overlay all the others. She put her gloved hands up to her temples and her face, breathing in short gasps.

It would pass. She knew this would pass, and leave her empty and safe. This was the worst. In London there would be Elizabeth waiting.

The road swung along the edge of the valley, turning so that she saw the house again, standing like a sentry on the moor.

Here's my tunnel, he had said, when he was deep in delirium. *Do you want to come in?*

"You won't stay," she whispered. "You won't, you won't."

But she was the one leaving. She chewed the knuckles of her glove, hunching in misery, watching the house disappear. She had a sudden vivid impression of her mother's voice, screaming, driving one of the servants out of the house—driving Zenia out of Dar Joon. She stared at the seat opposite. She remembered the night Mrs. Williams died. Zenia had shouted back at her hysterical mother for killing the only person Zenia had ever loved—and she could remember her mother looming over her, that white-robed figure, like a djinni, cursing her with Arab curses. She remembered the silent Bedu who had taken her away into the desert, into exile—all alone, all alone, terrified and alone among strangers.

Suddenly she seized the checkstrap, dragging frantically on it. The carriage ground to a slow halt. Mr. Bode drew back the little door in the roof. "Ma'am?"

"Turn around," she said, her throat so tight she could barely speak.

"Turn around, ma'am? Beg pardon, but the road's too narrow here, ma'am—and might be we will miss the train. Have you forgot something?"

She thrust open the door, with her mother's djinni shrieking a warning in her ears, blinding and choking her. She stumbled as she reached the ground, barely hearing Mr. Bode's voice.

"Turn around," she exclaimed. "I want to come in! *El-Muhafeh!*"

Her mother howled prophecies and threats; she blamed Zenia for the black draught that had killed Mrs. Williams, she called her faithless and cowardly and female, worthless and nameless; she raged against trust; only a fool would depend on love; what was love but a weak woman's delusion, a madness, a pestilence—he did not love her, but wildness and wilderness—he would go back to it, called back to it inevitably, not today or tomorrow, but just when she came to need and rely on him . . .

Zenia faltered, finding herself halfway up the road to the house, with Mr. Bode calling behind her. She felt the pull of her mother's life—she felt the fixed will in her own heart to clutch Elizabeth to her, to never let her go, the way her own mother had held Zenia and Mrs. Williams, alternating sweetness with dread, with the sheer force of her dominion over them—Zenia knew with a terrible certainty that she had the same power inside her and the knowledge to use it. She did not want to, but when she thought of being alone, of the days to come, she stood still in the snow, shaking with fear.

"I'm not like my mother," she gasped. "I'm not."

She walked a few feet, and then turned and looked back toward the carriage. It was moving away from her, down the hill. She felt a welling of panic.

"I don't want to be alone," she cried. She ran down, stumbling, slipping on the snowy slope. She stopped, panting. "I want to be safe! I hate the desert! You'll leave me!"

But she remembered his face. His face, and the rooms in a deserted house. And a man growing strange and lonely and remote, speaking to no one. While her mother's djinni roared furiously in the wind, dragging her ruthlessly away from him, promising refuge and peace, safety; promising no loss, because everything was lost already.

She began to run. She did not know if it was up or down, until the house loomed up in front of her. She was up the steps and into the dark passage, discovering herself there, the door closed behind her.

She swallowed her panting. Her heart was beating so that she could hear nothing, not even her own footsteps as she walked down the passage and stopped before the door of his room.

He sat at one of the desks, his head bent over a book. He was so still that he did not even seem real to her. He seemed like someone very far away.

He flipped the page, leaning over it: an English gentleman sitting alone, intensely occupied by the volume before him. Zenia could see the print. The engraving he was staring at so raptly was still covered by a leaf of blotting paper tucked in the spine.

"*El-Muhafeh,*" she said desperately, "help me!"

His head jerked up. He rose, knocking the book from the desk.

Her face crumpled. "There is a djinni!" she cried. "It's my mother!"

He stood gazing at her as if she were a supernatural manifestation herself.

She gripped the doorframe, shaking her head. "There are no djinn," she exclaimed. "It is all superstition and ignorance. It is unchristian."

His blue eyes narrowed. "What has happened?"

She closed her eyes. "I'm afraid! She's in my head. She makes me do things, and say things! She's making me the way she was! She's making me leave you." Her eyes opened. "Do you understand?" she cried. "You promised to protect me!"

She saw the elemental spring alive within him, the demon she had always thought she feared. With a sudden move, he stepped forward, his teeth showing in a fierce smile. "You're mine, little wolf. I won't let her have you."

"I'm afraid! I'm afraid you can't stop her."

"Who came for you," he said. "when you were alone at Dar Joon?"

"You came," she whispered. "You were never afraid of the djinn."

"Never," he said.

"They aren't real," she said. But in her heart she believed, she felt the malevolent power that reached out to tear her away. She looked up at him, ashamed to plead for reassurance. "But my mother—I dream about her. What if you leave me? What if you go away and I wake up and she's there?"

He did not touch her. He stood looking down at her, smiling his demon smile. "I'll write you a charm," he said. "To keep you safe."

While Zenia watched wide-eyed from the doorway, he caught the leather thong off the sculpture on the mantel and carried it to his desk. He lit a candle, and then tore a small strip of paper, writing on it.

Carefully, soberly, he rolled the scrap and held it in the smoke for a moment. Zenia watched his lips, but he spoke his short incantation silently, his face intent.

With a knife, he split the seal of the amulet, a little silver box the size of a sugar lump, and flicked the former contents into the fire. He placed his charm inside, resealed the silver band with a hard pressure of the knife, and rose.

"I said I would always be with you," he murmured, lifting the amulet about her neck. "Wolf cub. This holds me. This defends you. Forever."

She put her hand up, clasping it. She didn't believe in magic—that was her mother's influence, her mother's folly, the delusions of the East. But there was such a look of strong certainty in his expression, such an assurance . . .

For the first time, with the charm about her neck, she felt conviction spread through herself. It was like sweet water, like a mantle wrapped about her as she looked up into his face—his strong, harsh face that held no fear of demons—a pure, calm trust in him to stay.

SHE HELD ONTO the amulet all through their wedding, performed in the cold staircase hall before Mr. and Mrs. Bode. And when the curate copied out her marriage lines and gave them to her, she held them, too. She kept them in her lap through the surprisingly excellent dinner, put on by Mrs. Bode in the dining room surrounded by guns and maps.

There was an extra place cleared for the diffident young curate, who only blinked and discreetly applied himself to his soup when Lord Winter began, "Now that Beth's parents have made a Christian marriage—" And broke off in the middle of the sentence. "I mean to say—"

He apparently found nothing that he meant to say after that unguarded blunder. In the ensuing awkward silence he glanced ruefully at Zenia and made a faint gesture of regret with his hand. He seemed disinclined to say much at all after that, sinking into one of his bleak dinner-table silences.

But Zenia did not care. She felt pleased and easy with everything. After a long interval in which neither of the gentlemen offered to look up from their soup bowls, she even ventured to suggest that perhaps they could wait a day, or even two, to return to London, as Elizabeth was in excellent hands with Mrs. Lamb.

Lord Winter made a little grimacing glance about the room. "What a delightful place to honeymoon!"

"There is the cottage," Zenia suggested.

He looked at her, and then at the politely attentive curate, and positively blushed. She watched blood rise in his throat and cheeks. He cleared his throat. "Where the gamekeeper lives, do you mean?"

Zenia remembered that Mrs. Bode had called him a shy gentleman. It was such a wildly incongruous description of the man she knew that she had hardly paid it any mind. Reserved, yes—moody and difficult to understand—she curled her hand about her amulet and observed him curiously, his arrogant look down at the glass, black brows raised a little, as if he had been affronted.

You are shy, she thought, gazing at him with profound affection.

"It seemed quite cozy last night," she said placidly.

He gave her a smoldering glance, still red in the face, and then scowled at his glass, turning it around and around between his fingers.

It seemed her place, then, between these two backward gentlemen, to take the lead in conversation. She managed to carry them along, one after the other, with a speculation on the weather, and questions about the curate's parish duties, and a description of how Lord Winter's property lay in relation to the railway, but she did not engage them both until she happened to hit upon the topic of guns.

The curate, apparently too bashful to inquire for himself, eagerly seized her lead to enter into a torrent of queries about Lord Winter's collection. He was, it appeared, a devotee of shooting; he was inspired by several of the pieces hanging upon the walls and positively in awe when Lord Winter took down the Colt revolving rifle.

The clergyman listened with passionate attention to his host's description of the gun's action and performance in a series of desert encounters. They had it all apart on the table while the mutton grew cold and Mrs. Bode pugnacious.

"Something of a bachelor house," the housekeeper muttered audibly as she took away the plates. "Nasty guns all over, and my lady allowing it."

The curate instantly covered himself in stuttering apologies to Zenia, while Lord Winter looked up with a slightly startled expression. He sat down, leaving the rifle scattered between the green peas and marrowbone pudding.

"Lady Winter is familiar with guns," he said, with a trace of defensiveness. "She is a fine shot herself."

Zenia, afraid that Mrs. Bode had little respect for rifles, gathered the pieces up from between the dishes and put the Colt back together, as she had done a hundred times in the desert after cleaning and oiling it. She looked up to find Lord Winter smiling ironically at her, and the clergyman watching her in wonder.

"How you must long to be back in such marvelous strange places," the curate said warmly. "Do you plan another journey soon?"

Zenia touched the amulet about her neck. She curled her fingers around it.

"No," Lord Winter said, "I am a little weary of marvelous strange places. I am glad to be safe home." He gave Zenia a sideways smile. "If the chicken pox doesn't kill me."

The curate proposed a toast to Lady Winter. The conversation, easier now, led away to more mundane things, and the clergyman took his leave after an apple tart and port. Zenia went back into the dining room as the two men lingered at the foot of the front stairs. From the window, she saw the curate accept his vail, and give every appearance of surprise and heartfelt gratification before he went off in his little buggy.

Lord Winter stood watching after him a moment. Zenia waited, expecting him to come back, but he turned instead and vanished from sight around the corner of the house.

She sat in the window, trying to imagine the dining room without the gun racks and the jumble of books and charts. There were two pretty cascades of woodcarving, flowers and fruit and wild birds, framing the space above the mantel, and scattered about under the overflow of maps were side tables and needle-pointed chairs that seemed as elegant as the ones at Swanmere.

It *would* be pretty, cleaned and straightened, the rose-colored curtains renewed, the woodwork and brasswork polished. With a little wonderment, she realized that it was hers. Mrs. Bode had made a number of remarks implying that Zenia would be grossly derelict in her duty if she did not see to putting the house to rights, and sending the snakes and guns to some proper territory within it, masculine but strictly confined.

But Zenia was not certain what Lord Winter would think. Perhaps it would make him uncomfortable—more inclined to leave. Perhaps he wished her to live at Swanmere, so that he could keep this place for his own retreat.

Doubt began to possess her. Had he not sounded faintly troubled when he said he was glad to be home? And the rifle, the excitement in the desert—had he not had the same light in his eyes when he spoke of it?

He had not come back for a long time. She closed her eyes and put both her hands about the *hijab*.

She heard the sound of a horse and then his voice shout her name from outside. Zenia jumped up, leaning on the window.

He rode Shajar bareback, right up under the window, grinning at her. "*Yallah!*" The mare danced and reared, flinging her long mane as if she were ready for a *ghrazzu*. "Open up, beloved!"

She forced open the sash. Cold air poured in. "What are you doing?"

"Repeating my one success," he said, breathing frost as he reached up to catch her hand. "Abducting you again. You'll have to cooperate a little more this time, unless you wish me to drag you out the window."

"You are mad!" she cried, laughing.

"Well," he said, "it seems to work rather well."

"And Mrs. Bode says you are a shy gentleman!"

"Not much for small-talk," he admitted.

"May I come out the door?"

"No, beloved, that is entirely too sane and simple." He urged the mare up close. "You must come out the window, to prove you love me."

She sat on the sill. "I don't have a cloak."

"Such ladylike scruples! When it's your undying devotion at the test. Duck now, we're on our way."

With his arm about her waist, he pulled her down before him. Zenia had a moment of falling, tumbling, and then he drew her firmly between his arms as the horse reeled around, following the buggy tracks in the melting snow.

She looked back at the house. In the afternoon light, its golden stone and tall white windows made a fine sight against the open moorland beyond, where streaks of yellow grass and rocks were beginning to show.

"Will Elizabeth and I live here?" she asked, afraid to be more pushing than to put it as a question.

He laughed. "I sincerely hope so." Then his voice changed, and he said stiffly, "I suppose you would prefer Swanmere. It is far more civilized, of course."

"Yes," she said, "but this is mine."

He held her hard against him. "My opinion precisely, wolf cub."

"Perhaps you will not care for it so much if we put the guns into a special room."

"Mmmm," he said, nuzzling her throat. "Mrs. Bode has been working upon you, I see."

"May I buy some fabric for new curtains in the dining room?"

"You may take everything out, burn it, and start over. It's just a lot of old antiques. Burn the house down, if you like, and we'll sleep in our cottage."

"You are a horrid Philistine. Mrs. Bode says that you could just as well live under a bridge."

"That would make me a troll, rather than a Philistine. And I suspect there is something of a fortune in fusty old masterpieces somewhere in there, so perhaps you had best not put it to the torch, at least without an inventory."

The gamekeeper's cottage was in view now, tucked below the edge of the moor.

"What is a troll?" she asked.

"A demon, wolf cub. The djinn that live under bridges and under the ground."

"Oh," she said.

In the night, after he had entered her deeply and at sensuous leisure, and lay warm and asleep beside her, she stared at his face in the glow of the fire. She could feel the amulet about her neck, a silver shape pressing into her breast.

It troubled her. It had brought her instant comfort, but when she touched it, calling on its magic, she felt unchristian and un-English—she felt herself sliding into the old world of the East.

She had married him. He had understood her well enough to guess that in that moment of crisis, she would respond from her deepest fears, from the magical fantasy of her mother's faith, the realm of demons and supernatural powers. So he had written her a charm.

The worst of it was, she believed in it. Even as her reason fought the feeling, she was certain in her heart that this *hijab* held him. She had seen the truth of it when he looked at her; when he spoke to her; when he answered its magic.

She crept out of bed, kneeling beside the last leaping flames of the fire. He moved, and she looked up quickly, ashamed that he should see what she was doing, but he only shifted on the pillows, settling deeper. The light glimmered on his face and bared shoulder, on golden warmth and his black eyebrows and hair that blended with the shadows.

Zenia held the amulet, frowning down at it.

She did not need magic to trust him. She did not need magic to hold him.

With a deep, unsteady breath, she used a broad knife from the table to pry the silver seal open. She would put it into the fire, this charm.

The little roll of paper fell into her palm, smoke-scented and faintly darkened by the candle flame. But just before she threw it into the hearth, she hesitated—and then spread the ragged slip open.

Her heart contracted a little at the sight of the cabbalistic script, the mystical writing that was not Arabic or English or any familiar lettering. It flowed strong and black across the scrap, a strange elegance and power. It was fascinating and repelling at once, like his demon-look, an electric energy that made her loathe to toss it into the flames.

"I believe you have it upside down," he said.

Zenia looked up at him with a faint startled gasp.

He smiled lazily at her, lifting up on his elbow. "Turn it over, wolf cub. And then come back to bed."

She inverted the fragment of paper. And instantly the words were dark and clear.

I love you, her charm said. Her magical charm to hold him.

I love you.

Very carefully, she rolled the small scrap and put it into the amulet again. With the knife she pressed hard to reseal the silver strip that bound the talisman. Then she put it over her head and climbed into bed and buried herself deep and safe in his welcoming arms.

Historical Note

WHILE THE HEROINE of this novel, Zenia, is entirely my fictional creation, Lady Hester Stanhope and her young lover Michael Bruce were quite real, as fantastic and dreamlike as their story seems. I have adhered to the available historical facts about them, only extrapolating from holes in the record: while there is no evidence whatsoever for an illegitimate child of their love affair in the desert, there was in fact a period of time, immediately after Lady Hester insisted that Michael leave her in Lebanon, during which she fell ill of a malady she called the plague. She was certainly surrounded by a frighteningly severe bubonic plague epidemic, but her stated symptoms were not very plaguelike. During her long recovery, lasting some eight to ten months, she isolated herself even from her faithful medical attendant, Dr. Meryon, and then suddenly sprang up refreshed and ready to hunt treasure in the desert. There was even one rumor, pub-

lished in a French paper, suggesting she had one or more children by Bruce, but that is the sum total of historical evidence on
the matter.

To tell the story of Lady Hester Stanhope and Michael Bruce
would take a whole novel in itself. For those interested, I recommend the brief biography of Lady Hester in *Passionate Pilgrims:
English Travelers to the World of the Desert Arabs* by James C. Sim-
mons. Most of the earlier biographies are marred by unrealistic
allusions to Lady Hester as a wrinkled old crone at the age of
thirty-four and unsubstantiated pronouncements against Michael
Bruce's "weak" character, both of which do disservice to the very
real high drama and intensity of their affair. Bruce's and Lady
Hester's collected letters in *The Nun of Lebanon: The Love Affair of
Lady Hester Stanhope and Michael Bruce*, and *Lavalette Bruce: His
Adventures and Intrigues Before and After Waterloo*, both published
by his descendant Ian Bruce, give the reader a clearer and fairer
picture of an interesting and complex young man who—if he
failed to fulfill the vicarious aspirations to greatness which both
his father and his lover forced upon him to gratify their own
ambitions—as least had a life beyond Lady Hester Stanhope.

And as for aged crones who have passed the thirty-four
mark—well, humpf! Is it realistic to suppose that a handsome,
healthy male in his early twenties (who certainly proved in later
life that he could have any woman he wanted) was only interested
in Lady Hester's politics? In the end, outside of all the biogra-
phers' suppositions and historical evidence, I suspect that Lady
Hester's and Michael's real relationship can be most vividly imagined by listening to Rod Stewart's song "Maggie May."